I0703802

THE GUILTY

RODNEY JOHNSON

WORKBOOK PRESS LLC
187 E Warm Springs Rd,
Suite B285 Las Vegas NV 89119 USA

Website: https://workbookpress.com/
Hotline: 1-888-818-4856
Email: admin@workbookpress.com

Ordering Information:

Quantity sales. Special discounts are available on quantity purchases by corporations, associations, and others. For details, contact the publisher at the address above.

Library of Congress Control Number:

ISBN-13:   978-1-965732-01-4   Paperback Version

REV. DATE: 11/28/2024

The Guilty

A Novel

by

Rodney Johnson

CONTENTS

First Chapter

GOOD MORNING

The sky was dark, but the stars provided a few specks of light. There was a restfulness in the air confirmed by the full moon. Hidden in the darkness was an Elite Tactical Unit made up of eight men. They worked for the New York City Police Department. But they were trained by the C.I.A. at the FARM in Langley V.A. The new reality after 9/11. The Terrorism Response Unit (T.R.U.) was led by Lieutenant Robert Grey. He was third in line. That's where the supervisor stood in a tactical movement. They existed in silence and discipline. Shoulders touching as a sign to each other that they were all ready. They wore Kevlar vest and helmets. They carried Heckler & Koch MP5's. They used silencers. You can't wake the neighbors.

They were at 301 Baldwin Ave. The only sound was of crickets. It was suburbia a long way from where the drugs would be sold in the heart of city. The neighborhoods where the drugs were transported to and sold were loud and dirty. No crickets there. Just gunshots, screams, yelling, crying, and delayed police sirens. The Malo Cartel delivered their cocaine to the Italian Mafia at that house in that neighborhood under the cloak of suburbia. Grey's unit knew this because the "family" accountant Salvatore had snitched. He was arrested by Grey's Unit for selling drugs to minors. He was the supplier and his nephew the dealer to his old high school and new college mates. Their side money brought in fifty thousand a month. Kid's loved Cannabis, Ecstasy, and Spice. Sales' to minors, drug trafficking, and possession got you thirty years. The "Rat" had told Grey everything about his side hustle and all about the family business for a deal. Full cooperation and no jail time. Grey had studied the house and neighborhood in great detail for over six months. He could navigate the house in complete darkness. He had created a replica of the house so he could brief and train his Team on all of it. They were ready to arrest or kill. It was the bad guy's choice.

They waited for their go signal. The Drone above the house had enabled Captain Howard to see the delivery of a hundred kilos of cocaine. He was back at Headquarters with the rest of the Unit. The Bat Cave. That would make for a profitable summer. The Mafia and drug crews had eagerly awaited the shipment. Cocoa leaves, hydrochloride, corn starch, talcum powder, and caffeine created cocaine. Which was dangerous. But the men who protected the shipments and distributed it on the streets were far more dangerous. The goal was too let the gunmen inside the house relax. The two vans that delivered the product were stopped right before they hit New Jersey. It was twelve minutes after midnight. Howard made the call to 301 Baldwin. A man answered.

Tony says, "Hello?"

Captain Howard says, "Good morning. May I speak to Robert."

Tony says, "You have the wrong number."

Captain Howard says, "My apologies."

Howard then hung up. It took Tony a few seconds to realize that it was morning even though it was pitch black outside. There was no time for analyzation. That was the go signal for Grey's Team. They moved fast. The door was knocked down three seconds after the call ended by number eight. He then threw in a percussion grenade. After the blast number one went left, two went right. Grey went straight ahead, four went left, and five went right, six went straight with Grey. Seven stepped in and held the position. Eight stayed outside. They communicated with Kell pieces. Which consisted of an earpiece to hear and a mic to talk.

Grey was moving forward clearing space when he saw an arm with a handgun attach at the end of it. He raised his MP5 to eye level and took aim. He looked through the front sites and with his right index finger pulled the trigger twice. Hitting his target in the head with both rounds. Blood and brain matter flew everywhere. The target fell like a bag of bricks. Muscle memory. He moved forward in stride.

Grey and number six moved towards the basement. Six threw a percussion grenade and after the explosion they quickly went down into the unknown. Grey encountered a gunman laid out on the floor. He was disorientated but fired widely. Grey angled his weapon perfectly and fired two rounds and there was silence. Six saw a gunman in the back of the room and he told him to drop his weapon. He followed the instructions. He was handcuffed and debriefed. The kilos of cocaine were in plain view on a table. White bricks stacked neatly. That density caused chaos on the streets. The house was secure.

They were finished. No Crime Scene and responding supervisors. Other members from T.R.U. would clean this up. This was not a normal NYPD Unit. They didn't follow local protocol. They were trained by the C.I.A. and they operated under international law. After 9/11 the Mayor and Police Commissioner vowed to do everything necessary to prevent another attack. The result was sending Grey and his Unit to be trained by the C.I.A. More important deputizing them and letting them operate as federal agents. If it was related to Terrorism the gloves came off.

No one from the Unit was hurt. It was a "Good Morning."

Chapter 2

PHANTASM

Grey was in bed less than a few hours after he had killed two perpetrators. He was exhausted and fell into a deep sleep quickly. He should have went drinking like everyone else because he drifted into his recurring nightmare.

"I'm going to kill you! You took my father from my mother and I, destroying our lives. So now I'm going to rid the world of your evil existence."

The vivid sound of the gunshot caused Robert Grey to jump upright and awake from his nightmare in a cold sweat. Dazed, he looked around. Pamela was lying next to him, so he knew he hadn't killed anyone. Yet. The clock read 3:09 AM. In the light of the television, he watched the rise and fall of Pamela's chest. He didn't need his cop instincts to know she was pretending to be asleep. She was a great detective but a lousy actress who was used to his nightmares. He had the same nightmare almost every night.

He was awake but still fidgety, holding his 9mm Glock as he contemplated what to do next. His father's murder was his recurring dream. Tonight, was worse than most nights. They were beginning to feel more real. Which caused more guilt.

In his nightmares, he's standing on the street corner in Queens, exactly where his father was murdered. He's watching a young black male pull the trigger. Rob yells to his father to get down but his father can't hear him. He sees the bullet enter his father's back. He watches his father fall. Rob then tries to run to his father, but he can't. It's as if he is standing in quicksand. He is a small insignificant figure unable to do anything. All he can do is cry. He turns to his father's killers and says, "I'm going to fucking kill you," but what comes out was garbled, like he's underwater.

He sat up in the bed, still holding his Glock tightly, aiming it at the wall. In his mind he saw the person who killed his father. Jamaal Hall. He's been having a variation of this dream since he was sixteen. Twenty years of mental torture.

Rob went to the bathroom. He was drenched in sweat, so he decided to jump in the shower. He then got back into bed to get some rest before work. But he just stared at the ceiling.

I'm afraid of no one, he thought, *but this dream has conquered me. Owned me.*

Jamaal had just gotten out of prison one month ago. He probably was home, sound asleep before he went to work. Rob had waited years for this opportunity. Not knowing if he could actually act on his emotion, hate. So, he decided not to lie there; he was going to put an end to his nightmares. He jumped up and got dressed: black underwear, black Nike sweat suit, black Nike sneakers, a black Glock. He loaded a magazine, and chambered a round. Locked and loaded.

Pamela sat up in bed. A Gabrielle Union's twin. Simply beautiful. She was wearing her new Victoria Secret red pajamas. Her hair was in a bun. Most importantly she had her 9mm Glock tucked under her pajamas. She was locked and loaded as well. She had to protect Rob from any physical harm. She couldn't do anything about nightmares. She had been awake since the nightmare started a few minutes ago. She wished he would exert that energy towards fucking her, and then he would sleep like a baby.

"Want me to go with you, baby?"

"No," he replied.

As soon as the door softly thumped closed Pamela pushed off the blankets and strode over to the window. She flicked the curtain aside and watched Rob get into his car. His muscular frame and aggressive walk would be a problem for his intended target. She stepped aside before the headlights could illuminate her watching. She knew he didn't like that she worried about him. She walked to the night table and picked up her phone. She hesitated then, as the car's engine faded, she tapped out: *If you need me just call.*

Her next text was even more important. She texted Alex to let him know what had just happened. Everyone in the unit knew when the murderer of Rob's father was released from jail.

They knew because that was all Rob had talked about.

Chapter 3

CRUX

Rob pulled up in his Audi A8 in front of one of the most violent projects in South-Side Jamaica, Queens. Jamaal Hall would exit the building around five o'clock. Rob knew this was the time Jamaal left for his job at the NYC Parks' Department thanks to the wiretap he had placed on Jamaal's cell phone and the paperwork he got from his parole officer. All Rob had to write was: *Subject has a nexus to Terrorism.* No one asked any questions about granting a wiretap or subpoena after reading that in the explanation box. Gloves off, thanks to the Mayor.

Rob had been following Jamaal for four weeks, since his father's killer had gotten out of prison on parole. He had Jamaal's case file memorized since he first looked it up fifteen years ago when he was a rookie and got database access: Jamaal and an accomplice named Phil tried to rob a young woman as an initiation into the South Side Syndicate on Thursday, May 9, 1996, at 3:37 PM. During the course of the robbery, the victim ran. As she ran, Phil fired off two shaky rounds in the direction of the victim. He wanted to scare her and also prove his worth to the Syndicate. The victim was unharmed, but a block away Rob's father had been struck in the back by the stray bullet. He had died an hour later at Jamaica Hospital.

It was then Rob had decided to become a police officer. He'd grown up in Howard Beach, Queens, with both parents third-generation Italian immigrants. A normal lower-middle-class life, two-bedroom house, and a car. A typical Italian neighborhood of teachers, cops, and organized crime members all living together in harmony. He went to St. John's University where he received a B.S. in Criminal Justice. Boxing was his sport of choice, and he won the light-heavyweight division twice before his career ended. He went for the knockout every bout, Rocky Marciano style, and drove his coaches nuts. Two separated shoulders later, anger, instead of technique, ended his boxing career. This anger—at his father's killer and the terrorists who killed 2,977 innocent people on September 11, 2001—had brought him through the ranks to become lieutenant in charge of the most elite undercover unit in the history of the NYPD, the Terrorism Response Unit. Formed by a former CIA Officer, and trained by the CIA at the Farm in Langley, it was the first-ever domestic police department to receive this type of training.

And it was this anger that had brought him to 109-10 and 160th Street in Queens, with a loaded Glock 19 and forty-fucking-six rounds of ammunition.

Rob reached under his seat and felt for a box of blue latex gloves he always kept for legal and illegal use. He pulled out two gloves and snapped them on. He checked the time on his phone to start the countdown. 4:30. The date reminded him that his son's birthday was coming up. He already had bought his birthday gifts: a train set, a policeman action figure, and a police helicopter. They had been delivered by a friend, because Rob was in deep cover. His family's safety would have been at risk if the people he was hunting found him out. Anonymity protected you on the streets no matter who you were, friend or foe. Cop or Perpetrator.

Then he pictured his wife's face when young Robert opened the presents. Her face was like a shutter banging closed, hiding her emotions about his job that kept him away from her and the kids for so long. She never fully understood him or his job. She didn't understand how he could live without his family. Drugs, dealers, addicts, and crime were a part of the world. Good for some, bad for others. Good for the industrial prison complex, and bad for average citizen.

He and Loren had been high school sweethearts. Two kids, Robert and Anthony. Nice house. He'd not been able to stay in the house or see them since he started this new assignment. This being away from the family completely was rare. Loren was used to the long hours, but complete isolation was definitely new and strange. She hadn't signed up for this. The Unit.

He started to think that maybe shooting Jamaal might not be a good idea. He thought about his own two kids, and how he would hate for them to be tortured by something he did. *Best thing to do in a situation like this was to call a friend,* he thought. That's what Captain Howard would say. Captain Howard was Rob's boss and friend. Those lines never got blurred if you were a friend in blue you could ask for anything. No limitations; a loan (Gambling), alibi (Wife), or accomplish (Crime). They were both dark blue and on the same page. This new unit was important to them, the city, and the world. 9/11 affected everyone. So, they always worked together to arrest—or kill—anyone trying to do harm to the citizens of New York City. Captain Howard was old school: Blue before anything else. Take care of your people no matter what, even if they made a mistake or committed a crime. Rob was raised the same way. Blue.

Captain Howard was home sleeping next to his wife. So, the perfect person for this situation was Alex. The phone rang as he watched the entrance of the building.

Twelve years on the job, Detective Alex Dunne had no kids or family. He'd lost his parents, so Rob and the department were his family. His drug-addicted mother and father were both killed in a house fire when he was just ten. NYPD was his only family by circumstance.

Alex had joined H.I.D.T.A., the High Intensity Drug Trafficking Area unit, after being a plainclothes officer in the 40th Precinct, South Bronx. This was an FBI and DEA Task Force with extensive training. But he got injured while he and his partner were speeding to a 10-13 "Officer needs assistance" call while in the unit. He was lucky: a crushed collarbone and a broken left leg that left him with a limp. "Help's my cover, nobody would ever believe I'm a cop" he told Rob the day they met on the task force. They both laughed. His partner died. That left Alex with survivor's guilt.

For Alex, pain meant Vicodin, and Percocet. He added alcohol for liberation. After the prescriptions stopped, he turned to cocaine. He failed a drug test, but he blamed it on his girlfriend. He said she had a drug habit he didn't know about, and he had ingested it through her bodily fluids. Rob helped him keep his job, but he was given NYPD's harshest punishment for fuckups they don't want to fire: thirty and a year—suspended for thirty days and put back on probation for a year, for living with a convicted felon. He was transferred to the 28th Precinct in Harlem. He was put in SNEU, the Street Narcotics Enforcement Unit. This definitely helped him maintain his drug habit. Some drugs were vouchered more where consumed for personal use.

He put in for this new unit without ever thinking he would be chosen. "Nothing better than a drug addict playing a cop. It makes his cover seal tight," the chief said. A functioning addict, a hard worker, and as effective as any other detective in the unit. While he worked in H.I.D.T.A. Alex led the unit in arrest while he fed his habit. The quota was four arrests for the month; he averaged six. He was moved to the Terrorism Response Unit, trained at FLETC in Glynco, Georgia. His assignment in the unit was to act as a drug addict and sign up confidential informants—CI's—to gather intelligence.

On the third attempt Alex answered. Alex sighed. "Yeah?"

Alex had already read Pamela's text. Of course, he was up at this hour. He'd been up all night getting high with a female informant. Cocaine, which Alex had confiscated from another junkie. He was supposed to voucher it, but Lisa called him while he was en-route to the Bat Cave, and she was a better option than paperwork. Now he was driving to Jamaal's house. Driving too fast for a sober person. A person in his condition shouldn't have been driving at all. That's what friends are for.

"Everything okay?" Alex asked, rubbing his numb nostrils.

"I'm in front of 109-10 and 160th Street," said Rob.

Alex yelled, "Don't do anything stupid! I'm on my way."

Minutes later, Alex pulled up in his department-issued Dodge Charger, souped-up and seized from a drug dealer in Brooklyn. A present from the DEA. Lisa was with him. They both jumped out. Rob was about to walk towards the building. Rob looked and saw them both. He knew her face but had never been introduced. She was a part of Alex's other life.

Alex ran up to Rob. "Talk to me."

"I going to kill this piece of shit."

"I understand, brother. Your father—"

"He doesn't deserve to be alive. He's an animal so he will never feel the pain that my mother and I feel. So, he has to die."

"You can't let this mutt control your mind."

"That's easier said than done. I don't want to think about him at all. That's why I'm here to end this."

"You have a beautiful wife and kids. You can't jeopardize them." Alex said. "I'd trade lives with you in a second."

Rob looked into Alex's bloodshot eyes, and he knew he was high.

"Go home. Go back and fuck Pamela. Let that be your only sin for tonight."

Rob let himself smile. He would never cheat on his wife. Murder was justice so it was good. Adultery not.

Alex brought the subject back around. "Listen. I'm not going to let you do this. That's what friends are for, to help you in times of crisis and the contemplation of Premeditated 1St. degree murder."

Rob said, "It's judgment day and he's guilty! So, he must die." Rob took the 9mm Glock out of his waist, leaving the case file for Jamaal on the dashboard of his car.

Rob knew he should get out of there. Alex was right. This distraction created the reality check he needed. But it didn't help. He contemplated but his anger was present and real. He wanted to stop a heartbeat and gain his sanity back. What good was all his power if he couldn't stop evil? So, this was the right thing to do. Jamaal was liable, and death was his sentence. He has terrorized Rob's life. The weak criminal justice system had catalyzed Rob into action. Violence was appropriate. The city—the world—would thank him.

Alex stared down at the case file, his mind racing. If you can't stop him, join him. He followed Rob, and Lisa followed him.

Chapter 4

THERAPY

Alex dragged Lisa around to the southwest corner of Jamaal's building. They had only a few minutes before Jamaal would be leaving the building. It was 4:49 AM and the streets were quiet.

"Follow my lead," he told Lisa. He reached under her skirt and hooked his fingers around her panties and pulled. They ripped and she flinched. Rob watched what Alex was doing—providing incidental cover.

Just then Jamaal exited the building, leaving for work in his NYC Parks Department uniform. A job given to parolees. He wasn't a working man. He was a murderer wearing an ugly green uniform. He walked liked he was still in jail. It was a confident walk. He got his PHD in thuggery quite quickly. He entered jail as a kid, and then he had to become a predator while he was locked up. He did the fighting and slashing. He had to be violent in those walls. No one to protect you, definitely not the Correction Officers. They were in charge of the drugs, weapons, and money. They didn't have time to actually do their jobs. Gate kickers. He was out for a short time, but he would never be able to turn off his animal.

Alex kicked Lisa and she screamed, "Help, he's robbing me!"

Jamaal halted and looked at the commotion. He was wearing headphones and listening to Mobb Deep's song, "The Start of Your Ending." He barely heard the commotion, but when he did, he started toward them. Coolly, Rob waited till he was a few steps away. He stood in front of Jamaal and contemplated the twisted paths that led both of them to this moment. He stared at Jamaal, and Jamaal stared back and saw a stranger. Rob's stare urged Jamaal to run but he didn't. So, Rob aimed his weapon and fired two rounds, center mass, into Jamaal's chest. Jamaal's eyes opened wide as he fell to the ground. Blood poured out of his chest. There was a hissing sound as air tried to find its way in and out of his nose and mouth. Rob's eyes were wide too. Alex shoved Rob out of the way and then put Lisa's wallet into Jamaal's right hand and her panties into his right front pocket. He then took Rob's 9mm, and gave him his. These weren't regular cops. They didn't have department-issued weapons with serial numbers on them. Everything was street ready. No trace. Jamaal bled out fast. There was no more struggle. No need for air. His eyes were open, and his nose and mouth were slack, almost calm. Alex put two fingers on Jamaal's carotid, police training to confirm a murder victim. No pulse. He told Rob, "Get the fuck out of here. I got this." Rob felt relieved. He had overcome his guilt and depression.

Alex pulled out his cell phone and called 911. "Shot's fired central at the corner of 109 Ave and 160 Street. 10-13, Central."

Central responded, "All units 10-13 at the C/O 109 Ave and 160 Street. Shots fired."

#

Rob didn't remember driving home. He took a shower and went back to bed. Pamela had fallen asleep with the TV on so he switched it to Sports Center. He looked at the clock: 6:51 AM. He had a little less than three hours to rest. Alex was his closest friend in the police department, so his loyalty was unquestioned, but how do you repay something like this?

As he watched TV he got an alert on his work phone about a department shooting: *An undercover detective was involved in a shooting. No department personnel were injured. Because of the nature of his assignment, no further details at this time.*

He turned to Channel 1 to watch Alex's work on the news. The police brass and news reporters were all at the corner of 109th Avenue and 160th Street. They talked about a veteran narcotics detective who observed a vicious rape and robbery. NYPD Captain Frank addressed the cameras. There was a sheet over the body of the perpetrator. "At approximately 4:57 AM the perpetrator robbed the victim, and then attempted to rape her. The detective seeing this from his vehicle responded, and had to shoot the perpetrator to stop him. We don't have any eyewitnesses but we do have three people who say they heard the victim scream and say, 'He's robbing me!' We cannot disclose the identity of the detective because he was an undercover. This investigation is in the parliamentary stages, so that was all we have for now."

Without expression, Rob watched Jamaal's mother cry uncontrollably. Her body shook with a rhythmic violence. She was held back from entering the crime scene by four neighbors. "My baby, my baby," she wailed. The camera crew were just aiming their cameras at her. There was no need for the reporters to say anything. For the people watching the news the explanation was enough. For the black bodies gathered around Jamaal, there was no trust in the explanation or the police.

As Rob watched, he remembered his mother's shock when she found out about her husband, his father. Grief strikes everyone the same. It has no name or race attached to it.

Chapter 5

TAP DANCE

Detective Alex Dunne was at Elmhurst hospital being treated for trauma—department procedure for anybody who discharges their duty weapon. A duty captain was there trying to ask Alex some questions, but his Detective Endowment Association union delegate yelled, "Hell no, no questions for forty-eight hours."

"I'd love too, but department procedure," Alex said with a sly smile to the duty captain.

The duty captain didn't care about any rules; he wanted his questions answered for his 49, his incident report. He wanted Detective Dunne to talk, and he wanted Lisa the drug addict interrogated separately. He wanted to know where Detective Dunne was coming from and where he was going.

The duty captain leaned in close. "I've been around a long time, Dunne. And this story is too perfect. Deadly force is *never* this clear cut. Plus, you look like you've been up for three days with Charlie Sheen!"

Alex waved the captain off. He belonged to the most elite unit in the NYPD. He had already sent a text to the chief and knew all would be taken care of. As he sat on the hospital bed Alex slid his feet back into his shoes and went into the bathroom to get cleaned up. He leaned in close to the mirror and surveyed his bloodshot eyes and gray face. He flicked a hand over his hair. "I look better than Charlie Sheen," he murmured.

He'd be leaving with Lisa soon. Having sex, getting high, and listening to Metallica with his girl. "Sex, drugs, and rock and roll!" he laughed. He straightened up and stepped back into the hallway.

From down the hallway, the duty captain yelled, "I'm a captain in the NYPD, and I have a *sergeant* telling me to let you go. This is fucking crazy. Time for me to retire."

Alex smirked. The chief had received his text, deleted it, then called the police commissioner to contact the duty captain. Some sergeant from the PC's office had then called to tell the duty captain to let the detective, and the victim, go with any further questions. This was Alex's fourth department shooting, so he knew the drill. Besides, it was family business. He had worked up an appetite. He would wait for Lisa to be finished playing with the detectives, and then take her to breakfast. Eggs, pancakes, and cocaine.

Four rooms away, detectives on the Night Watch, the midnight-to-eight tour, were questioning the victim, Lisa Pearl. Even though the duty captain was told to let her go, he felt no reason to interrupt an interview already in progress. A civilian, she didn't get forty-eight hours. She kept her temper and answered their questions politely, remembering everything Alex had coached her to say. And to cry at the right moments.

Detective Scott said. "We know you have just been through a traumatic situation, but it was imperative that we talk to you as soon as possible. Are you physically able to do so?"

Lisa replied, "Yes sir. I was on my way to buy some crack in building 109-10 Apt.10 G, when this asshole came up from behind. Excuse me. This asshole came up from behind and snatched my wallet. I thought it was over but then he pulled me to the stairwell and put his hand underneath my dress. It felt like he was trying to penetrate me with his fingers, and he was unable to so, then he then ripped off my underwear."

She knew what Detectives Scott and Irving were thinking: she must have been something before she got hooked. That's where it stops for most men. They see the history on her face and move on. Except for Alex. Sex, drinking, arguing, stealing, and drugs. Now she had knowingly participated in a murder. But it was a great street marriage and as long as she had a steady stream of drugs she would be faithful.

"Was he saying anything while he did this?"

"Yes. He said this is *my* pussy now, bitch."

"Please tell me everything he said."

Lisa looked blankly at him. "That was it. It happened so quick."

"Did you hear the detective say anything?"

"No."

"Did you hear how many shots were fired?"

"No. I'm sorry, detectives, but I feel like I have to throw up. I need to go to the bathroom."

Lisa ran to the bathroom. After she closed the door, she stood a moment. A smile spread across her face. She was impressed with herself. An Oscar performance. It was easier than she thought, plus she was enjoying lying to the police. She had been doing so her whole life. It started off with her parents, then her husband, now the homicide detectives. She knew this would take her relationship with Alex to another level. He now owed her, and she would collect. She thought about how soon they could get high after leaving the hospital.

When she reentered the room, the detectives were packing up and told her to her surprise that she was free to go. Detective Irving muttered, "We have enough work as it is."

"Police shooting's high profile. Let Queens Homicide take over," said Detective Scott to him as if she was not in the room.

She knew this was not normal. It must be because her man was important. Detective Scott said to her, "We'll contact you if we need anything more. Thank you for your time. We can have a uniformed officer drive you home when you're ready. Here's my card, if you think of anything else."

In the hall Alex rushed past the detectives.

They turned, wondering where he was going so quickly. They watched him retrieve and then escort Lisa to the elevator. They exchanged glances. "Above our pay grade," said Scott.

Chapter 6

GENESIS

It's a beautiful summer day, the sky light blue, the temperature 84 degrees. There was a light wind, the time was 10:03 a.m. The young officer has parked his scooter and decided to walk a few blocks to get a feel of the neighborhood. He's working in the 113 Precinct, in Rochdale, Queens. He greets everyone he passes with "Good afternoon." People are happy to see this unusual sight; he is enjoying every minute of this. Other officers in the precinct hate dealing with the public, but he loves it. As he is walking he sees a pregnant women fall to the ground. He runs over to her and hears her say she is having contractions. The rookie shouts over the radio: "Central, be advised I have a female 27 in labor. Please send a bus to the corner of Guy R Brewer and Merrick Boulevard."

Central responds, "Ten-four, unit."

There is only one problem: the baby isn't going to wait. The rookie is terrified, his legs shaking. He tries to get control of them before she notices. It doesn't help that she is pretty. She does notice, and she thinks it is cute. He is afraid to look anywhere near her crotch area, but he has no choice because the baby is coming. She pulls her dress up above her waist. He nervously tries to look away but the woman grabs his wrist. Gulping for breath, he sees that the mother-to-be is calmer than he is.

"I'm going to lie back and push as hard as I can," she says, releasing his hand with a grimace. "It's your job to catch the baby."

He nods wordlessly.

A store merchant has brought out a dirty pillow for her head and a newspaper for the baby. "This is as good as it's going to get," the young officer mutters.

A crowd forms around them. With the young woman pushing as hard as she can, the baby's head begins to crown. At the sight of the pulse of the baby, the young officer feels woozy.

"Everything all right?" barks the patrol sergeant, who has just arrived. The rookie jerks himself back from his faint. If he goes unconscious now, the whole precinct will make fun of him. He realizes he is breathing as hard as the mother—the crowd around him notices, and laughs. The baby spills out into his arms. A girl—he blushes and hopes no one will notice he is blushing. Only then does the ambulance pulled up.

"Well done," the sergeant tells the rookie. "Nothing purer than delivering a baby."

The EMT takes the baby out of his arms to check her vitals. As the mother is put in the ambulance with her newborn baby girl, she asks the rookie his name.

"Officer Robert Grey," he stammers.

"Thank you, Officer Grey. My baby's name will be Robbie."

He smiles at the baby as the doors close behind her. He isn't sure if she is serious. If so he hopes the baby will have a better childhood than he had. He wants the baby to receive her parents' love for as long as possible. His father's murder destroyed five lives: father, wife, son, mother, and murderer.

Rob awoke from his dream. He was in bed, his alarm blaring. It was 9:55 AM. *How did I get from delivering a baby to killing people?* He thought about the night's events and what they meant for him in the long term. He got up and went into the bathroom to urinate and wash up, all the while with a clear image of Jamaal in his head. He laid back down in bed. He liked to watch his New York One Minute (NY1) so he could see what's going on in the city, his city. He liked the weather and any important news, which gave him a head start for the day. He was a news fanatic. Today he got to enjoy the news about his father's killer being dead. The police shooting was the top story this morning, so he watched again, so he could see the body lying on the sidewalk. This was closure for Rob, or so he believed.

Pamela walked into the bedroom with a cup of coffee for Rob. Black with no sugar. She had on a bathrobe, but Rob could see her bulletproof vest and Glock 19 handgun. He knew she some idea of what had happened a few hours ago. Rob trusted her with his life, but there was no need to involve her in this. He hadn't wanted to get Alex involved, but it was too late now. He wasn't worried about the truth getting out. The Blue Wall was real.

Pamela Brown was a thirty-four-year-old undercover detective with thirteen years on the job, unmarried, but had a six-year-old daughter, so playing Rob's wife was a big sacrifice for her. She had been personally chosen by the Chief.

She'd gotten his attention after, one night while in a beauty salon getting her hair done, two punks came in and announced a robbery. She shot one of them and arrested the other. She declined all news interviews, because she wanted to protect her young daughter. No Twitter, or Instagram. She already lived a covert lifestyle. This endeared her to police brass, and her humility and past training made her an easy pick for this new unit.

She was Rob's house security, and the eyes in the back of his head that he needed. She was well-trained and good at her craft; she had been trained at the CIA Farm for this assignment. She was also given heavy weapon and explosive training. So here she was in the most elite unit in the department with no baggage—just kills from the military and civilian world.

Pamela and other safety measures were put in place to protect Rob 24/7. The Italian Mafia had put out hits on a judge and two police captains the previous year. The captains were targeted because they led major investigations against the crime families. Rob was the highest-ranking supervisor in the field. This was mandatory to protect him.

Pamela loved and respected Rob. His reputation was true, and he was good people. Being away from her daughter was hard, but it was also the best live-in situation possible. The only thing that would make it better for Pamela was if she could have sex with Rob while they were together in this beautiful house. She was attracted to him, and his persona. She wanted to playhouse.

Pamela said, "Good morning," and handed him the cup of coffee.

"Good morning, Pam."

He never took his eyes off the TV. She stared at him for a moment thinking, *Every morning, same thing.* Most men watched sports but he was obsessed with the news. They had been playing husband and wife for over a year so she knew his tendencies. They had developed a rapport. Their relationship was real in the fact that they both believed in the mission and she was going to do her job and protect him while he was in that house.

They had been doing this for about a year. She had not seen her daughter doing this time. But if they could take the most notorious drug gang off the streets then it will be all worth it. The city and world will be a better place for her daughter and all the children of this great city.

Pamela concentrated on the police shooting. Rob informed her that it was Jamaal. He told her that he was dead. He was shot while robbing and raping a woman. Rob jumped up and got in the shower. She felt guilty because she called Alex and now Jamaal was dead. Pamela watched out of the house's front window to see if anything was out of the ordinary this morning. Everything seemed normal.

After Rob took his shower, he got dressed. The right side of thirty-six, he knew he looked good in anything because he was in great shape. It didn't hurt that he was six-foot-two, with blue eyes, muscular build, and decent looking. He was well-coiffed. He got that from his father. Best-looking man in a postal uniform. His father was always on his mind; he missed him dearly. The loss was never gone, always current.

Today Rob's attire was blue jeans, white French cuff shirt, and black Ferragamo shoes.

Pamela walked out the back door of the house and strolled the whole perimeter looking for anything suspicious. Everything was good. Under her bathrobe she still wore a bulletproof vest and carried a Glock 19 Handgun. Neither items were ordered from Victoria's Secret, but it all matched. Rob left out the front door and they kissed on the lips.

She told him, "Have a nice day, honey, and be safe."

It was for show. In case any eyes were on them.

He smiled and said, "I will. You, too."

Along with this house in Queens, the department had provided Pamela and Robert with two luxury cars, an Audi A8 and a Mercedes M350. This was part of their cover, to maintain their identity and lifestyle. The story: Rob owned and ran a deli in Queens, so his salary was supposed to reflect his earnings. This program cost the department a lot of the budget, but the rewards were great because the arrest, and asset forfeitures would be more than enough to pay for this covert program. You couldn't even begin to put a price on the news coverage with the police commissioner and mayor talking to the people of New York in front of seized weapons, drugs and money. When you take down a major drug crew; homicides, shootings, assaults, drug sales, and robberies all significantly go decrease. Crime down means a happy public and re-election for the mayor.

Rob jumped in his Audi A8 and was off to work, today's tunes on the MP3 player, RUN DMC. He was a Queens Boy through and through.

The Occhi deli was in the middle of everything on Jamaica Ave. It was set up upon the Chief's direction. It allowed Rob to be right in the middle of community he was protecting. It also provided a cover for him, acting as the owner. The Mafia traffic also added to his mystic.

There weren't many secrets in the hood. You could see who's selling what and where they were doing it. That wasn't enough to build a case on the kingpin and bring down a whole crew. That takes more effort and investigative work. That's what Rob's crew was doing.

The deli was equipped with the best video cameras on the market, NSA grade. They didn't stand out because in the hood, all businesses had video cameras. What people didn't know was that these had special zoom-in, audio-recording capabilities, along with facial recognition. And others, hidden from sight, had a 360-degree view inside and out of the property. The cameras were controlled off site at an undisclosed office where the detective investigators work. They called their office the Bat Cave.

The mission was called "Operation Raker," and their goal was to take down the most violent drug crews in NYC. There were four major crews and they had undercovers in three: Howard Beach Crew – Italians; Latin Cartel – Spanish; and Brooklyn Bullies – Jamaicans. The only crew they had not penetrated yet was the South Side Syndicate, but Rob had a personal mission to get one of his UC's, Dwayne Washington, in there. The other drug crews in New York all answered to one of the four major crews. So if you took down one crew, it was possible that ten might fall under them. If the unit could build a strong case on just one of the crews, it would be deemed successful. Lieutenant Grey had bigger plans: he wanted to rid his city of all of them. A clean sweep. He was ambitious and focused. That focus meant by any method necessary. When his father was killed he concentrated on just the two murderers, now he could take down the whole Syndicate.

#

Salvatore looked in the rearview mirror and didn't like what he saw. Nothing he could do about it. He was the man in the mirror. He used a paper towel to wipe his underarms before he got out of the car. He was parked in front of the crew's social club on Cross Bay boulevard. He was about to have lunch with his friends and then report what was discussed with the FBI. Salvatore Gravano was a "Lieutenant" in the Howard Beach Crew, but he was also a "Rat" for the NYPD Organized Crime Unit. He was caught selling heroin to minors. Facing eight to twelve, he easily cooperated. His main duties were to keep the department informed on the family's business. They set up a deal with him to stop by the Occhi Deli, and have conversations with Rob about nothing. The conversations with his crew were real. Salvatore's entire crew liked going to the deli because it had the best cappuccino in Queens, made on an original 1910 Ideale espresso machine. Salvatore didn't know why he was being asked to do this, but it was easy so he did it. The entire neighborhood knew who Salvatore was, because he was always on TV dressed impeccably. This gave the impression in the neighborhood that Rob was connected, so he got instant street credibility. Which allowed

Rob to walk around the neighborhood in cover. Perception was reality in undercover work and in life.

#

Rob thought back to when this unit first started, and he met the Chief. It hadn't been a great first meeting.

When the unit was first given the green light, they wanted the best the department had to offer. So they solicited the best officers, detectives, and bosses they had. It initially had over one hundred personnel. It was too much personality. Soon they realized that the smarter the individual was the more "What if" questions they had. The Chief knew that in order for this new unit to be effective he needed go-getters with a little bad boy in them. A small proactive unit with little supervision. He wanted men and women, who could interpret their new found power to their benefit. They would be dealing with US Code; US USC 2331 Chapter 113 B. Which was Domestic, and International Terrorism. They would have access to wiretaps, subpoenas, and warrants that don't require the same standards as the penal codes. Along with high-powered weapons and explosives. This was great power that if used correctly, could take down some big figures in the criminal world. So he personally went through the resumes and picked his personnel. He knew exactly what he was looking for, and he had a thousand applicants to choose from. The unit would be twelve people from top rank to bottom rank. He definitely wanted good, resourceful people. Usually if an officer had a lot of complaints on their record, a unit would not want them. The Chief saw it differently. If an officer used excessive force, or tainted evidence that was for the greater good. This was what he was looking for. No choir boys for this unit and mission. He wanted great mixed with devious. Also he wasn't from this department so he had no roots or ties. He just wanted a successful unit, anything negatives he could just blame it on "Dumb Cops." This would be his Dirty Dozen.

They were put together to arrest Drug Kingpins, Wholesalers, and Importers. Really bad motherfuckers. This afforded them great freedom, the greatest being not to arrest a felon, if it meant catching a bigger fish. This also helped with their cover, because a criminal couldn't imagine an officer witnessing a crime and not doing anything about it. They did track all crimes witnessed and filed paperwork at the Bat Cave. Murder and drug dealing only mattered if they could connect it to the boss. They were not limited by the penal code, or procedure. The Chief knew that federal agents would never go off script, and manipulate the law or their powers. Most of their great cases were from Joint Task Forces where they worked with local officers. So now he was given the power directly to the officers, hoping for "Rogue" tactics.

They were more elite than the Drug Enforcement Agency (DEA), Federal Bureau of Investigations (FBI), Homeland Security Investigations (HSI), High Intensity Drug Trafficking Unit (H.I.D.T.A.), and NYPD Narcotics. They were the shit. This was because of their training, and newfound powers. They would be treating American Citizens like enemy combatants.

The Chief personally wanted to interview the person who would be leading the unit in the field. So Rob's last interview was with the Chief, in his office.

The Chief had set up in the Garment District—he was able to use the department budget however he wanted, rent be damned. They came to him for help, so he was going to do this his way, these dumb cops need to follow and learn. They have signed off on everything so far with little questions. He does have the answers if they do ask. This was a covert location, in the center of the city. His office was huge with a lot of toys; Flat Screen TVs, Apple computers, and department radios. The Chief wanted to make this as informal as possible. He wanted to impress all that entered, including his girlfriends.

The Chief asked him, "Why did you join the department?"

Rob replied, "To protect and serve the public."

The Chief said, "Don't give me that standard bullshit. Tell me the real reason."

Rob looked at the gentlemen sitting across from him with his bow-tie and wing-tip shoes and felt no connection. He thought, this wasn't a cop. So Rob said, "Sir, that was the real reason."

The Chief said, "Come on, we both know you want to kill as many criminals as possible to avenge your father's death."

Rob said, "Fuck you." He stood to walk out.

The Chief said, "Two down. How many more to go to make you feel better?"

Rob's two department shootings.

Rob charged the Chief and threw him up against the wall.

The Chief spat out, "You think I'm afraid of you? I've been in the room with real terrorists who aren't afraid to die, Hamas. They got beliefs, passion, and suicide belts. Not the lowlife drug-addicted people you're used to dealing with, who kill innocent people. So get your fucking hands off me."

Rob let him go and walked out of the room. As he was walking out he said over his shoulder; "I only kill to defend this city, my city. Asshole."

The chief loved him for saying something so crazy and arrogant but Rob thought he would not be chosen for this assignment, and he might need to get union representation because of what just happened.

A week later he was told by the chief himself that he was chosen for the unit.

Rob headed into a coffee shop to quiet his nerves before a meeting. He picked up his macchiato and headed over to the milk and sugar station.

He heard a voice behind him. "Good morning, Rob."

He turned, macchiato in hand, and stood face-to-face with the Chief. Startled, he couldn't think of what to say at first. "Good morning, sir."

"Remember when I told you that you had been chosen for the new unit."

"Yes, sir," replied Rob.

The chief gripped his arm and moved him, slowly but steadily out the door. On the street, away from prying ears, he continued, "I said, 'Enjoy the training. It will transform you. There is only the trained and the untrained.'"

Rob nodded.

"I told you, 'Lead your men.'"

Rob knew then that the Chief had heard. About Jamaal. "I have," Rob replied, tightening the grip on his cup. "

The Chief glanced at Rob's white knuckles. "Relax. I told you then and I'll tell you again. When you get dirty, know that I have your back. Your training should've helped you understand what we were entrusting you with." He pushed close to Rob and twisted his hand on Rob's arm. Rob winced but held back any sound of pain. "Next time you go off and shoot a low-level thug, make better fucking sure nobody finds the body." He released Rob. "Good hunting."

"Thank you again, sir," Rob said automatically to the Chief's back as the man left.

The training. Robert Grey was trained at the CIA Farm, and at Glynco, Georgia. Heavy weapon and explosives. He had the most extensive training. A dirty-dozen unit to carry out the new program. They wanted no questions, just action and results. You didn't need a hook or a rabbi to get into this unit; you needed a tainted history.

The best trained intelligence unit in domestic law enforcement. This unit was *nonpareil*. Once an officer was accepted into the unit, the covert nature was explained. You were notified that if your identity was blown, you were able to retire with full benefits, no matter your time in service, and you were relocated if necessary. This was approved in advance for all officers. Chain of Command for the unit; Police Commissioner, Chief Frank Coppice, Captain Howard, Lieutenant Grey, and Sergeant Ling. Unit Command; Captain., Lieutenant, Sergeant, 4 Detective Investigators, and 5 Undercover Detectives. The Chief had picked Rob and Alex because of their prior shootings and the shade behind them. He knew they could put people down. Sgt. Ling hated the police department so his supervision would be minimal. This would allow the undercovers a lot of freedom to work and break a few rules, and laws.

Because the City Council had no oversight over the program, their methods reflected those of federal agents. Most people they came into contact with thought they were the FBI, Homeland Security, or CIA. The NYPD liked the illusion—most civilians didn't know that the CIA has no authority to act inside of the United States. Their budget was over three million dollars, and most of that was federal money. So this allowed for the second identities, and all things needed to secure their alias and support their lifestyles. They all had secondary homes and cars for their cover. Some of them had fake spouses as well, like Rob and Pamela. Full commitment from the department for great results.

The Mayor was in a re-election year so he wanted big televised arrest from this unit, so that he looked good and the city felt safe. He took the leash off and tagged all violent crime as terroristic. This allowed already broad powers to be stretch even more. So far the chief had been able to keep the mayor and his staff out of their business by promising big cases. Some officers, like Pamela, had been trained at the Farm in Langley. They had all been marshaled as federal agents so they had authority in all states as well, because of the New Jersey incident. The greatest resource for this program was the size of the department, and the minorities that work there. This allowed for believable undercovers who were of the same ethnic backgrounds as the subjects. Something the lilywhite FBI, and Ivy League grads at the CIA didn't have

Chapter 7

THE MYTH

The reporter was waiting at police headquarters to interview a high-ranking police official. There were whispers about a federally trained unit inside the police department. It was the first of its kind because it wasn't controlled by a federal agency. Just trained by them. Hank Reilly was a young reporter at the *Daily News*. He knew this story could elevate his career. He was excited. Captain Martin came out to greet him. They went into his office to talk.

Reilly said, "Thank you, sir, for taking this time for the interview."

Captain Martin replied, "It's my pleasure. We want the world to know what we are doing to protect our citizens. After 9/11, the mayor and the police commissioner did not want to rely on the federal government to protect the city from terrorism. The lack of cooperation and confusion prior we feel led to the success of the terrorist. The mayor told the PC to do whatever was needed to make the city safe and he would give him his full support. So the PC decided that the NYPD needed to revamp its Intelligence Division, and they decided to recruit somebody from outside of the agency."

Reilley prompted, "Wow. So who was that person?"

Captain Martin paced the office. "We got a thirty-five-year veteran from the CIA to head the division by the name of Frank Coppice. He is the first civilian chief in the history of the department. His reputation is of an arrogant prick inside the CIA, so the NYPD feels even more confident about our choice. We wanted a maverick. Whatever it takes to prevent another 9/11, we would do it. Needless to say, Coppice loved this idea and jumped at the chance to take this position."

Reilley paused in his notetaking. He had the feeling he should be asking more questions, like *Is this legal*? "Can you, uh, give me more background on the Chief?"

Captain Martin smiled as if he knew what Reilley was thinking. "Not that I can share."

Reilley asked, "Do you have a photo of the Chief?"

Captain Martin said, "No."

Reilley tapped his pen against his pad. "Is he an official member of the department? Does he follow department rules or does he have complete control? The unit has to obey and enforce the NYS penal code."

Captain Martin says, "He is the head of the department and acts under its rules and regulations."

Reilley wrote, *Under departmental control.* "What have been his initiatives, what's the mission?"

Captain Martin gave him a hard stare. "Because of the unfortunate incident that happened we don't want to give out too much operational information."

Reilley thought back and nodded. "Speaking of the incident. Flooding Muslim neighborhoods with detectives. In mosques, restaurants, and internet cafes. Then in 2009 the public found out about it. How?"

"Pillow talk brings down many dynasties. A detective was fucking his mistress in a surveillance apartment in Jersey City, New Jersey. Excuse my bluntness. Things went south between them and for revenge she called the FBI and said terrorists were living in that apartment. She even told the FBI when it would be safest to enter the home; she knew their schedule so well. So when the FBI descended on the apartment and found all of the professional equipment they thought they had a real terror cell operating there. The FBI set up twenty-four surveillances on the apartment to capture the terrorist. Needless to say the FBI, and governor of New Jersey, were very upset that the NYPD was operating in New Jersey. Cue a lawsuit followed by attempts for government oversight." He sat on his desk, looking down at the young reporter. "What I say now is off the record."

Reilley slowly nodded and put his pen down.

"The Chief, sensing an end to the program, switched direction from Muslims onto drugs, because the money in drugs can be traced to government, terrorism, and organized crime. Basically anywhere. And if the department investigated a drug crew and there weren't any terrorism ties, you still had criminals off the street. So crime would go down and everybody would be happy. The Chief gathered every ethnic group that had a political base in New York City; African Americans, Jewish, Hispanic, and Muslims. He explained that the unit's only goal was to protect the citizens of New York, and the country from any threat foreign or domestic."

"But this is true. This is laudable. I get it, follow the money. This should be publicized—why off the record?"

"With drugs, there's no worry about civil rights, or the ACLU knocking on the door. Democrats and Republicans can both agree on drugs being bad. The unit can investigate whatever we want, because now we have an answer for city, and federal government officials. But we do want to protect the identities and safety of our officers. They are most important. They are on the front lines. We had to learn from the recent Mafia hits on our people." Then Captain Martin pasted on a smile, extended his hand. "Storytime's over."

Automatically Reilley shook the captains' hand and found himself ushered firmly out the door.

"Have a nice day," the captain said. "On the record."

Reilley found himself outside police headquarters with a lot of words written in his notebook he could print. And many more he couldn't.

Chapter 8

THE HUNGER FOR MORE

Derek Mason stared at himself in the mirror. He flexed his arms to watch his muscles move. His appearance was everything to him, so he worked out daily. He was wearing his normal black 501 Levis Jeans with a wife beater, and he had his Smith & Wesson 380 tucked into his jeans; 380 M&P 380 Auto, double action. Since slavery, African American males have been getting their confidence and respect from their outer appearance, clothes and jewelry. *Not good or bad,* he thought. *Just a fact.*

Derek Mason was five foot nine. His height was the only thing that was average about him. He ran the most notorious drug gang in New York out of Queens, South-Side Syndicate. And he had a hunger to be number one.

In two weeks was the Memorial Day BBQ which meant the beginning of summer. Today Derek would plan to take over all the drug transactions in New York. Great summer. There were only two other major crews in the city, the Latin Cartel and the Brooklyn Bullies. The Italians just provided the products, but that was where the big money was, distribution. The Italians also charged a "Black Tax," because they were the only show in town. They controlled distribution through force, and police protection. So if the normal price of a kilo of cocaine was $25,500, they charged $35,500. This affected the drug crew's money on the street, because they had to make up the money through weakening the product. So depending on how potent or weak the shit was depended on the volume of customers. When the crew stepped on the product it was hard to sell.

The Italian's top accountant had been arrested, and was cooperating with the FBI, so it was only a matter of time before most of the rest of the family would be arrested. More importantly all of their money had been frozen, because the FBI had taken control of it. Between the cash-flow situation and the indictments, they were no threat to anyone. So Derek decided it was time to get rid of them, without spilling any blood. Everybody including the Italians knew that the indictments were coming down any day now. The Italians received their product from the Colombians. Derek had a deal with the Mexican Cartel to buy from them instead and distribute it to the major crews in New York. The Italians wouldn't be able to fight him. They were fighting the federal government. All resources directly toward it. The other crews would have no choice. If there was going to be any fighting over it, it would be over the border in Mexico. He was trying to time everything right. He wanted the Brooklyn Bullies and the Latin Cartel to eliminate or weaken each other, and indictments would take care of the Italians.

Derek had been in the game along time, and it had been thirty years since one crew controlled the whole city. That was Curtis Royal, and he was from Queens too. So Derek felt some crazy connection to him. Curtis was dead, but they talked about him all over the country, he was a legend. Black Entertainment Television (BET) even did a documentary on him. Derek wanted that recognition. Shawn, his number two, thought things were great already, money was flowing in and there were no real problems so why push it. He also knew why Curtis didn't last long: being at the top of the mountain gives everyone a clear shot; the police and rivals. Derek saw it as a challenge, and he thought Shawn's posture was the same as the other two crews. Weak. He had been studying the other two major crews and he saw that they were comfortable, which meant they were vulnerable.

Derek would start a war between the two, so that he could step in when the dust cleared. At the least the war would send both the other crews customers to Derek. Because when you were at war, there was no selling, you concentrate only on war. All your soldiers take it to the mattresses, locked and loaded all the time.

"For with great intelligence you can wage your war." Derek had learned this quote from his very religious grandmother, Proverbs 20:18. War was what Derek wanted, and if everything went according to plan, he wouldn't even have to get his hands bloody. His crew had Queens and the Bronx. All they needed was Brooklyn and Manhattan. Respect was what he wanted from the drug world. He would then be King of New York.

Shawn, his number two man, knocked at the door.

"What?"

On the other side of the door, Shawn said, "He's here."

Derek smiled. He always got excited about taking over new territory. "Give me a sec."

Nigel was a top lieutenant in the Brooklyn Bullies. If Nigel could take someone out for Derek, it would weaken or destroy two crews, and this would help Derek become King of New York. Nigel was his cousin, which meant more to Nigel than to Derek. He knew that Nigel was unhappy with his boss because of low pay and his iron fist. He knew this because of Portia.

Portia was a girl with natural beauty enhanced by her expensive style. She worked for Derek; she was his intelligence gather through sex. When men asked her to have sex, it was on her terms. Bondage, discipline, sadism, and masochism equaled ejaculation. These so-called bosses and thugs never controlled her, but they left satisfied. All business for her. She told Derek once that it took some of the control back from her being raped as a kid. Most men felt they could trust her with their secrets because they thought she was far removed from their underworld. They didn't know she used to run the same streets, until Derek saved her.

Derek's grandmother babysat her while their mothers ran the streets. She and Derek were the same: both with drug-addicted mothers, never parenting or showing love to their kids. When Derek saw her selling and using drugs, he pulled her off the streets and made her graduate high school. He even put her in the Borough of Manhattan Community College—the two-year party school in downtown Manhattan. But she dropped out like most of the student population. He then got her a job at a bank—the bank manager was a current customer, a straight crackhead and Wharton grad. But nobody rode for free, so Derek enlisted her to help in "Operation Take Over."

He paid for her apartment in Kew Gardens, and he brought her a Benz C250. The "Hood Benz." The fellas also gave her money as well—seeing that she liked to look good, they got off on buying her shit. Stilettos and La Perla lingerie worked for everyone. Looking good made her feel good, and she loved the fact that all the white women at work couldn't figure out how she can afford a ten-thousand-dollar Louis Vuitton bag; it drove them crazy. They paid special attention to her at work, the lead cashier watching her every move because they thought she was stealing. Only the bank manager knew her life style was supported by Derek.

Life was simple for her: clothes, BDSM, and Kerry Washington on *Scandal*. There was only one man Portia truly loved: Derek. He saved her and gave her a new life and for that she was forever grateful, and she enjoyed helping him. And if he ever wanted to settle down, the answer would be yes. More importantly she would do anything for him, including murder with pleasure.

Portia had worked her routine on Nigel, using chains and straps and the pillow talk flowed. He revealed that he wasn't happy working for his boss because he paid him less than the market rate, and made him live in his house so he could watch his every move and charged them rent. He was a modern-day George Pullman, controlling the wages, housing, basically the whole village. His whole crew lived in his building. Besides being greedy it also made them an easy target. This wasn't your uncle's old DC 37 Union, no stock options or free lunch, this wasn't Google. It was more like a Victorian workhouse: Spike, accommodations and employment.

Nigel Judas was twenty-six, and he was from Marcy Projects in Brooklyn. He was Derek's cousin through marriage. Once out of jail, he started selling weed because he loved to smoke it. He was at the right place and time when Trevor took over the Brooklyn Bullies. He rose quickly because Trevor couldn't trust any of the top guys, eventually becoming a lieutenant. But he soon realized that Trevor ran a tight ship. Trevor was all about money, but he had the business wrong. You have to feed your people, or their hunger will kill you.

So Derek had to find a way to use Portia's information to his advantage. He showed up at the club that Nigel frequented, and approached him. After buying him a bottle of Crystal and inviting him to sit with the big boys, the conversation flowed. Nigel wasn't used to getting attention from a big boss like this. Derek gave him some compliments and showed him some respect and then he made him offer. He also reminded him that they were cousins. Nigel ate it all up and told Derek he was ready to make a change to his crew because he saw how he treated his people. His reputation was solid on the streets. Derek told him he respected the time he had in the game, and if everything goes right he would offer him a top position in the Syndicate. He wouldn't have to start at the bottom.

Derek ended with, "Keep this conversation to yourself. We'll talk again soon." Only Derek, Shawn, Andre, and Nigel knew about the conversation. And only Shawn knew about the bigger plan to take over New York. Derek knew that loose lips sink ships.

Derek had built a strong empire, and there were three layers to his organization, Raekwon, Shawn, and himself. He and Shawn were able to stay away from the drugs while Raekwon ran the business directly. They saw him all of the time because they frequented the neighborhood where the product was sold. But they didn't contact Raekwon on the phone unless it was important. They made it almost impossible for the feds to build a case. They only worried about the NYPD because they knew that they would lie and plant evidence if necessary to make an arrest. Basically, out of frustration, do anything. So talking to Nigel was a risk, but taking over another crew was major, and Derek wanted to keep it quiet.

He opened the door and told Shawn and the young soldier to come in. Nigel approached, nervous and excited. Derek could tell—the way he was pumped up on feeling important, taking deep breaths. He was wearing a black-on-black shell-top Adidas. He was always fresh—part of the lifestyle. A lot of black in the wardrobe. Derek approved.

A flicker in Shawn's eyes got Derek's attention. Was Shawn thinking the kid wasn't ready? But a good soldier, Shawn waited for the boss to tell him. Derek looked Nigel up and down and decided that he was ready for what needed to be done. He nodded at Shawn.

Shawn looked the young soldier in the eyes and said, "You been asking to be a part of the Syndicate, right?"

"Yeah," Nigel replied.

Shawn stepped closer. "Well, we need you to take out Pedro, from the Latin Cartel."

Nigel knew that the Latin Cartel sold dope. They ran Spanish Harlem, as well as Jamaica, and Flushing, Queens, which was mostly Spanish clientele. Wanting to do this, to show and prove, he just said, "Fat boy on Jamaica Ave?" When they nodded he rubbed his hands together in anticipation. "I got this."

Derek liked his body language; he thought he might have a rising star here.

Shawn said, "Nigel, we need this done right away."

"What's the plan," Nigel asked. "Drive-by tonight on the motor bike?"

Derek and Shawn look at each other and then back at Nigel. Shawn said, "No, right now."

Nigel was thinking in his head, *these motherfuckers were crazy, it's almost noon. The avenue would be buzzing with people. They can't be serious.* He's down for the crew but this was just fucking stupid. He answered in the form of a question, "So you want me to kill him in broad daylight?"

Shawn said, "Yup."

Nigel knew it was a suicide mission because either the cops were going to catch him, or there would be a hundred witnesses. He shifted his stance and stared at the floor. Shawn and Derek noticed. They recognized the change in posture as fear. He was thinking, *what is this shit really about.* There were always numerous motives with street situations, so you have to think of every angle. Or you would end up dead. But if he said no, he would be dead by tonight, so he had no choice. He knew Derek wanted to take over the city.

Nigel said, "Fuck it. Let's do it."

Shawn handed him a defaced Smith and Wesson .45 semi-automatic handgun, and two magazine clips of thirty-four rounds so he had a total of fifty-one bullets. Derek thought that this was a can't-lose situation because even if something went wrong, there was still confusion from sending a shooter in the sunlight from a different crew. If everything went right Nigel would start a war that would help the Syndicate take over the city. If he was caught or killed the Brooklyn Bullies would take the blame. Shawn told the kid to come up on Fat Boy through the alley on 172th Street. "That'll be his blind side, he'll never see you coming." Fat Boy's concentration would be on his product and customers on 172 Street. The alley was his escape route; his back would be to it.

Nigel nodded. He understood that if he did this he would get his own corner because they could trust him with anything, and possibly soon he could be running the Brooklyn Bully turf for The Syndicate. Once Derek had a body on you, you passed the test to be a part of the Syndicate and to start earning some real dough.

Shawn looked at Nigel and said, "Let's get to it."

As Nigel walked out of the apartment, Derek paused and pulled out a wad of money and ripped off three one-hundred-dollar bills. Shawn knew what was going on. Derek could tell Shawn didn't think the kid was built for this, so he was going to take advantage of his doubt with a bet.

Derek placed the bills on the table.

Shawn placed three hundred-dollar bills beside them.

"Let's go see," Derek said. They waited a few minutes before trailing Nigel out of the apartment.

No matter what, it was going to be an interesting afternoon.

Chapter 9

ROUTINE PATROL

The vibrant orange sun had just begun to expose the day. It was a busy May afternoon on the streets of Queens. The ladies were wearing their summer dresses, and the fellas were staring. Whenever the temperature hit 80, people went crazy. Seemed like all the clothes came off, and the sunglasses came on, so fellas could be discreet perverts.

An eleven-year-old boy and his mother walked up Jamaica Avenue, and as usual the kid was mesmerized by all the people and cars, both moving at a frantic pace. The kid always noticed that men looked at his mom. She was beautiful, with her pretty brown skin. Today, she was wearing a skirt that was way too short for the morning hours, and definitely not appropriate while walking with your child. She knew better, but she always looking for mister right now to help with her bills. She and her son were both wearing the same Air Jordan's. She loved the attention, and the kid was used to it. He knew his mother was good-looking because there were always men at the house, and they always gave him money and video games to play in his room while they talked to his mother.

The kid eye's locked on a rare sight, two police officers walking on the avenue. The kid looked around for their patrol car but didn't see it, so he assumed they were harassing someone. But they were walking around like everybody else. The kid asked his mother, "Why Po Po walking around?" Even an eleven-year-old knew the cops just sped past with the windows up and their eyes straight ahead.

She turned to stare at them. "They look like rookies. Rookie have to walk."

The boy frowned. "What do rookies look like?"

"Like you," his mother said. "Babyface."

That confused him—since when did he look like a cop? But his attention span was short. His eyes had found the Toys R Us store across the street. He wanted to ask his mom to take him, but he didn't want to get her upset. Sometimes her anger lasted for hours. He knew they were broke, so he just stared at store until it was out of view.

Officers Alison Hale and Larry Cotten were indeed rookies and looked every bit the part. New uniforms, shined shoes, and visibly nervous on foot patrol on Jamaica Avenue.

Alison flashed a nervous smile at some of the gawkers. A toned five-foot-five, she looked great in her uniform and was very excited about the first week of patrol. She was the first cop in her family, and her mother was very proud. Ms. Hale loved showing off her mini-shield to friends and family, and it got her out of speeding tickets. Her father didn't like her risking her life for strangers, he really didn't see the logic. He wished that she would have put that St. John's education to use. But between *Law & Order SVU* and her Uncle Jack, a twenty-five-year veteran street cop, she joined the NYPD. She planned to be a detective in the Special Victims Unit.

Her partner, Officer Cotten, was looking around because he was nervous. He was a plodder, which was a name used by the Irish to describe big English police officers. He was big but not muscular, and he looked awful in his uniform even though it was brand new. He looked horrible, except for his baby face you'd think by his uniform that he had ten plus years on the job. Queens was much different from Ronkonkoma in suburban Long Island, where he grew up with his parents. He was not used to all of these people, and definitely not used to seeing so many minorities. Unlike Alison, he came from a family of cops and joined the family business because he had no idea on what else to do with his life. College wasn't for him; it took him almost four years to get the forty-eight credits needed to join the department. It should have taken him two years. His grandfather, father, and two uncles were all NYPD officers. His mother was a housewife, and she was the only one to encouraged him to join the NYPD. All of the uncles knew he was soft. His father always thought he was a little soft, so he just never talked about the

"Job" with his son, hoping he wouldn't be interested. So here he was, scared out of his mind, hand on his gun, walking through the hood.

Officer Cotten said, "How can people live like this? Trash everywhere and the constant smell of urine. Fucking animals."

Hale replied, "Relax, Long Island boy. They don't have homeless people in Ronkonkoma?"

"Nope. Just hardworking families, not a bunch of lazy good-for-nothings."

Hale hit Cotten on the arm and pointed to an old lady crossing the street. The light was turning yellow so she was not going to make it before the light changed. Hale jogged into the street to stop traffic, holding up both arms. She jerked her head at her partner; Cotten had no choice but to help the lady. He walked over to her and the lady immediately grabbed his right arm for assistance and they crossed the street.

When they reached the sidewalk the lady said, "Thank you, such a gentleman."

Hale thought, *this was what the job was about. There were not going to be too many situations where you were going to be on the news for saving somebody, so you have to enjoy the little stuff.* Then she saw the look on her partner's face—he'd clearly rather be somewhere else.

Hale had to ask, "Didn't that make you feel good?"

Cotten said, "Nah, I'm looking for some real action."

Hale replied, "Careful what you wish for, tough guy."

She thought, *His reputation through nine months of the academy wasn't good. He had mysterious injuries during Defensive Measures; Fighting, Speed Cuffing, and Felony Stops. And the infamous shin splints, he didn't participate in a run the last six months of the academy. His class instructor Officer O'Sullivan was trained by Cotten's father, Lawrence.* Fifty-five years of experience between them. They say he skated, so he's known as the "Skater." This was loyalty in the NYPD, his father's protégé would push through training a twenty-year problem for the department and the community. Officers were required to work twenty years, before you were eligible to retire. So for that span of time every officer and boss that comes into contact with him would be affected by his negative traits. These traits could get you hurt or killed. The citizens would be terrorized by his cowardice. His reputation has followed him to the Precinct, and most officers wouldn't work with him. They asked the sergeant to switch their assignment. Hale gave him the benefit of the doubt, because he wasn't in the same company as her, so it was just rumors. It said a lot about her character, because in this department a rumor can kill your career. There were twenty platoons of fifty cadets too equal 1000. They were split into two companies Alpha, and Bravo, 500 apiece. They alternated day (0700-1600), and night (1600-2400) tours. She was Alpha, he was Bravo.

Cotten looked at his watch. "What time do we go sixty-three, smartass?"

"Ten-six." Hale said. "Noon."

Cotten said, "Cool, we go sixty-three, in fifteen minutes."

A U.S. postal worker standing right next to Officer Cotton asked, "What is sixty-three?"

Cotten said, "It means meal time. We purposely use ten codes so civilians don't understand what we are talking about."

The postal worker says, "Got it."

Hale checked her memo-book, in which she, like all police officers, recorded her interactions with members of the public and any other pertinent information. She had learned in the police academy that they needed to write down meal times, and any inspections within her sector or place of patrol. Today they had two inspections at 1300, at Jamaica Ave and 161 Street, and another at Jamaica Ave and 165 St. at 1345. Both of these places had a Robbery Pattern, which meant people were getting robbed at these locations at those times.

As the young mother and her son walked by, she noticed Cotten giving her his full attention.

She poked his shoulder. "You would need an eighty-five with all that ass."

Cotten nodded in agreement. "Officer needs assistance, that's right."

They both laughed.

Hale decided she was still going to grab her usual chicken salad from the Oochi Deli. She was serious about not putting on the "Rookie Twenty," the traditional twenty pounds after the academy. Salad, jogging, and yoga would defeat it. "I'm going to the deli. Where were you going to eat?"

Lunch was Cotten's favorite part of the day, but he'd heard that when you wear a uniform in the hood, there weren't too many safe places you could eat. People often spat in your food, even a rookie knew that. So cops had to be strategic about where and how they ordered your food.

Today he wanted something different. He couldn't eat another hero, so he wanted the Chinese Buffet Restaurant around the corner. *They're aliens too*, he thought, *so they should appreciate his presence. Hey, they might even give me free food, one of the many perks of working in uniform.*

Cotten said, "Today I want Chinese. It should be safe they put the buffet out at eleven."

"Look at you, taking chances."

"I'll meet you back at the house, unless you want me to walk with you?"

I'm good, thanks," said Hale.

Cotten said, "See you in a few."

"Ten-four."

They went their separate ways for lunch but both looked down at their watches, something a cop always does because every second counts on patrol. The objective was to pick up lunch and be back in the precinct exactly when your lunch break started, without getting caught by the patrol sergeant. Hale entered the deli, and was greeted by Samantha and Rob. She was a familiar face to the deli workers. Samantha, working the counter, knew what Hale wanted. Chicken salad, no tomatoes.

Smiling, Hale said, "They tell me it's not good to be predictable in this business."

Samantha replied, "It's good to be certain in life."

They both laughed.

Down the block, Cotten entered the packed Chinese restaurant. He looked at the wrinkled old Chinese woman behind the bulletproof glass to maybe get some special treatment, but she wouldn't look at him. He skipped the line for the buffet and people were visibly upset but said nothing. He thought maybe he should have gone to the deli, but he was here now. Besides, he has eaten a hero everyday while he's been on patrol. No more. He still lived with mom and dad and thought tomorrow he would have his mother make him lunch, because this was too much. He packed a carton full of food, hoping that it would be free or discounted. He went to pay and the woman still didn't look at him, so he turned up his department radio, hoping she would recognize the sound, but still nothing. He'd be paying full price, nothing on the arm here.

The old timers told all the rookies that when they work in uniform, most of the food was on the arm, meaning it'd be free. If it wasn't minority owned. Reason being business people in the hood appreciate the police presence, and want police around as much as possible.

He put his back against the wall, his hand on weapon, and waited while the lady weighed and packs his food.

Chapter 10
NEW YORK MINUTE

Nigel loaded his weapon in the building's incinerator room and shoved it into his front waist. He then stepped out into the afternoon air, and walked south on Jamaica Ave. He planned on walking up to 172nd Street and making the left into the ally. He then could escape on 93 Ave, which was quieter than Jamaica Ave.

He would be in the alley in less than sixty seconds and he was in no hurry. His mind moved at a frantic pace; he knew this wasn't a good idea to do this while the sun was out. The Ave was buzzing. He also knew he had no choice, so just would have to be as careful as possible. If he was the one taking the risk, then he should have a say so in how it goes down. But Shawn called the shots. If he gave a command, the boss was okay with it. The boss didn't give such orders himself so he could have plausible deniability in court. Nigel knew this short notice was done by design; less time to think about it or tell someone. Derek didn't want to take any chances with this getting out.

Nearing the alley. Game time. He looked down at the weapon tucked into his waist. His lips moved, "Are you ready? Please don't fail me." Nigel looked up the alley to see Fat Boy pacing back and forth, his back to him. It was normal drug dealer behavior, looking up and down the block for customers—and cops. Nigel felt like he could get the drop on him. All he needed was a few seconds and he would win. He started up the alley, hugging the wall.

Fat Boy stared down at his phone. He glanced up and recognized a regular customer walking towards him. *'Bout time*, he thought. The minute he sold this last vial of crack, he was going to get some pussy from Maribel. The regular asked for a dime and Fat Boy pointed to the phone booth. The regular would know that meant there was a crack vial in the coin return slot. The regular took the crack, leaving ten dollars. Only three more left.

Already on his cellphone trying to set up an exact time with Maribel, Fat Boy was too busy to grab the money. Nigel had crept almost up the alley to where Fat Boy was talking on the phone. He knew he'd got the drop on him now. Then he saw the regular walking up the alley towards him and he recognized him. *Oh, shit. That's Dave. We played on the same football team together in High School.*

Dave saw Nigel and laughed loudly in recognition, "Yo, Nigel! You going to football practice today?" Clearly a joke, because they had been out of high school for over eight years.

Hearing the shout-out, Fat Boy turned and saw Nigel with his gun. Nigel knew he'd been spotted. *Shit, it's on now.*

Fat Boy ran to a nearby car and grabbed the gun hidden under the wheel barrel. He spun and started shooting at Nigel. There were dozens of people walking by on Jamaica Ave. They recognized the sound of gunfire and scattered. Nigel aimed his gun and started shooting back at Fat Boy precisely at the moment that Officer Cotten walked out of the Chinese restaurant with food in hand.

He heard the noise, but didn't believe it was gunfire. He froze in the doorway. Then as children, women, and men ran past him, screaming, he knew that it was. But his feet felt as if they were stuck in cement.

Hale was at the register paying for her food at the deli, Rob and Samantha behind the counter. She recognized the sound right away. Hale got right into a zone, her attention on the gunfire and her partner. It was seven blocks away but she ran towards the Chinese restaurant, her partner more important than the actual source of the gunfire. This rookie was sharp. She put a call over her radio. "Central, this was Two Frank Two, shots fired. I'm at 165 Street heading east towards Jamaica Avenue."

Rob followed her out but stopped himself from running like a cop. He kept a safe distance as not to scare her and divert her attention from the perpetrator.

People ran past Cotten and pointed in the direction of the shots. He managed to turn in that direction but he at the thought of getting shot or fighting, his legs went stiff. He thought he should wait for backup. *Why do I need to be first on the scene?* he asked himself.

Fat Boy was crouched behind a car shooting at Nigel. His big fat hands were holding the gun so tightly that he cut his middle finger on the trigger. Nigel was firing back. Fat Boy's shots missed widely because Nigel had good cover behind a car. He was damn near dripping from fear. Fat Boy just wanted to let him know who he was messing with. Nigel wasn't good with a gun so he just aimed in the general direction of Fat Boy. The aim was too high and to the left of Fat Boy, so Fat Boy knew he was amateur. This gave him confidence so he stood up and shot at Nigel until his magazine emptied.

Then Nigel's clip emptied. He pulled out another clip to reload his weapon to see Fat Boy advancing, gun pointing at him. Nigel's hands shook as he hurried with his reload. He needed to get off one more round and then get out of Dodge. Without looking back at Fat Boy he fired a round that bounced off the pavement and smacked Fat Boy in the right thigh.

There were too many people around and the cops would be here shortly. He muttered, "Shit, I didn't want to run on the ave, but I have no choice."

He had played wide receiver on the football team and all they did was send him deep because of his speed. He's been a decoy his whole life. He would make a left on Jamaica Ave, and he'd be gone. He ran, checked back for Fat Boy, not knowing if he'd floored the motherfucker with a leg shot. When he turned around, he saw a cop standing in front of him—a big one, holding a takeout container in front of the Chinese restaurant.

"Oh shit." Nigel still had the weapon in his hand. But the look in the cop's eyes—the cop was going to piss himself with fear. So Nigel didn't stop but ran right by him.

Cotten dropped his takeout. He didn't pursue or even put it over the radio. The cashier from the Chinese restaurant went to the window to watch. She saw the man with the gun run right by, and the officer do nothing. "This would not happen at home with Chinese police," she told the waiter in Mandarin. "He would be dead already."

In the alley Fat Boy looked down at his leg. It was clean shot, in and out. More importantly, not a lot of blood. He ditched his gun and limped to the corner, flagged a livery cab, and jumped in.

Hale ran at top speed towards the Chinese restaurant when she turned the corner and collided with Nigel. His gun flew into the air and they both fell to the ground.

Hale saw the gun flip over her head and knew she had a second. *Control your breathing, think*, she told herself. She had to gain control of the perpetrator because if she pushed off and went for her weapon he could get to his gun on the ground.

She saw everything in her mind in slow motion, as if she was previewing a game. *Even if I get to my weapon an innocent person might get shot, so I'm going to play defense until my partner arrives.* She grabbed him and twisted his arm.

As they tussled, Nigel punched her in the face, but they were so close it didn't have the effect it should. Dazed, her motor skills direct her to punch back. She counter-punched him with little effect, hurting her left hand. Then she was just holding on tightly to him for her life. A crowd formed around them, shouting as loudly as if they were at a Knicks game. Hale heard their shouts as if they were muffled, as she focused on the gun and Nigel.

Rob stood at the edge of the building. Every instinct told him to dive in and haul the criminal off the rookie but he held back, his fists white-knuckling in his pockets. He was under strict orders to stay out of anything but his assignment, deep cover. The department has invested too much into his alias, and the program. But he followed Hale out of the deli, and she was fighting for her life. *Where the fuck was her partner or the backup?* He couldn't tamp down the adrenaline and his concern for the rookie. No matter how many name changes, no matter how much training, he would always be a cop.

He felt a crowd coming closer, so he stepped in finally to put his foot on the weapon. This was the hood, and that weapon would disappear fast. Nigel was swinging her around like Jeff Van Gundy on Alonzo Mourning's leg, but she was holding on. *Tough girl*, Rob thought.

Hale managed to elbow Nigel in the ribs, which knocked the breath out of him. She then pushed him off and pulled out her weapon.

"Don't move, motherfucker!"

Her hands were shaking, but Nigel looked into her eyes and knew she would shoot him out of fear. Her nerves meant his life. He froze.

Rob told the officer, "I got his weapon. Cuff him."

Hale looked up and saw the owner of the deli. The weapon was under his foot. With Nigel frozen, she tried to put her location over the radio. Holding the weapon in her right hand, she tried to pull her radio out but her hand was in too much pain so she just held down the button.

Very loudly, she said, "Central, be advised I'm at the corner of Jamaica Ave and 169 Street holding the suspect, 10-85."

Central responded, "10-4 Unit. All units be advised 10-85 at the C/O Jamaica and 165 Street."

Rob was impressed that she didn't call a 10-13, which was the most severe call for officer assistance. 10-85 was the Ten-code for Officer needs additional units.

Hale looked around at the crowd and wondered where her partner was. She was in too much pain to try and cuff the shooter. She repeated her location too Central on the radio. Hearing the sirens in the background, she nearly dropped in relief.

The female cop had only one hand on her weapon. She hoped Nigel didn't see her wincing in pain. She noticed he readied his quick feet and turned to flee. Just as Nigel hit his stride, Rob stepped in his path and hit him with a two-punch combination, dropping him. His head hit the pavement, and he felt his wrists getting cuffed. Rob was a former Golden Glove Champion for light heavyweight, 178 pounds. He still wore the chain. He used to think he would be the next Rocky Marciano, until he tore his rotator cuff. Just like that, his career was over.

Rob gave her the weapon and when he saw the patrol cars pulling up, he walked away. Hale's attention was on Nigel. She placed the weapon in her waistband. The backups burst through the crowd and grabbed the perp, and they threw him in the back of the RMP—Radio Mobile Patrol.

Sergeant Donnelly asked Hale, "Are you okay?"

"Yes, but I don't know where Cotten is."

At that moment Officer Cotten waddled up. "There you are. You okay?" His heart was racing, and sweat was seeping through his uniform shirt.

Sergeant Donnelly said, "Let's get the hell out of here before there's a riot."

All of the officers move, everybody jumping in a car and speeding off with lights and sirens.

Sergeant Donnelly put over the radio, "Central, we have one under and we were headed back to the house."

Central responded, "10-4 Sergeant, any injuries to officers or prisoner?"

The Sergeant Donnelly said, "Unknown at this time Central, Have EMS respond to the precinct I'll sort it out there."

Central responded, "10-4 Sergeant, all units the 10-85 was over, slow it down, and resume patrol."

The Duty Captain comments over the radio, "Central, have the Sergeant take the officers and prisoner to Jamaica Hospital. I will meet him there."

The Sergeant told his driver to head to the hospital. The driver flipped on the siren and changed direction. He knew that the Duty Captain was right.

Fat Boy was in a livery cab headed to his cousin's house. He was shot and he needed to money and to get to a doctor. He was picking up his cousin in case he passed out or died. He also needed ten thousand dollars in cash to see the doctor. Time was of the essence.

#

Derek and Shawn sat in a black SUV across the street from the action, watching the officers put Nigel in the back of the patrol car. Derek wasn't worried about Nigel giving any information to the police because loyalty was the number one code in the crew, and on the streets. Even the cops respected the code. The Stop Snitching campaign and the Blue Wall of Silence were the same.

Shawn wasn't that confident about anybody. The only people he's sure of were Derek, Raekwon, and himself because they had been tested on many occasions. There was a time when it was just them running around the streets of Queens, so the trust was there. Derek was more intuitive; he went off his gut. Besides, when you were a part of the crew they knew your whole family. Which would be Nigel's girl and two kids. So if you do "RAT," your entire family would pay.

#

Inside the deli, Rob made a phone call to Captain Howard and told him to check on the female officer he had just helped. He shouldn't have gotten involved. But he was glad that no officers had been fatally hurt. In his mind he could handle any situation without identifying himself as a cop. In fact, he was not a cop, he was a Centurion.

"Fucking hero." Captain Howard said. "Don't get involved in street matters."

Rob didn't answer. In this elite unit, the Captain was the only supervisor Rob answered to, and Captain Howard reported directly to the Chief. With all of the training he had received from the CIA and the great responsibility the unit had to take down major drug games this could not be jeopardized doing normal patrol.

Chapter 11

THREE SIDES

Sergeant Donnelly was running on adrenalin through the hospital trying to sort things out before the duty captain arrived. Everywhere he looked, he saw officers trying to look busy so they wouldn't get assigned an official duty from him. Nigel was in one room, half-conscious. Officer Hale was in another room that was filled with officers worried about her. Cotton was alone.

It didn't hurt that she was pretty—not just cop pretty, but really pretty.

The elevator stopped on the third floor and the squad appeared. Four detectives and a sergeant. They were all from the 103th Precinct so on a first-name and poker-debt basis.

The detective sergeant found Sergeant Donnelly. "Relax," he said. "Don't worry about the duty captain and his fucking 49. All that matters were your cops were okay. We'll help you sort this shit-show out."

They both laughed.

Officer Cotten paced nearby. He spoke up to impress the other cops. "He's lucky I didn't get there earlier, because he would be dead. Bang. One shot, one kill."

No one paid attention to him except the hospital staff. If it were anybody but a uniformed officer, the person saying these words would be called an emotionally disturbed person (EDP) and admitted.

Through all of the confusion, nobody saw Officer Armetta go into Nigel's room. He had a crush on Alison, so he had taken the attack on her personally. He felt safe from identification because he was in plain clothes, shield tucked under his New York Yankees shirt. His plan was to make sure Nigel had a black eye and a broken hand, the same injury as Alison.

Nigel saw the officer approach and knew it wasn't good from the look on his face. Armetta stood on Nigel's right side and grabbed a pillow with his left hand and put it over Nigel's face to muffle any noise. He shoved Nigel's left hand between the metal bars on the bed and pulled straight up, snapping his wrist. Nigel was in excruciating pain but his cries were muffled by the pillow. Armetta lowered it and punched him in the face. A couple of times just to make sure.

Nigel's eyes swam shut.

Armetta left.

#

A few rooms away, Sergeant Donnelly escorted the detectives to Officer Cotten.

Cotten saw them and raised his voice for effect. "Fucking piece of shit. I wish I could get my hands on him."

Sergeant Detective Ryan introduced himself. "Detective Johnson and White will be interviewing you."

Detective Johnson found an empty room and motioned for the officer to follow. Cotten was still muttering, but the seasoned detective paid no attention.

Detective White told Cotten to have a seat and then he went through his spiel. "Listen, I'm not a boss so I'm not here to jam you up. All we want is information to complete our canvass so we can create a timeline. So give us as much details as you remember. What was the scenario?"

Officer Cotten said he was ready to answer any questions to help them in the investigation.

Detective Johnson said, "Well then, tell me where you were when you heard the shots, and what transpired thereafter."

Officer Cotten started stuttering as he began, trying to think how to frame the story in his favor. If the other officers in the precinct found out he didn't respond, his career would be over before it even started. He already had a bad reputation. Cowardice was not tolerated in the NYPD or the streets. The game didn't allow it, period.

He started by saying he was in the Chinese restaurant when he first heard the shots. He then dropped his food and responded toward the shots, or where he thought the shots were coming from. "When I came out of the restaurant I initially went to the right, which would be north on Jamaica Ave. I soon realized from what people were saying that I went the wrong way. So, after fighting through people I started after the perpetrator, but he was running like a gazelle. When I finally caught up, the backup was already there and they were putting the perp in the RMP."

The detective thought for a moment and then asked, "Did you and your partner get separated? Because she beat you to the scene."

Officer Cotten explained they had gone to different places for lunch. The detective wrote this on his pad.

The duty captain arrived with his own entourage. He took a look at the chaotic scene and yelled, "Judas Priest. What is going on here. Can we establish some order? Where is Sergeant Donnelly?" Nigel was yelling at the top of his lungs that some cop just beat him up.

"Place a uniformed officer in that room for prisoner security!" the duty captain said. "Have we forgotten the prisoner's well-being is our number-one priority while he is in our custody."

Sergeant Ryan walked into the room and said the duty captain wanted the perpetrator interviewed right now.

Detective White dismissed Cotten with, "Thanks, Officer."

Cotten said, "No problem, anything to put this piece of shit away."

As they walked away, Detective White turned to Detective Brennam. "Why does it seem like the officer was lying?'

"Maybe not. He's just a nervous rookie."

Detective White said, "You're probably right." Under his breath he muttered, "Because he's an officer or are we going with the facts?" His gut told him the latter.

They entered Nigel's room. Nigel was cuffed to the bed with a uniformed officer standing guard next to him. Nigel had a massive headache from his latest beating, but he still felt lucky to be alive. He knew assaulting a cop would lead to this, especially a female cop. This was part of the game, and he accepted it. And he knew these guys in suits were detectives, so he was on guard from the jump.

Sergeant Ryan introduced himself, Detective Johnson, and Detective White.

Sergeant Ryan said, "This is your opportunity to tell us your side of the story and then maybe we can do something for you. If the other guy started shooting first, then it was self- defense. Tell us if there were any mitigating circumstances. We just want to hear from you."

Nigel cradled his throbbing wrist. "Get the fuck out of my room. I got nothing to say. Find the officer who fucked me up. Solve that case, Batman."

Detective Johnson smiled and pulled out his notepad.

Sergeant Ryan explained that he needed them more than they need him, because there were at least thirty witnesses on the street that could identify him, and soon there would be a gunshot victim at the hospital.

What the detectives didn't know was that the drug gangs' "Stop Snitching" campaign was winning. The community was scared. There were no witnesses.

Detective Johnson warned him, "If that victim you shot ends up dying, this is a murder charge."

These motherfuckers are lying, Nigel thought. *I didn't hit Fat Boy. He was still standing last I saw. This must be a trick.*

A custodian outside of the room was listening to the conversation as he pretended to mop the floor. He was one of Shawn's people. It pays to have people everywhere. People would do a lot to feel important, and for fifty dollars.

Nigel told them to fuck themselves and turned his back to them, forgetting he's cuffed. He had to turn back over because the cuffs tightened every time he moved. He was double cuffed. He was in excruciating pain but he was trying to be cool.

Detective Johnson pulled up a stool and sat down. "Hey, tough guy, we have you dead to rights: attempted murder, assault, chambered round, two fully loaded magazines, hollow-point bullets, felony assault on a police officer, and resisting arrest. That's the scenario. All great reasons to make a statement. A shoot-out in broad daylight wasn't too smart. So this is your chance to tell us your side of the story."

Nigel said, "Suck my dick, you fucking sell-out. Go arrest the white cop who fucked me up."

Detective Johnson's face swelled as he held in his anger, but he tried to maintain his cool.

Detective White told Nigel, "Okay, we'll see you again, but the next time would be in court and there would be no deal."

They all started to walk away, then Nigel yelled, "Wait!"

They smiled because they thought he'd come to his senses and was going to talk. They returned to his bedside.

Nigel said, "No one likes a coward in this game. Whoever that big white officer was I passed, he wasn't doing shit. Just stood there like a pussy. That lady cop, she got heart. It wasn't like the movies and some Tomb Raider Angelina Jolie type shit, but I'm here." He lifted his wrist cuffed to the bed. "She did have some help from Brave Heart–looking motherfucker," Nigel finished.

The detectives looked at each other.

Nigel said, "You're welcome, you rude motherfuckers."

Sergeant Ryan turned back to him, "Was Brave Heart a cop?"

Nigel didn't know, so he just shrugged. The detectives left the room, satisfied that they would find enough witnesses to put the prisoner at the scene, and maybe someone who actually saw him firing the weapon. Or maybe some videotape from one of the businesses along Jamaica Avenue showed the shootout and both shooters. That along with DNA from a blood trail should be enough to catch the other shooter. The blood trail should go from the alley to the street. They were guessing he got into a waiting car.

Just a matter of time.

Down the hall, Dr. Wright was finishing up his examination of Officer Hale under the watchful gaze of a few of her fans.

Sergeant Donnelly stepped into the examination room with Dr. Wright, Officer Hale, and her fans. With pen and pad in hand he asked for the official diagnosis.

Dr. Wright answered, "Officer Hale has fractured her phalanges bone in her left hand. Also, the officer has blood leaking into tissues under the skin in her right eye, and it's causing the black-and-blue hue."

Officer Hale whispered, "Doogie Howser in the flesh." Her fans all laughed.

The nurse translated, "The officer has a broken left hand, and a black eye."

Sergeant Donnelly, laughing, thanked her.

The detectives entered the room, pushing aside the large contingent of male officers around her. Sergeant Donnelly announced to all the caring officers, "I know all of you Neanderthals are sincerely concerned about this beautiful young officer's health." He paused and rethought his words. "And by beautiful, I do mean internally." They all laughed. "The officer has a black eye and broken left hand. She is going to make a full recovery. She is tougher than most you'll."

They all clapped. Alison was embarrassed but felt a secret glow of pride. She thought, *this must be what all the instructors at the police academy were talking about: "the Blue Family."*

"Now get the hell out of here and get back on patrol before we lose the borough of Queens."

Everybody was all smiles as they hugged Alison and left the room. Except Officer Armetta. He was extremely upset. He wished that he could protect her all of the time. Alison had a dark guardian angel, and she didn't even know it.

After introductions by Detective Johnson and White, Officer Hale told them everything that happened.

She said, "I was in the restaurant when I heard the shots. I knew my partner was in the area so I headed towards him. I was running east on 165th Street and I made a left on Jamaica Ave and I literally fucking ran into the perp. His gun fell to the ground and I tried to subdue him. We tussled for a while and I was able to pull my duty weapon out and stop him."

"Is that all?" asked Johnson.

"No, something else. There was this civilian, a male white who put his foot on the weapon, which was a big help because the crowd was going crazy. This allowed me to concentrate on the perp."

Detective Johnson asked, "Do you think he was an off-duty cop?"

Hale said, "Male, white, about thirty years old, that's all I got through the chaos."

She didn't feel the need to give any more information on the deli guy because if he wanted to cooperate he would have stayed on the scene. She was grateful.

Sergeant Ryan ask, "Where was your partner?"

She didn't know and she was not willing to say anything negative about him until she spoke to him herself. But she was wondering the same thing. *He should have been on the scene first,* she thought.

Detective Johnson watched her face. Something… But could be looked into later. Maybe the perp was right. Her partner might be a coward. His gut said she knew, but that she wouldn't say anything. Not his business. The officers of the 103rd would deal with him. It wouldn't be hidden for long.

They thanked her and left.

#

Officer Armetta entered Nigel's room, but halted at the sight of a uniformed officer. Nigel saw him and yelled, "Are you fucking kidding me?"

Armetta asked the officer to leave the room, but the officer informed him that he was ordered by a captain not to leave the room for any reason, unless told so by a ranking officer. Armetta reminded him that he didn't patrol with bosses, but with officers. He reminded him that he was a rookie, and there was a lot he didn't understand. His best bet would be to get the fuck out of the room.

The rookie reluctantly started to walk out but Sergeant Donnelly entered and shouted, "Armetta, get the fuck back on patrol."

Nigel shouted, "That's the motherfucker who did this to me. He was coming back to kill me. I'm not safe here."

Armetta left without saying a word, and the uniformed officer remained in the room. Sergeant Donnelly again reminded him not to leave for anyone. "Rookie, this will be the easiest assignment you will ever have. Just stand still."

#

The detectives were satisfied with Officer Hale's narrative. As they walked towards the elevator, Detective Johnson said, "Her story makes sense."

Detective White nodded.

Sergeant Ryan's phone buzzed. It was Captain Howard. Ryan told his guys, "I have to take this. Give me a sec." He stepped to the side to give the captain his full attention. Ryan listened to Captain Howard tersely outline his request. He and Captain Howard were old friends, so the communication was smooth. Forty thousand-plus officers, but still a small department for the active guys.

"No problem," he said then pocketed his phone.

"What did the captain want?" asked White.

"A copy of the case file when we're finished."

"What does he want with—" White shut up at a look from Ryan.

Ryan shrugged but in his mind he was wondering the same thing: *Why is the captain interested in this low-level street dispute?*

Officer Armetta entered Hale's room. She was alone. He was a plains-clothes officer from her precinct. He hit on all the female officers, and he hit on Hale in the past. He had a reputation for being a creep.

Officer Armetta said, "Hey Alison, can I give you a ride home?"

"Really?" said Hale.

Armetta said, "I was just trying to be nice."

Hale said, "Right. No thanks."

Chapter 12

OUTPATIENT

Fat Boy's cousin Hector was waiting in front of his building when he pulled up in the livery cab. His cousin jumped in. Fat Boy whispered, "I got hit, but the bullet went in and out, not much blood."

His cousin stared at the hole in his thigh, amazed at the lack of blood. Fat Boy turned on his side and showed him the exit wound on his buttock.

His cousin blurted, "So we going to Jamaica Hospital?

Fat Boy grimaced with pain. He said through gritted teeth, "I can't go there. We going to the Hood Doctor. You got the dough I asked you to bring?"

They pulled up to the back of a project building in Queens Bridge Projects. Once the car pulled away, Fat Boy limped over to a park bench and leaned on it. Hector stood there not knowing what to do or what was happening. He sent a text message and waited by the door. This was a hard number to get. If you had it, you're supposed to have it. When you lived by the gun you needed it. A criminal perk.

Soon after, a huge white guy opened the door and told them they both had to be searched before they enter. Safe to assume that the man searching you for a gun has one. Once inside, an old Russian lady told them that it would be ten thousand dollars cash to see the doctor. Fat Boy gave her the money, and then she locked the entrance door.

She told them, "Only the injured boy will see the doctor." She unlocked another door and he limped in.

Hector took a seat in the makeshift waiting area. There were two old *People* magazines on a table, one with Heidi Montag on the cover, the other Jennifer Hudson. He picked one up and looked through it to pass the time.

One hour later, Dr. Vlad cleaned out the open wound, peered in, and said in a heavy accent, "Nothing too bad. I've seen worse in the Ukraine."

He gave Fat Boy a shot of ampicillin and then put a gauze pad on both wounds. He told him to change the gauze pad once a day to prevent infection. Simple, he was sent on his way. Modern-day outpatient care.

Pedro Diaz, better known as "Fat Boy," was twenty-nine years old. He was from Astoria, Queens, where he grew up with his four siblings and parents. He was the baby of five with a fourteen-year difference in age between him and his oldest sibling. So he was picked on a lot by his siblings. They called him a mistake. Food became his comfort. When he was locked up for selling weed at York College during his junior year, he met a member of the Latin cartel in the Puerto Rican section of the yard. The Puerto Ricans had the Latin Kings and Netas, the Dominicans had Dominicans Don't Play, the Mexicans had La Nuestra Familia, and the Salvadorians had MS-13, the most powerful of them all. They would unite to fight another race, but they would also fight each other. After he got out of Riker's, the Latin cartel controlled drugs in his neighborhood, so with his connect he started to work for them. The jails were a recruiting place for criminals.

He was a loyal soldier; proud of his Puerto Rican Heritage. He had taken an oath to the cartel and it was easy for him to honor it. One of the few things he learned from his father was loyalty and heritage.

He spent his money on Air Jordans, pussy, and food.

Not necessarily in that order.

Chapter 13

HEADQUARTERS

Derek was at his usual hangout spot, the strip club. He liked the loud music, which kept people from recording his conversations. He sat at a back table to see all who enter and, of course, he loved the naked women. This was his office. There was no business done here, just a meeting point for the crew. For all the important people: Shawn, Raekwon, Andre, and Jocelyn.

Shawn sat the table with Derek, looking at him watching the girls. Shawn could fuck anyone he wanted, and he often broke in the new girls. Derek was a little jealous of that.

Shawn made a call on his phone to the hospital custodian.

The custodian answered on the first ring.

"Was it a long or short conversation with the police?" Shawn asked.

"A very short conversation," said the custodian.

Shawn told the old man that he would take care of him by the end of the week.

The old man knew Shawn was a man of his word; he always paid in a timely manner. He had been working for him for years. They used him often. Many victims that came into the hospital were part of the crew or victims of the crew.

Shawn was happy because Nigel had nothing to say to the police. His next call was to their lawyer, and he gave the name: Nigel Judas. The lawyer would track him down in the system, and keep Shawn updated.

"All set," Shawn said to Derek over the pounding music. "My guy will find him. He's the best."

"Cool," Derek said.

Derek had learned this the hard way. After he was busted on a second armed robbery charge, a young lawyer gave him an education. While reviewing his case, the young male white public defender said in a low voice, "You niggers are stupid. Trying to be tough, you pick the worst crime you can—armed fucking robbery. Every judge and prosecutor is afraid of you. You represent the worst and most violent people in society to them. You will never get any mercy from the court. Even Al Sharpton can't defend you. Drug dealers get pleas and sympathy all day long. No one cares if only black people were using and dying from drugs. All you fucking idiots should read the Penal Code before you commit a crime. Every goddamn library has a copy. I do know this for sure, if you get arrested again for this you were done. Three strikes and you're out! They throw away the key on the third violent felony and max your time, twenty-five years! Stupid motherfuckers. Waste of my time. The prosecutor won't take a plea offer on this."

He was right. No plea was taken, and Derek got five years. It was also the last time he robbed anybody. He was rehabilitated by a racist rant. Poetic justice.

Derek read the penal code in the prison library, and also minutes for big trials. It was entertainment and education all in one. It was funny to read how some of the biggest cases were started. He saw that drug offenses got big time as well, but it was harder to build cases, if people were smart. The Mafia bosses rarely got arrested for drugs as they didn't directly touch them. He knew from personal interaction with those bosses that drugs were a major part of their business. Even though they said otherwise. So Derek devised a strategy to run his crew without touching the product, and without him having a cell phone. It had taken years, because for a while it was only Shawn and him. Then Raekwon and a few soldiers joined the team. The system worked.

Raekwon Griffin was a small-time hustler who had been murdered when Raekwon was three. His mother had been on public assistance Raekwon's whole life. Raekwon hit the streets early because he knew he wanted to eat something better than government cheese, and wear something other than Sketchers. He met Derek on Riker's Island in the Queens Section of the yard. They connected right away, and when Derek was set up he called him to work for the Syndicate.

Raekwon was all street, violent and tough, so Derek was constantly teaching him about consequences. Derek could teach a person how to play chess on the streets, but he could never teach a person to be tough. So Derek knew Raekwon had the heart. He taught him to see the frame, not just the picture. Raekwon picked up the finished product from Jocelyn and he handled the daily street matters for the Syndicate. This cut down on indictments. He would be the next to move up away from the product, but right now he loved it!

Jocelyn was the drug courier because Derek and Shawn didn't touch any drugs or money directly. She had two special assets: she was gorgeous and she was white.

Jocelyn had been using that her whole life. She went to BMCC and actually graduated, because people did her homework for her and the male professors took care of the rest. She had an Associate Degree in Business Management but she was too lazy to use it. She also loved weed, so she couldn't pass any city employee drug test. So it was inevitable she worked for someone like Derek, where she could have all the money and weed she could ever want.

Her good looks let her maneuver through the city with kilos of cocaine. She was a brunette who changed her hair to blond, and was always trying to throw off cops, rivals, and stick up kids. She even threw on a gray wig, and glasses sometimes. She used the train, Uber, and rented cars to transport the Syndicate's drugs. She carried the drugs in an expensive Louie Vuitton Bag that had a special perfume to throw off the dogs. She was not worried about getting caught because she believed the judge would go easy on her pretty white ass.

The system pretty much ran itself, so there was no need to for them to actually touch anything. While Raekwon ran the streets, they had Andre running the muscle side of things. So if the competition, rivals, or stick-up kids attacked, Andre handled all.

It had taken years to perfect this system but it had a proven track record.

"Derek, hand over that three hundred dollars," Shawn said. "Even though it was sloppy, the kid performed."

Derek felt that it would be just a matter of time before both crews were at war with each other. This kept all the other crews on their toes. Which was exactly what he wanted, because soon he would run the NYC drug trade by distribution, and sales. That meant he would get a piece of everything moved through the city.

Shawn was done arguing his point. It's too much responsibility, and it made them a bigger target to the police and rivals. He turned his attention back to the half-naked women dancing to the loud music.

Derek really hadn't thought about all of that, he just wanted the top spot. He was confident he can get it.

Chapter 14

POISE

Rob stood at the front window of the deli watching the neighborhood. After the shooting, everything seemed quiet. He got a phone call from Captain Howard to say he would send him the case file as soon as he got it. As usual, Howard always came through. He would see him later tonight.

Rob was impressed by Officer Hale's actions. He knew she was nervous, but that was actually a good thing. He was impressed that she was aggressive and tactical all at the same time. He had seen a lot in his fifteen years on the job and knew quite a few male cops who wouldn't have acted as heroically as she did. He was not easily impressed, but he was by her.

Rob had a lot of energy after the fight, still an adrenaline rush, so he decided to take a run. Samantha could handle the deli while he was gone.

#

Derek's crew stopped by the strip club as soon as they got word about the shooting. News traveled fast on the street, but, just like the news, it was usually based on rumors. They wanted to know what happened, so they were there for the hood news. Facts!

Derek told them that it was just some regular street beef, probably over a girl, but definitely no war. Nothing to worry the Syndicate business. His crew never questioned his word so with business done they directed their attention to the strippers.

They knew that Derek put a self-imposed tax on all money earned, a lawyer fund, so if anybody got arrested Derek would supply them with a lawyer. This also helped his chances of his crew not ratting on him.

The lawyer made for loyalty from his crew, and an inside track on all investigations on the crew. Think Puff Daddy and Shyne. Puff paid for Shyne's lawyer. If you control the money, you control everything. Shine went to jail, and Puff Daddy didn't.

So Nigel would have a good lawyer—even though Derek hadn't told the Syndicate yet. Anyone on Derek's crew knew he took care of them no matter what. If anything happened to them, their families would be taken care of—if they obeyed the code. On the flip side if they snitched, their families would be executed. Buying Nigel a lawyer was buying his loyalty. Just good business.

They worked and played hard. It was stripper time. Shanika, the manager of the strip club, pushed the new girls toward the crew. She was happy when Derek and his crew showed up so she could watch her man. With all of the money he had, women threw pussy at him daily, and there wasn't much she could do to prevent it. She loved him, so she tried to make him happy as best she could. So far, so good. She clapped her hands and the top talent appeared on the stage. It was going to be a profitable day for the girls because his crew threw a lot of money around.

She told new girls she owned a modeling agency, but it was a prostitution ring, and the girls didn't have a choice. Sex was not optional. Shanika would physically convince them to provide all services on the menu. She had about twenty girls at any given time, with the occasional pregnancy, or runaway. But there was always new talent available to work for her.

Shanika and Derek had an agreement. As long as she was there he could sleep with any stripper once. If she was not there, she would kill the girl and hurt Derek. Derek didn't know how serious she was, but he enjoyed threesomes so her word hadn't been tested yet. She told all of her new girls to stay away from her man, or else. They believed her.

#

Fat Boy arrived, still limping, at the pool hall, which was his boss's office. He told one of the soldiers what happened and waited for an okay to talk to the boss. He saw the soldier talk to the Lieutenant and got scared. Sosa was the boss, but he wasn't the one who ran the Cartel. Sosa was the older brother but his Lieutenant, his brother, was more streetwise. Sosa was boss in title only.

Sosa Colon had grown up in Queens with his younger siblings, Carmen and Louie. His parents were both born in Puerto Rico as was Sosa. His younger siblings were born in New York. His parents were both musicians and drug addicts. To them heroin was another instrument. So there were always small-time drug dealers around the house. So little Sosa used to run errands for them which led to him working for them. He climbed the ladder and he was the boss now.

The Lieutenant told Sosa that Fat Boy was downstairs. Louie told the boss that Fat Boy was too hot right now, so deal with him in a few days, as things smoothed out. Sosa liked that idea and nodded.

Fat Boy eyed the door when the Lieutenant walked over to him, but all the Lieutenant said was, "Lay low for a few days and we'll contact you."

Fat Boy was confused and scared. What did that mean? But there was nothing he could do about it. So he said, "Cool, you know where I'm at."

Fat Boy limped away wondering if he was in trouble, which would mean he was dead. He limped to the Chinese restaurant around the corner so he could sit down and think about what just happened. He thought that he had done nothing wrong. It was not smart to have a shootout in broad daylight, but he didn't start it, and he had to defend the Cartel's turf. He even paid for the hood doctor himself, because if he would have gone to the emergency room the detectives would have picked him up.

It was what it was. No better time to call Maribel for a therapy session. He called Maribel on his cell and told her he was coming over right now, and if there was anybody there when he arrived they were dead. He hung up to make his point. His attention then went to the smell of General Tso chicken. There was always time for that.

Maribel was alone, and shocked by his words. She was also very street smart and had just learned how much Fat Boy liked her. It would reflect in the price: the usual three hundred dollars would now be five hundred dollars.

She considered it a last-minute appointment fee.

She jumped in the shower and lathered with strawberry body wash to prepare for Fat Boy. His favorite.

She was a professional. Know thy clientele.

#

Rob was taking a run through the neighborhood, another way to see what was going on. He noticed none of the drug crews were out, but that was normal because after a shooting, police activity was high. The drug crews knew this and just cut their losses by pulling their soldiers off the streets. The neighborhood was actually peaceful, and he wondered why it couldn't always be that way, but then he would have been out of work.

Rob felt good, so he would easily run five miles. He had a long day ahead of him because he had a wedding to go to later. He felt guilty because his wife wanted to attend, but he felt it was too dangerous. He knew this would cause more stress in their already difficult marriage. Rob felt that his wife should understand his work, and how important it was. His wife, Lora, didn't care about any of that. She wanted a husband who was present, and more importantly wanted their kids to know their father. Rob felt it would all work out, and if explained properly by her to the kids, they would understand.

This was a never-ending battle, with no winners.

#

Big Andre walked into the strip club. He was so big people felt his presence before they saw him. Derek and Shawn motioned him over. He was the crew's muscle on the streets, and they didn't have any problems thanks to him. Andre did his job very well, knowing when to put the smack down on addicts, competition, or anybody who warranted it. He walked over to their table and took a seat. He was smiling. They knew what was coming.

He said, "Why you keep letting these young thugs put in real work? And this kid wasn't really a part of our family."

Shawn just shrugged because he agreed with Andre.

Derek said, "This was all part of a master plan, so don't worry. If it's really important, you know we'll come to you first."

Andre didn't want the work because while he liked killing, he hated sloppiness more. He knew sloppy work meant indictments. Which would put the whole crew in danger. A trial could wipe out entire crew out faster than anything else, even a war. But the boss had spoken so there was nothing more to say.

Derek pointed. "If you want to party with the girls, we got you."

Andre shook his head. He was married and very happy with his wife of five years, and their son. He met his wife Kim at a Nas Concert at Madison Square Garden, and they had been together ever since. He had never seen his father cheat on his mother, raise his voice or hand to her. So he emulated that, never doing the same to his wife. They were a great team.

He told them he would see them later tonight, and left the club.

He straddled his new Ninja H2 motorcycle. It was big, all black with chrome accents, beautiful. He loved the excitement of any type of motorcycle, and rode often. It was in a killer's profile to take unnecessary risk all of the time, out of guilt.

He had grown up in 40 Projects on the South Side of Queens, like Derek, considered by some as the toughest projects in the New York City. Andre had enlisted into the military to follow in his father's footsteps, even though his father was against it. Ironically, Andre was dishonorably discharged because he knocked out a Lieutenant. While stationed in Iraq, he felt the black soldiers were being put in more danger than anyone else. There was enough stress from being in a combat zone, you didn't need the added stress of your commanding officer trying to expedite your demise. From the kills Andre recorded and all of the other stress, he developed Post Traumatic Stress Disorder (PTSD). That energy and mindset was being used to protect the Syndicate. His mother blamed the father, because she felt Andre took his dad's attitude into the military, and probably overreacted to the situation. The father believed it proved his point that the U.S. Army was a racist organization.

When Andre was released he went into a depression because you can't get a city job with a Dishonorable Discharge. He got into a fight at the club Encores on Jamaica Ave over someone else's girlfriend. He hurt the guy pretty bad and was sentenced to four years for felony assault. In jail, he met Shawn. They were close. After his release, Andre began working for the Syndicate.

The security guards outside the club were mesmerized by the bike. Dre, knowing this, threw on "I Teach You How da Stunt," by G-Unit.

He zoomed off, smiling. Helmet half on, strap loose. The security guards both smiled out of amazement. As he pulled out, two cops in a patrol car heard and then saw him. They decided to pull him over to fuck with him.

They made the U-turn and flipped on the lights and siren. Andre saw them in his right rearview, and knew he was being fucked with so he decided to have some fun. He sped up, and the RMP did as well. They didn't put the pursuit over the radio because they were not allowed to chase motor bikes—innocent civilians usually got injured. But in this patrol car, Officer Doherty was a cocky veteran, and he wanted to chase this guy. It was personal.

His partner, Officer Washington said. "Hey, should we be chasing him?"

Officer Doherty told him to shut up and relax.

With that the pursuit was on.

Andre, smiling, decided to show them his skills. He jumped into the bus lane and was moving fast. The RMP finally got over and they picked up speed. Andre slowed down to let them catch up. Once they did, he was gone again. He decided to cross the divider so he could go up a one-way street. The RMP would never be able to keep up with him. He jumped the divider effortlessly, but as he took the turn a kid ran into the street and he had go around him. He lost control and went head first into the sidewalk. The loose strap couldn't hold the helmet, and the impact crushed his skull.

Events happened so fast for no good reason.

In the hood there is always senseless death.

The officers saw this from their car, but Doherty kept driving. His partner knew this was wrong but said nothing. When the call came over the radio they responded to the scene, hoping nobody recognized them. They were the second car on the scene and nothing was said, so Doherty felt they were safe. He helped the EMTs put Andre in the ambulance.

Officer Washington was disgusted with Doherty, but he said nothing. It was just easier to fit in than to say something. The Blue Wall was real. There was little room for honest cops. If they couldn't trust you, your life would be in danger. The EMT searched Andre's pockets for a license so they could fill out the paperwork. They closed the door and Officer Minuto, another rookie, escorted the body to the Jamaica Hospital. This was procedure until the desk sergeant notified the next of kin. The EMT handed the driver's license to Officer Minuto so she could fill out the aided card, the official police form for any sick, injured, or dead person.

#

She called it in and the desk sergeant had an officer run the driver's license number, which came back with a long and violent arrest record. *At least it was a mutt who lost his life, no loss to society*, thought the desk sergeant before noticing the phone number listed.

The procedure was to have a officers respond to the home address and make the death notification. The officers could only make the identification to an adult, which was then recorded in their memo books. But Sergeant Saint was feeling self-righteous and decided to make the notification himself over the phone. Drug dealers and murders didn't deserve the same treatment as others, so he made the call.

Andre's eleven-year-old son answered the land line. "Hello?"

The sergeant, hearing the youthful voice, didn't ask any questions. He knew he couldn't make a notification to a minor so he didn't ask his age. He stated, "This is Sergeant Saint of the 103 Precinct. I'm calling to notify you that Andre Young was killed this evening at 5:03 PM in a vehicular accident. You need to go to the morgue at Jamaica Hospital to identify his body."

The sergeant hung up the phone.

On the other end of the line, Andre's son couldn't speak.

His mother walked into the living room and twice asked, "Who was that?"

He didn't answer. His back was to her. She grabbed him and said, "Boy, do you hear me talking to you?"

She saw his face and knew it wasn't good. She knew the business her husband was in and she had heard about the shootout early today. She'd called him right away and had been so happy he picked up the phone. She always called when the streets talked. Maybe he got hit in retaliation. She couldn't bear to ask her son what happened.

They sobbed together until Kim passed out from the thought of Dre being dead.

Chapter 15

CELEBRATION

Rob was back at his fake home, getting ready for a real wedding, with his fake wife. His life was sometimes confusing, but all Rob had to remember was the feeling he had as a kid being told his father was shot and he felt all of this was for the greater good.

Pamela was walking around in just panties and a bra. Pamela finally put on her formal dress because Rob was paying no attention. She looked stunning. She too thought this was crazy at times, but for a young girl who grew up in the hood surrounded by drugs, it was worth it. They left the house looking great together even if they both didn't feel that way. They both were armed with their Glocks, hers under her armpit, his on the waist.

Tonight Detective Investigator Shirley Gaglio was marrying the love of her life. This was a real wedding that had had to be cleared by the department. The department would rather Detective Gaglio get married a City Hall; they even offered to pay. They hated even more that the whole unit would be together. This was really risky, and they had to make sure no one saw them together. They were having the ceremony at a private location. Rob was excited to have the whole team together, and Captain Howard was as well because he had less contact with them than Rob did. A real Italian wedding with pasta and Frank Sinatra to match. A fiesta.

They arrived at a private hangar at Floyd Bennet Field in Brooklyn, a police facility. They had done a great job transforming the place into the dream wedding that Shirley wanted. She was very happy; Pamela went to see if she needed anything. Rob headed over to the boys.

Shirley Gaglio was a thirty-seven-year-old detective with ten years on the job. She was a gorgeous woman and knew it. She did not look like a police officer; she looked like a model. She grew up in the Belmont section of the Bronx which was Italian. She grew up with her older brother and parents. Her father was a masonry worker who had helped build the Bronx Zoo, her mother was a housewife. Her brother Salvador was forty and he had a hard time as an older brother. He got into a lot of fights defending his sisters honor in High School. Shirley has always been easy, and they threw this was Salvador's face often. Just kids being cruel, which was normal. She has navigated her way through the department the same way. She slept her way to detective. Right out of the academy she did clerical duties at the 32nd Precinct. No street time because she was fucking a Lieutenant there. She then was picked up for narcotics where she was given drug arrest by her boyfriend Detective Cart who was the best detective in Manhattan North Narcotics. He could afford to give away arrest to his girlfriend he still led the unit in arrest the whole time he was there. She gladly took the arrest which helped her get 2nd grade Detective. Which means you were paid sergeants pay without the responsibilities. Cart didn't even get promoted to second grade. She was picked up because she didn't look like a detective so they could use her to penetrate the Italian Crime family, The Howard Beach Crew. She could use her special talents to get information. She had been penetrated. She was trained at FLETC in Glynco, Georgia. Her assignment was a "Moll" in the Italian Crime Family, Howard Beach Club (HBC).

The Dirty Dozen would all be at the wedding. They used special skills, along with rogue tactics to complete the mission and live up to the title. They would all be here tonight, against the department's wishes. Some with their real families. There would be a lot of drinking, and bad jokes. Rob was at a table with Sergeant Jeremy Ling. They saw each other often, it's the under covers who they didn't see, and most times when they did there was no interaction, just a visual verification that they were alive.

Sergeant Jeremy Ling was forty-four years old with ten years on the job. He grew up the only child with his parents. They both work as waiters in a local Chinese restaurant. He was college educated, he studied marketing a Baruch college. He started a career in marketing but was bored, so he filled out the NYPD application and never looked back. He married Lucy Xing and they had three kids, Jeremy Jr., Lucy, and Zach. Jeremy started his career in the 5th Precinct, which was Chinatown. He got caught up in an Organized Crime Case involving the Triads, a Chinese gang that specialize in drugs and racketeering. There was no clear evidence he was involved, so he was an unindicted coconspirator. He had a gambling problem and they manipulated that. He tipped them off about police raids. He was launched out of the 5th and sent to the 44th Precinct in the Bronx. He hated the new assignment and he became disgruntled. Most people would be glad that they kept their job and avoided jail, but he was mad at the department. He was also not allowed to be promoted above the rank of sergeant. The Chief loves that the sergeant resents the brass, which means lax supervision on his part. This means that the new tools can be manipulated by the detectives. The sergeant was trained at FLETC in Glynco, Georgia. He was the sergeant investigator at the Bat Cave.

The supervisors drank, and there wasn't much talking. The food and the alcohol were plentiful.

#

Derek felt it was time for a toast, so he got every one's attention by tapping his glass with a fork. Everybody looked up. Derek climbed onto the table, and slowly looked at everyone. Unnecessary dramatics, but he was making sure everybody was paying attention.

They all stared back; he had their full attention.

Derek said, "You know I love all of you, and I'm glad to call you all family. We are the baddest motherfucking crew in New York City, and those who don't know that will very soon know."

Carla cleared her throat to keep him on message.

"But tonight we celebrate Shawn's first born, Lorenzo. I'm honored to be his godfather; I take this title very seriously, so I will definitely look forward to being a part of his life. Taking him to his first strip club, you know be there when Shawn gets on his nerves." They all laughed.

"Bow your heads please. Heavenly Father please forgive us for all our sins. We will do better one day. Now put your glasses up and let's toast to family." They all put their glasses up and cheered. Derek looked around the room and felt a stirring of unease.

Shawn asked one of the crew, "Has anybody heard from Dre?"

He answered, "Last I saw him at the club." It didn't feel right. Mac and cheese, and LL Cool J. They partied on.

#

The wedding was beautiful and Shirley was very happy.

She went over to talk to Rob alone. She expressed how much she appreciated him pushing this up the chain of command, so that it could happen. Somehow he found a way to classify this as a department expense. Safety. This was no easy task! Rob wanted no credit for this, because it was the right thing to do. She was sacrificing her life so the least the department could do was pay for this. He was a little sad that his wife wasn't there, but it was his idea that she didn't attend. He felt them seeing each other would create more want and need between the two, so he would rather wait till the assignment was over to see her. Of course, his wife wanted to see him any chance she got, and she loved Shirley and wanted to be there for her. He was regretting his decision.

Shirley had something important to tell Rob, but she was nervous. She took a sip of Champagne. No better time like the present. She told him that she wanted to start a family right away, and to do that she would need to transfer out of the unit. Rob couldn't believe what he was hearing. So he tried to make it right in his own ears.

Rob said, "Take a leave of absence. Your position will always be here."

Shirley said, "No, I don't want to be separated from my husband. I want out now. I don't know how you and Lora do it. God bless."

Rob said, "Okay."

In his mind, he thought he would convince her later, but today was her day. Shirley was summoned away by her husband, and there were envelopes to collect, stuffed with money. As they walked away, you could see the love between them. Rob was happy for her. Captain Howard was alone at the bar putting away a lot of Jack Daniels, and his wife was dancing with some of the kids on the dance floor. Detective Dwayne Washington was there and he had on his arm a beautiful young lady as always. She was a lieutenant at the Employee Personnel Department, at One Police Plaza Headquarters.

Detective Dwayne Washington was forty-two tears old and has twelve years on the job. He grew up in Hollis Queens with his parents. He has two half-brothers that he was not close with. He and his brothers share the same father. He went into the Army right after High School where he did two years of active duty as a Military Police Officer (MP). He was currently in the reserves now. He has two kids from two different mothers, but he was a good father. He started his career in Transit District Two, which covers South Ferry to 34 Street everything on the Westside. He was an undercover because of his baby face. He soon went to narcotics where he flourished because of his looks, he made a lot of arrest. Between his good looks and street smarts he became a great detective. His looks were also his downfall because he didn't have a filter for women: he fucks them all. He has never been in a monogamous relationship. He was fucking the female sergeant in his unit and the borough captain at the same time. When they found out about each other they conspired to destroy his career, and end his life.

Technically he did nothing wrong according to department protocol and the penal code. He was guilty of a moral felony, breaking two hearts. They tried to have him killed while he was working by sending him into a drug location where they tipped off the drug dealer. They were told that the "Courier" was an informer. Luckily Detective Washington had some street smarts from growing up in Hollis Queens. He knew something wasn't right so he didn't enter the location with the buy money. The department found out because they had a wiretap on the drug dealers phone. And they heard him put a hit out on the police informer. They arrested the drug dealer and cancelled the hit. The sergeant was terminated because she made the call to the drug dealer, and the captain was let to retire because there was no real evidence on her, just hearsay from the sergeant. The sergeant told the truth but there was no real investigation, so no one went to jail for this crime, because the victim was an African American male. His judgment left a lot to be desired, the Chief can use that for the unit's advantage. He was in this unit because of his street smarts, and detective skills. His looks were a gift and a curse.

The Chief interviewed and chose him.

The Chief said, "I find you very interesting because I can't interpret your body language. I think because of this you would be a great field agent."

Detective Washington said, "Thank you, sir."

Chief said, "You have a steady poker face. Amazing. Enjoy your transformation."

Detective Washington said, "Thank you, sir."

He was trained at the CIA Farm, and FLETC in Glynco, Georgia. He went undercover school and was given heavy weapon and explosive training. He fucked both his CIA, and FLETC handler, and both women still called him. Yes, he penetrated the feds.

His assignment was a smalltime hustler, awaiting an opportunity to penetrate the South Side Syndicate. He was Rob's ace.

The two Spanish detectives, Stella Machado and Juan Vasquez, were dancing to merengue music as everybody watched them. People thought they were probably sleeping together, with the precision at which their bodies were in tune with the music and each other.

Detective Juan Vasquez was forty years old and he had ten years on the job. Detective Vasquez grew up in Spanish Harlem with his eight siblings, and parents. He had six brothers and two sisters. His father was a maintenance man, and his mother was the neighborhood babysitter. Detective Vasquez lived a normal Puerto Rican life growing up in the city. He spent his summers in Vieques, along with his siblings. He graduated from Humanities High School in Manhattan. He was on his way to be a dope dealer when his best friend and cousin were killed picking up a shipment for the Spanish Cartel in Harlem. He was supposed to be there but his father got last-minute Yankee tickets and he was made to go to the game. His short time in the street gives him the upper hand he needs with dealing with local drug dealers. That incident gave him a second life, so he had been on the straight and narrow ever since. He was in the 30th Precinct's Street Narcotics Enforcement Unit (SNEU). He was known as a great investigator, and received all the big cases in the unit. He was an honest cop; he didn't steal any drugs or money. But he obeys the laws of the Blue Wall of Silence, which was the same on the streets, "No Rats." He provided an alibi for his partner, because he needed it for an Internal Affairs Bureau, his unit really respected that. He also got the same partner help for his alcoholic problem, which allowed him to keep his job. He was in this unit because he was a great investigator, and he obeys the code. He was trained at FLETC in Glynco, Georgia. His assignment was a low-level dealer for the Spanish Cartel.

There was a loner in the group, Detective Kingston Campbell, drinking in a corner watching everything. He had brought his real wife to the wedding, but their lack of contact showed the stress this assignment had put on them. He enjoyed the work and if it meant his marriage would fail, he was okay with that. His job was his identity.

Kingston Campbell was twenty-nine years old with eight years on the job. He grew up in Kingston, Jamaica, with his two older brothers, Vernon and Langston. His father came to New York first and once he was established he sent for the family. They lived in Mount Vernon New York, which has a large Jamaican population. He and his older brothers were raised in a strict household. They all went into the Marines and their parents were very proud. Vernon, the oldest at thirty-four, was still in the Marines, planning to do twenty years. Langston had his own shipping company business. He shipped anything in bulk to Jamaica. He lived a good life. His mother did the books. Kingston had decided to go into the police department right after he got out of the Marines. He was married to Mary Wright, and they had a four- year old daughter, Adelaide. Kingston loved his wife but they had major communication problems, so he had a girlfriend that he saw often. She was aware of his wife and daughter. He started his career in the 121st Precinct on Staten Island. He was in the Elite Street Crime Unit and had an excellent arrest record. He had a reputation of being heavy handed. He would only tell you something once, and then he would make you do what he wanted. He had numerous excessive force complaints, but his supervisors loved him. Other African American officers felt he was too aggressive with his own people, but he didn't see the world that way. He had no special empathy for African Americans, he only saw right and wrong. This was why the supervisors loved him, and others hated him. He hung with the "White Boys." The Chief wanted him in the unit. He was trained at FLETC in Glynco, Georgia. His assignment was a low-level dealer in the Brooklyn Bullies.

Detective Stella Machado was thirty-five years old with fourteen years on the job. She was a divorced mother of two. She has two daughters that were six and eight. She was basically a single mother. She grew up in the Castle Hill section of the Bronx, a mixed neighborhood. She grew up with her two siblings and parents. Her sister was thirty, and her brother was twenty-eight. She was the oldest and most of the time was in charge of her siblings. Her mother and father both worked twelve hour shifts at a plastic factory in the Bronx. The mother worked the mornings, and the father at night, so when they were home they slept. Stella saw how hard they worked, and she worshipped her mother. Her father has a drinking problem which led to numerous other problems. Her mother wanted better for her and never wanted her to work in a factory or the equivalent. With her freedom Stella spent a lot of time in the streets, even though she never got into any trouble. Her friends all had drug-addicted parents, so even though her parents weren't home it wasn't a negative experience for her. She did the normal teenage stuff, smoked weed, and occasional sex on the project roof. No bad habits formed from that. But her mannerisms were all street. If she was not in uniform it was hard to believe she was a police officer. Stella graduated from Harry S. Truman High School in the Bronx. She took the police exam while she was there because she had a crush on the NYPD school safety officer. So she took the police exam while she was there, so she took the job at the age of twenty-one. She started out in The Housing Bureau PSA 6, which was West Harlem. She was made an undercover early because of her street savvy. She was put in the housing plainclothes unit after having two years on the job. She soon met her husband, he lived in Grant Houses. He wanted her to quit because he was insecure, and believed she was sleeping with every male partner she ever had. She wasn't. He started physically abusing her, and during one of those beatings she shot him and killed him. Battered wife syndrome, and self-defense was used successfully at the trial. In this unit she runs the street as a small-time dealer who occasionally works for the Spanish Cartel. She gathers intelligence with her many street contacts. She was the most important person in the unit, because she gets information faster than anyone which gives the unit a strategic advantage, and helps to protect the under-covers. The Chief personally notified her.

Chief said to her, "I just wanted to congratulate on being chosen for this new unit." Detective Machado said, "Thank you, sir."

She was trained at the CIA Farm, and FLETC in Glynco, Georgia. Her assignment was a field intelligence detective.

The two clerical nerds of the unit were here alone, Detectives Lance Banner and Joseph Rogers. Neither one of them have alias families, or girlfriends on the side. All they have was each other. But they can say they belong to the most elite unit in NYPD, no matter what their duties are. Anyone from any other unit would switch places with them if that meant they could be a part of this.

Detective Lance Banner was twenty-eight years old and has six years on the job. He grew up in Floral Park Queens with his parents. His parents were both professors. Lance spent a lot of time alone as a kid, so his energy was put into computers. He learned every aspect of computers, building, programming, and hacking. He graduated from Stuyvesant High School in Manhattan early at the age of sixteen. School made him bored so he never wanted to go to college. He was picked on a lot throughout his life, so joining the police department and carrying a gun made perfect sense. He excelled quickly because of his intelligence, but was hated because of his arrogance. He didn't have a girlfriend or any social life what so ever, computers rule his life. He was in the unit because he was great at what he does. With his skills the unit could do wiretaps and hacks with no trace.

He was the computer guy at the Bat Cave, and went in the field as a Con Edison worker as his cover.

Joseph Rogers was thirty-one years old with ten years on the job. He grew up in Flushing Queens with his older brother John and their mother, Mary. His father was a murderer; convicted of a vehicular homicide. He was drunk and drove his car head on into oncoming traffic killing a family of five. His mother took a job at Target soon after the arrest. This happened when Joseph was twelve, and he was embarrassed throughout High School, because the whole neighborhood knew about his father. He and his brother graduated from Flushing High School. The detective that handled the case made an impression on Joseph. Even though he arrested his father he was amazed at how he caught him and the professionalism showed throughout the trial. He also noticed that his mother appreciated that as well, he went out of his way not expose the family. It was actually a reporter who notified the neighborhood. He loved his father, but he killed a family of five. So he would want the same justice if it was his family. He has always been this logical. He visited his father for a while, but his father went into a depression and didn't want any more visitors. Joseph got a swim team scholarship and attended Boston College for two years. The coach, a Boston native, hated him because he was from New York. He was always yelling at him and berated him in front of everyone. He followed details precisely but was told he was wrong all of the time. The stop watch said he was the best swimmer on the team. But the coach treated him as if he was the worse. So he filled out an application for NYPD online, and when they called he left school in a hurry. He started his career in the 101th Precinct in Far Rockaway. He wanted to be a detective, so he was an active uniform officer and was placed in the eighteen-month investigative program. If you make it through you get your detective shield. Which he did because he really enjoyed the work and became great at it. He was in the unit because the current Police Commissioner was his Precinct captain when he was in the 101. Young Joseph saved the captain by catching a newly released felon who went on a violent robbery spree within the Precinct. If not caught the captain would have been transferred and never promoted to Deputy Inspector. Joseph along with his partner caught the perpetrator by hiding in a makeshift construction box for six hours. The perpetrator even leaned on the box and cased victims. The police Commissioner felt he should have at least one pick for the unit. The chief had no problem with that—he knew how to play the game. Besides, Joseph was a great detective. He was an investigator and prepared all of the department paperwork for the unit.

It was time for speeches, so everyone returned to their tables. The best man gave a great speech about the couple, and then the bridesmaid did. Next up was Rob, who loved to address the troops. He went to the front of the room with a bottle of champagne in hand. All eyes were on him and he knew it.

Robert said, "I love everybody in this room and I'm so glad that we all were here together tonight." I have known Shirley for ten years, and I can't believe she found someone to marry her." They all laugh. "But in all seriousness, I'm so very happy that Shirley and Francesco have found each other, and I wish them a hundred plus years together, and thirty kids. Everybody raises their glasses.

"We all know how dangerous our work was, even if the brass didn't realize or understand what we do. So I promise my full support to you, no matter what happens in the field, please do whatever you need to do to come home to your families, both families. I'll back you no matter what you do. We do God's work."

Someone yelled out, "We were Old Testament in this Unit."

Rob slurred, "Also I just want to say thank you to Teddy, I couldn't ask for a better boss.'

Shirley yelled out, "We love you, old man."

Chapter 16

QU–HECTIC

Derek lay awake in bed, Shanika curled up next to him, too far for him to reach out and touch her. She had gone back to the strip club after the baptism. She had to collect that money and she didn't have an assistant or trusted staff to rely on. Her theory was "Born alone, die alone." So besides Derek, she had no friends or family. This was one of the things that he liked about her, because he didn't have to worry about her people being in his business or asking for money. Their relationship was simple. What he hadn't considered was that he was all she had so she would do whatever she could to protect and preserve that.

Derek looked at his phone. Still no response from Andre. Derek went into the subway to use the pay phone to call Shawn. He told him to stop by Andre's house, to see what was going on. In this business, when routine was broken there was always room for concern. Shawn was on it; he too was worried about Dre.

#

0700 at the 103rd Precinct. Second Platoon Roll-Call.

Sergeant McMullan was talking to the twenty cops about to hit the streets for their 0700-1630 AM shift. He told them that there was a shooting yesterday afternoon, so for the immediate future there would be full enforcement on Jamaica Avenue from 175th Street to 155th Street.

"For all you rookies, this means everybody you come into contact with gets arrested or a summons, no discretion. Hit people hard—we can't take another shooting in this Precinct. We have Comp. Stat coming up at the end of the month, and the Captain doesn't want to have to stand and explain numerous homicides. So be where you were supposed to be, because the sergeants will be out there checking on you. I expect at least ten arrests from this tour today. The plainclothes guys will be out hitting the known players, so the radio will be busy. Queens is Hectic right now, so let's bring it back to normal. Let's go hunting."

Martin, a black cop, said, "Why were we punishing the whole community for a drug beef?"

Short, a white cop beside him, said, "You got a better idea?"

"Yes, provide the community with omnipresence so they feel safe where they live and pay taxes. And hit the known players who were committing the crimes."

"I just work here, so I do what I'm told. Plus, I could use some overtime, so somebody was getting arrested."

"We were punishing the people that were under siege already. This was fucking stupid."

Sergeant McMullan said, "No two-hour breakfast today, hit the streets."

Officer Armetta was a part of the Anti-Crime Unit, which consists of ten plain clothes officers and two sergeants. They studied the crime reports and deployed to high crime areas to catch criminals when they committed crimes. Within each precinct the anti-crime units and the high-profile perps everyone knew each other. So it became a game between the two, cat and mouse. The cops were filling a quota, so they arrested when needed; the perpetrators gave tips when they needed competition gone. They addressed each other by name. Today though the unit hit the street and arrested all of these players so that they could put out the message that a shooting was bad business for all. The unit would also try and get some information to help the detectives solve the case. The people in this unit were trying to become detectives, so they were a proactive unit: arrests were their goal. Today the roll call was brief.

Sergeant McMullan shouted, "Let's solve this shooting and prevent any others."

They all prepared for patrol. Yankee shirts and tucked shields.

Officer Armetta had been at the precinct for five years, but he was new to the unit, so he felt he needed to be aggressive to fit in. His dream was to become a detective, so he would do whatever was needed, plus some.

As soon as Quale stopped talking, Armetta said to anybody who was listening, "I can't wait to become a detective. I'll do whatever is necessary." He was already leading the unit in arrests, with fourteen for the month. The quota was five, and the other guys didn't like this grandstanding. He was already an outcast. So he was eager to hit the streets with this directive to be heavy-handed.

#

It was 7:03 AM, and already a beautiful day, enhanced by the quiet streets without the city noise of traffic and yelling. It was about to get hectic.

Two EMTs were sitting in their ambulance waiting for their tour to end in about an hour. EMTs Joy and Onus were both twenty-five, with four years on the job. They were listening to the morning radio that Onus chose and Joy hated. Right-wing propaganda. They worked in the confines of the 111th Precinct, in Queens. They received a call from dispatch that there was an officer in cardiac arrest at his residence. Officer down at 58-10 215TH Street. EMT Onus threw his coffee out of the window and sped toward the address. EMT Joy sent over the radio that they were responding. The lights and sirens were on and Onus was pushing the ambulance as fast as it can go. He almost broadsided a car, but he was in a zone. EMT Joy said nothing about the reckless driving, because "officer down" was the most serious call to get. This was their first. They arrived at the address and there were already two patrol cars there. They grabbed their equipment and rushed in. They could hear a woman screaming.

Maureen watched as a sergeant from the 111 Precinct was trying to do CPR on Captain Howard as his body was slumped in his recliner. His face was grey, and his body was stiff. Onus pushed them out of the way and started doing chest compressions. Joy started to get the defibrillator ready. Onus called for the defibrillator, and Joy handed it to him. He put the two electrodes on Teddy's chest. He yelled, "Clear!" and pushed the button to deliver a therapeutic dose of electric current to Teddy's heart. The counter shock didn't work, so he tried it again. More officers rushed into the house. He looked like a cop, but no one knew him and nobody better not ask Maureen at this point in time.

Onus and Joy both knew that he was gone but they put him on a gurney and continued to work on him as they rushed to ambulance. The officers helped them load Teddy into the ambulance and they were off to New York Hospital Medical Center. Onus was in the back of the ambulance with Teddy, and an officer from the 111th Precinct. Onus was driving, he has called ahead to the hospital. He has a police escort so it was a straight drive. Maureen was in a RMP right behind them.

When they arrived at the hospital, the chief surgeon was waiting outside with his staff. Joy pulled right in front of the emergency room entrance and the staff pulled Teddy out and started working on him as they rolled him inside. Onus was exhausted from working on Teddy even though he knew he was deceased at the house. This was for Maureen. Better if he was pronounced dead in a hospital by a doctor. Maureen ran into the emergency room and she watched the doctors work on her Teddy. She said, "Theodore, please wake up. You can't leave me like this, please." She was escorted out by a nurse.

The team was franticly working on him everybody doing something; three nurses and a doctor. They started with mouth to mouth, and then went to the defibrillator. No movement.

The doctor stopped working on him. Everybody knew this was not good.

A nurse said, "The time is 7:38 AM."

Teddy was gone.

It was 8:01 and everyone in the neighborhood was off to work. Jermaine starred at the light blue sky from the passenger seat. He was dreaming about what he was going to do with quick money he going to make from this robbery. Curt readjusted his Glock. He was always readjusting it in his waistband. It made him feel strong and confident.

He didn't know if he could use it but the sight of it made people freeze so he hadn't been tested yet. Jermaine had used his gun before. He was a horrible shot but unafraid to pull it and let some bullets fly.

Jermaine says. "Yo, we in and out. Quick fast. Nothing heavy or big. It will slow us down Sow means caught. Money and jewelry is what we want. You stay on the first floor and I'll hit the second. Make sure you check all the rooms before you start packing da bag!"

Curt says, "Cool. I know the drill. If I find a housewife or kid just tie them up and gag them. I'm ready!"

Jermaine says, "Yeah no unnecessary violence or sex. We here for straight cash. Nothing else. Remember we leave out of the front door. We are a Carpet Cleaning crew."

Jermaine had stolen the uniforms for the company he used to work for. He worked at Carpet Cleaning Pro for over a year. He was fired for being excessively late. While there he always felt it would be easy to rob the places he cleaned. Most of the times no one was home. They were let in electronically. The other times it was just a housewife. Easy money. Once he was fired he revisited the houses with the electronic locks. He already knew the layouts so he was in and out within fifteen minutes. He made 5K his first month. He knew he needed a partner to could grabbed more stuff. So he brought in his neighborhood friend Curt. Curt was slow so Jermaine manipulated that. He controlled him and the money.

Today they were in Ozone Park, Queens. He hit a few times in this neighborhood with ease. It was a nice middle class community where everybody worked. The house they were hitting this morning belonged to a single man who left for work at 7:30. Jermaine had his power drill so they were in the house in less than sixty seconds from van to living room. Curt went to the furthest room in the back on the first floor. Jermaine headed upstairs. Rob was deep into his nightmare. The theme of this one was a never ending chase. He was being chased by a Pitt bull on Jamaica avenue. This really happened to him when he was a rookie. The sounds in the nightmare were so real. Rob heard a yell. He looked around and didn't see anyone else. It took a minute but he was now awake. Did Pamela yell? Wait it sounded like a man. He reached for his gun under the pillow. It was too late. The first shot woke him fully. He stayed low. He figured he had a better chance if he played dead. The second shot came with a loud thump.

Curt says, "J, you okay?"

Pamela heard them enter the house and she was on her feet with her Glock before Jermaine hit the top step. She was always locked and loaded. She had decided not to move to Rob because she might draw the gunfire to him. She was there to protect him with her life. When she saw the "Tango" she waited for him to go right to Rob or left to her. He went right to her. The first shot was center mass. She took a second to analyze if he was a pro. He was not. The second shot was a kill shot to his forehead as she walked past him. That was the loud thump Rob heard. Precision point shooting. She was the best. She knew there were at least two in the house. Pamela closed Rob's bedroom door and was moving to secure the second Tango.

Pam says, "Stay down until I secure the house."

Rob of course did not stay in his room. With Glock in hand he was moving also. She opened the hallway window and climbed down to the backyard. Curt heard the shots and he was frozen in the kitchen. She was opening the back door within thirty seconds. She was even winded. She moved to Curt. When he saw her he was shocked that it was a woman. He reached for his gun but by the time he gripped it she had shot him in the shoulder. The next shot was quick. The headshot put him out of his pain. Pam heard footsteps so she stepped to the side of the refrigerator for cover and to change her magazine. She was ready. He ran through the door with aggression and purpose. She raised her Glock and quickly realized it was Rob.

Rob says, "Are you okay."

Pam says, "I'm good. Watch him while I clear the house and make sure there's no getaway driver."

Rob feeling uncomfortable says, "Okay."

He was used to being in charge. This was a first. Pamela was back in two minutes.

Pam says, "All clear. We have to call the Chief."

Rob called the Chief and Pam searched the bodies for identification. They both had driver's license on them. The Chief was able to check them out to make sure they were burglars. They were.

When the Clean Team arrived they took pictures of the subjects and then removed them. They cleaned the house spotless. When you work in the most powerful NYPD Unit created after 9/11 this is what happens when there is a shooting. No crime scene or Duty Captain. Their location and identity had to be preserved. The Chief took care of everything. Their cover was secure.

9:03 AM. It was a deadly morning.

Chapter 17

ILLEGAL SEARCH

Officer Ametta was in his unmarked patrol car with his partner, Officer Donald Blake. They were about to hit the weed block. This was on 166th Street, and they sold marijuana up and down the block. They turned the corner onto the block and they saw a group of five men standing in front of 94-12 166th Street.

Just neighborhood guys talking sports, no drug dealing going on here. It was animated because the subject was the New York Knicks.

Brian said, "It's May and as usual the Knicks season was over already."

Paul said, "They fucking suck."

Jason said, "They gotta spend money if they want the chip."

Paul said, "They used all their money on Carmelo, and it ain't working."

Brian said, "Fuck Carmelo."

Paul said, "It ain't his fault. He does his part. Look what he did with an old Jason Kidd. Get him some help and he's great."

Jason said, "I don't know about great."

Paul said, "He was the best player to ever wear a Knicks uniform."

Brian said, "You crazy."

Paul said, "He was the best scorer in the league."

Brian said, "He ain't better than Curry or Durant."

Paul said, "He was. He can shoot jumpers or he can score on the blocks the other two can't. They just have better help."

Brian said, "You crazy."

Jason said, "I see your point. You explained it well."

Brian said, "They need something cause what they got ain't working."

Jason said, "True."

Paul said, "You'll see one time creeping on us?"

They all looked towards the unmarked police car that pulled up. Armetta and Blake got out. They were both wearing jeans and Yankee polo shirts with their shields visible on their neck chains. The five guys saw them coming, but weren't worried. They were just chilling. They knew that the precinct would crack down after the shooting, so nobody was holding weapons or contraband.

The officers approached the group.

Officers Armetta asked, "Do any of you know anything about the shooting yesterday?"

The group laughed and kept talking.

Officer Armetta said, "What's so fucking funny?"

They kept laughing.

Officer Armetta said, "Everybody hit the wall and put your hands up."

Jason said, "Why you fucking with us? There's no law against standing in front of your own house."

Officer Blake said, "Relax, guys."

Officer Armetta said, "It is if it was a known drug location."

Jason said, "We're not doing anything wrong. We can't help it if you're suspicious of us."

Armetta said, "Shut up and put your hands up."

Brian said, "Don't talk to us like that."

Armetta grabbed Brian and slammed him to the ground. He then went through his pockets searching him. He was only supposed to frisk him. This was illegal. Officer Blake knew this was an overreaction, but he had to back up his partner.

Officer Blake said, "Everybody on the wall look away from us, turn your heads to the left."

The guys reluctantly complied.

Armetta said, "When I tell you do something, you better fucking do it. No questions."

Brian said, "Fuck you. This is an illegal search. I know my rights!"

Armetta said, "What the fuck, did you say. You motherfuckers better stay in your place or else."

Armettta punched Brian in the face.

Brian began yelling.

Officer Blake stared at Armetta but maneuvered his body to hide his own shield number.]

Brian said, "Why did you do that?"

Officer Armetta put his hand on his weapon. Brian saw this and understood what could happen next.

Armetta said, "Shut the fuck up." And cuffed him.

To break Armetta out of his zone, Blake told him to stand him up. It worked; Armetta's eyes lost their crazy glare.

Brian said, "This was bullshit. Straight police brutality. I want your shield number."

Armetta said, "I'll give you my fucking shield number. Nine-one-one. Asshole."

Officer Blake tried to gain some control over the situation. "Frisk him, and then do a warrant check."

Officer Armetta said, "Yeah, okay. Okay."

Blake hoped this would end the confrontation that had gotten out of control. If he had a warrant then he would be arrested; if not, he got a summons for loitering.

Officer Armetta was searching Brian, going through his pockets and throwing his property on the ground. This was against the law and the Constitution.

Blake muttered to him, "He'll make a complaint. He's got your name." He took over and Armetta got the idea and sat in the car. He did a warrant check over the radio.

Central said, "Negative results on Brian Thompson, unit."

Officer Blake said, "Write him and then cut him loose. Let's get out of here."

After writing the summons,

No one said a word.

Officer Blake looked at Armetta as if to say, let's get out of here. Armetta uncuffed Brian, tucking in his shield so no one could read it.

Brian said, "You fucking racist. You hit me for nothing."

To deescalate the situation, and to make Armetta think he was backing him up, Officer Blake said, "You got off easy. You could have been arrested for disorderly conduct, and resisting arrest. So get the fuck off this block and stay off the block."

Officer Armetta said, "Get the fuck out of here, now."

Jason told his friends, "Let's just leave."

Brian shouted, "I'm going to make an official complaint.

Officer Blake wanted to tell his partner that he didn't appreciate him putting his job on the line for nothing. If you can't keep your composure, then you shouldn't be here. He wanted to say that but the Blue Wall prevented him. Once they kick you out then it's impossible to get back in. The crazy thing was he knew Armetta was a punk, and if it were not for the badge then he wouldn't be so physical. Sometimes this job sucks not because of the danger but because of the racism, it affects all, even the oppressor. The biggest thing was this was a waste of time. They were supposed to be arresting people, getting information about the shooting. Here they just wasted time, with the possibility of getting a complaint. No apology or even a word of remorse from Armetta. On to the next confrontation.

#

Surrounded by people talking, consoling each other, weeping, remembering Dre, Derek sat alone on the couch, a bag of cash at his feet.

"It's okay if you want to go," Kim said.

He stared blankly at her, his head still buzzing with the news that Dre was gone.

"Family isn't your thing," she said. "Go on. I know you loved Andre."

Derek nodded and stood. He nudged the bag of cash further under the couch out of sight. "For anything you need. Funeral expenses, whatever... And Mohamed is outside. He'll drive you anywhere you need to go. Errands, security if needed..."

"Thank you," she said, her eyes filling again with tears. He didn't hug her. He wasn't the hugging type. He didn't even kiss Shanika. His kids' mothers just wanted his money; they even gave up custody of their kids for a small fee. The kids lived with his grandmother. She loved taking care of them and most importantly having them all together. Derek had moved them to the Poconos, where they had a big house with a pool. The kids loved it they all went to school together as well. Derek let the mothers visit whenever they wanted, as well as take them for sleepovers. He still paid them child support. This all kept the peace.

Derek jerked his head at Shawn and they got in the car, Shawn driving. Without asking, Shawn head to the strip club, because they needed a drink. The car ride was quiet, nothing to say. Shawn had sent a kite to the team about what happened, so they would be waiting at the club. Dre was the man. The only thing that made this bearable was the game didn't take his life. So everybody was sad, but not angry. There would be a lot of Hennessey consumed tonight.

At the club, they brushed by Shanika breaking in a new girl, a nineteen-year-old Puerto Rican chick. Shanika was saying, "Sofia, you break that rule, you're gone and I break your hands." The rule: splitting whatever money she made with the house, fifty-fifty.

Shawn and Derek took their usual table. Derek's eyes lingered on the new girl, Sofia. She by far was the best-looking girl in the current bunch. She looked quiet and shy so he knew this helped to make her beauty acceptable to Shanika. Shanika resented her beauty, but she would be a cash cow, because the brothers loved Spanish women. That's a fact. Sofia caught his eye then looked away. He smirked. He recognized that kind of girl. Pretty but hood certified. On her own and ready to shake that ass.

He turned to Shawn, who was still staring into his drink. "Who should we move up to take Dre's place?'

Without looking up, Shawn said, "Too soon, man."

"It's just business. We have to replace him so we can keep things running."

"Not business for me. He was my brother."

"And why you'll never be the boss." Derek knew that replacing Dre wouldn't be easy because he was truly one of a kind. Since he had been the muscle there had been no arrest or even any investigations pointing at the crew. Dre's work was clean. South Side Syndicate had been off the NYPD's radar for some time. He wanted to be King of New York. He could taste it in his spit. Nothing, not even tragedy with stop him.

Derek stepped off to go see Shanika. He'd told her over the phone what happened but now he wanted to talk to her. When he entered her office, he couldn't help but notice the beautiful Spanish girl sitting there. He stared for a moment and she did as well. At that moment, Shanika walked in, and she could sense that her man liked the new talent.

Shanika said, "Remember the motherfucker I told you to stay away from. That's him."

Sofia said, "Okay."

She then told Sofia that she could go out on the floor.

Derek and Shanika hugged and they both sat. Derek told her that he couldn't believe that Dre was gone. This shit was crazy. She was in tears. He told her that she should call Kim and give her condolences. Shanika agreed. Shanika said that she actually was going to stop by the house later. Dre was family.

Shanika felt the need to make him happy, because this situation was fucked up. She had an idea how to cheer him up. She told him she had to text a friend. She sent out a text to Sofia to come back to her office.

When she arrived, Derek knew right away what was about to happen.

Shanika said, "I know you need this."

Derek said, "Word up."

Shanika looked at Sofia and said, "No kissing. Everything else is cool."

Sofia walked in front of Derek and dropped to her knees and unzipped his pants. Derek smiled as she went to work on his penis. Shanika took off her own clothes then Derek's shirt, and then started licking his chest. Derek was in ecstasy. Shanika was enjoying this just as much. Sofia stood up and walked over to the desk and took off her panties then bent over the desk and looked back at Derek. Shanika handed him a condom. He took off his pants and started fucking her doggie style. He was going to work on her.

She looked back at him and said, "Fuck me daddy."

He grabbed her throat and started to choke her. She loved it. Shanika got a little jealous of the eye contact and fun, so she started to kiss him to break it up.

Shanika said, "You like that."

Derek said, "Hell yeah."

Shanika started to kiss Sofia. With that Derek couldn't hold it, he bust his nut right on her back. Derek sat in the chair and watched as the girls went at it. Sofia started to suck on Shanika's breast, as she stared at Derek. He walked over to them, but Shanika pushed him away. So he just stared. Sofia then went down on Shanika, and Shanika leaned back to enjoy it. The whole time she was staring at Derek. Sofia brought her to a climax and tried to come up and kiss her but Shanika turned away. "It's over," she said. This was for Derek. She only enjoyed it because he did. She would never bring a woman home to their bed.

In this office, it was always business.

#

Rob flew down the highway as if he was in a patrol car. Maureen had called him from the hospital even before she had called her two kids, he was that important to the family. Rob pulled up to the emergency room and didn't even park his car. He jumped out and ran into the emergency room, where Maureen was standing with her head down in deep thought. He hugged her, asking what had happened.

She told him that Teddy had had a heart attack caused by his binge drinking last night. He was pronounced dead about two hours ago. Rob was in shock. He couldn't believe it. He had just lost a friend and colleague. He directed his attention to Maureen.

He asked, "What do you need me to do?"

She told him she was unsure of what to do on the department side, because the unit was so covert. Rob told her he would take care of it.

One hour later, the hospital was crawling with police brass. Rob had made one call and they had come, bosses and old friends. A white shirt approached Rob and introduced himself as Captain Gallagher. He let Rob know he was aware of the secretive nature of their unit, and if there was anything he needed in the immediate future, please call. He handed him his business card. Physically there, Robb was mentally out of it. "Thank you, sir," he answered.

It was no mistake that Gallagher was there. Word had already gotten to the Chief that Teddy was gone, and he then had to notify the police commissioner and mayor. The mayor was up for reelection and he was looking for some big arrest to boost his image. He knew this unit can do that for him, so he called the PC directly, and said he wanted his guy in there to direct things. The PC could do whatever he wanted, because if he got reelected that meant four more years for him as well. The mayor wanted his nephew, Captain Mike Gallagher. He was a real tool because the mayor had his back. He supervised like a Chief. Speaking of which, the Chief didn't like him, nor would he put him in the unit. But there was a mayoral race, and he had no choice. He was told in the beginning this was his unit, but the polls were down. So the Chief had a decision to make: would he stick around if he lost control.

From this point on NYPD would help Maureen with everything, and they would still be there after the funeral. This was what they did, and they did it well. She would have a police escort, and honor guard at the service. They had an employee relations unit dedicated directly to this type of tragedy. This was besides the monetary and medical benefits. This was the Blue family. Captain Howard had earned it.

A young woman ran up to Maureen, throwing her arms around her. Abigail, her oldest at twenty-one, and she was in her last year at Holy Cross College, studying law. They hugged and cried.

Rob backed away and went out the doors to his car, still waiting at the emergency room entrance.

The funeral would be hard for all them. He had to tell his mother before she heard it on the news. That would be breaking protocol, but he had to tell his mother about Teddy.

Rob hadn't seen his mother in over a year. He bumped the horn even though she heard the car pull up. It was an old tradition that his father used to do, blowing the horn every time he pulled into the driveway. He entered the house with his own key. His mother was on the couch with a glass of wine in her hand.

Rob said, "Hey mom, I missed you."

His mom said, "I missed you too, son. Is everything okay?" They kissed and then hugged each other tightly for a few seconds. "Are the kids okay?"

He told her that Lora and the kids were fine and sat next to her. He told her that Teddy had passed away early this morning.

Shaken, she asked, "What happened?"

He told her it was a heart attack.

"Oh my God. I can't believe it."

Rob said, "I know, it's crazy."

She asked if this secretive work was over now. Rob really never thought about that. But the work always continues, no matter what. The work was more important than any one person. She asked about Lora and how she was holding up with not being able to see him. He let her know that they were dealing with it, but it was hard. He reminded her that she could call or go see Lora and the kids anytime she wanted. She told him that she was busy, and she'll call Lora soon. Rob knew that was a lie—his mom was jealous of his relationship with Lorna—but this wasn't the time for an argument. He asked his mother to make him some pasta, and she happily obliged. She told Rob how proud she was of him being a police officer.

"I miss your father so much."

Rob said, "I do too, Mom."

Mom said, "I still can't believe those Moolies killed your father."

Rob said, "Mom, please." "Moolie" from *melanzane*, "eggplant" in Italian. Eggplants have black skin. So this was a derogatory nickname for black people.

Mom said, "You're not going to defend those fucking animals, are you. Killing for a five-dollar hit?"

Rob said, "I'm not going to condemn any group of people but some of the white people in this very neighborhood have done some pretty bad things."

In silence they ate their meal. Rob sighed. He tried not to resent her. She'd grown up in a different time. What he was sure of was that his kids would give everybody the benefit of the doubt, unless that person—black, white, or whatever color—proved otherwise.

"Gotta go, Mom. Thank you for dinner."

As he stood up, she asked eagerly, as if to keep him with her just a little longer, "How you sleeping?"

"Much better these days. Thanks, Mom." He kissed her cheek and left. No need to tell her about Jamaal.

#

It was 9:51 AM and Pamela was leaning her ass on Rob's penis as they lay in bed. He was rock hard even though he was asleep. Jamaal was dead, so now he could sleep. The alarm went off at 9:55 am and he turned it off, he was not a snoozer. He soon realized that Pamela had her ass on him, he backed off and went to the bathroom. He was still rock hard; he thought about his wife at that point, and it went away. Pamela was lying in bed happy that she made him hard, but upset that she couldn't relieve him. Rob jumped back in bed to watch the news. Pamela got up to take a shower and get ready for his departure. While trying to get Rob excited, she made herself horny. So she had no choice but to masturbate in the shower, it was an easy climax as she thought about Rob.

Good morning.

#

It was the end of tour and everybody was preparing to go home. The desk officer was looking over the numbers for the day. Uniform officers had six arrests, and Anti-Crime had eleven. Good day. The only negative was one complaint. Against Officer Armetta.

Sergeant Donnelly looked up and saw Armetta down the hall. "Hey, Armetta, let me talk to you for a moment."

Armetta ambled over and said, "Yeah, what's up, Sarg."

Donnelly said, "Complaint against you today. I just wanted to give you a heads-up."

Armetta said nothing.

"Does any situation come to mind that somebody would have complained about?"

Armetta said, "No."

Donnelly tapped his pen against his desk. "I'm not asking you if you did something wrong. I'm asking if somebody was so mad at you that they would make a complaint."

Armetta winked, "No, I'm just out there doing what needs to done."

Donnelly just shook his head. "Well, it's for excessive force so you and your partner will be receiving a notice from IAB to appear."

Armetta shrugged, "Thanks, Sarg. Can I go now?"

The sergeant knew something happened out there on the streets but it was not his job to investigate it. He had stopped him at the hospital from assaulting a prisoner, again. Armetta was not worried, because his partner would never give him up so this would go away. As Armetta was leaving the precinct he saw Officer Hale in the 124 room taking civilian walk-in complaint reports. He admired her great body, and then approached.

Armetta said, "Hey, Alison. How you feeling?"

Hale said, "I'm doing okay. Thanks for asking."

Officer Armetta stared at Officer Hale like he wanted to eat her.

"Good to hear. Just to let you know I got a little payback for you today on patrol."

Feeling Armetta's eyes on her, Hale shifted away. "What do you mean?"

Officer Armetta said, "I did some smack face in your honor today."

Officer Hale didn't like what she heard. "Don't do that for me. Besides, the guy who did this *to* me was arrested *by* me."

Armetta said, "We have to keep these animals in line, you know what I mean?"

Hale straightened the stack of papers in front of her before she spoke. "I don't know what you mean. I'm here to protect and serve not to prosecute. Remember, we are held to a higher standard."

Armetta shrugged. "Sometimes you have to keep people in line, and you need to that with force."

Hale snapped, "Don't take everything so personally."

Armetta leered and said, "Be safe, Alison."

Chapter 18

BUSINESS

S osa's ashtray was overflowing.

"You're smoking too much," his brother said. Louie was bent over his phone, sending text after text.

Sosa lit up another one. "Nigel shooting at Fat Boy. Louie, are the Brooklyn Bullies coming at us?"

Louie didn't look up from his phone. "That's what I'm finding out."

"Maybe it's personal. Nigel and Fat Boy." Sosa dropped his cigarette from his shaking fingers, picked it up again. "Maybe this shit is about a female. You know how Fat Boy falls in love all the time. You know how most thugs are motivated by money, but this guy literally fell in love with hos and tries to make them housewives."

Louie grunted. "Maybe."

"We have to make sure another crew isn't moving on us, because if so we need to make a plan."

Louie glanced up, shutting up his brother with a cold stare. "I'm handling it."

#

Maribel wanted Fat Boy out of her bed. This was business, he should not still be here. Maribel had been here before. These Drug boys always fall in love. How can they not tell that I don't love them back. She was walking around the apartment making as much noise as possible to wake him up. He was sound asleep. She decided to wake him and ask if he was hungry, get him going. She took the covers off him and stared at his stomach. She thought that he couldn't be good at his business if he slept this hard. She shook him a few times and he opened his eyes. He smiled as soon as he opened his eyes and saw her.

Maribel said, "Are you hungry?"

Fat Boy said, "I'm always hungry."

He rubbed his belly and laughed. Maribel was not laughing. Maribel said, "Your phone was ringing off the hook. Probably your girl looking for you."

"He rolled over and looked at the number. Shrugged. "No one I know." Slung the phone back on the bedside table. It was the Cartel. This could be the end, so it was no need to rush death. There was enough time for a last supper. He said it as cool as he possible, "Want to go to IHOP?"

She snorted. "I don't have time for all that."

"You have somebody coming over?"

Maribel said, "None of your fucking business."

Fat Boy said, "Let's go to IHOP. I'll give you more money."

She said, "No. And you can't spend the night here."

He said, "What? You know how much I like you."

"I'm calling the police if you don't get out of here!" she screamed.

Fat Boy got out. He could take a hint. Rejection and death coming at him all at once. Fat Boy was stressed. Strawberry syrup was the cure. He went to IHOP.

#

Two stickup kids were hanging outside of the club. The younger one asked, "How we going to do this?"

The older kid said, "We'll follow the person that's driving the Range Rover and get him."

"Why can't we just hit them right here?"

The older kid pointed to the cameras on the building. The younger kid hadn't noticed them. Panicked, he pulled his hoodie over his face. It was why the older one was the leader. He was why they were wearing masks and hoodies.

A well-dressed couple walked out of the club and got into the Range.

The two stickup kids got into their Honda Accord. "We'll take them a few blocks from here," the older one said. "Remember, don't touch the car, just cash and jewelry, nothing traceable."

In the Ranger Rover, Derek put on his music. Tonight strictly Fifty Cent. Hard. He and Shanika were both exhausted and couldn't wait to get home. Shanika was wondering if Derek had had too much fun. She always wondered this after they had a threesome. Derek was thinking about food. He noticed the Accord behind him, so he decided to take a couple of turns to make sure it wasn't following him. He took a couple of lefts. The Accord was still behind him. Derek opened his middle console and pressed a button. A panel open and he took out a Smith & Wesson 45. He handed it to Shanika. He already had his in his waist. War was in the air.

"What's going on?"

Derek motioned to the rearview. She glanced into it and then took a better look out of her passenger's side window. She held the gun on her lap, ready. "Who?"

Derek was trying to figure out who it might be. Latin Cartel, Brooklyn Bullies, or stickup kids. "Stickup kids," he finally said. "Professionals would have something else, we would never see them coming."

He told her at the next light he was going to get out, but she was to stay in the car. Her gun was for her own protection. A last resort.

"You're by yourself, this is too dangerous," she said. "Let's just jet on them? Call Dre!"

"Dre is dead, and I don't run from nobody," he said. His tight grip on his gun told her he not going to do much talking. He thought the message was clear he was not to be fucked with. It would be crystal clear in a few minutes. He slowed down to get caught by a red light. When the light turned red, he put the truck in park. He opened the door.

The younger kid was confused, but the leader knew that it was on. He put the car in park and went for his Glock. Then froze, because Derek's gun was already in his friend's face.

Derek said, "Come out and I won't kill you." Derek had known the steering wheel would give him a few extra seconds with the driver. So he had gone to the passenger's side first. The younger kid made a movement—and Derek squeezed the trigger. The younger kid was hit three times in the upper chest. As the older kid jumped out of the car, Derek shot at him. He fell, but got up again and ran to the rear of the Accord.

Shanika, scared for Derek, stepped out of the Range Rover, her Smith & Wesson shaking in her right hand. She was nervous not scared. The older kid aimed as Derek took cover at the front of the Accord. The older kid never expected this shit. He'd been robbing motherfuckers for years, and he had never been caught by the police. Being shot at by the victim was never even considered. He didn't want to run out of bullets, as he only had one magazine. He wasn't expecting a shootout. He was trying to remember how many times he shot his gun. Maybe the best thing to do was run? Suddenly bullets sparked against the side of the Accord—from the Range Rover. He saw Shanika, her hand shaking but advancing. As he aimed his gun in her direction, Derek came around the car and shot him in the leg. The kid fell to the ground and threw his weapon to the side. Street version of a white flag. But he was in the West Bank!

Derek leaned in, gun pressed against his head. "Who sent you?"

"Nobody!" the kid gasped. "I was trying to get some quick money."

Derek said, "You picked the wrong guy."

"It ain't personal, I'm just robbing to eat!"

"Pointing a gun at me and my girl *is* personal." Derek shot him in the head.

Without looking away from the bloody mess of the kid's head, he asked Shanika if she was okay.

She said yes. He knew she was going to say more. She always had more to say.

"No, we won't be connected to this," he said. "It'll look like a simple carjacking. I'll get the Range Rover burned—you report it stolen tomorrow."

They both jumped in the Range Rover and pulled away. Derek turned to Shanika. "And I thought I told you to stay in the fucking truck."

Shanika said, "Fuck you."

#

Midnight at Queens Central Booking was packed. Nigel waited in the cell with about a hundred other young black men. There were four cells in total with about a hundred prisoners in each. Nigel had been locked up before, so he was cool but it would have been nice to see a familiar face. He looked around and saw nobody he recognized. He took a seat. He should be here till the morning, when hopefully Derek would have a lawyer waiting in the courtroom.

The correction officers came around with dinner: bologna and cheese sandwiches with milk. Nigel passed. The lawyer would have breakfast for him. The hardest thing would be staying awake for the next nine hours. All of the pain from his numerous injuries he had would help keep him awake. A correction officer asked Nigel if he wanted food. He told him no. One thing Nigel wouldn't do was talk shit to a CO. They were known for their legendary beatings. You don't fuck with transit cops and correction officers; it was known on the streets.

Danger! Nigel recognized the tall thin Jamaican staring at him. He walked over and sat down next to him. "Trevor know you're here?"

Nigel stared at the floor, thinking fast. Last thing he needed was Trevor to step in and "help" and screw up his chances with the Syndicate. Or worse, find out about the takeover. "Nope. This is on me. Got into a fight with my girl. She called the devils on me. She lied and said I beat her up. So they fucked me up and then charged me with assault on a police officer, and resisting arrest. Still can't believe this shit. We fucked then I go take a shower. She answered my phone and then forty-five minutes later I'm in a cell." The thin man just shook his head in support. Family shit, he would stay out of this.

#

Trevor figured the cops had beat the shit out of Nigel for jumping on a female cop and put him in the hospital. But he didn't know for sure. He sat in the backyard of his natural juice bar, smoking a blunt. His niece and her best friend were working hard inside, serving customers. He had a successful business. He was a Rastafarian so he took this juice shit seriously: vegetarian juice, Bob Marley, and cannabis. He would've made his parents proud. He'd moved from Kingston, Jamaica, to Brooklyn when he was twelve. He'd grew up with his parents, both hardworking people. The mother a home attendant, and the father, a former soldier in Jamaica, a security guard. They were poor, so Trevor got picked on for the cheap clothes he wore. The kids also made fun of his heavy accent. He was always behind in school, because the schools in Jamaica were horrible. This led to his dropping out. It wasn't long before he started selling weed on the street corners in East New York, Brooklyn. It took him almost twenty years to become the top man. It happened because was at the right place at the right time—the day his crew was raided he was at an abortion clinic with his girlfriend. All the top bosses of his organization got arrested, and they started ratting on one another so they were all convicted. Trevor was the last man standing, so he took over, outshooting anyone else who wanted the position. Which is why he didn't know exactly where Nigel was, he mused. He didn't trust anyone to collect information for him. he didn't trust anyone to watch his back. But someone had to know where Nigel was. All he had to do was be patient and he would hear.

His phone buzzed. He recognized the number and picked up the phone. "Talk to me."

"This is Sosa."

Trevor said, "I'm listening."

"We should meet up and talk."

Trevor said, "Good idea."

"You name the time and place."

Trevor liked that idea. "11:00 PM at the Q Club." It was public and loud. He hung up.

Chapter 19

IDLE

Kim had to bury her husband in five hours. Restless, she wandered around her house, finally going into the kitchen to check over the supplies for the meal after the funeral. She figured that she needed more paper towels. She grabbed her keys and was out the door. Her sister and son were both sound asleep upstairs. When she exited the house, she could see Mohammad sleeping in the car. He'd been here all day. She knocked on the car window, and he opened his eyes. She got in the car and told him she needed to go to Pathmark. They took the short ride over to the supermarket.

They entered the store together, and she grabbed a cart and left him behind. She had a short list, but she wanted everything to be perfect. Then a maintenance man mopping the floor blocked her access to the paper towels. He had on his Beats headphones and tried to go around him, but he hit her shoes with the mop. She slipped and fell. But she was up before her ass could touch the floor. She jumped in his face and screamed, "You fucking idiot. You put that dirty mop on my shoes!"

The maintenance man protested, "I'm sorry, miss!"

"You don't know how to say excuse me. You stupid motherfucker!" She swung to slap the shit out of him but a hand gripped her wrist. Mohammad.

Mohammad knew what needed to be done. He pressed Kim behind him then punched the guy in the face until the man buckled to the floor next to his mop. The Mohammad opened a bag of paper towels and wiped his bloody hands. A small crowd had formed. He turned and without thinking Kim pushed the cart out of the store with the merchandise still in it. Mohammad followed. Kim and Mohammad were silent the entire way home.

\#

It was an extraordinary morning, the sky a perfect blue, the sun shining. This morning the hood was burying Andre Smith. This day was not wasted on just a funeral. The weather was giving the mourners comfort, and a reason to wear their best with no coats and don't forget the shades. Kim was in the limo with her son and sister, while Andre's parents had their own limo. Derek was driving his black Cadillac Escalade; his was the third vehicle in the procession. Portia, Carla, and Shawn were all in the vehicle. No one said a word. Portia was looking for the right music. She tried old school R&B and then smooth jazz. Nothing felt right so she turned it off altogether, and no one cared. They pulled up to the church and got out of the SUV. Portia had been crying all morning. Carla was crying, because this could have been Shawn. She was wearing heavy makeup and sunglasses to hide the bruise under her eye. That morning Shawn had hit her to stop her from yelling at him to get out of the life. The fellas were just trying to keep it together; this was their first loss since they established themselves three years ago. They had seen death many times but not someone so close to them—it hit everybody hard. They thought they had built a wall to prevent anything like this. In the streets there is no security. They had to be reminded.

Kim had to be held up by two ushers. Her sister was holding little Dre's hand; he was crying but under control. Dre's parents were both crying, and they consoled each other. They all entered the church packed with people from the neighborhood. Some people had on their Sunday best, others were in jeans and Jordan's. Raekwon was there with his girlfriend, Tasha. They were the best dressed—they just couldn't help themselves. All black underwear, socks, belts, watches, suits, and shirts. Gangsta.

The service was being performed by Reverend Clark this morning. He was a family friend; he had known Andre's mother for over forty years. He was shocked when he got the call, hard to believe anything could get the big man. Derek and Shawn sat a few rows back, so as not to upset Andre's parents. The service was long, almost two hours. After the service the funeral procession drove through 40 Projects past Andre's childhood home, there were people outside to salute him. The limos honked the horns and kept moving. They were then off to Calvary National Cemetery in Riverhead, Long Island and then to Kim's house.

Derek had asked Mike if he'd taken care of everything. He didn't tell Shawn—no need and by the sound of things Carla was giving him grief about the life anyway. Mike had it all covered from what Mike told him. He had taken off the license plates on Derek's Range Rover and off the Van Wyck at Linden Boulevard he'd driven down the back streets to find a good spot to torch the Range. He'd found a secluded area and pulled over. Without hesitation he'd poured gasoline on the ground underneath the truck. He'd lit a match and thrown it down. It had taken three minutes and thirteen seconds for the truck to be up in flames. Derek was a victim of a carjacking. He killed the stickup kids. Now he could actually receive insurance money for a new car. The game!

At five in the evening, it was still beautiful outside. The weather wasn't wasted on this sad day, because everyone was spread out from the house to the front sidewalk. The sun made it a holy day; the skies had opened for Dre. Kim and Dre's mother walked through the crowd together. Dre's father was eating with little Dre. The Syndicate was outside, and Derek was leading the conversation. The topic got to best rappers of all time, and Queens rappers' place in history.

Derek said, "My top five are: Jay, Biggie, Fifty, DMX, and KRS One."

Shawn said, "You got Fifty over Nas?"

Derek replied, "Yes, because he and DMX were the most authentic rappers ever. They wear their emotions on their sleeve."

Shawn said, "Cool. I get it. My top five are Jay, Nas, Fabulous, Jada, and Rakim."

Shanika jumped in eagerly. She loved rap and felt she knew more than the fellas. "My top five are Fifty, Jay, Biggie, Ray, and Ghost."

Shawn said, "Yo, your list was crazy."

Everybody looked at Carla, but she didn't want to participate. Rap was not that serious to her. Derek continued, "More importantly, my top five rappers of all time from Queens is Fifty, Nas, Cool G Rap, Run, and LL Cool J."

Shawn said, "Nice. Mine are Nas, Fifty, Nikki Minaj, LL Cool J, and Q Tip."

Derek said, "I'm not crazy about your list."

Shawn retorted, "It's my list, motherfucker."

Jocelyn asked, "Can't a white girl get her rap on? Mine are Wu-Tang, Mobb Deep, Boot Camp, Nice and Smooth, and Onyx."

Everybody agreed that her list was good. Kim walked over and thanked everybody for showing their support. She motioned for Derek to walk with her.

Kim said to him, "Thanks for everything."

Derek said, "I didn't do anything, I just gave you a few dollars."

Kim said, "If you only knew. It made everything else easier. There was so much going and I didn't anticipate going to war with his mother. I mean, we were legitimately married. You would think I was a side chick with the way she treated me. I think she associates me with the work he did. Like he met working for you. No disrespect to you. But Dre and I met at a concert and we were in love and did everything right out of respect for his parents and still I get no respect."

Derek said, "Don't take any of that personally. She just hated that he was in this life, so she automatically associated you with it. Not knowing you were the best thing to ever happen to Dre. I think over time she would realize that."

Kim said, "Thank you. For little Dre I would hang in there. They don't have to see me to have a relationship with him."

Derek said, "Trust me, they were going to latch on so hard to both of you, it would be hard to breathe. You're gonna wish for these days. Because with love comes opinions and advice."

Kim said, "You crazy, but right."

Derek said, "You'll see. Listen, I don't want to talk money today, so just know you would be receiving a package for you and little Dre soon."

Kim said, "You already have done so much. Thank you."

They hugged and kissed. Tonight Derek would hang around as long as needed. Today was all about little Dre and Kim.

When the time came for Shawn and Carla to leave, Carla took the keys, because Shawn had had too much to drink. They were driving on the Van Wyck, which was always crowded no matter the time of day.

Carla said, "You need to get out of the business, now."

Shawn jerked upright. He'd been dozing. "What the fuck are you talking about."

Carla said, "You need to stop selling drugs."

Shawn said, "Not this shit again."

Carla snapped, "Yes, this shit again. Don't you think about Lorenzo and me? I don't want to have to go through what Kim did today."

Shawn stressed, "Andre died in a motorcycle accident."

Carla said, "He was your fucking hit man. That was karma."

"Chill," said Shawn. "Too much information."

Carla thumped the steering wheel. "I'm not playing. You need to get out. We have enough money to start a business."

Shawn said, "*I* have enough money."

"Fuck you, negro," said Carla. "Whatever. You could be investing your money in real estate."

Shawn said, "I told you I don't know nothing about houses or a restaurant. I only know the streets."

Carla said, "You're acting like a pussy. The same way you learn the streets is the same way you learn anything else."

"I ain't no fucking pussy."

"You can't do this forever. You know my uncle—you say he was a perfect gentleman—well, he was the baddest Dominican you ever met in the eighties."

"Uncle Tito," Shawn said.

Carla said, "When he was in the game he literally chopped heads off and killed anybody who got in his way. But it was all business. He started making so much money he couldn't trust anyone, not even his own people. So he left with no warning. He was smart enough to leave his number two with the connect and control. There was no bitterness. A brilliant exit. He can walk the streets with no worries. He set up a livery cab business, laundromat, and cleaners. He's a family man now. Just like Joe Kennedy, so hopefully his children would become senators or presidents. Don't be stupid, but more importantly, don't be a follower. You don't owe Derek anything. He has your loyalty—you would never rat on him. So it's time to start putting this family first. If he's your friend, he'll understand. You sold drugs, but now you can run a legitimate business and employ your own people so they have a better path than you. The only reason why I tolerate Derek he is an excellent business man. But he doesn't have an exit strategy. You started doing this because you had no other options. Now what? You can take this dirty money and do good in the hood. Hire who you want and save some lives from the game. Your hunger was for respect and survival. Then it was cars and toys. What's your hunger now?"

To end the conversation, Shawn said, "I'll look into it." His head was spinning from the conversation. She had fucked up his high.

Carla said, "You better make it quick cause I'm not hanging around forever."

Shawn turned to her. "What?"

Carla said, "You heard me. And if you ever hit me again you'll never to be able to sleep because the minute you close your eyes, I'm going to kill you."

She had more to say. Shawn stared out of the window.

When, after midnight Carla was still talking, Shawn sent Shanika a text to Derek to call him, no emergency. Derek called him right away from a pay phone. Shawn picked up on the first ring and said right way, "Cool, I'll pick you up in a few."

Derek said, "Cool."

When Shawn pulled up to Derek's home, Derek was waiting out front. He got in the BMW 550i X Drive, Gran Turismo. Shawn rarely drove this baby. Derek knew something must be up.

Derek said, "You brang the toys out. Crazy."

Shawn said, "Yeah I needed to get out in style."

Derek leaned back in the seat. "You doing it."

"I forgot how bad she was. Leather, wood panel. Perfection."

Derek waited. Then asked, "Everything okay?"

Shawn admitted, "Carla was on my ass today. Or should I say in my ear."

"What did you do?"

"She was bugging cause of Dre's death. She's just paranoid right now."

Derek shook his head. "That shit will pass."

Shawn said, "She has been talking about this for the last five days, nonstop."

"Oh." He waited again.

Shawn said, "Let's not talk about that bullshit. Let's hit the block in honor of Big Dre."

Derek nodded. "Sounds good to me."

Shawn spun the wheel and jammed the accelerator. They'd go find Raekwon. He was probably in the Little Dragon restaurant on Hillside Ave. They pulled up, and there he was. He saw them and headed out and got in on the rear passenger side.

Raekwon said, "What up, fellas. I was expecting you."

Derek stared at him. "What?"

Raekwon said, "The God knows all."

Shawn shrugged. "Whatever. We decided to hit the block for old time's sake."

Raekwon laughed. "So you'll need me to get you in. Got you."

Derek said, "Fuck you."

Raekwon looked around the interior. "Damn, this car was nice. I need a raise."

Shawn said, "Stop spending your money on your girl."

They all laughed. Shawn turned up the Cool G Rap, Ill Street Blues playing on the MP3. They all relaxed and enjoyed the music and the ride. Destination unknown.

At five in the morning, Derek, Shawn, and Raekwon were still in the hood. They were parked in front of White Castle, eating burgers and drinking beer and talking about Dre. Derek and Raekwon had had a bet on how many green lights Shawn could hit on Queens Boulevard. Derek's record was ten, but Shawn hit eleven. If Derek's record held, they'd have gone to IHOP, but if Raekwon won, White Castle. So here they were talking shit on the corner, like old times.

Then an old Ford Explorer pulled into the parking lot with three young brothers in it, very drunk. One of the young men decided to stare down Shawn, but Shawn was cool. He recognized that he was young. You get no credit for knocking out a pup.

The kid started talking shit. "I feel like fucking somebody up tonight."

He stopped in front of Shawn, and Raekwon started to walk towards him, but Shawn stopped him. Shawn was cool, no worries here.

Shawn said, "Have a nice night, brother."

Then Shawn intentionally turned his back to him. The young man was feeling himself and wanted to pursue this situation. So he stepped closer to Shawn. Shawn still under control, turned around and looked him in the eye and said, "Get the fuck out of my face."

Raekwon was ready to handle this. Derek was cool cause he knew what his boy was capable of.

Raymond said, "Fuck you."

Derek said, "What would Dre do in this situation?"

Nothing more to say, they square off. It wouldn't be a long fight; Shawn could see it in his eyes: the kid was having second thoughts. The kid threw a knockout punch that missed by a mile. Shawn hit him with a combination and dropped him. Derek was laughing, and Raekwon was hoping one of his boys said or did something. They didn't—they were scared out of their fucking minds. His friends helped him up and they got back in their truck and drove away.

Derek, Shawn, and Raekwon laughed.

Shawn said, "I really tried to avoid that but I needed it."

Derek asked, "Cause of Dre?"

Shawn sighed. "Carla on my ass. And of course Dre."

Raekwon chimed in, "I wanted to get him, bad."

Derek nodded. "I saw. I think we got soft."

"Not soft," Raekwon said, "but I know your guns are warm."

Shawn said, "Hopefully one day soon your gun will be warm."

They all laughed.

Derek said, "Let's finish off these murder burgers. Killers."

Chapter 20

DEJA VU

When Rob entered the room from a door in the back, Officer Hale recognized him immediately as the man who had helped her with the arrest.

Rob said, "Hello, Officer Hale. I'm Lieutenant Robert Grey."

Stunned she shook her head. "Oh my god, I thought you worked at the deli!" Hale was sitting at in an office with a cast on her left hand. She was on light duty, doing clerical work at the precinct until she healed. Today she had been told to go with an officer to Police Plaza to be interviewed by the Internal Affairs Bureau but instead she was following the lieutenant through a door and into a setup so high-tech it looked like the CIA.

She stared at the monitors connected to camera systems in the deli, rooms in houses, and in cars. Also on the walls were all the organizational charts for the Top Drug Crews in the city, from drug lord to the street pusher. Rob introduced Hale to the four detective investigators: Detective Gaglio, Banner, Machado, and Rogers.

They then went into Rob's office and he motioned for her to take a seat. He explained that he was about to discuss something with her that she couldn't speak about once she left; it was top secret. She said she understood. Rob told her that he wanted her to join the unit as a Detective Investigator. He explained that her duties would be to do computer checks on suspects, complete DD5s, surveillance, arrest, raids, serve warrants and subpoenas, interviews and interrogations, and court testimony.

Hale said uncertainly, "I'm a rookie, I don't know how to do all of that."

Rob replied, "We would train you. But we'd need you to commit to us. The unit works hard. Don't be afraid to challenge yourself and make a real difference."

He watched her, waiting. He wouldn't tell her about the alias, and all the high-speed training until she accepted the offer.

"I like uniform patrol. I felt like I'm helping people."

"Take your time," he suggested. "Think about it." They had plenty of time to work on good recruits like Hale.

#

At 7:47 AM on Friday morning, at the Church of St. Augustine in Bay Ridge, there were already thousands of police officers lined up for the funeral service of Captain Theodore Howard, their dress blues coloring the streets for blocks. Inside the church Maureen sat with her children, Abigail and Thomas. They had a lot of family there as well. The church was packed. In a rear room of the church sat Rob's unit. They weren't supposed to be there but Rob told the department to "Go fuck themselves" when they told them to stay away. An officer stood at the door for security. It was a somber mood in the room with little conversation. At least he didn't die as a result of their work, that was the only solace. Rob wished that he could be out there for Maureen. Rob was even more upset that Teddy was not receiving an Inspectors funeral: a memorial service that the mayor and police commissioner attend with full honor guard. But it was not a death in the line of duty. Rob felt that with all Teddy had done for this city, cleaning up drugs for thirty years, he warranted it. The mayor and PC could have come, but he knew they always changed the rules when it benefitted them.

A knock came at the door, and Rob opened it. There was a vaguely familiar face in a captain's uniform standing there.

Captain Gallagher asked, "May I enter."

Rob let him in. "What can I do for you?"

Captain Gallagher said, "I'm your new boss. I'll be at the office on Monday so we can work on finally getting some big drug arrest and seizures. Long overdue."

Everybody looked at each other with surprise.

Detective Dunne said under his breath, "Get the fuck out of here."

Rob shot Dunne a warning glance. "Hold it, sir. This conversation is inappropriate right now. We just want to bury our friend with respect."

Captain Gallagher got the message. "We'll talk soon."

Rob slammed the door behind him. Detective Dunne let everybody know that he had a bad feeling about the new guy. Rob told him to relax; they have to give him the benefit of the doubt, for now. They stayed in the back for the duration of the service, which was a little over an hour, and waited for everyone to leave.

In the backroom of the church was a window. Rob could see Lora leaving. She was not supposed to be there either but he knew she probably said, "Fuck the department," as well. Maureen and Teddy were family. He yearned to comfort his wife. This assignment was crazy, but he still believed in it. He wanted to hope that she would understand.

#

Rob and the unit retreated to the Bat Cave to drink and reminisce. Everybody was drinking Jack Daniels in honor of Captain Howard. Rob had his own bottle. A lot of stories were told about Captain Howard, until everybody was laughing and enjoying them. This was how officers cope with death within the ranks. Alcohol, jokes, and revenge. The revenge would be paid on the drug crews they were investigating. They had to make Captain Howard proud so there was a new dedication towards their work. Pamela, Alex, and Rob lingered at the end.

Pamela said, "Alex, what the hell really happened that morning?"

Rob gave Alex a quick look and poured out the rest of the Jack Daniels into Alex's cup.

Alex took his glace as warning and just said, "It was a crazy night."

Pamela said, "I bet."

"And after that night, I was driving through one of our areas of interest and by chance I saw this piece of shit on top of a woman."

Pamela said, "Thank god you were there. It's almost impossible to mentally recover from a rape."

Alex said, "I was just glad I was there."

Changing the subject Rob said, "I wish Teddy was here."

Pamela said, "I can't believe how much I miss him already."

Alex said, "If first impression were true, then we were really going to miss the big guy. Gallagher is going to be an asshole."

Rob said, "He tries to mess with the unit, we'll have to set him straight. But maybe it was just the funeral." He felt uneasy though. There was no way the unit could be shut down.

Pamela said, "It was awkward for all of us."

Alex said, "You motherfuckers were disregarding your greatest gift as a cop, your gut."

They laugh. He was absolutely right. Rob lifted his cup, they both followed.

Rob said, "To Teddy."

"To Teddy."

Rob couldn't help think of Officer Hale, and the way she said she had to think about joining them, as if she wasn't sure what she was getting herself into. Rob grabbed the bottle but there barely a swallow left. He tipped the bottle up to his mouth, finished it.

#

At 8:45 AM, the Bat Cave was empty. Rob was alone in his office and not looking forward to meeting with Captain Gallagher. He was signing Teddy's name on paperwork to make sure expense reports got through. It would take a long time with a new boss and things would be scrutinized more. At 8:58 he heard a buzz from the door, and Rob saw through the camera that it was Gallagher. He swept the forged paperwork into a drawer in his desk and buzzed him in.

Rob said, "Good morning, sir."

Captain Gallagher said, "Good morning. Where is everybody?"

Rob said, "We do a noon-to-eight tour, unless otherwise needed."

Captain Gallagher said, "Interesting."

They walked over to the large conference room, which was equipped with flat screen TVs, boards for charts, and telephones. Captain Gallagher looked around.

Rob said, "Have a seat wherever you want."

The captain took a seat and Rob sat across the table from him.

Captain Gallagher said, "This office was very impressive. How long have you been here?"

Rob said, "A little over a year."

Captain Gallagher said, "Nice. I read up on the unit and it sounds very high speed."

Rob said, "We're the best. The federal training, we received puts us ahead of all law enforcement."

Captain Gallagher said, "That's what we need to talk about. What do we have to show for it? There haven't been any arrests at all."

Rob said defensively, "It isn't that type of unit. We build big cases here. We don't go after the small guys."

Captain Gallagher leaned forward. "I was in narcotics. I know how this works. All you need was one good confidential informant."

Rob shook his head. "Not with these guys. There is no C.I. who can catch us the top boss in any crew. They are all too smart. They stay away from the daily routine of the drug business."

Captain Gallagher said, "So what's your plan?"

"We build our cases over time using CIs, wiretaps, and other investigative methods. An investigation can take over a year."

Captain Gallagher stood and walked by the TVs. "Well, you might have to change your methods, because we need arrests to justify your budget. The mayor has a link to Comp Stat now."

Rob said, "Have you talked to the Chief?"

Captain Gallagher swung around and stared hard at Rob. "Just a brief conversation when I was chosen by the mayor."

Rob didn't back down. "I advise you should do that before you do anything with our budget."

Captain Gallagher said, "I'm telling you as your supervisor we need arrests. This is an election year so the mayor wants some big drug arrest and seizures. If you can't produce that…then we'll find someone who can."

Rob leaned back, eyeing the captain. "Are you threatening me?"

Captain Gallagher said, "What I'm saying directly to you is the budget for this unit was 3.5 million dollars. We need productivity."

Rob snorted. "If you're looking for a better bang for your buck this is not the unit. And if you'll excuse me, I have work to do." He started to the door and held it open politely, but inwardly he was seething. All he wanted was to be able to take down the gang who was responsible for his father's death. Before Derek Mason, the Syndicate had been a small-time operation. If Gallagher didn't interfere, they stood a chance.

Captain Gallagher walked through the doorway and halted right in front of Rob. "Sounds like you either need better supervision or a new assignment. I'll figure out which, real soon."

Rob said tightly. "We have a mission here and a way to execute it. The Chief can explain it to you."

Captain Gallagher snapped, "I need expense, intelligence, and tactical reports."

Rob said, "I'll jump right on it, sir."

Rob has no intention of doing any of that. As soon as the new captain left, Rob called Detective Stella Machado, the unit's intelligence officer.

"We may have a problem," Rod told her, relaying his conversation with Gallagher. "Are we close to making any arrests?"

Stella confessed she didn't think so. "The Italians have indictments so they're laying low waiting for the arrest warrants. That recent shootout? That was between the Latin Cartel and the Brooklyn Bullies. The streets are saying that the Bullies were making a move on the cartel. No news from the Syndicate."

Rod mused, "The Syndicate could be starting something. A drug war."

Stella said, "Definitely possible. It would be a smart move on their part."

Rob said, "Are we close to getting Dwayne in the Syndicate?"

Stella nodded. "They just lost Big Andre so there's a chance."

"Good news," he said.

Another buzz from the door made Rob look up. Officer Hale. He got up to let her in. She was dressed in business attire, because she didn't know the dress code.

"I wasn't sure you would come back," he confessed.

Alison said, "You sent the address. I knew that meant you had confidence in me."

They sat in his office.

"Ready when you are, sir," she said.

Rob said, "Do you know who Louie Sojo is?"

She shook her head.

Rob said, "You're not a Yankee fan?"

She laughed. "No. I'm from Queens. Go Mets."

Rob said, "I should be a Met fan too. I'm from Queens as well."

Alison smiled. "Traitor."

Rob laughed and said, "Louie Sojo was a utility player for the Yankees. He did everything."

"Um, okay?"

Rob could tell she didn't get it. "Well, you certainly fucked up my analogy. I want you to be *my* utility player."

Alison stared, "Oh. Okay. I understand."

Rob said, "I want you to learn. Computers, UC work, wiretaps, warrants, and subpoenas. Everything."

Alison said, "That sounds like a lot. I'll do my best."

"You got this. In eighteen months you'll receive a detective shield. How does that sound?"

Alison said, "Remember, I'm a rookie, so you're really going to have to train me well."

Rob said, "We'll start slow. First because you're injured you should learn computers. After you're back on full duty, we'll send you away for training."

Alison said, "Sounds good. What tour am I doing?"

Rob said, "We work a noon-to-eight-thirty tour. An old transit police department tour. We tried to preserve some of the history after the merge in March of 1995."

He didn't think she knew what that was but she nodded and said, "When Mayor Giuliani merged the NYPD, NYC Transit Police Department, and the NYC Housing Police Department. The Transit Police were about to get a big raise, and the city didn't want this so the mayor got the merger through. A bad deal." She smiled. "I like the hours. I can hang out and not have to be up early."

Rob said, "We'll have to put your paperwork in for your security clearance. This is a covert unit. I'll tell you more in the next few weeks. By the time you go away to training you'll be squared away."

Alison asked, "You keep saying 'go away to training.' We train in Queens?"

Rob said, "Virginia."

They heard voices as the door opened and banged shut. The detectives were starting to come into the office.

Rob said, "Go and meet your co-workers."

Alison went out into the bull pen. The first work day since Teddy's funeral, they were all upset but they said hello. She met Sergeant Ling, Detective Banner, Detective Machado, and Detective Rogers.

Detective Machado asked, "Where did you work before coming here?"

Alison answered, "The 103."

"Busy house," Sergeant Ling said.

Detective Banner said, "How much time you got on?"

Alison knew it was the standard cop question when you first meet another cop. "A year."

Detective Machado said, "What?"

Sergeant Ling said, "Rob must have his reasons. Let's lighten the mood." He opened the bottle of Jack Daniels and poured everybody a glass. When he tried to hand Alison a glass, she politely declined.

Sergeant Ling said, "How am I supposed to trust you, Rook?"

Officer Hale said, "I don't drink."

Detective Machado said, "Of course you don't. You're not old enough."

They all laughed, except for Alison. She excused herself to go to the bathroom and instead went to Rob's office, where she knocked on the door. He waved her in.

Alison said, "I don't think I fit in here, sir. I don't drink but even if I did I wouldn't do it on duty."

Rob told her to relax. The reason why she was here was because she wasn't status quo. He wanted her to be herself, and everything would work out.

Rob said, "Listen, take the rest of the day to clean out your locker at the precinct and get yourself together. I'll see you tomorrow afternoon."

Alison nodded then as she was leaving said, "Hey, I never thanked you for helping that day. You throw a nice combination."

Rob said, "No problem. Safe home."

Chapter 21

PROJECT PRINCESS

Fat Boy had been calling Maribel all day and she hadn't answered. He was calling Maribel as if she was his girlfriend, but he couldn't help himself. He had fallen hard again. Fat Boy decided to try and call Maribel again. He called her twice leaving a message both times. He then sent her a text: *I'm sorry for showing up at your crib. Let me take you to dinner to make up for my mistake.*

She responded with: *Don't fucking call or text me anymore.*

He decided to go to a strip club on Queens Boulevard, because he had too much energy. Strippers and alcohol, guaranteed relief. Home of the project princess.

Fat Boy entered Scandals Strip Club in Long Island City with his cousin Hector. The club closed at 5 AM, so he had about an hour to find someone to take home. Hector was just tagging along. He had a girlfriend and no money. As soon as Fat Boy entered, Juan from the Latin Cartel saw him and called Louie.

Louie said, "Dime?"

Juan said, "Fat Boy just walked into Scandals."

"Is he by himself."

Juan said, "He and his cousin."

"Throwing money around?"

Juan said, "No, he's chilling. He's walking around looking for a date."

Louie said, "Okay, just watch him."

Fat Boy gave his cousin some money to get himself a drink. He had a wad of money in his left hand to attract the fish. The money was spotted, and a stripper approached him.

Candy said, "You wanna lap dance?"

Fat Boy said, "I'm looking to get out of here, with you."

Candy said, "No, I don't do dates."

Fat Boy said, "Cool. Point me in the right direction."

He held up a twenty-dollar bill. Candy pointed to two girls in the corner. Fat Boy headed in that direction. They were both decent looking, but he went for the skinny one hoping it would be less work.

Fat Boy said, "Hey *flaca*, you are beautiful. What's your name?"

"Susana. You wanna lap dance?"

Fat Boy nodded.

She took his hand and led him to a set of chairs by the wall. She sat him down and then straddled him. He leaned back in the chair to enjoy it. She started to grind away, gazing into his eyes. Fat Boy had a good feeling about this.

Fat Boy asked, "Where you from?"

Susana wiggled her ass. "I'm Puerto Rican."

Fat Boy said, "Me too. *Eres hermosa*."

Susana purred, "Thank you."

Fat Boy saw Juan watching him, and he felt uneasy. He suggested to Susana that they go for breakfast so they could talk, and then he would take her home. She asked, "You got me?" He told her yes and he would be in the front of the club in the black Range Rover. He handed her three twenty-dollar bills. He knew the big tip would set the right tone. He knew Juan was watching him, but he also knew if the Cartel wanted him dead it was nothing he could do to stop it. He grabbed Hector and strode out the front door, attempting to show no fear. Once outside he gave Hector money for a taxi, and he told him he would see him tomorrow.

Juan was impressed that the fat motherfucker pulled a girl so quickly. He also figured that pussy could be the reason they might go to war with the Brooklyn Bullies. He called Louie and told him what he observed.

Fat Boy was sitting in the Range with his Hector Lavoe blaring. El Cantante fits any mood. Susana came out, her sweatshirt's hoodie low over her face. She got right in the truck. Covert stripper movement.

On their way, Fat Boy asked her, "So how old were you?"

"I'm twenty. What about you?"

Fat Boy said, "Twenty-nine. How many kids do you have?"

Susana said, "Two. A boy and a girl. You?"

Fat Boy said, "None. Do they live with you?"

"We all live with my grandmother."

They had pulled into the parking lot of the diner. He had all the information he needed. The hood interview was over. Time to close.

Fat Boy said, "You are so beautiful."

Susana said, "Whatever, *papi*."

Fat Boy said, "I want to spend the night with you. What do you think?"

Susana remembered he was walking around with a wad of money in the club, and he just paid the bill with a hundred-dollar bill. She was in control here.

Susana said, "I don't usually do this, but you seem cool."

Fat Boy said, "Yeah, *calinda*, I'm cool. I'm just really feeling you. So I felt I would keep it one hundred with you."

Susana said, "No doubt. If I stay with you I'm going to miss work in the morning."

Fat Boy said, "I told you, I got you. Don't worry about anything. You good."

Susana said, "So there's no problems, what number are we talking about?"

Fat Boy said, "Five hundred?"

Susana was very happy with that number. She would have said three, because she ain't got no other job but shaking her ass. What she didn't know was she could have gotten him for eight hundred. For now, they both got what they wanted.

#

The juice bar was closed, so Trevor was smoking up a storm. The hood news said that Nigel was in the hospital and then jail. So it made sense there was no contact. Everything seemed to be calm on the streets, so maybe Nigel had some side business that got him in some trouble. His phone vibrated. Kim. No time for pussy. He needed to figure how he was going to replace Nigel's production. He didn't want to lose out on any money. He would deal with Nigel in due time. For the money bag!

As he smoked, he thought about all the possibilities, Bob Marley playing low in the background.

Chapter 22

DA STORY

The correction officer finally came to get Nigel for his arraignment. He sat up when they called his name; he was ready to see the judge. They handcuffed him and then escorted him to the courtroom, where he took a seat. He was put on a short line; he could see his lawyer; defense attorney Gerald Weiss was waiting. Weiss was wearing an expensive suit—this wasn't a court-appointed lawyer. Nigel hid his smile. It wouldn't help his case to look like Derek and the Syndicate had his back. Weiss had told him then he would take care of everything. The lawyer had even said that the injuries were good, because it made him look more like the victim.

The court officer called his name.

He stood and waited to be moved. He knew his way around a courtroom. He was taken to the table with his lawyer.

His lawyer whispered, "Act timid, because you know nothing about guns. You were the victim."

Nigel was prepped.

The judge looked at the prosecutor. ADA Kristen Gate was young, energetic, and inexperienced at her job. The ADA said, "Your Honor, we have serious charges against the defendant: criminal discharge of a weapon, possession of a firearm, possession of hollow-point bullets, loaded magazine, chambered round, assault on a police officer, and resisting arrest."

Weiss broke in and said, "Allegedly. Your Honor, my client was actually the victim in this case. He was shopping on Jamaica Avenue, when a gentlemen attempted to rob him with a firearm. The same firearm recovered at the scene."

Gate asked, "Your Honor, if he were a victim, why then did he assault a police officer?"

The judge looked over his glasses at Weiss. "Gerry?"

Weiss said, "My client was scared out of his mind. He literally ran into the officer and was arrested. There was no intentional fight."

Gate's rolled her eyes. "He broke her hand, and gave her a black eye."

Weiss said, "Your Honor, again he was running for his life. He sincerely regrets what happened to the officer—he truly was in a moment of hysteria. Regardless of that he was still a victim of an attempted robbery and police brutality. I have pictures of my client's injuries right after the attack. He was viciously beaten at the scene. An officer broke his hand at the hospital. As you can see now, he was still recovering." Weiss pointed to Nigel and the visible black eye, and broken hand. "He has the exact same injuries as the officer. Do we think that this was a coincidence? We also have the name of the officer who did this to my client. His name was Armetta and we would like this to be investigated."

Gates asked, "Do you have any witnesses?"

Weiss said, "I have two witnesses that can testify to Mr. Judas's character. His boss is here, along with his pastor."

Nigel tried to disguise his shock as he scanned the courtroom for his boss and pastor. He had never worked on the books in his life, and he had never been to church. Weiss motioned for both of them to stand.

Judge said, "I will let both of them make a brief statement."

Daniel Jacobs approached first. He was sworn in and took a seat on the witness stand,

Weiss said, "Sir, please state your name, title, and where you know Mr. Judas from."

Daniel said, "My name is Daniel Jacobs. I'm a bank manager at Jamaica Savings bank. Mr. Judas is one of my employees. He is the janitor."

Weiss said, "How long has he worked for you and what type of employee is he?"

Daniel said, "He has worked for the bank for eighteen months. He is a very hard worker who was always punctual. In fact, we let the other maintenance man go because Mr. Judas does such a great job by himself."

Weiss said, "Any issues with him?"

Daniel said, "None. He is a pleasure to supervise every day."

Weiss said, "Nothing further, Your Honor."

Judge said, "ADA Gates, any questions?"

Gates knew she was beat. "No, Your Honor."

Pastor Banks took the stand, and was sworn in.

Weiss said, "Pastor, please state your name, title, and where you know Mr. Judas from. Thanks."

Pastor Banks said, "My name is Earl Banks. I am the pastor at Allen Methodist Church in South Jamaica. Mr. Judas is an usher there, and he has been in that capacity for about two years. I see him every Wednesday and Sunday."

Weiss said, "This was a voluntary position correct, pastor?"

Pastor Banks said, "Yes. It takes a God fearing man for that type of commitment."

Weiss said, "Nothing further, Your Honor."

Judge said, "ADA Gates?"

Gates said, "Nothing for the witness. I just want to say for the record that people saying he is a great guy means nothing to the facts of the case."

Weiss said, "Yes, he is. And I do think it says a lot about him that his boss and pastor have taken the time to address the court."

Nigel couldn't believe what was happening, but he knew it was good.

Judge said, "Okay, counselors. We will hold Mr. Judas on the charges of assault on a police officer and resisting arrest. This should give you time to build a case for the other charges."

Weiss said, "So the other charges are dropped?"

Judge said, "For now. I would see you both on Thursday morning."

Nigel knew he was lucky because if they dropped the other charges he would have an opportunity to plea the other charges. He was very happy, because he had been prepared to do some serious time. Derek had hooked him up with a great attorney. Nigel faced Weiss and whispered, "Thank you."

Weiss told him that they would keep him in that cell until Thursday. He would send him some decent food in the morning. Nigel was ahead of the game. No matter the outcome, he was at peace with his decision to make a move on his boss. Something had to change, so this was the best option. If it paid off, he could hold rank in the baddest crew in New York City. It was worth the roll of the dice. He would get street cred for the shootout, for having taken a beaten by the cops, and, most of all, for keeping his mouth shut.

#

Hector walked into Louie's pool hall with two of his friends as if they owned the place. After a few glasses of Bacardi and Coke, Hector thought he was a tough guy, so along with two of his tough friends they were here to raise hell. After a few games of pool and drinks, they got louder.

The waitress thought it best to get their money ahead of time, and Hector said, "Fuck this place, I ain't paying for shit."

The waitress got Ricardo to tell him those guys didn't want to pay. Ricardo approached the three *amigos*.

"Gentlemen, is there a problem with the service or bill?"

Hector said, "We just ain't paying the fucking bill. Motherfucker."

Trying to figure out their deal Ricardo said, "Really." He nodded to the waitress: *get Louie.*

Louie and Juan came downstairs with their Louisville Sluggers. They walked over to the confrontation. Ricardo let them know he had it under control. Juan recognized Hector right away and he let Louie know.

Juan said, *"Ese pedazo de mierda con* Fat Boy."

Louie said, "Interesting."

Ricardo said, "What's the deal, guys?"

Hector shouted, "We don't respect people who don't take care of their own."

Ricardo didn't know what the fuck they were talking about. But Louie knew this was related to Fat Boy so he gave his bat to Juan, saying, "Gentlemen, we don't want any trouble so let me take care of the bill for you. Hopefully you would come back and everything would be better the next time."

Hector said, "Now I know you're a bunch of *coños.*"

Louie held Ricardo back and just replied, "Have a nice day and don't drive drunk."

Stumbling out the door, Hector said, "Fuck you."

"Get the car ready," Louie told Juan. He gave the waitress a hundred-dollar tip and told her to take a break. The patrons went back to drinking and playing pool.

Chapter 23

QUESTION

The blackness of night was the perfect mood lighting for killing someone. Louie and Juan were parked in front of 4-25 Astoria Boulevard, Astoria Projects, where Hector lived. Weaving a little, obviously drunk, Hector walked into the building just as they were getting comfortable in the car for a long night.

Juan grunted, *"También."*

Louie got out of the car and followed Hector into the building. Juan was right behind him. In the elevator, Hector tried to press the sixth floor, but Juan pushed the button for the top floor, seven. Through his haze, Hector recognized them. He felt around in his pants pocket for anything that could be a weapon. The elevator passed six and Hector knew things weren't looking up for him. Juan stood in front of the door and brandished his nine-millimeter at his waist. Nothing Hector could do at this point. Hopefully they wouldn't beat him too bad.

The elevator stopped at the seventh floor and Louie got out first, then Hector, and Juan followed. They walked out onto the roof and went to the corner farthest from the door. Hector pressed his back against the wall. "Sorry about the pool hall, guys. I can pay the bill."

Louie said nothing.

Juan said, "We ain't here for that. Where's Fat Boy."

Hector shrugged.

"Tell us about Fat Boy's side business."

Hector protested, "Fat Boy never had any side business. He's loyal to ya'll. That's why I was shooting off my mouth. I was high, that's all.

Like I said, I'll make good." He began to reach into his pocket for his wallet then froze when Juan's hand next to his nine-millimeter twitched.

Juan said, "And the shootout?"

Hector said, "The dude just started shooting at him. That's why he's upset with the Cartel."

Louie chuckled.

Juan said, "*He* is mad at *us*?"

Hector felt a little better when Louie laughed. He had this. "Yeah, because nobody had his back. He paid for his own doctor and he avoided the police. He felt all alone. Except for me—I take care of my *familia*."

"And you don't know where he is."

Eying the gun, Hector gave them Maribel's address.

Louie nodded at Juan.

Hector took that as a good thing. Tell the truth and you go free.

Juan said, "You made a big mistake by disrespecting our place of business."

Hector pleaded, "I'm sorry, *primo*. I was trying help my cousin."

"Big mistake." Juan pulled out the nine-millimeter.

Hector knew this wasn't good. "Please let me go. I'll never come into the pool hall again."

Juan said, "I know."

Juan shot Hector twice in the head. Juan and Louie picked him up and threw him off the roof. Juan took the gun apart, wiped it down, and threw different pieces down different pipes. Louie was already walking to the elevator.

The sky was a perfect purplish black.

\#

The sound of the front door closing awoke Fat Boy. He sat up in bed and stretched and yawned. He wanted to get something to eat. He was very happy. Susana had spent two nights with him and he felt that maybe they had a connection. He always brought females back to his apartment because it made him feel like he was in a relationship. Plus, he wanted to impress them with his toys. This was a violation of the street code. You never bring a stranger back to your crib. Especially not a ho.

He looked around and didn't see Susana. Fat Boy called out, "*Miel! Miel?*"

He took a shower and got dressed and went to put on his Rolex and Cuban link chain but they were gone. He noticed that his wallet wasn't on the counter. He walked closer and saw that it was on the floor. He picked it up. It was empty. It had had around two thousand dollars in it.

He sat down on the bed. He thought she had really liked him— she'd even introduced him to her grandmother and her kids when she stopped by her apartment to pick up some clothes. But this bitch had stolen from him. He was furious. He called her phone. No answer. He left a message: "Listen *puta*, if you don't return my money and jewelry I'm going to slit your fucking throat." But she knew where she lived. He texted Hector: *Meet me at McDonald's on Linden.* His life might be in danger, but he had to take care of this business.

\#

Three in the morning and Little Italy was still buzzing with tourists and natives craving great food, so it took a few minutes for Shawn and Derek to find parking.

Derek said, "We should start using Uber."

They were early. So they sat for a moment in the car, getting a feel for the night.

Derek asked, "What up, you think?"

Shawn said, "This has to be about the indictments. They might talk tough so they don't look weak as long as they don't raise the price on the bricks."

Derek said, "I was thinking the same thing. We know it's their last stand."

Shawn said, "You do the talking. Just don't let them know we think they are weak."

Derek said, "No doubt."

They got out of the car and walked toward the restaurant. Upon entering, they were immediately escorted to the lower level. To their surprise, Capo Francisco was seated at the table in back with his Lieutenant Tony. Tony was who they usually dealt with, so Francisco being there was a big deal. Derek knew right away that if the boss from the Queens Family was here this was a show of force. Francisco and Tony had already started to eat. It was four people for a Thanksgiving feast. There was a security guy near the steps to stop any intruders or nosy workers. They shook hands and hugged, greeting each other as family, although Derek knew these Italians were racist, evident in the "Black Tax" on the product. But the Italians also appreciated the money the Syndicate brought in, so face to face they were very respectful. The tax was ordered all the way from Palermo, Sicily. The tax ensured that the New York family and Sicily all ate very well. Francisco gave Derek his respect as a boss.

Francisco said, "Please sit and eat. I couldn't wait. It has been a long day."

Shawn knew that he had been at court all day. His girl at the Queens Court House had let him know all of this.

Derek said, "Thank you. No problem I understand. It's good to see you."

Shawn said, "Yes it has been a while since we've seen you." He gave his polite comment so that his presence would be acknowledged.

Tony said, "Yes, I was getting tired of Shawn's face."

They all laughed.

The Mafia was run like a paramilitary organization. So they had a rank structure and it was respected. Just as Derek had taken the advice of the defense attorney, he also took the rank structure from the Queens Family and used it for the Syndicate. Derek studied everything and he took the good things from all situations.

Derek said, "How are your wife and kids?"

Francisco said, "They get on my fucking nerves but I love them."

Everybody chuckled. Francisco looked at Derek. "You have to start a family soon. You can't spend all your money on cars and diamonds."

Derek nodded. "You're right." He was glad he had been able to hide his kid's existence from his rivals.

"And for you and your newborn." Tony handed Shawn a Catholic cross on a chain as a gift. Shawn covered his scowl. This meant that the Family was watching him.

Francisco said, "Let's talk business."

Derek nodded.

Francisco said, "We know you might have heard on the streets that we were having some problems. I just wanted to let you know that as far as our business together, we are fine."

Derek said, "We're not guided by the streets, but it's good to hear that directly from you."

Tony said, "We want to maintain our good relationship because we know a lot of times when families have legal troubles, people think it's the optimum time to make a move. We just want to keep things peaceful and proceed as we are."

Derek and Shawn knew they had just been officially warned and threatened.

Shawn spoke carefully so that there was no mistaking his meaning. "Loyalty is important to us. We'll stay with you as long as you can deliver our product."

Francisco nodded after a pause then gestured to the food. "When business is done, it is time to eat." Shawn got up and made a plate. Derek followed.

Chapter 24

ACCESS

Captain Gallagher had a list of the supervisors and investigators but he didn't have access to the case files and undercovers' identifications. He knew this was for their safety because they have been killed in the past from dirty cops giving out their information, but he was supposed to do his job, he wanted that information. He called Detective Murchado and told her to meet him at his office in 1 Police Plaza. He told her he wanted to go over the active investigations in the unit. She replied, no problem, she'll be right over. But it *was* a problem.

She got Rob on the phone next. "We've got pressure from Gallagher. I'll need to give him what he's asking for."

"We need time," he snapped. "Stall him."

"He's our new captain."

"You're not paid to second-guess my orders," he snapped.

Stella was speechless—she'd never heard him talk like this before. "Yes sir," she said and hung up.

By the time she arrived for her meeting with Captain Gallagher, Stella had come up with a plan. She arrived early but of course Gallagher made her wait. She did, fuming. At last, the captain's secretary called her into the office. The captain was standing when she entered.

Captain Gallagher said, "Good morning, Detective. Take a seat. How is this assignment going for you?"

Stella said, "The assignment is going great. I don't have it as bad as the undercovers so I can't complain."

"Good to hear. I wanted to be updated—fully—on the investigations and any pertinent information. As the intelligence detective I know you know all. So I wanted to talk to you." He clasped his hands on his desk and looked her in the eye in a way to show her how much he valued her input. "I'll give it to you straight. It's an election year and the mayor is looking for arrests to help his approval numbers."

Stella gritted her teeth but made a show of looking eager to help. "Of course. There is a major case on the Queens Italian Family. There should be arrests coming imminently."

The captain leaned back in his chair. "Tell me about the case."

"They arrested the accountant and he gave up all the top bosses. He also had control of their money so that was frozen."

"Why was he so cooperative?"

Stella knew he was hooked. "He was caught selling ecstasy to minors at John Adams High School. So he was facing twenty-plus years. He doesn't have the physical or mental capacity to do major time. He would rather hide out with the protection of the U.S. Marshals."

The captain said, "Win for us. I'll need a case file that I could brief the mayor with. As soon as possible."

Stella said, "No problem." She would take her time getting the brief together for him.

The captain stood up and extended his hand. "Thank you detective. It has been a pleasure to meet someone as helpful as you."

Stella said, "Oh, thank *you* sir."

The smile on her face was still there by the time she got to the Bat Cave. She saw the new recruit, Alison, filing paperwork with Detective Banner as she walked into Rob's office.

Stella said, "Can I close the door?"

Rob said, "Of course." Before Stella could start talking he apologized. "You didn't need that," he told her. "It's just . . . we're so close to nailing the Syndicate. And Gallagher could screw up everything. I shouldn't have taken it out on you."

Stella held up her hand. "It's okay. Apology accepted."

Rob said, "I told him to talk to the Chief but I haven't heard back yet and—"

Stella interrupted and couldn't help feeling smug. "I bought us some time. Told him about the Queen's Family."

Rob said, "Genius."

Stella laughed. "FBI Joint Organized Crime Task Force. The Unit has nothing to do with that case."

"Gallagher gets some information to chew on for a while and the unit can keep going without interference. We've got till Memorial Day."

"Memorial Day?"

Rob nodded. "Dwayne met one of the Syndicate's top men—made some IDs for a couple of people in the guy's family. Guess they're tight now. He's got an invite to their annual BBQ."

"Clone some phones so we can start making cases. Big ones."

"That's the plan," Rob said. His phone buzzed and he held up a finger as he answered it. "Chief, glad you called. I think we have a work around for Gallagher——"

Stella gave him a thumbs-up as she left his office, but she could overhear him say tightly, "I'll be there."

Rob and the chief met at a coffee shop far from the office. Rob shook his head. "So you're saying the Unit's days are numbered. This fucking guy meets with you, and doesn't even listen?"

Chief said, "They picked this guy because he's married to the mayor's daughter. And the mayor wants to have a press conference with some arrests. So what the mayor wants, the mayor gets."

Rob said, "Jesus."

Chief said, "I told Gallagher that's not what we do here. We build major cases without any restraints or timeline. He told me with our budget that was unacceptable."

Rob said, "This was what we were promised wouldn't happen."

Chief said, "He then started talking about justifying the—"

Rob interrupted angrily. "Justifying the power. I got the same thing from him. So what do we do now?"

The Chief said, "Just keep working for now. He already has control of the budget."

Rob said, "Stella distracted him for a while. He wanted information on arrests so she told him about the organized crime case."

The Chief shook his head. "I don't think he was someone you should lie too."

Rob said, "You might be right but we need time."

Chief warned, "Just remember that same awareness you use in the streets you have to use within the department. He could take the Unit down. He could take you down."

Rob muttered. "I don't care about me."

#

Louie parked in front of Maribel's apartment with Juan. Juan had ordered takeout from the corner Spanish restaurant, and he knocked on the door, with Louie out of sight. Maribel asked who it was. Juan put up the food blocking the peep hole, "Your delivery from El Caridad."

Maribel said, "I didn't order any food, but she opened the door. Juan and Louie pushed their way in. Maribel tried to scream but Juan covered her mouth. He then took out his Heckler & Koch VP9SK, nine millimeters, and pointed it at her. Louie showed her his Heckler & Koch SP5K automatic gun.

Juan said, "*Callate o te matare!*"

She understood. She saw in his eyes that he would shoot her.

Louie looked around the apartment to see if there was any sign of Fat Boy. No clothes, no Jordan's. And no snacks.

Juan shoved her, "What's the deal with you and Fat Boy?"

Maribel said, "There ain't no deal. There's nothing you *putas* can do to me that would make me see him again."

Juan said, "When was the last time you saw him?"

Maribel said, "It has been a while."

Juan said, "Do you know if he had any side business going on outside of the Cartel?"

Maribel said, "Not that I know of. I do know he was loyal to y'all. Always yelling he was in the best crew. He was a proud Boriqua."

Juan said, "Has he brought any expensive things lately. Car, house, or jewelry?"

Maribel said, "No! Listen I don't fuck with your guy no more because he's a stalker."

Juan handed his gun to Louie and proceeded to put on his black gloves. Maribel said scornfully, *"Esa mierda no me asusta."*

Louie knew she wasn't lying. Not a scared bone in her body. He did just notice how fine she was standing there in sweatpants, T-shirt, and a handkerchief wrapped around her head. he spoke courteously to her, as if she was his niece. "All we want is information. We're not looking for Fat Boy."

Maribel answered, "That's all I know."

Louie said, "Let's get out of here, *primo.*"

Juan was looking forward to punching her smartass in the mouth but he took off the gloves and winked at her. She spits on the floor and he hefted the takeout food and threw it at her.

Juan said, "Enjoy."

Maribel said, "I will, asshole." She opened the food because it did smell great.

#

Fat Boy was eating breakfast when Carlos walked into McDonalds. All-day breakfast was one of the greatest things created because every hustler started his day at noon. Carlos asked Fat Boy, "No word on Hector?"

Fat Boy shrugged. "He's done this before. Gets a girl and no word from him for a while. He'll be okay. Anyway, this fucking stripper robbed me last night while I was asleep."

Carlos said, "Damn, kid. Crazy."

Fat Boy said, "I know where she lives so I want to go to her crib."

"Are we shooting or cutting?" Carlos asked.

Fat Boy said, "I just want my shit back. I got too much other stuff going on right now."

"Easy."

"Cool."

Fat Boy tried Hector one more time, then they headed to Susana's.

There Fat Boy and Carlos sat on the steps waiting for somebody to open the front door. The front of the project building was busy with the tenants. There was loud music coming from the playground where a bunch of teenagers had taken it over from the kids. As the old Jamaican lady approached, they stood. She didn't ask any questions and let them in. If they were going to rob her it would have happened already. But she would not ride the elevator with them and stayed by the mailbox until they got on the elevator.

They went straight up to Susana's apartment. They listened outside the door. They heard the TV blaring a telenovela. Fat Boy knew that this meant that the slightly deaf grandmother was home watching her shows. He knocked loudly, like the police would. Her heard her shuffle to the door in her slippers.

"Who was it," she said.

"Tito." She called him Tito because he reminded her of Tito Puente.

"*Aquanta mi amor*," she said and opened the door.

Fat Boy said, "Is Susana here?"

Grandma said, "*No carino.*"

Fat boy pushes past her to check for himself. "I think I left my chain in her bedroom. I want to see if it's there."

He rushed straight to the bedroom and searched it thoroughly. Nothing. The kid's clothes were gone too. He figured if the kids were gone she was smart enough to take everything. Carlos was in the living room with grandma.

Grandma said, "*De donde es tu familia?*"

Carlos said, "*Aquadilla.*"

She smiled and patted his hand.

Fat Boy walked back into the living room.

Grandma said, "Did you find what you were looking for?"

Fat Boy said, "No. Do you know where Susie went?"

Grandma looked him up and down and as if realizing that Susana might be in trouble, she began to quaver, "She left this morning with the kids. Maybe she went to see her sister."

Fat Boy said soothingly, "Okay *abuela*. Maybe you can call Susana's sister. Go ahead, just find out where she is. We won't hurt her. We won't hurt anyone."

One phone call from Grandma, and they left her in the apartment, listening to the telenovela.

#

"You can find me in the club, bottle of bub. Look mommy I got the X if you into taking drugs. I'm into having sex, I ain't into making love. So come give me a hug if into getting rubbed." Fifty Cent was blaring through the speakers and everyone was enjoying it.

The crowd was a nice size tonight. Now it was time to make some money. All eyes were on Susana but she was looking for any hint of money. She hadn't rubbed against a big dick all night. Easy work. She couldn't sense it from the clothes or swag because there was none. So she stood by the bar and it took only a minute to see an old man take out a wad of money to pay for his drink. She closed right in on him. She walked over to the bar and bumped him. He turned and she apologized. She then placed her hand on his back as she ordered a glass of rosé. He looked her over and paid for the drink.

Susana said, "Let's find some privacy."

Carlos entered the club and sat at the bar. He ordered Hennessy and Coke. He sipped and waited for a gorgeous skinny Spanish girl to appear. It took a while but when Susana walked past he knew it was her. The description was perfect. She was gorgeous, so gorgeous he forgot about the other guy he was supposed to look for and warn Fat Boy about. He sent Fat Boy a text that she was here. He finished his drink. Fat Boy texted back saying to stand near her.

Carlos first went to the bathroom and got his nine-millimeter that was stashed behind the last toilet in the men's bathroom. Twenty minutes earlier he had paid the janitor a hundred dollars to sneak it in and place it there. He tucked into his waistband and then covered it with his shirt. He then went to find Susanna.

Fat Boy approached the bouncer.

Fat Boy said, "What up, big man." Always gotta hit the big man with a compliment.

Bouncer said, "What up. Have your ID out. Everybody gets searched."

Fat Boy said, "Listen, this shit is embarrassing but my mom's sent me here to bring my sister back home. I don't want no problems from you. I just want to get her out of here but I know she is going to fight me because she is addicted to this life."

The Bouncer answered, "I can't be having no problems in here from nobody."

Fat Boy protested, "That's why I'm talking to you first, big man. I wanted to give you that respect."

Bouncer said, "Who's your sister?"

"Susanna Rivera."

The bouncer put some deep thought into trying to figure out who that was but then he realized that he only knew the girls by their stage names. "Describe her."

"*Flaca* with long hair."

Bouncer knew right away who he was talking about. But he said, "I can't make a grown woman leave with you."

Fat Boy handed the bouncer a hundred-dollar bill. The bouncer took a quick glance at the money and let him in, trailing behind Fat Boy just in case.

As Fat Boy walked up to him, Carlos said, "Oh shit. Your brother's here." He said it loud enough for the bouncer to hear. It was the confirmation the bouncer needed. He believed.

Susanna stared at the guy she'd never met before talking to her about her brother. At that moment she saw Fat Boy.

Fat Boy grabbed her and said, "I'm taking you home to Mommy."

Susanna screamed, "He ain't my fucking brother!"

Carlos kept saying, "Don't fight with your brother. *Tranquillo.*"

Fat Boy covered her mouth as best he could. A crowd formed but the bouncer was working for Fat Boy. He provided a personal escort right out of the strip club. Fat Boy carried her right out in her stripper uniform which was matching black bra, panties, and black stilettos. He threw her in the backseat and jumped in with her. Carlos was at the wheel and as soon as the door closed they were gone. She was screaming at the top of her lungs to let her out of the car.

Fat Boy punched her in her solar plexus and told her, "Shut the fuck up."

She was gasping for air and decided the best thing to do was listen.

Fat Boy said, "Where the fuck was my jewelry?'

Susanna groaned, "At my sister's house."

"Who the fuck is home right now?'

Susanna said, "Just the kids and my sister. The jewelry is in the bathroom closet in a laundry bag. Tell me you won't hurt them."

Fat Boy ignored her. "No men. Boyfriends?'

Susanna wept, "No. Please don't hurt them."

Fat Boy said, "Direct us."

They drove to her sister's house. They pulled into the complex and Carlos parked. Fat Boy said, "Me and you are going to go up and get my shit."

Susanna said weakly, "I'll go up and bring it down."

Fat Boy took out the nine-millimeter and pistol-whipped her. "Are you fucking crazy? I'm going with you." He dragged her out of the car and followed her upstairs to get his jewelry. They entered the apartment and he was out in less than two minutes. He brought her back downstairs with him. She knew this wasn't good, but she was glad he didn't hurt her sister or the kids. So she didn't scream. She just awaited her fate. It didn't take long. He took her over behind the trash binder. With one motion he cut her face from temple to chin. She wasn't going to make any more money with that pretty face. She fell to the ground in a fetal position and cried in silence. Fat Boy was gone.

Chapter 25

POSITION OF POWER

It was an array of puffy white clouds mixed with the Maya blue sky. It was a beautiful spring day. St. Albans park was full; everyone was enjoying the day. Derek and Shawn were meeting here to discuss business over a game of chess.

Derek was early so he could do his usual countersurveillance. He watched from the southeast corner. but today he noticed nothing out of the ordinary. He saw Shawn pull up so he walked across the street to greet him. Shawn saw him approach.

Shawn said, "What up. How long you been here?"

Derek said, "Just got here."

Shawn said, "Yo ass probably been here for at least an hour."

They both laughed. They walk over to the painted chess tables and sat down at their usual spot.

Setting up the chess pieces, Derek said, "So what do you think about the meeting."

Shawn said, "It was pretty light on their part. You still sticking to your plan?"

Derek nodded. "I feel good about the way things are unfolding." He made his moves on the chessboard without much thought, while Shawn took his time. Similar to the way they both moved in the streets.

Derek continued, "Think about it, the feds are taking away the Italians. The Jamaicans and Latins will destroy each other. It's perfect timing. Now it's just falling into my lap. I can't say no. King of New York. Can't say no. Wish Andre was here to enjoy this."

Shawn said, "Talked to Mike. He wants us to meet this guy Dwayne. Thinks he'd make a good soldier."

Derek moved his rook. "Check. Good time for it. We need another person especially now."

Shawn saw the rook close to his king but in the path of the queen. He pondered the board, trying to figure out if Derek was being reckless or had some big plan in mind. "I don't know. Everything's running smooth. I don't see the need to fuck with things."

Derek said, "I think the risk is worth it." He held Shawn's gaze. Shawn looked down first.

Shawn said, "Just thinking worst-case scenario. I'm the eyes in back of you. You shoot, I shoot." He took the rook with his queen.

Derek said, "My man." He moved his knight.

Shawn said, "Damn."

Derek said, "Yup. Checkmate." He smiled, leaned back, and crossed his arms.

They packed up the game, said their good-byes, and parted ways. Shawn drove aggressively up Merrick because he had a lot on his mind. He didn't agree with Derek but he had his back. Then he saw Smooth Steve in his wheelchair chilling. He used to be the biggest thing in Queens until some dirty NYPD cops shot him up. Shawn pulled over and got out the truck. Steve was still fresh even in the wheelchair. He had on new kicks and a fresh haircut.

Shawn said, "What up, OG?"

Steve said, "What, Shawn. I see you riding nice. Business must be good."

Shawn answered, "Business was always good. The only problems were the cops and the stickup kids."

Steve nodded. "You know… I know."

Shawn sat beside him on a bench. "Man, you look good."

Steve shrugged. "I do what I can do to look okay in this fucking wheelchair."

"I hear you brother. You gotta keep your head up."

Steve continued, "My whole world is trash. But I did this so I can't complain."

"Why you say that?"

Steve said, "Dirty grimy cops shot me for nothing but I killed a lot of fucking niggas that nobody knew or cared about. So it was written."

Shawn shook his head. "Damn. I don't agree but I see what you saying. I feel like they gave us drugs and now have the nerve to investigate and arrest us. The game is crazy."

Steve said, "You went deep on me. That Reagan Iran Contra shit."

"Yup. No disrespect to you. Just my thoughts."

Steve quickly replied, "No disrespect taken. Don't feel sorry for me. Learn from me. You know my story so analyze it and get the fuck out da game. Cause you can't win. The game will always win and leave you dead or in jail. Which is a slow death."

Shawn said, "You right."

"I had jealousy from within my crew, streets, and the cops. I had no chance. Even my girl Melody loved the life more than she loved me. The moment I was in this chair she left to be with another hustler. She dropped our kids off at her mother's house and kept it moving."

Shawn said, "My girl wants me to start a business and get out."

"Listen to her. There's no wins here. None."

Shawn said slowly, "I'm glad I ran into you."

Steve pointed to his head. "Listen."

They hugged and Shawn was out.

\#

At 6:00 AM in the squad room, there was already a new case on Detective Mullen's desk to investigate. He sipped his coffee. He would get to it in a minute. He had to send a text to make sure his boys were up for school. Single parenting was hard as a police officer but he made it work.

Cases in the squad were given out on the wheel. All detective names were put in seniority order and the cases were given out. Next case, next name was the way it's supposed to work. But this morning the slimy guys came in early to steal the domestic violence cases. Detective Palermo and O'Shea always did this. They liked domestic violence cases because it was a known perpetrator. Not much to investigate. Most importantly after they locked up the husband or boyfriend they fucked the woman. To the women they were saviors. And all they had to do was just call the phone number provided by the victim and explain the circumstances and make an appointment for the arrest.

Mullen opened the homicide case and looked over the pictures. Two black males killed. No urgency or First Forty-eight here. There was a note from the night-watch detective, his opinion being that this was a carjacking gone wrong. Subjects stopped at a traffic light and then were fired upon by one or two perpetrators. The resistance from the victims made the perpetrators flee. As he looked through the case, though, he wondered why anyone would carjack a 1998 Honda Accord. Maybe if they were drug addicts or fleeing felons. Maybe a gang shooting. He ran the names of the victims and they both came back with numerous arrest including grand larceny.

Perp.#1 had been arrested four times for armed robbery and two times for drug sales: Timothy Stanley. Perp.#2 arrested two times for the sale of narcotics and one arrest robbery: Gary Follows. Maybe this *was* a carjacking gone wrong—but they were the carjackers. They could have tried to carjack the wrong person. He would need to go to the scene to put it together. He had to wait for his partner, Detective Wagner, to come in. Wagner arrived, still smelling like his alcohol. Mullen didn't say anything, and just poured him a cup of coffee and got him to the car.

Detectives Mullen and Wagner pulled up to the busy intersection and parked right where the victim's car had been. Mullen snapped on the take-down and hazard lights. Wagner was sound asleep. Mullen didn't bother to wake him. He was getting drunk from the fumes coming out of Wagner's pores. He got out and walked over to the southeast corner with the case file in hand. He opened it up and examined the photos. He visualized the scene. He then walked over to the northwest corner and looked for bullet holes in the store windows or wall. He found two and marked them. He then went back over to the car and figured where Victim #1 was standing. He walked in a straight line to the nearest structure, which was a billboard. It was an advertisement for Nike. As he looked around he found a bullet hole in the Chinese restaurant window. He marked it. He then went into the restaurant and identified himself and asked to see the video camera footage. They were happy to show it. It wasn't clear but you can see the Range Rover slowly pull up to the light followed by the Honda. Then after a few seconds he saw the bullets. No faces or license plate numbers. The owner let him take the tape. This was the Hood, no subpoena or hesitation. Mullen checked around for any other tapes but there were none. He called the Crime Scene Unit (CSU) and gave them the Omni Form number and told them about the bullet holes. He then dropped off the tape to Technical Assistance Response Unit (T.A.R.U.). He hoped that they could enhance it and come up with a plate number or better.

#

Mike waited for Dwayne in front of Fantasy so they could walk in together. Dwayne was on time. They embraced. Mike told him to say as little as possible and just be chill. Dwayne already knew that saying nothing was saying a lot. He played it cool, didn't look around or say much. All he had to do was shadow Mike. His posture said confident and quiet—just what was needed in this business. Mike introduced him to some low-level soldiers but kept him away from the Syndicate bosses. Dwayne shook hands and didn't say much. Derek, Shawn, and Raekwon were watching him from their table. He knew they were there but his eyes stayed disciplined. Mike was in a good mood—if this worked out he would be the one to bring down the biggest drug crew in New York City. Derek and Shawn just watched; they thought Dwayne looked and acted like a street kid. Mike decided to sit at the bar and see if his protégé could drink and hold a conversation. Dwayne ordered Hennessy for both and paid. Off to a good start. He drank it like a grown man, not fast but steady. Raekwon wanted to test him so he sent over a stripper. She approached Dwayne and introduced herself as Peaches. "Can I sit?" she asked.

Dwayne shrugged. "Why not."

She sat and started feeling him up. No wire but a lot of muscles. She liked what *she saw and felt. "You want a private dance?"

Dwayne nodded.

She grabbed his hand and escorted him to a private booth. Once inside she started kissing his neck. He followed her lead and started feeling her up. She brushed against his penis and felt that it was rock hard. He was trying to finger pop her but she knew how to make it difficult to do. This was the point when a stripper knew she was about to make some money.

Peaches said, "You want a blow job?"

"Yes."

Peaches said, "Hundred."

Dwayne said, "I don't pay."

Peaches pulled out his penis and started stroking it. "Let me take care of this. A hundred ain't nothing for a baller like you."

Dwayne repeated, "I don't pay."

Peaches pleaded, "Don't let this go to waste. I guarantee you I will make you explode."

"I don't doubt your skills," Dwayne said. "I just don't pay for sex."

Peaches sensed the seriousness in his voice and gave up. "That's all right," she cooed. "With that face you don't have to pay for sex."

They both left the booth, and Dwayne headed back to the bar where Mike sat.

Peaches went straight to Raekwon.

Raekwon asked, "What happened?"

Peaches answered, "He didn't flinch when I touched him. I pulled his dick out and everything. I told him a hundred to fuck. He said he don't pay for pussy. He was grabbing all over me I had to hold his hands. He tried to stick his middle finger in my pussy. He ain't no cop. Truthfully that nigga was so fine I would have fucked him for free but I was doing Syndicate business."

Raekwon gave her a hundred-dollar bill and head back to Derek and Shawn. Jocelyn walked in the club and caught up to Raekwon. "Why we gotta be here?"

Raekwon said, "Boss was thinking about adding to the crew."

"Who."

Raekwon glanced in the direction of Dwayne. Jocelyn studied him. "I think I know him. I definitely know his face."

Raekwon asked, "Cop?"

"No," Jocelyn answered. "I talked to him in a club. He asked for my number."

Raekwon nodded, satisfied. He reported to Derek and Shawn and they had seen enough. Shawn gave Mike a head nod. Mike knew what that meant.

Mike said, "Let's get out of here and get something to eat."

Dwayne said, "Cool."

They left the club more quickly than they came in. Mike felt that it went good. He knew not to ask Derek and Shawn; they would let him know.

Chapter 26

TIMES UP

Fat Boy cleared his throat. He loved the ladies, but he wasn't a punk. If they killed him, so be it.

Louie and Carlos had called him to the pool hall. The back room of the pool hall was set up like a VIP area. It had a special pool table with a dark blue felt. The walls were also blue and the furniture was dark brown. It had all the toys as well; four flat T.V.s, wet bar, DJ booth, and a humidor. It was Louie's de facto office. Louie sat down at the desk staring hard at Fat Boy standing in front of him. "You got one shot to be honest with me, *popi*, if not you're a dead man. *Tu muerte*. The shooting. Why?"

Fat Boy explained that Nigel started shooting out of nowhere. No words, nothing.

Louie asked, "When was the last time you seen this dude?"

Fat Boy said he couldn't remember.

Casually, as if he was talking about the weather, Louie said, "I'm asking again."

Fat Boy said maybe he saw him on the street sometimes.

"Did you have any side business with this fucking guy?"

He looked into Louie's eyes and began to sweat. "No." He wished he was back with Maribel.

Louie kept his hard stare on Fat Boy. "Was this over some pussy?"

Fat Boy said, "I'm telling you the truth, I haven't been making any side money, and this ain't got nothing to do with no pussy. *Honestamente.*"

After a moment, Louie threw a wad of money at him.

Fat Boy picked it up. "What's this?"

Juan said, "Time missed. And how you handled getting shot."

Fat Boy gauged it was maybe twenty thousand dollars. Fat Boy said, "Cool."

"Pack a bag. I'm sending you out of town for a while," said Louie. "Get out of here until I call you. And when I call you, you *will* be ready."

Fat Boy knew he didn't have a choice.

As soon as Fat Boy had left, Louie sent one of the waitresses to get Sosa. Sosa entered the room with his signature glass of dark Bacardi in hand.

"Fat Boy's dumb," Louie said. "But he's loyal. This has got to be the Jamaicans."

"This changes the meeting with Trevor."

"We're past communicating."

Sosa nodded. "*Que estamos intentando hacer?* How do we do this?"

Louie said, "We sell the rest of our product, and we hit the Jamaicans hard. We take all their real estate. We'll be number two in New York. That ain't bad. Maybe someday we'll be number one."

Sosa said, "Really?"

Louie said, "I think it would be easy. And then we would be as strong as the Syndicate."

Sosa asked, "And what about the Syndicate?"

Louie said, "We were hit first so the rules of the game are with us. This takes no money from the Syndicate so they won't care."

#

Mullen walked into the squad room with his usual cup of coffee. He looked over in the corner and Wagner was asleep at his desk. Same clothes on from yesterday. Drunk on duty again. he said nothing, the Blue Wall protecting them both.

He noticed the envelope from T.A.R.U. sitting in his mailbox. It put a smile on his face. Time to investigate. He opened it and there was an enhanced photo of both vehicles with license plate numbers. He ran both plates. The plate from the Honda came from a Campbell Young. The plate for the Range Rover came from Loretta Mason, who lived in the Poconos. It had been reported stolen the day of the shooting. Detective Mullin ran her name in the NYSID–NYPD computer system and got a phone number. He then ran the phone number in the BADS NYPD computer system, which told him everybody who had called this number after they were arrested. Only one person, numerous times. Derek Mason. He knew Derek was one of the biggest drug dealers in the city. So he figured the perpetrators in the Honda tried to carjack Derek and he killed them. The rap sheets, the car, and the sloppiness said so. Excited, he told his sergeant that he had tracked down the perp. The sergeant was happy that this case could end with an A-1 closing, an arrest. They high-fived each other.

An alert came to Sergeant Ling's phone that an extensive computer check was done on Derek Mason. He called Rob and let him know.

Rob said, "Find out who and what's it about. Then stop it."

Sergeant Ling replied, "I'm all over it." He pulled up Detective Mullen's case file and read the work done on the investigation. He then called over to the squad. Sergeant Iles picked up the phone.

Sergeant Ling introduced himself and gave the case number. Sergeant Iles pulled it up on the computer, and Sergeant Ling told him firmly to stop the investigation immediately. "Stand down. I will provide through department email my name and the supervisors of this unit for your clarification. Thanks in advance for your cooperation."

Sergeant Iles called Detective Mullen into his office to notify him of the bad news. "That carjack case you've been working on?"

Mullen nodded, "I'm going to make a collar just give me a few days. I got this."

The sergeant shook his head. "Actually, Mason is a big fish and we were told to leave him alone."

Mullen gaped. "Get the fuck out of here."

Iles said, "There's a big investigation going on with him and the feds."

Mullen groaned. "Shit. That's crazy. Can I continue once they arrest him?'

Iles shrugged. "I didn't ask. They just said for now stop all investigations regarding Mason."

Mullen slammed the phone down. He had looked forward to cooking Mason. But he would fall back.

#

The line for IHOP was long, so Mike sat in his car waiting for Shawn. When he saw him pull up, he got out and waited for him to park. They gave each other dap and walked into the restaurant.

Mike said, "It has to be at least a forty-five-minute wait. You wanna go to the diner?"

Shawn walked in right past everybody on the line and just sat at a table. Mike followed. A waitress came over and said, "Did someone seat you?"

Shawn said, "Can you please clean the table."

The waitress did just that and apologized. "I'll be right back to take your order."

Confidence. Mike just smiled and shook his head.

Shawn said, "Listen, invite your man to the BBQ."

Mike said, "Cool. So he's in?"

Shawn nodded. The waitress placed two glasses of water and two menus on the table. Shawn winked at her and she smiled. Shawn explained to Mike that it's a crazy time on the street. "So be on your square."

"Always," Mike answered.

Shawn nodded. "That's what I like to hear."

After breakfast, Mike drove straight from IHOP to Dwayne's crib. He wanted to sneak up on him. He knocked on his door. Dwayne answered in his bathrobe and let Mike in. Dwayne was always in work mode. The apartment and car all part of the cover. The chick from downstairs in 3B was taking a shower. They talked in the living room.

Dwayne asked, "What's good?"

Mike said, "Just wanted to let you know that they want you come to the big Memorial Day Basketball Tournament and BBQ." He gave him the time and place.

Dwayne said, "I'm there. Appreciate this, bro."

Mike said, "I see you're busy so I'm out. Hit me on the jack later."

Dwayne said, "One."

Mike said, "One."

#

The building was sixty floors. It looked like glass but it wasn't. It looked like money and it was. Jocelyn was the manager of the cleaning staff. This position was given to her by one of her many rich admirers. It was a no-show job. She could stay home and collect a paycheck every two weeks. Fifteen hundred dollars to be exact. But she had keys to every room in the place and the perks were even better. Derek and she decided that this would be a great place to cook and bag their drugs. There was no trace to anybody from the Syndicate to this building. And she had access to a hardworking Hispanic staff that loved making extra money. So they could show up on their days off and cook cocaine and no one in the hotel knew. The other managers left Jocelyn alone because she ran her department well. Raekwon would pick up the finished product and take it to the block. Today he was here waiting downstairs by the trash contractor. He usually smoked weed there and the garbage covered the smell. Today Jocelyn joined him. He passed her the blunt and told her about Frog.

Raekwon had been on the block driving through the neighborhood making sure everything was running smoothly. He was in his black Tahoe; the music was blaring. Today was Fabulous on the stereo, "Summertime Shootout." Raekwon loved driving through the hood, and everybody knowing he was running things. He saw a dice game, and decided to pull over and make some money. He jumped out of the truck with his Glock 45 showing in the small of his back, three chains on his neck, and Nikes on his feet. Nike sweat suit with the left pocket bulging with cash. Street uniform.

Raekwon said, "Don't worry, this wasn't a stickup. But I did come to take your money."

The cipher opened for him. Respect. He loved this shit. He crossed his arm and just wanted to watch and get a feel of the game. One of his soldiers was there, "Frog." They call him Frog because he had green eyes and the police could never catch him, he leaped fences faster than anyone. Frog was nervous because he should have been in the building watching the two thousand vials of crack that were stored under the first-floor staircase. It was in a makeshift port in the wall. Raekwon saw, but he would address that later. For now, it was all about that seven or eleven.

"How'd you do?" asked Jocelyn.

"Quick thousand for an hour's worth of dice rolling," he said. He didn't tell her he then headed to Suptin Ave. and Foch Blvd. to see why Frog wasn't taking care of business. This sloppiness was how you get robbed or arrested. He pulled around the corner so he could enter the building from the back. The lookout saw him, and let Frog know that the boss was coming. Frog was expecting it. He had fucked up. Raekwon entered the building and motioned for Frog to follow him back out to the rear. Frog followed.

Frog asked, "What up, boss man?"

Raekwon said, "Cut the bullshit, man. You know you fuck up."

"My bad, black."

Raekwon said, "There was always a consequence for your actions."

Shawn learned that from Derek. Frog was nervous, because he didn't know what to expect.

Raekwon said, "How much dough you got on you?"

"The stash has five thousand in it."

Raekwon gave him a hard stare. "Not the stash. Yo pocket."

Frog shook his head.

"Count it, motherfucker," commanded Raekwon.

Frog pulled out his money and counted two thousand dollars. Raekwon took his money from him and put it in his own pocket. "You on my time. So today I'm docking your pay. You working for free. Don't get comfortable out here. That's how we get hit from the goons or the blue ninjas. Stay right."

"Cool," said Frog.

Raekwon casually said, "Next time I'mma break your jaw, and move you back to lookout on the corner."

Frog nodded hastily. "Won't happen again, brother."

Raekwon walked away, headed straight back to his car. He got in and drove over to the soup kitchen. He gave the two thousand dollars to the guy who ran it. He didn't say a word, he just handed him the money and was gone. Raekwon was righteous. He believed in food, clothing, shelter.

Jocelyn nudged him. "What are you thinking about?" she asked.

Raekwon just said, "What do you think about the added security for the pickup?" Derek had put two guys in a jeep on the north side, one guy selling newspapers in front, and a girl riding her bike with a messenger bag around the blocks.

Jocelyn shrugged, "Security is always good."

Raekwon took a hit. "I just don't like change. I wonder if something else was going on we don't know about."

Jocelyn said, "Well, I trust Derek so . . ." She plucked the blunt from his fingers.

Raekwon said, "I trust him too. but I always go with my gut feeling. It just seems that there is more."

"You might be right but I'm going to follow D."

Annoyed, Raekwon said, "Stop sucking his dick. I hear you. I'm going to do the same. We got this new guy coming in too. It's a lot going on."

Jocelyn gave the blunt back to Raekwon. "It'll be ready in thirty."

Raekwon nodded.

#

Dwayne entered the deli wearing all black clothes with a black Mets cap. Rob was at the grill in conversation with an employee. He glanced at Dwayne and saw that his cap was tilted to the right. Rob rang Dwayne's a six-pack of Heineken.

Rob says, "Afternoon sir. How's it going?"

Dwayne says, "I'm great thank you. Can I have a box of Magnums, please."

Rob says, "Good to hear. No problem. That will be $17.56."

Dwayne was in and out of the deli in less than two minutes. Rob couldn't control his excitement. That brief conversation and the purchase of the condoms let Rob know that Dwayne had penetrated the

Syndicate. He called Stella and Alex and told them to meet him at the Bat Cave. He drove so fast he was the first one there. Alex arrived next. Hungover as usual. They hugged.

Alex said, "I need something to drink." He poured himself a glass of Jack Daniels.

Stella walked in with a smile on her face. She knew she was about to hear good news.

Rob said, "Dwayne was in with the Syndicate. The final piece. Now we can start putting the pieces together."

Stella crowed, "I knew it was good news. This will keep the fucking captain off our backs."

Rob nodded "I was thinking the same thing."

Alex said, "We can finally start making some arrests. It's been over a year. Did you call the Chief?"

Rob smiled grimly. "No, this a face-to-face announcement!"

Alex said, "You're right. Let's take these motherfuckers down!"

Rob poured Stella and himself a Jack. They toasted. "To taking these motherfuckers down," Motherfuckers!"

Chapter 27

SOLSTICE

Sergeant Agnes was giving the Second Platoon roll call, explaining to the rookies that Memorial Day was the official start of summer—and one of the most violent weekends of the year.

"We usually take an average of fifty shootings on this weekend. Last year forty-six people were shot. Thirteen died. The innocent law-abiding people of this city shouldn't have to deal with this so it would be a full enforcement weekend. Summons and arrest! So make sure you have a full book of summons and be careful out there. Don't be afraid to call for backup. For tomorrow's basketball tournament there will be a detail of two sergeants and sixteen officers. This event is usually peaceful because all the thugs are playing ball."

Everybody laughed. Except for Officer Dan, who grumbled, "This is another excuse to abuse a poor community. We should arrest people who commit crimes. Full enforcement doesn't deter crime and picks on everybody."

Officer West pointed out, "You might be in the wrong business."

"I'm actually in the right profession. It's not a business," Officer Dan snapped.

Officer West shrugged. "Let's go, Malcolm X."

#

The white clouds looked like cotton candy. Ramon thought this must what Heaven looks like. In an instant, it got a hundred times better as the New York City skyline appeared. First he saw the Statue of Liberty and then Manhattan. It was big and beautiful. And intimidating. Ramon was a twenty-two-year-old Dominican. He was on a plane for the first time in his life. His partner, Hector, sat beside him sound asleep. Which was great because he talked too much and he would have fucked this moment up. Ramon continued with his fantasy but was interrupted by a flight attendant announcing their arrival over the loudspeaker.

The flight attendant said, "Welcome to JFK. The time now is 7:03 AM and it is 81 degrees Fahrenheit and clear. We will be landing in thirty minutes."

The message was repeated in Spanish. Hector woke up and stretched. He pointed out the Brooklyn Bridge and the Freedom Tower. He had been to New York a few years back for his grandmother's funeral and stayed for the entire summer. He knew the streets.

After they landed, Hector drove Ramon around the neighborhood to get him familiar with it. He showed him where the spot was and then the escape route. They avoided the bridges because they all had cameras. After the hit they would be staying in Queens for a week and then get back on the plane—they couldn't leave too quickly because the Feds would figure it out. Ten days on the ground was how long most tourists stayed.

Ramon loved the neighborhood and wished he could stay. This was business so he knew he had to leave or they would be shooters on him. Maybe in a few years from now, if he saved his money, this could be a reality. For his half of $20,000, it was worth the risk. He could live off of that in Santo Domingo for five years. Being a mechanic back home meant he was lucky if he made a hundred US dollars a month. Hector, on the other hand, had already spent his money in his head. Watch, car, new apartment, and bitches. He lived fast. He had been in this business for ten years so he thought the money would be coming in forever. New York always had business for him.

#

The park's courts had new rims and nets. There was additional seating to view the big game. There were lights put up so they could play the championship game at night. The game tonight would be Far Rock against Southside. A rematch from two years ago. This was decided over the four prior weeks in a twenty-team tournament. Southside had Jason, the Archbishop Molloy High School phenom so they were favored. Derek had a lot of money on the game. He and Rodney from Far Rockaway, a longtime friend and a small-time hustler, had a $50,000 bet.

Food was in abundance, with two grills going. One was for hamburgers, hot dogs, and sausages. The other was for chicken, steak, and ribs. The music was loud you could hear it blocks away. Derek was the DJ for a while. A passion and hobby for him. He would take his seat in about an hour for the big game. Of course his seat would be center court row one. Shanika, Shawn, Raekwon, Jocelyn, and Kim would be right beside him. It was going to be a great game.

Shawn and Raekwon were talking shit about the Knicks while Jocelyn stood by eating a hot dog. "I'm a Knicks fan," said Shawn, "but I know they aren't any good so I root for LeBron."

Raekwon countered, "That doesn't make any sense. You have to be a fan in the good and bad times."

Shawn said, "There's no good or bad times, just incompetence."

They both laughed.

Carla and Kim were talking about getting out of this life. They both didn't understand how much money it would take for Derek and Shawn to walk away. Too much time in this life equals jail or death. Facts! Shanika was talking with Rodney about the people they knew in common. It was pissing Derek off only because he hated Far Rock on this day and everybody from it.

Portia made a grand entrance. She parked the Benz on the sidewalk. She gave a crackhead a twenty-dollar tip. She had decided on white linen shorts, a blue wife beater, and blue and red Gucci sandals. The key to the outfit was no bra. The twins were loose and happy. She walked over to Derek and gave him a kiss. Shanika was watching and was glad to see he didn't stare. Portia took a seat a couple of rows up.

Dwayne and Mike had just arrived and they went straight to food. They grabbed burgers. Dwayne asked no questions and look at no one, even though every eye was on him. Raekwon was the one he worried about. He could tell he didn't trust him. Raekwon was a follower of if we do time together then we do crime together.

Detective Murchado stood on the project's roof with Detective Rogers to collect intelligence and take photos. They wanted to see how Dwayne was doing now that he was in. From the roof they could see all the hustlers out and they getting photographed. Pretty girls were everywhere looking to meet and leave with a boss. They wouldn't even eat, but just stood trying looking cute. Then they spotted Louie from the Latin Cartel with a few soldiers, then Trevor with some Brooklyn Bullies standing close but not too close. Stella pointed them out. "It's like they're just hanging out, like law-abiding citizens."

Rogers peered at through binoculars at the crowd. "The Cartel knows we're watching. They're gathering in a public place for an alibi."

The sun had set and the game was starting soon. Everybody started to take their seats. Derek saw Rodney and they nodded at each other. The DJ turned the music up and the crowd went crazy. Both teams came out at the same time. They were staring and taunting each other. Then they started the lay-up line which quickly turned into a dunk show. Each team had guys that could jump out of the gym so the dunks were crazy. The music just enhanced the show.

Jason, the phenom, dribbled the ball up court and looked at the scoreboard. It said 1:03. They were down eight. He pulled up to the three-point line and without hesitation he shot a three. Nothing but net. The crowd went crazy. Derek was quiet because he had $50,000 on this. More than the money he wanted bragging rights. He shot a glance over at Rod. Soul on Ice. You couldn't tell if he was happy or sad. He had the same expression all of the time.

Jason and the rest of the team were back on defense. Carl the point guard from Far Rock was getting directions from the coach so his full attention wasn't on Jason so he charged him and Carl lost control of the ball. Jason grabbed it in stride and ran to the three-point line and hit another three. They were down by two with thirty seconds left. Far Rock called for a timeout. Carl was angry. Cursing at himself. The crowd went crazy again. Rod was cool and Derek was trying to stay cool. Shawn and the crew had a couple of thousand each on the game but like Derek, this was about bragging rights.

Dwayne and Mike sat on the top row enjoying the game. Dwayne had attracted three beautiful young ladies and they were sitting next to them.

Mike commented, "We gotta tie this and win it in overtime."

Dwayne eyed Jason. "If Far Rock misses they should take the three."

"But if we miss we lose," Mike said. "The percentages say drive and take the two with a chance at a three-point play with a foul."

Dwayne replied, "This was why you don't do good with the ladies. You always go for the win." Dwayne kissed the closest girl.

Mike said, "This was more than a game for us. Trust me on this. If you're gonna be down with the Syndicate, then you better start shouting Southside. We need this win."

Dwayne said, "Southside!"

Shanika was sitting next to Derek but he made her move because she was rooting for Far Rock. Loudly and proudly. She had her Far Rock shirt on. Custom made of course. He was furious, which meant rough sex later. She went to sit with Shawn and Carla. Carla was actually having a good time even though she didn't really understand the game. Shawn had no patience to teach her. She did know the bragging rights were very important. Derek wasn't alone, as Kim was there. It was good for her to be out and she was having a good time.

Far Rock was going to drive the ball to the rim and hope for a lay-up and foul.

Southside was going to push the ball to the left because nobody could drive the ball from that side. Everybody was right handed. If they got a steal or rebound, they were going to push the ball up the court. Jason was supposed to be the decoy and drive the ball and then throw it out to Don or Bruce who would be set up on both sides of the court behind the three-point line. They were going for the win.

Everything was peaceful. The police were offered food and they obliged. No need for full enforcement here. Everything was going smoothly.

When they came out of the timeout everybody was quiet. They all stood. Far Rock inbounded the ball and Southside pushed it to the left. Steven from Far Rock looked at the clock and got nervous. He didn't want the ball in his hands so he tried a cross court pass. Khalil stole it for Southside and immediately passed it to Jason. With a big grin he pushed the ball up. Don and Bruce flanked him. The crowd was going crazy. Rod was the only person sitting. He still had a clear view of the game. Respect. Derek was standing and he was sweating. He wanted this to be over. Shanika was yelling defense. Jason looked up at the clock: ten seconds. Don and Bruce ran to opposite corners. Khalil went to post up for a pass or rebound. Matt set a pick for Jason and he had a clear path to drive. Carl was a step behind him. He knew Jason from AAU no way he was going to pass the ball. On cue, Jason decided to take the three so he could be the hero. It's in his blood. Far Rock coach was yelling, "Don't foul," because he thought Jason was going to drive. Jason took a jab step and then stepped back to take the three. He made the last two. Carl was behind him and in bad position but he goes for the block and gets it clean. It's over and Far Rock wins. Bragging rights for a year! The coach and Jason yelled at the referee for a foul.

The referee shouted, "No foul. Maybe next year."

Matt punched him in the face. The coach and team quickly broke up the fight, with the coach slipping three hundred dollars into the referee's pocket. The police saw the punch and approached. The referee walked right by them as they asked what happened. The police didn't push the issues.

The Far Rock team carried Carl off the court. They were going crazy, way over the top. Shanika was crying tears of joy. Rod was cool. He nodded at Derek. He would get his money later. Derek was angry but he tried to maintain his cool. The whole Syndicate was upset.

The music was turned up and the DJ shouted out, "Far Rock!" The crowd mingled and ate.

As Dwayne and Mike talked to the girls, they knew it was a sure thing. The girls were fighting over Dwayne. He would have fucked them both but he was trying to get into the Syndicate. So he had to share.

Jason sat crying on the bench. A few teammates consoled him. Others thought it was his fault. Jason said, "I can't believe we lost. I put my life on the line for this. I would literally die for this. Die on this or any court. No ref should decide this. That was a foul."

#

Loud lightning and thunder. The sky finally gave in to a thunderstorm. The truck with limo tints on it looked like a taxi. Hidden by the tinted windows, the two Dominican gentlemen inside loaded up their Heckler and Koch SP5K, automatic weapons. They didn't need pinpoint accuracy for these. Just point and shoot. They got out of the truck and crossed the street, the weapons concealed under their black trench coats.

When they were in front of Trevor's juice bar, Hector kept his weapon trained on people walking by who froze in terror. Ramon shot into the juice bar, directly at the girl at the register. Shirley, Trevor's cousin, he had been told. He then aimed high above the heads and the customers and the other workers. He finished off the magazine. One hundred rounds in twenty-three seconds. When Ramon was finished he said, "*Terminado*." Hector on cue aimed high and shot randomly into the air. He yelled, "Get down on the ground. Don't look at us!" People dived for cover and covered their heads. They walked across the street and Ramon got in the truck and pulled it out into traffic while Hector watched the ongoing traffic for cops. When he climbed in, they drove off.

Inside the juice bar glass and juice made a mess. The screaming customers couldn't see Shirley's body slumped behind the register. Her co-worker, Jackie, huddled behind the counter and sobbed. The customers were screaming because they were frightened; Jackie was screaming because Shirley was dead. It was done with precision. Hector and Ramon only wanted to kill Trevor's niece. It was personal to draw Trevor in and so he would be sloppy. Personal was always sloppy.

But shooting randomly on the street can't be done with precision. In a building three blocks away six-year old Elizabeth was doing her homework at the kitchen table. She was hit with a stray bullet in the head. It exploded on contact and she was instantly killed. Her mother was on the phone in the living room and heard the glass break. When she entered the kitchen she was in shocked to see her little girl lying there in a pool of blood. The primal scream she let out could be heard for miles.

The war had started.

Chapter 28

ORDER

The duty captain didn't like basketball or groups of black men. He referred to the NBA as the African Ballet and a group of black men were a wolf pack. He was looking for a reason to break up the fun. Noise, a fight, something soon! He got what he needed. A call came over the radio for the shooting at the juice bar—a Level 3 Mobilization. He ruled the Queens tonight.

Central said, "We have a shooting at 666 Linden Blvd. The perps are outstanding. No description at this time. Level 3 Mobilization for South East Queens."

One sector from each Queens command would respond to the scene. The duty captain advised his lieutenant to clear the park. The lieutenant had no problem with the order. He told his sergeant. The sergeant knew it wasn't right but he had to follow orders. He was from the neighborhood so he knew Derek. He figured he would go right to the boss. Which he did. He told Derek it was out of his control but he was told to clear the park. The permit said 10 P.M. It was only 8:39. Derek knew he couldn't fight NYPD. He gave Shawn the nod that they were leaving. Shanika was the only one that was upset and she gave the cops hell. She cursed them out and even spit at them. "Why you fucking with us, pigs? Everything was peaceful. This shit ain't right. Motherfuckers."

The Syndicate formed around Derek for protection and guidance. When he moved they all moved. The duty captain thought they weren't going fast enough so he told his people to move the people out of the park now. One of the officers started to push people. He pushed one of the girls who was leaving with Dwayne.

She yelled, "I'm leaving—why were you touching me? He got that little dick syndrome. Asshole!"

The young officer shouted, "I will lock you up. Don't test me."

Dwayne knew this wasn't going to end well so he tried to intervene and grab her.

The officer grabbed her other arm and said, "You're going."

The girl didn't know what that meant but Dwayne did.

The officer said, "You and your boyfriend were under arrest."

The officer told his partner to grab Dwayne while he slammed the girl to the ground. The Syndicate held back, waiting for Derek to give the word—this girl wasn't part of the family.

Thinking on his feet, Dwayne threw a telegraphed punch, hoping the officer would duck. He did, letting Dwayne finish strong, so it looked as if he caught the officer in the face but he didn't. The response from the other officers was immediate until the sergeant cuffed him and ordered the officer to get both out of the park.

Shanika couldn't believe what Dwayne had done. She would have slept with him at that moment. She got everybody excited about what had just happened. Even the fellas were impressed with what they saw. They all headed to the strip club for alcohol and strippers, while Trevor and his crew stood by, watching the free entertainment from the Syndicate. Then Trevor got a 911 call from his sister to go to the juice bar. He never got emergency messages from his sister. He ran out of the park.

The Latin Cartel on the sidelines was watching his every movement. They knew why he left in a hurry. They continued to talk and eat. Louie wanted to be told by the police to leave. So they waited for the sergeant to make his way to their corner of the park. Which he did and they peacefully left. Alibi secured.

On the roof, Stella had enough photos of the three crews to update the crime chart. She was pleased with her work. She headed straight to Rob to tell him about Dwayne and the reconnaissance work. A call to the Chief would help Dwayne's situation.

#

Trevor tried to turn onto the block but there was a police car blocking traffic. He knew this had something to do with his sister's call. He parked his car around the corner and introduced himself to the police as the owner of the juice bar. The uniform called over a white shirt.

Sergeant Vasquez said, "Sir, do you own the Caribbean Flavors?"

Trevor said, "Yes. What happened?"

Vasquez said, "Do you have a driver license or some form of identification, sir."

Shaking, Trevor gave her his driver's license. She let him through the police tape. She handed the I.D. to the detective and then she escorted him to the store. The detective went to do an extensive background check on Trevor.

Trevor picked his way through the broken glass to the doorway of his juice bar. When he saw his sister, their eyes met. He knew his niece was gone. She fell into his arms and he could barely hold her up. They walked towards the store. There was a blanket covering a body.

Tonia said, "My little girl. My little girl. Cedella."

"What the fuck happened?" Trevor shouted at Vasquez.

Vasquez said soothingly, "We don't know yet. We were going to need to you to speak to the detectives."

Trevor looked around the store to take in the whole scene. *Who would kill my niece*, he thought? All he could think of is that it had something to do with Nigel.

Hours later, he was still sitting in an interrogation room as if he was under arrest. This made him hate the police. In business, he respected his opponent and his enemies—if they obey the code. He didn't care if he got arrested, because it's not personal and this was the life he chose. But the NYPD always treated black citizens like animals. He had lost his niece and he couldn't be there for his sister. He was locked in a room and couldn't leave. Detective Wiley walked into the room and sat down. He introduced himself and showed his I.D. Wiley said, "Sorry about your loss tonight, Mr. Rohan. It must be a tough night for you."

Trevor shook his head.

"Where were you prior to coming to the juice bar?"

Trevor said, "I don't appreciate being treated like I did something wrong."

"I assure you," said Wiley, "that by answering my questions it will help solve this case."

Trevor said sullenly, "I was at a basketball tournament in Baisley Park." When asked, he provided the time and the names of the people he was with.

"Do you know of anyone that wants to hurt you?"

Trevor said, "Hurt me? No."

"The reason I ask," said Wiley, "is because this was not a robbery. We believe it was for other reasons."

Trevor said, "I don't have any beef with a nobody."

"In your line of business you always have some type of beef."

Trevor arched a brow. "In the juice business?"

Wiley shook his head. "In the weed business. Trevor Rohan arrested four times for sale and two for possession. You were currently running the Brooklyn Bullies weed gang."

Trevor didn't answer. "I just lost my niece so I need to get to my sister, sir."

Wiley paused then said, "Okay," letting him go.

Cazembe was outside waiting for Trevor.

"What are you doing here?" Trevor asked.

"It was the Cartel," Cazembe answered. "We're getting you out of town. Going to Amityville—"

"Not my ex's house," Trevor interrupted. "She'll give me up out of revenge."

"No time to argue," pointed out Cazembe. "We can park a car on each end of her block watching for any shooters. Now get in the car." Trevor slide into the SUV and looked back, something catching his eye. A Hispanic woman on the corner, staring hard at them, talking on her phone. He didn't know for sure, but maybe the Cartel already knew where he was going.

"I'm sending my sister and girlfriend home to Jamaica," he said. "Right after the funeral."

"You're not going to the funeral," said Cazembe.

"My sister needs me," he answered, and Cazembe knew that was what would happen.

At Trevor's ex's house, Trevor decided to have a meeting about their next move in front of her. Cazembe was thinking about tactical privacy while Trevor was thinking about pussy. Cazembe thought to himself that it was idiotic to try impress a girl you were already sleeping with. Forget about the disaster it would be if she told someone.

Trevor said, "We have to hit back at the Cartel hard and quick. We should hit their stash apartment in Astoria tonight."

Cazembe shook his head. "They probably already moved out of there anticipating our retaliation." He paused, knowing what he was going to say would light a fuse under Trevor. "We better to hire a professional to do this."

Trevor yelled, "You don't tell me anything! I pay these motherfuckers to do whatever I tell them. My niece was killed so I need to see who is loyal to me about this life. All these Ras Clots always talking about shooting. Well, I need to see it."

Cazembe waited until he had finished. "Respect. I wasn't telling you what to do. I'm just saying that the police are out heavy after the shooting so it'll be hard to move with hardware. If you use your own people it could be traced back to you. If they get caught this entire conversation would come up in court." He didn't say what he knew to be the case: *It could get messy because they don't know what they're doing.*

Trevor said, "Fuck this. These are my guys. Let them put in the work. Hit that apartment tonight."

Cazembe said, "Okay, boss." He left that apartment feeling defeated. But he was built a certain way so he would do what he was told. That code was crazy. It controls you even when you know it's wrong.

#

The fight with Dwayne made the Syndicate feel as if they had won something. They invited Far Rock back to the club. Everything would have been free. Far Rock declined, wanting to go back to their hood and party without looking over their shoulders. So at the club Hennessy flowed and naked girls danced.

Shanika was happy because of the game and the fight. Also her girls were gonna make some good money tonight. They had invited D.J. Clue—a legendary Queens product—to spin. They thought they would be celebrating a championship, but the party must go on.

Derek and Shawn beefed up security at their stash houses and other real estate. They used contractors for this. Derek told his guys not to strap up because the police would be out aggressively putting hands on people. It was just a precaution. The war was between the Latin Cartel and the Brooklyn Bullies. "We are officially neutral. This should boost up our sales by 200 percent. Leave your guns at home. Be careful and get that money. Watch out for stray bullets."

Meanwhile Shanika was horny. Derek was in one of his moods so she had to look elsewhere. She could fuck anytime anywhere. He had to be in the mood. He overthought everything even sex. He was upset about the game and he was thinking about war. The little girl getting shot was also on his mind. Heavy. It made him think about his kids. He missed them, it had a while since he had saw them. The ghetto news had spread about the shooting at the juice bar. He knew it was the Latin

Cartel. He was trying to think a couple of steps ahead. Shanika started flirting with Portia but was quickly brushed off. She then turned her attention to Sofia.

She was going to take her to Edgemere and fuck her all night. It was rare that she went home because she usually stayed with Derek. What a night to go home with victory in the air. Sofia would benefit from it all. In Shanika's mind sleeping with a women was not cheating on Derek. Besides he did cheat on her so she felt it was justified. As long as he didn't disrespect her. He never had. Sofia did what she was told. She like working at this place it was better than the last where she had to fight different girls every night who were trying to steal from her. Here Shanika was the boss and she kept the order. She could survive in a place like this. Plus, she was looking forward to fucking Derek again. Hopefully alone. Tonight she would be alone with Shanika.

Shanika called for an Uber and they were in her living room forty-five minutes later. Shanika told her to take a shower. Sofia did so. When she got out she gave her a drink and told her to wait for her in the bedroom. Shanika then took a shower. When she entered the bedroom Sofia had dozed off. She grabbed her and started kissing her. Sofia was awake. She turned Shanika her on her back and kissed her way down to Shanika's sweet spot. She opened her legs wide so she could lick and suck until she caused an orgasm. It didn't take long. She was good at it. They ground on each other into the night.

#

Louie put the word out, telling the Cartel to be ready. Then he got call from the Dominicans. He frowned. This was against their contract but it might be an emergency.

Hector said, "*Buenos noches.*"

Louie answered politely, "*Buenos noches, el hermano. Como estas?*"

"*Adelante.*"

Louie heard the TV in the background. "*Y Ramon, como esta?*"

"*El es Bueno,*" began Hector. "*Necesitamos alcohol y mujeres.*"

Louie knew he had a problem. The deal was no alcohol or women. They were supposed to lay low and leave in a few days. Louie didn't have the manpower to watch these motherfuckers. Worst-case scenario there was no connection between them.

Louie said, "*No, hermano. Esto es negocio.*"

Hector said airily, "*El negocio esta hecho. Trabajo facil!*"

"*Tenemos un trato,*" said Louie sharply. "*Si usted quiere conseguir pagado siga las instrucciones.*" If they didn't follow the contract, no pay.

"*Primo Ahora necesitamos mujeres y alcohol. Si no nos lo traes nosotros vamos a comprar boletos y salir. Hijo de puta* JetBlue."

The threat made it an easy decision for Louie. Even if they made it back to Santo Domingo that didn't guarantee safety. If they bragged to the wrong person it could come back and indict him. So killing them was the only sure way to silence them. There would be a knock at their door later but it wouldn't be alcohol and women. It was going to be bullets.

Louie took a walk to the neighborhood butcher and went straight to the back. It was a few customers in there but nobody paid attention because he walked as if he knew where he was going. Diego was smoking a cigarette and cutting up chickens. Quite sure this wasn't USDA approved. This was a neighborhood place with its own rules. Louie never said a word; he just handed him an envelope and walked out. Diego Blades thumped his cleaver down to the bone, splitting a whole chicken in two. Ten thousand dollars, and he would be able to slaughter human flesh.

Chapter 29

OPTIMUM

The reporters gathered around the podium waiting for the mayor to speak. All of the heads of departments were starting to arrive, including councilmembers and the state senators. The mayor's assistant yelled out, "One minute." Then the mayor appeared and stepped to the podium. His navy blue suit, white shirt, and blue tie were perfect for getting re-elected.

Mayor Lowry said, "The city is in mourning. We have lost an innocent young citizen. Little Elizabeth, six years old, was at the dinner table doing her homework when she was struck by a stray bullet." The mayor held up a photo of Elizabeth in her first grade Catholic school uniform. It was a photo op. And it worked. It was hard not to look at the photo and feel anger towards the person or people who did this. "This cannot be tolerated in a civilized society. We will not be terrorized. And make no mistake this was an act of terror."

One reporter shouted out, "Is it appropriate to call this an act of terror?"

Mayor said simply, "Yes. This is not Iraq, this New York City. There will be order."

The reporter continued, "Mayor, sadly kids get killed in this city every day and you have never used that term. Is there a reason why? Does color play a role in this specific case?"

The mayor answered smoothly. "Color definitely wasn't a factor. If anything, it was a mistake for me not to have said it earlier. The police commissioner will speak next."

The police commissioner said, "This is a tough time for the city. Be assured that my department will do everything in its power to bring the perpetrators to justice in this case. For now, we were offering $50,000 for any tips that lead to an arrest in this case."

Another reporter asked, "Do you think the bullet could have been from the earlier shooting on Linden Boulevard?"

The police commissioner held up a warning hand. "We have determined that the stray bullet that struck her was in fact from the shooting on Linden Boulevard. That's all we can release now because we don't want to jeopardize the case. I assure you that we were working diligently on this."

The mayor wanted to pull attention back to his show. "Here we had a family of two. A divorced mother working two jobs to put her daughter through private school. They both represent what this city is about: fighters. And in an instant it was destroyed by a terrorist. On 9/11 we lost 2,606 people in the World Trade Center and a few of those were from cancer due to the toxic air from the buildings. That was a terrorist attack and no one would ever argue with me on that point. Since January 2002 we have lost 11,134 people to violent murders in this city. That is terror as well. We must take this city back from rapist, murders, and thugs because they *are* terrorists. Whenever we have to alter our lifestyles because of criminals, that is terror. So if I'm reelected I plan to hire more than ten thousand officers so that we have the personnel we need to patrol this city properly. Until then I'm authorizing as much overtime as needed for the police department. The police commissioner knows he has my full support and confidence to patrol and control this city as he sees fit."

Another reporter shouted out, "Mayor, can you explain why this shooting has touched you so much? Last week three children were killed in Brooklyn. Also there was another young lady killed in the shooting at the juice bar. You haven't even mentioned her name. The only difference between the victims is race."

Mayor said, "I've said his has nothing to do with race. It is time to get tough. Individuals that act inhumane are animals."

Another reporter said, "That sounds like code for the cops to use excessive force. We all know excessive force is only used on black men in this city."

The Mayor scolded, "You should be ashamed of yourself. The police go to where the crime is. That's in poor areas of this city, which were populated by African Americans. So the high number of contacts is not the fault of the police. You can't think that the police want to injure innocent people."

"There's no excuse or rationale for police brutality," the reporter answered.

The mayor's assistance checked her watch and decided it was enough. Any more questions could hurt the mayor's polls. "The mayor has to attend to a crisis."

As the mayor and police commissioner left the news conference, a reporter yelled out a question. "Councilman Roberts, do you agree with the mayor?"

Roberts answered, "The mayor has my full support in cleaning up this city and preventing innocent kids from being murdered."

Councilmen Jackson was not planning on speaking but he couldn't in good conscience say nothing. He sprang up and faced the cameras. "Every life in this city has to be valued equally. It seems that when an African American youth is killed it is business as usual. I don't want *any* kids to be murdered. I don't want anyone of *any* age to be. I agree that we have a duty to protect those who can't protect themselves. But all young lives matter. With respect to the police department, I want them to do their jobs in accordance with the law. I don't think they need extra powers or incentives. The words used by the mayor and commissioner could lead to excessive force on the minorities of this city. I think it is incorrect to refer to any citizen of this city as a terrorist. There are, of course, cases where that label would be appropriate. But definitely not en masse. We must be careful with our language and actions in the heat of the moment. The other young lady who was murdered last night by thugs was Cedella Rohan. Both funeral services will be posted online at the official city website."

#

The Third Platoon roll call was packed. It was the busiest time in the precinct, 4 PM to midnight. It had an extra twenty-officer today because the mayor had authorized their overtime. It was hard to find room to stand but everyone was in a great mood, as they all loved their overtime.

Sergeant May said, "This was coming from the top. Full enforcement tonight and for the foreseeable future. We want arrest over summons. Arrest. Arrest. Let's take control back of the city. Be careful out there."

The officers mingled after roll call, talking shop. Most talked about little Elizabeth. Others talked about the extra money they would make. Officer Armetta was ready to patrol with this new mandate. He was physical already this made it easier for him to justify it in his own mind. He was hoping that his partners felt the same. He was ready to do his part and protect the city from animals and terrorists. Maybe this would expedite his path to detective.

Nearly an hour later, Armetta and his partner Scott were sitting in a Dunkin Donuts looking out the window for anything suspicious. It was perfect weather, 81 with a breeze. The streets were quiet. Then a man ran by wearing a hooded sweatshirt with the hood over his head. That was enough for Armetta. He would put his hands on this mutt and maybe get a weapon or drugs. At the least it would be a UF-250, "Stop, Question, and Frisk Activity." He started in a foot pursuit. His partner followed. Everybody was in a slow jog.

Armetta yelled, "Hey bro, stop! Bro, stop!" He sped up and grabbed the runner's shoulder.

Malik, startled, stopped and took out his earbuds, loud music spilling out from them. He figured it would be a cop. "What's up?"

Armetta said, "Take your hands out of your pocket where I can see them."

Malik replied, "Why are you stopping me?"

"Shut up and listen. Where were you coming from?"

Malik warily replied, "The gym, Officer. I'm asking again, why are you stopping me?"

Armetta said, "There's a lot of crime in this area. You were acting suspicious. Do you have I.D. on you?"

Malik shrugged. "I'm not answering any more questions until you tell why you really stopped me. I'm not acting suspicious. You're suspicious of me."

Armetta's partner Scott waited, watching the interaction. He had been warned. He thought everybody had been overreacting but no, they were all right. Scott knew a cop could stop someone, be polite, and still search them. So like every other cop in the city, why couldn't Armetta just apologize and say, "We just got a call with someone fitting your description so we need to search you. Sorry sir." The person would be angry but he would comply. That's excessive force with a smile. Armetta had an anger and hate in him that had to be stopped.

Scott interrupted, "Sir, we are just doing our jobs."

Malik said, "Being unprofessional is doing your job? That doesn't seem right. I'm asking you yet again, why are you stopping me?"

Armetta snarled, "See, it doesn't pay to be nice. You have to control animals."

Malik yelled, "Who the fuck are you calling an animal?"

Noisy Rosie heard the yell from her third-floor apartment window. She looked out, help up her smartphone, and started filming. Whenever the police stopped someone in this neighborhood it caused a scene because the people hated the way they were treated by them.

Armetta said, "Turn around and put your hands on the wall, tough guy." He spun Malik, who slipped and fell. Armetta jumped on top of him, placing his knee on his chest.

Malik gasped, "I can't breathe."

Armetta hissed, "Stop resisting. Stop resisting."

Scott tried to help him out by grabbing Malik's hand. "Stop resisting so we can stand you up."

Malik choked, "This is bullshit."

Armetta punched Malik in his face and then kicked him. Officer Scott shielded Malik's body, absorbing some of the blows, and he stood Malik up and then cuffed him. Out of breath, Armetta had no more fight left in him, while Malik was in shock, quiet and cooperating. Officer Scott patted him down and then told him he was under arrest for disorderly conduct and resisting arrest. Armetta called for a patrol car to pick them up.

Rosie couldn't believe what she just witnessed. She couldn't wait for her daughter to get home so she could show her the video.

#

Captain Gallagher had called an early morning meeting for the Unit. Mandatory attendance except for the undercovers. Everybody was there. This was Hale's first big meeting so she was nervous. Pamela, Alex, and Rob arrived together. When the Captain walked in at 7:45, he went right into the conference room. Everyone followed. He went over his notes and at exactly 8 AM he stood up.

"Morning, everybody. We all know about the shooting last night, which was gang related. This shooting has shaken up the city and the Mayor wants arrests. We are supposed to be a high-speed unit—we need to produce some arrests so the Mayor can calm the people of this city."

Rob interrupted, "As I told you before, we can't rush what we do."

Captain Gallagher retorted, "Fuck that. We need to make arrest and parade people in front of the news cameras. Now!"

Rob coolly replied, "We just penetrated the most notorious gang in the city. The Syndicate. If you give us some time, all the dominos would fall. I guarantee it."

"We don't have any more time," Captain Gallagher replied. "The Mayor won't hesitate to shut this unit down if we don't produce. It's been over a year and nothing."

Detective Stella said, "Maybe you should go to Narcotics and they could help you. Here we make cases."

Capt. Gallagher said, "I don't know what you have because I don't have full access yet." "That's policy," Rob replied, "until your secret clearance is finished."

After a pause, Captain Gallagher merely said, "I'm going to do you a favor and tell the mayor we will have something in a few days. So when I leave, get your stubborn asses to work or this unit is finished. I give you my word on that." He walked out of the room.

Alex looked around in the silence and said, "This guy is a clown. He doesn't understand what good police work is."

Detective Stella shrugged. "It's not entirely his fault. He's getting pressure from above. It also really shows how great a boss Teddy was."

Rob shook his head. "I'm not compromising anything for him, so I might be the one leaving."

Alex said what was on everyone's mind. "If you leave we leave."

Rob stalked out of the room without answering, heading to the Chief's office in the Garment District. He knew the mayor was looking to capitalize on the incident, which made him even more upset than he was about the death of Elizabeth. Good police work couldn't be rushed. If only he could just kill all those responsible for the murder. He felt a pang, missing his kids and wife. He wondered what his wife was thinking when she saw the news about Elizabeth. Hopefully it made her appreciate his work more.

Right before he knocked on the Chief's office door, he heard footsteps behind him. Alex. They entered to office together.

Five minutes later, Rob was frustrated. The meeting with the Chief was not helping matters. Rob wanted to talk about Gallagher and the

Chief did not. Rob wanted direction. The Chief wanted him to use all of the tools that he learned at the CIA Farm.

Rob said, "This guy is out of his mind. I can't work for him. I think the right thing is for me to just leave the unit."

Alex said, "Don't be a pussy. We can work around him."

The Chief snorted. "I wish I could give Alex a battle field promotion so we could have some leadership here."

Rob bit back his retort. He knew he deserved that.

"You keep worrying about someone who was inconsequential to you and the unit," the Chief said. "You have the power to do what you want to take down these violent gangs. You're still looking to do things the NYPD way. The unit you are supposed to be leading has broad powers. You don't need probably cause for anything. You just had the mayor today deliver you a gift. He called the same people you were going after terrorist. So treat them as such. Which you should have already been doing. You have heavy weapons and explosive training, interrogation skills, and wiretap authority. Use them all. Surveil and then capture or kill the terrorists in this city. Whatever you do, stop coming here because you can't get along with your commanding officer. I'm here to help the unit with legal issues. I'm not a therapist. Get to work. Let's try to prevent any more innocent babies from being murdered."

Alex nodded. "Let's take these motherfuckers out before Gallagher can interfere."

Rob looked at them for a moment before answering. "You're both right. Chief, send Hale away to the Farm and give her the full training."

The Chief said, "No problem. Done."

Chapter 30

ACCIDENT MURDERERS

Glenmore and Gerald pulled up to 4-25 Astoria Boulevard. They each carried an Uzi and a 9mm. Glenmore, born in Jamaica, had a heavy accent so that alone scared most people. He always talked about all the bodies he had put in the ground in Kingston—but Trevor always suspected he was all talk and no action. Gerald was Nigel's friend so Trevor needed to know if he could trust him. So they both had to show and prove.

Glenmore and Gerald went up to 5C to let the world know that the Brooklyn Bullies were not to be fucked with. They kicked down the door and emptied their weapons. No precision, just shooting until the magazines went empty. They then walked back down the stairs to their car parked right in front of the building. But the apartment was empty—the Latin Cartel had already moved their stash out of that apartment. They could hear the screams though. There was no one home in 5C but the bullets had penetrated the thin project walls into 5B and 5D. Mr. Benson in 5B was struck in both legs. The Rodriquez family in 5D lost three-year-old Mary, eleven-year-old Juan, and father Carlos. The mother was the only one to survive. A family murdered as they watched T.V. together and their mom cooked them dinner. When Trevor heard, he made an announcement that this was the Brooklyn Bullies—he was making a statement.

Trevor also had them hit the Latin Cartel's main spot, the pool hall. He had them hit it in broad daylight. But the Cartel's business had moved. A local hustler had rented it out. It was now part strip club and pool hall. They hit just as the school across the street let out. Of course Glenmore and Gerald killed two innocent kids. They wounded a few strippers and customers. It was a bloodbath. They were able to escape because the school buses blocked the responding police cars. The news reported it as an ongoing drug war—something the Police

Commissioner and the Mayor didn't need in an election year.

Another violent night in the city had become the norm. Councilmen Jackson wrote an op-ed piece for the *New York Times* about race. Commonsense things that needed to be said at this time. He explained the relationship between slaves and the police all the way up till present time. Black men were always afraid of the police. If you're innocent, you worry about jealousy. If you're guilty, you worry about the police being the judge and executioner. He felt the mayor had a responsibility to speak to all citizens of the city and to govern them all as well. Giving the police more power was not the way to stop violent crimes. The city council had discovered that the NYPD had a unit that was trained by the CIA and it was operating in other states, which was illegal. The council was currently investigating the unit. He knew it was only a matter of time before there was an incident between the police and an African American male. He believed even criminals deserved a certain amount of respect.

#

Pamela, Alex, and Rob were having breakfast at the house. Pamela had made a feast for them. They all were drinking vodka and orange juice. For Alex it was a chaser. For Pamela and Rob, it was relaxation. A way to take the stress away from missing their families.

Alex suggested, "Let's do as the Chief instructed and use all the tools we have to take down these gangs."

Pamela added, "You should always listen to the Chief."

Alex laughed, "You're his favorite. That's just loyalty speaking."

Rob mused, "His words hit me hard today. Maybe I have misunderstood what this unit represents and the power we have."

"We should use all the power granted to us," Alex said. "We are the good guys so let's do what we need to do to take down the bad guys."

Pamela laughed, "You sound like the mayor."

Rob said snidely, "The mayor was a lot tougher."

They all laughed.

"So we were going to get to work?" asked Alex briskly.

Rob finished his vodka and orange juice. "I'm going to be off the grid for twenty-four hours. When I get back, we can get started immediately."

Pamela rested her hand on his arm. "You have to at least let me know where you're going. Because if something happens to you and I don't know where you are, that makes me look like an idiot and puts my position in jeopardy."

Rob said, "Trust me on this. I would not put you on the spot with anything I do. Just give me a little room so I can clear my head."

Pamela nodded.

#

Shawn and Derek were at the back table in Peter Luger's Steakhouse on Long Island. Derek toyed with his drink then finally spoke up. "Corrupt cops, rivals, and stickup kids are all fair game. We try to stay clear of innocent bystanders."

Shawn shrugged. "Part of the game. You want to be king. Well, this comes with it."

The waiter brought over prime rib for two, medium well with a mixed green salad, French fried potatoes, and fresh broccoli.

Derek cut the steak. "You're right. But it still is on my mind. It might be wrong to say but everything else is working out fine. Our sales are up and all our people are good."

"What do you want to do with Dwayne?" Shawn asked.

Derek paused. "The arrest was legit?"

Shawn nodded. "Lucky for him the cops lied so bad in their report it just didn't add up for the judge. So he was released. No protective custody or high-profile lawyer. He was in population and he had one of the regular public defenders. I think we can give him some more work."

Derek said, "Cool."

Shawn said, "That thing we talked about before. You laying low. I think you should take a vacation because even though we are not at war there is a war going on and you have to be protected. That's the rules."

Derek said, "You right. I'mma lay low."

They ate.

#

The weather was a steamy 86 degrees. A family had been murdered, and the mayor was looking to stop the bleeding so he gave the NYPD unlimited O.T. But he wanted results. At the Bat Cave, Captain Gallagher wanted the names of people that they were going to arrest. He wanted to be the one to deliver a major arrest for the city. All this would get him promoted and make him a TV star. So he was pushing. He had called Rob and left a message for him to meet him. There was no answer and Rob was a no-show. Sergeant Ling was at the Bat Cave and he updated Gallagher on Dwayne penetrating the Syndicate, which was considered the most notorious drug gang in the city.

Gallagher brusquely interrupted. "Let me see the jacket on Derek Mason." It didn't take Gallagher long to see that Derek Mason killed two people and he was still walking the streets.

Ling explained that it hadn't been investigated in this office as a homicide. "We're trying to take him down as a kingpin and we can use the possible murder as leverage."

Gallagher snorted dismissively. "We should use the two murders as the leverage to make him talk about the drugs."

"Usually that doesn't work because the major time comes with being declared a kingpin," said Ling. "That title comes with mandatory minimums."

Gallagher threw up his hands but he understood. "Fine. Let's arrest anybody in the Syndicate for anything. I'll leave Mason alone but you have to give me something. Let's arrest one of his soldiers and maybe we can get him to talk, which could expedite the case on Mason. We do agree murderers shouldn't be walking around on the streets."

Ling agreed and started to do basic warrant checks on all the names listed in the Syndicate. Raekwon Griffin had a suspended license. That's all he came up with after checking eighty-seven names. Gallagher's thoughts went back to his days in Narcotics. It was usually the low-level targets who turned on the boss. Between jealousy, low pay, and fear of jail they talk. This was not the method of this unit but the city was on fire. He needed something. Gallagher would work this separate and if he got nothing, no one would know.

Alison Hale sat at her desk filing, but she was observing everything. She had a feeling that what was going on was of a bigger magnitude than an argument between the two men. As she filed she got a notice that she was going to training in Williamsburg, Virginia. She was going to Camp Peary better known as the "Farm." Alison's orders had read that she would be arriving on Sunday and training would begin on Monday. She was instructed not to tell anyone of the training. She didn't understand the magnitude of that as well. She was honored that Rob saw something in her that she wasn't sure she had. The little that she knew about the unit impressed her. She was looking forward to the training and coming back and being an asset to the unit and the department. She didn't know that the Chief had made it happen—that he was fascinated by her last name as he and Rob had a feeling that the Unit's days were numbered. Nathan Hale had been the first CIA spy to die for the country. During the American Revolutionary War, Hale had joined the Continental Army as a commissioned captain. He volunteered to go behind enemy lines in the Battle for Long Island, gathering intelligence on British Troops, which was considered an act of spying. He was captured and hung by the British Army on September 21, at 11 AM. Honored by the CIA as the first American spy to be killed in the field, he had a statue at CIA headquarters. The Chief wondered why Robb wanted to protect Alison Hale. He trusted Rob though. No matter what happened to the unit, ultimately she was going to receive the CIA's full training and be deployed to the streets of New York.

Chapter 31

ROAD TRIP

"Mama Said Knock You Out," by LL Cool J was blasting. Driving to the Poconos to visit his kids and grandmother, Derek was listening to the entire album from beginning to end. Shawn wanted him to keep a low profile. Plus, he missed his three kids. So he was taking a two-hour drive which was therapeutic for him. He like road trips for the food and music. He stopped at Roy Rogers and Arby's all of the time. He didn't tell his grandmother he was coming, as he wanted to surprise her and the kids. He knew they would be happy to see him. It had been about four months since he was last there. He talked to his kids like they were adults. He told them they would have a much better life there with grandma. So they missed him but they understood. This was to protect them.

#

The only way to listen to "My Life" by Mary J. Blige was to blast it. Kim was on the road to Charlotte, North Carolina. Little Dre was in the back with his headphones on watching T.V. Kim decided not to tell anyone she was leaving or where. She couldn't call Derek but she would get word to him later. She would call her sister and Dre's parents from Virginia. There was no trail: Dre taught her well. She wanted to leave and then see where everything was at in a year. People would be upset but she didn't care. This was survival. She had paid her sister's debt off so she had no reason to be mad at her.

Everything should be about little Dre. So if they cared then they would understand. She wouldn't be apologetic about her method. Derek would be the one person who understood. Dre's parents would be the only foreseeable trouble. Kim could handle them. After a year if things were okay she would give them the new address and visitation rights. For now, she was enjoying the road and thinking positive thoughts about the new beginning. She had sold the Range, Benz, and the house. She had put $100,000 in a fund for little Dre for college and life. She was going to buy a small house for Dre and her and live simply. She was going to find a job that allowed her to work around her son's schedule. This was all to protect Dre.

#

Rob always listened to Run DMC when he was on the road. He was going up to Camp Talcott to visit his family. His kids were in camp and his wife was a volunteer. For their protection and his, they didn't know he was coming. Between Elizabeth and the Fernandez family being murdered he needed to get away. Gallagher breathing down his throat didn't help matters either. He felt the guilt of maybe he could have done more. Now a family was feeling what he felt about his father being murdered. This hurt him more than anything else. Alex and he had decided that they would do whatever was in their power to put a stop to the violence in the city during their watch. He would do anything to protect his kids from this pain.

Chapter 32

CHASER

"This is Harry Sleezer. I handle civil rights cases. Do you want the video in your possession to help bring a corrupt cop to justice?"

He had Juanita's attention. Like everyone else in the hood, she thought the police were too aggressive and did what they wanted with no consequence. She had posted her mother's video on Facebook and Instagram with a few comments. It hadn't taken long for it to spread. She started getting calls from all of her friends about another case of police brutality. The call she wasn't expecting came from Sleezer. He needed no introduction his name, the sloppy suit, and dirty shoes said it all. Ambulance Chaser. He just needed to know if she was the original videographer. She admitted that her mother gave it to her. Mr. Sleezer saw no problem with that. He just asked her to post a message asking if anyone knew the man being assaulted by police.

Within minutes of her posted query, she had the assaulted man's name, phone number, and address and gave it to Sleezer, who called a reporter to let him know that he was representing Malik Sanders. He told the reporter there would be an official news conference at Malik's house.

When Sleezer showed Malik's mother the video, Mrs. Sanders believed every word Malik had told her when he called her from jail, so she told Sleezer all about him. He was a college kid who worked out all the time. He had never given her any issues growing up. So for him to be arrested was a shock.

Once she saw the video she was angry. Sleezer promised vindication and money. She thought that all sounded good. Sleezer was pleased to have another person onboard with his plan. Usually the mother was the hardest to turn. The next step was getting to Malik in jail. He needed

Ms. Sanders help with that. She agreed. Before they walked out together to his news conference, Sleezer said he would do all of the talking. He told them both not to hold back any tears. The reporters were already lined up outside.

Sleezer began, "Thank you all for coming. My name was Harry Sleezer and I'm a partner at Sleezer and Barnes. At my side today are Malik's mother, Mrs. Barbra Sanders. She has just observed the video of the police beating up Malik for no reason. We believe the stop was unlawful and all actions after that were illegal. This video has confirmed that the NYPD are a rogue bunch. The mayor of this city bears responsibility because he has given them a pass to do whatever they want. They have shown this behavior many times before. Yet he continues to support them. Today this stops. We will work on freeing Malik and then we will file a hundred-million-dollar lawsuit against the city." While the reporters buzzed, they retreated back to her house.

Chapter 33

STAY

Derek was lying on the floor playing with his three kids: Derek was ten, Mark was eight, and Sharon was four. They were very happy to see him. His grandmother was as well. His daughter was named after her. They were extremely close. She didn't like the life he chose but it was partly his mothers, fathers, and her fault. She did what she could raising him right. She let him know all the time that he should get out. She did notice how good he was at his business. She told him all he needed to do was ask God for forgiveness and give the rest of his life for redemption. His mother was an addict who sold. Bad combination. He was a businessman. She was cooking his favorite tonight; Fried chicken, yams, and greens. He wanted to play around on the turntables for a while. He went down to the basement to play some music. He mixed and cut up "Good Times" by Chic for a while. It was his go to mix. He was rarely there but he still had a man cave. Two flat screen T.V.'s mounted on the wall. Sectional couch and pool table. Simple but good. The hardest thing will be leaving. He could never stay long enough. His kids and grandmother always wanted him to stay. His kids because they missed him. His grandmother because she always knew it could be here last time seeing him.

#

There were kids everywhere but if they didn't move she would have knocked them over. Lora Russo had gotten a call that she had a visitor—her husband. She ran into the office and right into Rob's arms, startling. They both cried. She felt him all over to make sure he was okay.

Lora said, "What were you doing here? Are you okay?"

Rob laughed, "Wow. I thought you would be happy to see me. How are the kids?"

Lora said, "They're fine. Really, what's going on?"

Rob shrugged but evaded her eyes. "Nothing. I just wanted to see you and the kids. That's all."

Lora didn't pry any further. "How long can you stay?"

Rob said, "I'm staying the night. If that's all right?"

Lora answered, "Of course. Let's go get the kids."

Rob said, "Let's not interrupt their day. Let's get something to eat. I'm starving."

They walked hand and hand to the chow hall, smiling and kissing all the way there.

#

Kim checked into the Sheraton in Virginia Beach. She was tired. It had been a six-hour drive. Dre wanted to get in the pool but she wanted to take a nap. Realizing that taking him to the pool now would ensure him sleeping tonight, she took him to the pool. When they got back to the room she made the easiest call first. Her sister understood and told her to call often. The second was harder than she thought. Dre's mother couldn't even talk to her. Between the crying and cursing there wasn't much expressed. Dre's mother handed the phone to her husband. He told Kim he was very upset with her. But at this point just call and let them talk to Dre every day. She agreed.

Chapter 34

BODY IN THE TRUNK

"You learned nothing. You didn't case the apartment before the hit. They'd already left and you shot up the projects. You parked right in front of the apartment building!" Glenmore and Gerald shifted uneasily but didn't reply.

Cazembe had known it was a bad idea to have two unproven soldiers do a hit. But he had been overruled by Trevor. Now he faced a dilemma on what to do with the two knuckleheads. He'd send them underground. He gave them some money and took their phones. He put them on a bus to Maryland and told them he would come for them when it was clear. They were so scared they listened to everything he said. They had just created even more heat on the Brooklyn Bullies. He didn't think that was possible.

His phone buzzed in his pocket. He glanced at the phone and slid it back without answering it. Trevor had been calling him nonstop but he shouldn't be calling. Even though Trevor was his boss Cazembe wasn't going to make it easier for police to arrest him.

"I need some pussy," he muttered. Damien, his right-hand man waiting in the kitchen, came in and told him to hurry up. He would grab a few things and then he was going to one of his girls in Rosedale to fuck. After that it would be all business. He went upstairs to grab some clothes. Cazembe turned the light on in his bedroom and heard the two shots that killed Damien. He knew he fucked up, he should have moved before he relocated Trevor. Rookie mistake. Trevor had rubbed off on him. Now he had a gun pointed at him.

Cazembe went down to the garage, the gunman behind him. There he saw garbage bags laid out across the floor. Cazembe took all of it in and started to plead for his life. He offered money and to leave town, the country, whatever. Paco stepped into the garage, dragging Damien's body. The gunman, Diego, put his apron on and took out his cutting tools.

Cazembe's eyes opened wide. "No, man. Not like this." He tried to run but Diego sprayed him with something from a canister—as the mist settled over his face, he lost control of his body and fell to the floor. There he lay, fully conscious but unable to move.

Diego leaned over him. "Cazembe, I'm going to cut you up and deliver you to your boss. This is not personal. It's business."

Cazembe concentrated on his lips and found he could speak. "We from the same world," he slurred. "I'll see you again in Hell."

Paco said, "You thought you was with a real crew. Stupid *Negrito*."

"*Estupido*." Diego spat.

Cazembe's eyes remained open but he could only lie there with his new Queens hoodie and Cuban Lynx chain.

Paco took out a bottle of Hennessy and two cigars. The alcohol was for horrific nature of the work about to start. The cigars were for the smell. Diego, who could smoke his without taking it out of his mouth, worked with precision. He hacked the head off first then the arms and legs. The rest was easy. Humans were different than the beef and pork he cut up. It took a little longer, but it wasn't hard. After he was finished he placed the head and body in a garbage bag. The bag was scented with vinegar and baking soda. The trunk was scented with coffee grounds. He placed it in the trunk and drove it to Fat Boy's house.

Once he left, Fat Boy took a photo of Cazembe's head when Diego was gone, following Louie's instructions. Then Fat Boy leaned over the head and peered closely. "Damn. I know this kid from Jamaica Avenue. He used to work at the barber shop. We couldn't have just shot him. Old-school shit."

He didn't want to drive with the body alone so he called Carlos.

Carlos asked, "What were we transporting?"

"There's a body in the trunk, son."

Carlos, not knowing what to say, said nothing but came over. Fat Boy keyed up "Body In the Trunk," by NORE! Fat Boy turned up the music and they drove into the night.

They dropped the bag at Trevor's front door. He then sent a picture of the head to Trevor's phone. Of course Fat Boy was using a throwaway cell phone.

And of course Trevor was still using his own phone, although Cazembe had told him to throw it away. When he received the picture, he sat in shock. his girlfriend threw up and fainted.

#

Raekwon was fucking the shit out of Jocelyn inside his apartment. This was a new romance. Weed and talking had led them to the bedroom. Jocelyn came and then Raekwon right after. He always jumped right in the shower after he busted off. He went to turn the water on in the shower but there was nothing. He tried the sink, nothing. He ran to the kitchen and tried the faucet there. Nothing. He was sharp. He knew the police were about to raid his apartment. They always turn off the water so you can't flush any evidence. He ran into the bedroom and hissed at Jocelyn to get dressed. She was half asleep and not moving at all. He grabbed her and carried her over to the closet. He said nothing in case they were listening.

"One of your girls at the door?" Jocelyn sleepily asked. He pulled up the carpet and opened a latched door and shoved her down into the crawlspace. She started to scream but he jammed his hand over her mouth. "Shut the fuck up." He then threw down her clothes. He started to jump down as well but then he decided not to run. If you run, they always catch you and it just makes everything worse. They tear up your mama's house and everybody else's.

He closed the latched door and fixed the carpet and then moved the safe back over it. The safe was empty—it was just there to cover the door. He could hear the footsteps in the hallway. He turned on the light in the bedroom and got back in bed. It took thirty seconds for the Emergency Service Unit Team to get into in his bedroom and then he was cuffed and on the floor looking up at them. They dragged him outside in his underwear.

They could have searched his clothes and then given them to him but they wanted to humiliate him. He didn't know why this was happening but he wasn't worried about it. No drugs or guns in the apartment. Derek's rules. They had nothing extra on him.

Gallagher, feeling empowered, starting talking shit to him. "You fucking mutt! We got you for selling drugs and murder."

Raekwon didn't react. He was cool. Gallagher knew he was on thin ice. All they really had was a suspended license. Gallagher had had to convince the commanding officer of the ESU that his men storming the apartment was appropriate for a person with a suspended license. He had told him that the Mayor and Police Commissioner wanted this. Ling, on the scene, texted Rob with no response.

Jocelyn had slipped down the crawlspace to the first floor. Hearing the commotion, she realized he had saved her. She did nothing wrong but she didn't need the inconvenience of being arrested. This nigga was too fly! She was highly impressed and thankful. There was nothing in the house not even weed. She knew the Derek rules! Derek had taught him well. She would thank him for this later. Right now she was going to tell Derek in person what happened. No phones!

#

Dwayne wasn't home for more than forty-five minutes before Mike knocked on his door. He let Mike in. "Yo. How did you know I was out?"

Mike looked over Dwayne's black eye, busted lip, and a chipped tooth and said, "The Syndicate knows all. Welcome home, champ."

Dwayne shook his head. "Good to be home. I hate fucking cops." He disguised the relief he felt. What he had done had earned him big points with the Syndicate. He also knew the Chief would take care of the legal side. He had looked convincing in front of the judge and his attorney. Charged with disorderly conduct, resisting arrest, assault on three police officers. Then the judge asked for all the medical reports. Dwayne was the only to have any. The officers had none, although on their paperwork they were listed as severely injured. He'd gotten a summons for disorderly conduct and then got out of that courtroom.

Mike sat. "Fuck those motherfuckers. Yo, you knocked that pig the fuck out."

"He put his hands on the sister for nothing," replied Dwayne. "I had to do something. Crazy shit. Bout to call that ho now. I took a beating for her so she gotta let me beat it up."

They both laughed.

#

Detective Daly finally stepped into the room after Raekwon had been sitting there for two and half hours. The room was cold and bright but Raekwon was cool. He knew there was a separation between him and Derek. He also knew he was always very careful. But he was curious to see what they had.

Gallagher had said to let him sit for a few hours. Let him shiver and think. He had called an old detective he worked with in Organized Crime to interrogate Raekwon. He promised the Second Grade Detective, First Grade Lieutenant's pay. Detective Daly would have done it without the offer. He loved to interrogate and for an old friend he would do anything. The Blue Line.

Daly introduced himself. "Mr. Griffin, my name is Detective Tyler Daly. I want to talk to you about your position within the Syndicate drug gang and your activities. Your incentive to talk to me is that we have you on murder, narcotic sales, and possession." It was a lie, but it was legal to lie to a perpetrator to obtain information.

Raekwon replied, "I got nothing to say."

Daley crossed his arms. "You sure about that? You think Derek Mason gives a fuck about you. If it's you or him, believe me it's going to be you. I've seen this a million times. It's not who talks—it's who was the first to talk."

Raekwon shrugged. "I don't give a fuck what anybody else does. I don't talk. For nothing or nobody. I live inside my head."

Daly tried again. "So you're okay with never seeing your family again for some rats?"

Raekwon stared back at him without expression. "What's my charges?"

"I already told you," said Daly. "We can bury you in jail. Help yourself. All I need you to do is confirm that Derek Mason is the leader of the Syndicate. Tell me where the drugs come in and how they are distributed. We'll give immunity."

Raekwon said, "I don't know a Derek whatever you said his last name was. But nobody I know talks to the police. Can you tell me the evidence against me?"

Daly replied, "I'm *trying* to help you. We have enough to lock up your whole crew and I guarantee you one of them will eventually talk. I'm just giving you the first crack at it. No pun intended."

Raekwon shrugged again. "I'm only concerned about me, so I need a lawyer. Thanks."

Daly said, "The best deal is sitting on the table now. Immunity for testimony."

Raekwon knew his rights so he said nothing else. Daly knew he was dealing with a seasoned criminal. The interrogation was over.

He stepped out of the room, closing the door. "No deal," he told the waiting Gallagher. Gallagher yanked the door open. "I'm going in to talk to this piece of shit."

Daly knew it was time to leave. He figured if the promotion was gone in the wind, so was he.

Gallagher stormed into the room. "Listen you motherfucker, you're going to tell me everything about the Syndicate and then maybe I would give you a deal if I like what I hear. I'm in charge, not you!"

Raekwon kept a straight face. In his younger years he would have had more to say with a lot of laughter. But Derek had taught him that this was all business—just shut up and wait for your lawyer to talk for you. Today he was following that advice. He felt in control of the situation.

Gallagher paced. If he didn't get any information from Raekwon, he didn't know what his next step would be but it would damn well be frustrating and embarrassing. Then Gallagher grabbed Raekwon by the neck and threw him to the floor. Handcuffed to the chair, his arms twisted and his wrist snapped with a crack. He was in pain but he didn't give Gallagher the satisfaction. Some uniforms rushed into the room when they heard the commotion. In true NYPD fashion they beat up Raekwon, who was lying on the floor.

Remembering Derek's lessons, he didn't resist. He didn't even ask for medical help. Gallagher stood there and said nothing. Ling observed it as well but said and did nothing.

#

As Shawn and Carla entered her apartment, Carla threw down her purse and keys and stormed into the kitchen. "I don't even know why I ask you to go with me to look at restaurants. I don't want to argue with you in front of that white woman again. Fuck."

Shawn said, "Is that why we're arguing now? I'm writing the check so I have a lot questions. Running a business is hard so location is very important. It's half the battle. That lady is going to tell you every location is great so it's up to us to do our own research."

Carla muttered, "Now you're fucking Gordon Ramsey."

But Carla knew what she was feeling was bigger than a spat about location. She believed that she was disrespecting her son by staying in her relationship. She wanted to stay with Shawn but only if he got out. She didn't know for sure if he was responsible for the little girl getting killed but she wanted no part of it. What she didn't know was the man sitting next to her on the couch had changed his mind. It had taken an old hustler like Steve to open his eyes. But now they were wide open. He was looking for an exit. He knew how the story was going to end with Derek. He would become kingpin number one but that wouldn't last long. Shawn couldn't rationalize seeing the bullet coming and not ducking. He owed it to his son and his girl.

She was done beating around the bush. "What happened last night?"

Shawn answered, "Business."

Carla snapped, "It's not normal to do business at four in the morning."

Shawn shrugged. "It's not normal to ask your man for $50,000."

Carla took a step back. "What? Fuck you."

He wasn't in the mood for her smart mouth so he said something slick. But he had gone too far.

"The norm is going to be you jerking off for a while."

Shawn said, "You're so childish sometimes."

Carla snapped, "Seep on the couch like an adult. Asshole."

Shawn was happy to get away from her mouth. Smiling all the way downstairs, he turned on Sports Center.

Chapter 35

JOURNEY

It was 5 AM and already Rob was on the road. He had had a great time with the family. After dinner the last night, they had sat and talked by a campfire. The kids roasted marshmallows while Laura and Rob cuddled. He had said good-bye to Laura this morning but he couldn't say it to the kids. Laura would do that when they woke up. His head was clear now. So he was ready to do what needed to be done without anyone influencing his decisions; Laura, Alex, or the Chief. He was going to do his job. He would arrest or kill the criminals his Unit was charged with taking down. He turned on the radio and put on the cruise control.

#

Derek was on the road. The radio was too loud for the morning but he needed it to go along with the thoughts in his head. His thoughts were violent and graphic. He was going to be King of New York no matter what it took. He thought it would be easy but if it wasn't bang, bang. His grandmother had told him that no matter what you do in this world you can always ask God for forgiveness. He was going to need it.

#

Kim was driving in circles. She was looking for an address and she couldn't find it. She had decided to drive to Union, South Carolina, and rent a room. She was originally going to settle in Charlotte but she was so paranoid she thought the extra sixty-six miles would make a difference. Andre had always told her paranoia was good. It was on her shoulder and she couldn't shake it. It would guide her through the next year.

Chapter 36

STANDING ROOM

Malik's head spun. Why was the judge apologizing to him? The courtroom was packed with reporters, family, bad guys, and a few clergy members. He saw his mother, but he didn't know who the gentleman was who was sitting with her. He just wanted to kiss his mother and then go the gym and then eat some home cooking. He was allowed to leave right away.

His mother greeted him with a hug and a kiss. "My baby. I'm so glad you're all right."

Malik said, "Hey, Mom."

Almost pushing Mrs. Sanders out of the way, the gentleman introduced himself. "Your unlawful arrest was filmed," Sleezer said. "And I'm the one who is going to sue the city upon your behalf for millions of dollars."

Malik knew the guy was full of shit. He wanted no part of him but they were rushed out of the courtroom together by reporters. Malik found himself out on the courtroom steps among waiting reporters for the scheduled news conference. Sleezer fixed his tie. His mother was in a dress, having been directed by Sleezer to do so. Sleezer stepped up to the mic.

"Malik's mother and I are glad that we were able to get him out of jail safely. Malik is not the kind of kid who should be locked up. Malik is in college and holds a full-time job. His mother has proudly told me that he has never been arrested or even gotten a speeding ticket. He is a good kid. We are going to sue the city for millions for what they have done. Ms. Sanders will say a few words now."

Nervously Malik's mother stood in front of the microphone. "I want to thank Attorney Sleezer for getting my son released before he was harmed in jail. He is a great kid. I have raised him alone and he has never given me any trouble. The police department is supposed to protect kids like him but instead they beat him up and arrested him. They will pay for this."

Malik couldn't believe that this was his mother. She was always so quiet. Maybe her baby being arrested was what it took for her to show this side. It was genuine but it was instigated by a crook. So he still was reluctant to be a part of this. Sleezer asked him if he wanted to speak. "The people will understand if you don't want too. This has been a crazy ordeal for you," he said in Malik's ear, hoping the kid would not want to. He didn't know what Malik would say and knew that the public would have more pity on him if they thought he was traumatized.

But Malik stepped up to the microphone and gazed out at the assembled reporters. "I'm meeting this man for the first time and I can tell you that he will not be representing me. I don't want money from the city. I want justice. I want the officers responsible for this to be terminated and arrested. What I want most is for these officers to be never again be able to do this to another citizen. Thank you."

Sleezer and his mother stared at him in shock. Malik grabbed his mother's hand and they headed for the subway. Sleezer escaped in his waiting limo. Everything was caught on live national T.V.

Finally, home with his mother, Malik explained to her how angry he was at how these officers treated him. His priority was to get them off the street so that they couldn't do this to anybody else. No money would enhance that. "I just want to finish school and become a journalist. I don't need this attention. It's not cool."

After a moment, his mother said, "I'm proud of you, Malik. Everything you're saying is what I should have said to that lawyer."

He hugged her. Malik said, "Don't worry about him. Nobody can come between us."

She shook her head. "I messed up. If anything, I should have let you talk to him before I agreed to let him represent you."

Malik replied, "Nobody was hurt. You didn't sign anything, did you?"

"No. He had papers for you sign today."

When he smiled she laughed. "The next time the cops beat you up," she teased, "I won't talk to any lawyers. I'll wait for you to make all of the decisions."

They laughed and hugged again

#

Shanika waited for Derek in Edgemere. He'd offered to pick her up and she had been startled but said okay—he didn't usually offer to do so. She made sure she was downstairs on time. He would be angry if he had to wait. Like a boss, he didn't like waiting for anything. Sometimes she tested him by being late or telling him what to do in the bedroom. But she knew it was a thin line.

When his Jeep pulled up, she hopped in. They kissed.

Shanika said, "Hey, baby. I missed you." He missed her but he would never say it. Against the rules of the hood. "You hungry?"

Shanika shrugged. "I can eat."

As he pulled into traffic, Derek said, "I'm going to stop by that Spanish spot to get some sandwiches."

Shanika nodded. "Popitos'. Okay. You remember how to get there?"

Derek said "Yes, but I know you can direct me the cab driver route."

They both laughed.

Shanika said, "Make a right at the next corner."

At Popitos, Derek asked Shanika what she wanted. She replied, "Same as you. And get one for Sheila."

He got out of the Jeep and walked toward the restaurant. A young lady was walking in as well so he held the door for her. He could feel

Shanika's eyes on him. She was always watching him around women. He let the young lady order first and then Derek ordered his three fried chicken sandwiches. He went over to the drink station and positioned himself so that when he returned to pick up his order, he could get a better angle of the girl. He noticed that she had a Metropolitan Authority Agency I.D. on her neck. She was beautiful. He decided to make small talk. He heard the slam of the Jeep's door. Shanika was heading into the restaurant, so he didn't have much time to make this young lady's acquaintance.

Derek asked, "What did you order?"

She looked around, making sure he was talking to her. "I got the grilled chicken with peppers. How about yourself?"

Derek replied, "I always get the fried chicken but now I might try your healthy one."

"I don't want to be healthy. I'd rather have the fried chicken."

They both laughed and then Derek introduced himself.

"Monique. Nice to meet you, Derek."

Derek said, "Nice to meet you. Enjoy."

Monique grabbed her sandwich just as Shanika entered the restaurant. Shanika gave her the death stare as she left. Monique paid her no mind. Ms. Tough, meet Ms. Tougher.

#

Nigel was taking his second shower of the day. All the other inmates got to shower four days out of the week. He took his time, enjoying the luxury. After Nigel was finished with his shower, he got to sit in the TV room alone except for his personal bodyguard, C.O. Brandon from Baisley Projects. Brandon had grown up with Shawn and was on the payroll. He and a few others were to take care of any inmates that Shawn asked them too. Nigel ate his Popeye's spicy three-piece dinner with French fries, washing it down with grape soda.

"Not as good as being at home," said   Brandon, "but this is about as good as it can get in this jungle."

Nigel leaned back and pushed away his cleaned chicken bones. Trevor didn't have this juice because he would never pay the money needed to do it. Trevor failed to see the bigger picture. If you don't take care of your people your empire will crumble.

Then the door swung open and he looked up and smiled. Dessert had arrived. C.O. Jackson walked into the T.V. room, shaking that ass, as C.O. Brandon walked out. Jackson was not on the payroll; she just liked fucking inmates and she'd been told to fuck this important person. Always the same routine. She pulled her pants down and bent over the table. Sixty seconds later it was over. Easy work for her. They didn't talk much. No kissing or touching. Back to work for her. Back to the cell for him.

He got the hood news every day, so he'd heard that the Latin Cartel and the Brooklyn Bullies were at war. He also heard that the Cartel was winning. It made things in the jail heated between the Latins and the African Americans. More than usual. There was no contact between him and the Syndicate. The lawyer wouldn't even tell him anything. All he had to do was wait. Which he did as a well-fed, clean, T.V.-watching inmate. He was even getting pussy. He couldn't wait to tell his cousin Greg; the street dudes wouldn't believe it.

#

Rob had watched the news conference with Malik and Sleezer. He had been very impressed with the young man. Most people were motivated by money. Especially young people. So to have that much integrity at that age was amazing and rare. Rob had been sued through the department and personally many times. He knew ambulance-chaser lawyers like Sleezer who prayed on poor people. Who could blame someone for suing if they were truly a victim? But mostly those lawyers exploited the situation and the victim. They could burn down the city with their rhetoric. Rob thought that officers were probably wrong. But it had been an isolated incident. No need to condemn the entire department. Discipline the two and get on with life.

He called Stella and Alex to meet him at the Bat Cave. He wanted to make sure that Dwayne was going to be okay. The arrest had been easy to void—the Chief had taken care of that. It helped that the officers had trumped up charges on him, so it looked like they were lying about all of it. Dwayne's cover hadn't been jeopardized—he was out and mixing in with the Syndicate. Everybody he was next to; their phones were now tapped. So the case on the Syndicate was proceeding. It was good news to tell Captain Gallagher.

Stella briefed them on the Raekwon arrest and what a disaster it was.

Rob shook his head. "Only good thing about it is it'll slow down Gallagher and let us work."

Alex said harshly. "He want results but doesn't know how to get them correctly. He doesn't understand investigations and he's too stubborn to listen and learn. The best bosses, like Teddy, just get out of the way and let their men work."

Stella then explained that the shootout in the alley was no doubt tied into the current war between the Latin Cartel and the Brooklyn Bullies, although she wasn't sure who started it. She outlined the battles, ticking them off on her fingers. The shooting at the juice bar had been a contract hit ordered by the Cartel. That killing had led to little Elizabeth being killed. The family killed at the Astoria Housing Projects was retaliation from the Brooklyn Bullies.

"Wiretaps?" asked Rob.

"On both crews," she answered. "Nothing from the Cartel but a lot of chatter from the Brooklyn Bullies."

Rob said thoughtfully. "War means less activity from both sides, so less evidence. The Syndicate will increase their activity and will be the only crew selling. So here's an opportunity to make some cases." He would take the Chief's advice: he didn't need probable cause to bring someone in. "We'll bring in Trevor to talk to him and maybe stop some bloodshed."

Alex said, "Those motherfuckers responsible for killing the two girls don't deserve a trial. They should be executed on sight."

Stella replied, "You're crazy."

Alex retorted, "Am I? Should the tax payers have to pay for their lawyers, room and board, and food? *That's* crazy. Rid society of their evil."

Rob said, "He's right. If you can prove they're guilty, why waste time." He dismissed them. "Keep me posted on anything new with the crews. If we need to pull Dwayne, let's do it right away. Let me clear any updates for Gallagher."

Stella nodded. "I won't speak to Gallagher without first speaking to you."

Alex said, "Hopefully Dwayne can find something quick. He's good at his job so the possibility is there."

As Stella was leaving, Rob said to her, "Oh, and do a full workup on a Malik Sanders. Thanks."

Stella asked, "Part of the Syndicate?"

Rob said, "No."

Stella knew enough not to ask him any more questions. "Okay. No problem." She gave both of them a kiss and she was off.

Alex and Rob sat down to talk.

Rob said, "I'm all in."

Alex peered closely at Rob. "As in *all* in?"

Rob said, "Yes, all in! Let's use all of our resources like the Chief said. I'm ready to arrest or kill. Whatever gets these animals off the street."

"That's what I needed to hear. Let's focus on the contract killers first. I can't sleep after what they did to those girls. Then after maybe you let me kill Captain Gallagher."

Rob gave him a warning glance. He didn't want to touch that. He knew Alex was serious about killing Gallagher. "Let's hunt."

Chapter 37

ACCOUNT-ABILITY

As Shanika and Derek entered the club, they saw Jocelyn and Shawn seated at the Syndicate table in the back. Derek headed toward them while Shanika went to check on the girls.

Derek sat and said, "What's good?"

Right away Shawn replied, "Raekwon got arrested."

Derek narrowed his eyes. "For what?"

Shawn spat, "Suspended license. But they lied and said it was for murder and sale of narcotics."

"And?" asked Derek.

"He didn't bite," Shawn answered. "He wouldn't even give his full name."

Derek said, "Never doubted his loyalty. NYPD just probably picking up niggas cause the little girl got shot."

Shawn nodded. "I was thinking the same. He should be out soon."

"We need somebody to make the deliveries," Derek told them.

Shawn said, "I'll do it."

Derek warned, "You gonna get your hands dirty."

Shawn waved off his objection. "Nobody else we can trust with something so important. I got it."

Derek replied, "Cool. We have to be careful with this war going on. We have to watch out for the cops and stray bullets. Jocelyn, you okay?"

Jocelyn nodded but said, "It's fucked up that Ray got arrested."

"It's part of the game," Derek replied, leaning back in his chair. This was new; she never showed any emotion or concern.

"I think we got a winner with Dwayne," Shawn said. "He's working well with Mike."

"Raekwon doesn't trust him," Jocelyn cut in.

Derek laughed. "He doesn't trust anybody."

Jocelyn grinned. "Not a bad way to be. Fewer mistakes that way."

"Cartel seems to be bringing it to Brooklyn," said Shawn.

"No surprise there," answered Derek. "Trevor is only built for the good times. How's Nigel doing?"

Shawn gave a thumbs-up but added, "He better be an earner cause his protection was costing us a lot."

Derek answered smoothly, "If we come out on top after this war, then it's all worth it. He pays for himself."

#

It was 5:45 AM and Francisco Santore was sitting in his living room recliner for the last time. He had on a black Adidas sweat suit and a black-striped Adidas shell top. He had an appointment to be arrested. Serious shit. Sale of Narcotics, Possession, Distribution, Racketeering, Money Laundering, Extortion, and Murder. The cops weren't going to bust down his door like they did Raekwon's. White murderers get arrested differently. Francisco had a rat in the department who told him when and who was going to arrest him. The agreement was he was going to walk out of his house at 6 AM and surrender. Even a minute later and they would knock down the door. Tough stuff.

Francisco had sent his wife and kids away to make it less painful and embarrassing for them. Also he wanted to do it as early as possible so the neighbors wouldn't see it. His lawyer was already at the precinct.

Once he and lawyer got all of the evidence then he would figure out what to do. The business would run without him. Everything but the drugs. Only Tony and he knew the connect. The other bosses wouldn't push the issue because drugs were forbidden. But they were the biggest money maker so everybody did it. Tony was already arrested but he couldn't contact Francisco so he didn't know what was going on with him.

For now, he had to worry about himself. Jail time was the easy part. He would have to worry about his own people sending killers after him if they believed he talked. And he worried about who would run the business for him. The next up was Phil. A complete idiot. He was full-blooded Italian and loyal but needed a level-headed guy beside him at all times because he had no common sense. He could destroy the families twenty-million-a-year business in just a few months, but if Francisco wasn't loyal to Phil it might cause a civil war. So Phil would be in charge.

All the family's money was frozen. A lot of guys were hurting. Francisco had money stashed away so that he could pay his lawyer. His wife and kids were also taken care of. If he was convicted, the plan was for her to move with the kids to Miami, where she had family.

Francisco watched the clock and shook his head. A fucking "Nerd" had taken down an Italian crime family. They had trusted him because he was a genius with money. He got greedy but guys like him don't do time. Witness Protection or suicide. When most people were presented with time, they take a shortcut out. They sign that paper quick. Facts. As for the connect, they couldn't go anywhere near drugs with the feds all over them. And handing off the connect to Derek was bad business. He could only hope that the Syndicate feared the Italians enough that he wouldn't move on his own. Unlikely. Drug dealers need drugs to sell. So they would find their own connect. The Italians would deal with that problem when the government was finished with them. But right now it was all about survival. Francisco sat in his recliner watching the clock. 5:59 AM.

#

Taking a shower, Nigel turned around and saw two Spanish dudes with shanks in their hands. He yelled for the Batten and grabbed for his towel—his only weapon. They rushed him. He did his best to hold them off, swinging his towel wildly, cursing himself for getting soft and careless.

He ran at one of them, surprising him enough to knock him down, then he felt a piercing pain in his back—he'd been stabbed. Through a blood-red haze he saw two more guys enter the shower area.

Nigel woke up in the infirmary, shocked to be alive. He didn't know what to do or say. He craned his neck and saw that the place was full of inmates, which made him even more nervous. He figured he had lost his protection and that because the guys were Spanish, the Cartel sent them. But it could have been Derek. The life of a rat, he knew. Who can you trust? Batten had clearly been offered more than what Derek and Shawn were paying him.

An inmate mopping the floor began to move toward Nigel's bed. Nigel tensed but was too weak to get away. He put up his hands defensively.

The inmate swirled the mop beside his bed and muttered, "Shawn sent me. You got stabbed by a Cartel member. You were saved by our people."

Nigel said, "What about the C.O.?"

Willie said, "He must have been paid off. I'll be watching you while you're in here."

Nigel nodded. "Thanks."

He was scared now. He would request to see his lawyer and if he was still representing him then he would know that Derek still had his back.

Chapter 38

REAL TALK

Captain Gallagher wanted to meet with Rob alone. He didn't want Alex or anybody else to influence him. They met at a diner. After their breakfast orders came, Gallagher said, "I'm sure you heard about the arrest the other night. We got some stuff off him but nothing major."

On guard, Rob merely replied, "Okay."

Gallagher continued, "This is coming from the top. We need some major arrests made soon or we don't exist anymore. Do you understand that?"

Rob kept his temper under control. "We can't rush on our end to make cases. We need time. I know the mayor wants to get reelected but that's not our concern. We do things a certain way."

Gallagher pointed his finger at him. "I don't give a fuck about how you normally do things. This isn't normal times. The city is under siege. We have to do something."

Rob stood up. He was not going to play this game.

Gallagher stood as well, blocking him from leaving. "If by next week your unit hasn't made an arrest I'm transferring you to Transit. You'll be back in uniform signing memo books with rotating RDOs."

Rob said nothing, sidestepping Gallagher to leave. Gallagher sat back down and finished his omelet.

#

Fat Boy was more than a little nauseated after delivering the body to Trevor's doorstep. He wanted to get back to making money and bagging bitches. He was relieved that he was all good with Louie because otherwise that would have meant death. He had been shot, lost his girl, robbed by another girl, and now war all within a few weeks. It was a crazy life and he was living it to the fullest.

He was supposed to go right back to the house. But he couldn't resist IHOP. Plus, who the fuck could he run into in an IHOP? As soon as he was seated he started checking out the waitresses to see if he could get a number. Nothing really there so he concentrated on breakfast. He got his usual; Three pancakes, three strips of bacon, three sausage patties, and three scrambled eggs. Strawberry syrup on everything. It was good. Just as he sat back with a sigh, pushing his empty plate away, he noticed Jay from the Brooklyn Bullies walking in with two other dudes he had never seen before.

Quickly he pulled his hood over his head and kept his head low. They sat down and didn't seem to notice him. The only problem was he had to walk by them to get out. Unarmed, he was naked. He waited. Sure enough one of the dudes went to the bathroom. He grabbed a knife from the table and followed him into the bathroom.

He pressed up against the guy with the knife. "Give me the gun."

The guy froze. "What?" he croaked.

Fat Boy said, "Give me the fucking gun." When the guy's hand whipped to the weapon in his waistband, he sunk the knife deeply into his back. The guy fell to the floor and Fat Boy pulled the gun from his fingers.

He exited the bathroom and ducked into the kitchen. He'd leave out a back door to avoid Jay. But Jay had heard the commotion in the bathroom so as Fat Boy exited the bathroom he had two motherfuckers coming at him quick. He pulled the Glock hoping they would stop. They didn't so he let off a few rounds.

With everyone in the restaurant screaming, Jay let him go. He was smart. He knew there were probably cameras on them so he didn't pull out. He went into the bathroom to check on his boy. He saw the red shirt and that he was alive. He hesitated but he could hear the sirens already. He had to make a decision to take him or leave him. All that blood would have been a trail for the police, so he bent down to his boy and told him to tell the police he was robbed. He and the other guy left through the kitchen—no one followed.

#

Standing in front of Malik's door, Rob knew what he wanted to say. He just couldn't predict what the response would be. He knocked on the door. Malik answered. Right away Malik knew the man in front of him was a cop. He just didn't know why he was here.

Malik politely said, "How can I help you?"

Rob introduced himself and asked for a minute of his time.

Malik asked, "Is this about my arrest?"

"No. This is about you."

Thrown by the answer, Malik paused. "What about me?" he asked. "You don't know me."

Rob asked, "Can we talk outside?"

Malik looked behind him and saw his mother sleeping peacefully on the couch. There was something about this NYPD lieutenant that he trusted. He nodded and they walked downstairs together. They sat on the building steps.

Malik said, "What's up, Mr. Grey?"

Rob said, "You're right that I don't know you. But hearing you speak at the news conference allowed me to witness a lot. You displayed more integrity and character than anybody I have ever met. Your only agenda was justice. That lawyer of yours could have gotten you a few million dollars. Yet you walked away from that without much thought. You didn't tweet or use any Instagram to cash in on the fame. That's just not normal for a millennial."

Malik sat up straighter. "I really just want those officers terminated so that no one else will ever have to feel what I felt when they assaulted and then unjustly arrested me. They deserve to be arrested."

Rob held up a hand. "I actually don't care about them. It's you that I care about. Only a person like you can really rid the world of that kind of hate. So I'm not going to fight them. I'm going to build you."

Malik blinked. "Build me? What the fuck are you talking about? My mother and father built me."

Rob said calmly, "I'm only saying that most people fight evil. I have done enough of that. I want to build positive human beings to be able truly fight evil."

Malik shook his head. "I'm lost."

Taking another tack, Rob asked, "What are you studying in college?"

Malik promptly answered, "Journalism. I want to write for the *New York Times*."

Rob nodded slowly. "That would be a great career. Why do you want to be a writer?"

"I want to communicate to people. Tell them what is going on in the world."

"That sounds great," said Rob after a pause.

Malik watched him closely. "But?"

Rob took a breath and plunged in. "When I watched you on TV, I saw a man who could create change in the world. Change for the better. Now you can do that through journalism but you would eventually be censored. I can offer you a position that will never be compromised. You will be able to change the city and the world by your actions."

Malik asked, "What's the position?" "A NYC Police Officer."

Malik laughed. "That wasn't your average recruitment speech. I think you might have oversold it. A bit." Then Malik turned serious. "Cops have to listen to their supervisors and if that supervisor is evil in any way that evil is now perpetrated through all of those officers. If you don't believe in the mission, you can't create any change."

Rob nodded. "Good points. There is no greater sacrifice than your life. If you are willing to risk your life for your fellow citizens, there is no evil in that."

Malik said, "Agreed."

Rob continued. "You are an intelligent, charismatic young man. You will never be a follower. You led when you walked away from that lawyer. I want you to join the department because you will be an asset the minute you were sworn in. Shit, you already have made the department better because those two knuckleheads were exposed."

Malik looked down for a moment then up at the lieutenant. "Why me, Mr. Grey?"

Rob looked him right in the eyes. "I want to send you away for the best training in the world. I never want you to act and think like you're the average street cop. The training you will get will put you at an advantage amongst your peers. This will allow you investigate and arrest anybody that is committing a crime—cop or civilian. The reason why I think you can do this with ease is because your integrity and character are real and I don't think it will ever be compromised."

Malik said, "Wow. You have said a lot."

"Listen," Rob continued. "I want to be completely honest. I've done some things I'm not proud of and I'm about to do some more. I sincerely want to put you in a position to change the department and the city. You will have to put your trust in me because I can't tell you a lot about the training and what you will be doing after it. If you make it through the training, you will be paired with a person quite like you." He wanted to tell Malik about Alison Hale but he stopped—Malik would get to know her soon enough. "I know you and her will work great together. What do you think?"

"So," Malik said slowly, "I guess I won't be working overnight walking on Martin Luther Boulevard in any borough in the city?" They both laughed.

Rob said, "With this training, you will be investigating real crimes right away."

Suddenly doubtful, Malik said, "I don't know if I'm even worthy of that."

Rob said, "After what happened to you and your reaction, you have earned it. Just don't change."

Malik said, "This was a lot to think about. Do I have some time to think on it?"

Rob shook his head. "My sins are catching up to me. You'll have to leave soon."

"Your sins?"

Rob continued, "There is no negative here. If you fail out or don't like it, then you go back to being a journalist. If you accept, you will not be writing about people who change the world—you will be that person."

"How will I know what to do and where to go?"

Rob said briskly, "You'll be leaving within the next forty-eight hours. You'll face someone I respect. Answer his questions truthfully and you'll be all right. We good?"

Malik paused and then said, "Yes."

Rob stood up and shook hands with the young man. "We won't talk again until you've finished your training."

Malik said only, "Damn, Mr. Grey."

#

Ms. Homes said, "So, what do you think?"

Shawn had on his poker face. He wanted to buy the brownstone but he was trying to act like he had a lot of other options. The great thing was Ms. Homes was fine. They had chemistry.

Shawn said, "It's okay but for 1.5 million I don't know. I think it's more around 1 million. There's no land and it needs a major renovation.

Ms. Homes said, "This was prime real estate. It's a corner property and the renovation would be cosmetic. The structure is great. New roof and finished basement."

Shawn asked, "If I was buying right now how low could you go?"

"I probably could go to 1.3."

Shawn countered with, "If you go down to 1.3 million, I'll buy right now."

Ms. Homes said smoothly, "I would have to check. Give me a sec." She took a walk down the hallway to get some privacy as she called the owner, which gave Shawn time to visualize his family living and running a business here. He could see Carla in the kitchen working her magic. The restaurant full of happy people enjoying her food. They could live above the restaurant. It even had backyard space so he could barbecue. Or Carla could barbecue.

But Ms. Homes was walking back. "How much money would you be putting down and what bank are you using for finance?"

Shawn said, "I'd be paying cash."

Even the professional Ms. Homes seemed fazed by that. "Wow. Okay. Give me a second."

As she walked away again, Shawn went back to daydreaming. He wanted another kid so he pictured his young daughter chasing her older brother around the house. Then he stopped with a jolt. He had been thinking about being out of the game more and more often. Maybe it was time.

Ms. Homes touched him on his shoulder. "Let's have a seat in the den."

As they sat on the couch, Shawn said, "Talk to me."

Ms. Homes replied, "What would you say if I told you that I could get them down to $900,000 for the house and a $100,000 tip for me?"

Shawn laughed, "I would say you can take the girl out of the hood."

She smiled. "So?"

He could afford it and he didn't mind giving a sister a payout. She was still saving him $300K. He respected her directness, gangster. But no one rides for free! Instead of answering directly, Shawn leaned back casually on the couch. "So where you from?"

Ms. Homes answered, "Grant Projects in Harlem. How bout you?"

"Southside Jamaica," he said. "So that's where the street smarts come from. What would you say if I told you I wanted to fuck you in that dress on this couch?"

Ms. Homes looked him straight in the eyes. "I would be flattered."

Shawn held up one hand. "I'm buying this for my family. Just so there's no confusion."

Taking off her glasses, Ms. Homes purred, "Understood."

He reached over and unbuttoned her shirt and started sucking on her breast. She moaned as he sucked her nipple. Her hand went straight to his dick. She took it out and stroked it. He slipped his finger through her panties and could feel how wet she was. He turned her around and lifted up her dress. He moved her panties to the side and entered her. He fucked her doggy style till she came and then so did he. The deal was done.

Chapter 39

COUNTER

The rain was coming down like it had an intended target. The religious would say the heavens were crying. Today was Cedella's funeral. The church had just twenty people mostly watching Cedella's mother, Tonia, weep inconsolably. Then, when Trevor walked in with an entourage, rage eclipsed her sorrow. Her daughter's death was Trevor's fault. She watched as Trevor made the rounds hugging and kissing everybody. With an entourage for protection, along with Cecil, his armed bodyguard, he brought everything that caused her daughter's senseless death to her funeral. When Trevor reached out to hug Tonia she attacked him. She punched and kicked him until people pulled her off.

Tonia hissed, "You fucking Blood Clot motherfucker. There is blood on your hands."

Trevor grabbed her. "What the fuck are you talking about?"

"*You* are responsible for my baby's death. *You* know your blood clot business."

Trevor clenched his fist, about to strike her. "My blood clot business pays for your house and food. Fuck you." Then Cecil pulled him away, saying in Trevor's ear, "Relax, boss man. Let her vent."

Cecil made Trevor sit a few pews behind his sister so that she would calm down. Detective Shaw waited for them to sit and then took a pew behind them. From the decoy unit, he was of Jamaican decent and he spoke patois. He was wearing a dashiki with the Jamaican flag colors, green, black, and yellow. He fit right in. No one gave him a second look.

But people were looking at Trevor. Embarrassed and furious, Trevor felt not only was he losing the war but his sister was blaming him. He needed a win.

He leaned over and whispered into Cecil's ear, "We need to kill some of their people soon. They killed my niece and Cazembe."

Cecil murmured back, "I'll handle it myself, boss. We'll hunt tonight until we find one of them."

Trevor said through gritted teeth, "Two or three of them. They didn't disappear off the face of the earth."

Cecil nodded. "I'll be on it."

Trevor looked at the casket. "I want you to take care of this shit right now. I'll ride with my uncle to the burial."

Feeling alarmed, Cecil advised, "Boss, let me at least get you home safe and then I'll take care of business for you."

Trevor shook off his hand. "I'm good. I need you to kill some Puerto Ricans."

Cecil said softly, "Okay, boss man."

After the funeral, Cecil and a few of his guys left. Detective Shaw had heard the conversation so he had an undercover car follow them.

Trevor hugged and kissed his sister. Weeping, she didn't have the energy to fight him. He murmured into her ear, "I'm sorry, baby girl. I wish it had been me."

Tonia looked straight into his eyes. "I wish it had been you too."

#

The long funeral procession pulled up to the church. A large crowd had already gathered outside, with police barricades controlling the news media. Ms. O'Sullivan stepped out of the limo with the help of her brother Connor. Her numerous family members pushed to come close to her. Her mother and father were too poor to travel from Ireland to New York. But they would get their chance to say goodbye to their only grandchild because Elizabeth was taking her daughter home to be buried with her younger brother. A member of the Irish Republican Army, her younger brother Aedan had been killed by British troops in 1983. A hero to the family.

The mayor and police commissioner were present along with both senators, and many city council members against a backdrop of hundreds of New Yorkers who had been touched by the tragedy. Cardinal Dolan was performing the service. It was a star-studded event. Standing room only. News cameras were allowed in the back of the church. Security was everywhere. There were snipers on the roof and helicopter flyovers. The hour-long traditional Protestant service was a beautiful service deserved by little Elizabeth, but no one mentioned young Cedella. It was a divided city.

#

Derek moved as if he was being followed. He borrowed a car from one of his soldiers and was soon in Far Rockaway, constantly checking his rearview mirror. He was looking for the girl he met in the deli. Because of the MTA badge around her neck, he figured she worked at the train station at Beach 44 Street and Frank Avenue. He descended the steps with a bounce and a smile on his face. His face got poker-face serious when he saw Monique in the token booth. He wasn't sure she remembered him.

But she smiled when he appeared in front of her.

Derek said, "Hi, my name is Derek, I'm from Queens."

She laughed. "LL Cool J. I remember you, Derek from Queens. How can I help you?"

"I need your number so we can arrange a good time for dinner. Please."

Monique answered, "I don't give my number out to strangers. But I'll take yours."

He hung his head. "Well, I don't carry a phone."

"I guess arranging dinner is impossible," she said briskly. "That sucks."

Derek said, "Where there is a will there is a way. You should write your number down for me and I'll text you a time and place."

She smiled but shook her head.

Derek pleaded, "Listen I'm just trying to get to know you. There has to be more than just your beauty. Give a brother a chance."

Monique hesitated then replied, "Tell you what. Let's figure out a time and place now and then we'll meet there."

Derek almost broke his poker face with a smile. "That'll work. What are your days off?"

Monique said, "I'm not going to tell you my schedule, but I will say Thursday is good for any time after 6 PM."

"You're too much. What's your favorite type of food?"

Monique said, "Besides Chipotle, Thai."

"Holy Basil on Austin street at 7:30 PM. Cool?"

She nodded.

"Aren't you gonna write it down?"

Monique answered airily, "I got it."

Derek said, "See you then!" But he walked away with no confidence. She should have at least written it down to make it look good. But he would show up at the restaurant anyway.

#

Rob had just got off the phone with Stella. She had told him that Malik Sanders was completely clean. Nothing. That was great news. He walked into the Chief's office for the first time without being nervous.

The Chief said, "What's up, brother?"

Rob said, "Alex and I were about to get to work. Just wanted to let you know that I thought about what you said and the power and training I was given. I'm ready to utilize it."

The Chief nodded. "Good to hear. It's hard to get out of that police officer state of mind. You were put in a unit with awesome power and training. It's easy to justify interrogations and murder. It's little things like summons that turn into arrests that get you in trouble. There is a narrative for using physical and deadly force. So don't be afraid to use it."

Rob said, "I got it. Speaking of thinking like a police officer, I want to put a young man through the Farm training straight off the street."

The Chief waited, listening.

Rob continued, "I want to swear him in as a NYPD officer and then send him straight to CIA training. I think he would be able to get along with Allison to really make an impact in the department. He won't have to worry about forgetting any military or police training or bad habits. He could just hit the streets running."

The Chief looked skeptical. "Hopefully he has some streets smarts to make up for the lack of local training?"

Rob nodded. "He'll be able to blend in and I think be a great officer. He'll be able to arrest anybody, perpetrator or corrupt officer. This mold could change everything. It's a big risk but I feel he is worth it. He's a rare talent."

"Have him train with Alison Hale. That way they will build a rapport. We will also have to keep his lack of training a secret as well. Is it possible to hide his last name?"

"That isn't a problem. Give me his information. Let me talk to him." Rob had Malik's information ready for the Chief and handed over the folder. He hesitated. "We might not be talking for a while because Alex and I are planning on getting to work soon. So just know that I respect and appreciate you."

Chief said, "I feel the same."

Another hesitation and then, as awkward as it was, Rob leaned in and hugged him.

#

Driving to the precinct, Alison wished she had eaten more at breakfast. But the image of her mother praying on her knees for her that morning had made her upset. She had gone over her parents' house to tell them that she was going away to training for the next six months. "Will you be able to come home on the weekends?" her mother asked. "Are you in trouble?" her father asked. "Is this remedial in any way?"

Allison said, "No, no. I do what the department tells me so I have to go."

Her father had persisted. "Why is this so shady? It's like you're in the CIA. This is the NYPD and you can't tell me what kind of training it is and where?"

Allison said regretfully, "Sorry, Dad. I'm just following orders. You understand. You were in the military."

He insisted, "But you're not in the military. You're in a local police department."

Allison looked up. "The best police department in the world."

At last he relented. "Well, at least you won't be on the street. So it isn't so bad."

Allison's mother patted her hand. "You make sure to call us as soon as you can."

Allison said, "Of course, Mom. I will."

"Prayer will make me feel better about this." Mrs. Hale got on her knees and prayed until it was time for Alison to leave. She kissed both of them. She couldn't wait to get out of there. She hated lying to her parents.

She drove to the precinct—there was just one last thing that Alison needed to do before she left. At the desk, she asked for Officer Cotten. The desk officer said he was in the break room. Of course he was in there eating Chinese food. When she walked in, he put on a fake smile. "How you been? How's your hand?"

Alison said, "I'm all good, no issues. How about you?"

Officer Cotten nodded. "I'm good. Just trying to make it off probation."

Curious, Alison asked, "What do they have you doing?"

He replied, "Transport truck. It's a pretty good gig. No complaints."

Wryly, she said. "Anything is better than foot patrol. They have me doing clerical work since I got injured."

Cotten looked away and cleared his throat. "What do I owe this visit?"

She sat opposite him at the table. "I just wanted to ask you a question about the day we had the shooting."

He nodded. "Shoot."

She could feel the table start vibrating—his legs were shaking. Alison said, "Interesting choice of words. I'm still confused as to how I got to the shooter before you did. Maybe I'm missing something."

Cotten answered nervously, "I went the wrong way so I think that's how you encountered him first."

"It wouldn't matter which way you went," she said slowly, staring hard at him, "if the shooter was on that same street. You would see him no matter what."

He gathered up his lunch without looking at her. "I never saw him because if I did I would have killed that motherfucker. It's better that you got there first. Trust me on that. I do wish I saw him first because that would mean you never got hurt. It still bothers me. Trust me on that."

Alison knew he was lying. She stood up. "Be safe out there."

Cotten said, "You too."

She stepped away from his hug and left. She would have accepted

"I fucked up" or I'm sorry." But not a lie. He would be exposed soon. Hopefully before he got someone else hurt or even killed.

\#

The Chief asked, "So, what is important to you in life?"

"My mother," Malik said, "and my health and integrity. I think my integrity reflects my health."

The Chief asked, "Do you find it hard maintaining your integrity? Is it a daily struggle?"

Malik shook his head. "Not at all. It is habit. I'm not a religious person but I do pride myself on being a good human being. But it is not difficult. Eating healthy is difficult and running is difficult."

Malik started to laugh until he saw the Chief wasn't. The Chief did find it funny but he was working. Doing the thing he loved most. Interrogating.

The Chief leaned forward. "Would you die for your country?"

Malik took a moment. "Honestly, I don't look at that way. If I were to die while I was working, I think I'd be dying to save a fellow human being. So I would be all right with that. Best believe though, I would do everything to avoid it."

The Chief couldn't believe the realness coming from this young man. He was used to standard answers from recruits. He liked Malik. "What does patriotism mean to you?"

Malik stated, "If you're a good human being, it fits into patriotism. You are doing for your city and country through your positive actions. It might sound corny but people like that make the world a better place to live in."

"What does it mean to you to be black or African American?"

Without hesitation, Malik replied, "I'm extremely proud to be African American. I read a lot about my history as well. From Africa to the slave experience in America. It means I come from a great ancestry that started civilization. It's an honor, not a burden."

"What do you do when you are faced with racism?"

"I respond to it," said Malik levelly. "But I don't overreact. Watch me on TV."

The Chief nodded. "Checkmate. Do you think you can survive in this world of law enforcement? You aren't choosing it; you have been chosen so the commitment might not be there. I've seen stronger men than you cower."

Malik replied slowly, "I visualized it when Rob discussed with me and I think I can do it."

Chief said, "I think so too. Be ready to go away for training. It should happen in a few days. It's usually on a Saturday morning around 11 AM."

Understanding that he was dismissed, Malik stood. "Thank you for your time, sir."

The Chief stood as well and extended his hand. "The pleasure was all mine. Be safe."

They shook hands and Malik was off. The Chief really liked him and he saw Rob's vision. He also thought that Rob was about to get his own hands dirty with the training he was taught at the Farm. Malik and Alison would be his redemption.

Chapter 40

THE FOUNDATION

Derek was at the bar trying to play it cool. As usual he had a seat against the wall so he could see all who entered. He planned to wait for Monique until 8 P.M. Drinking Coconut Cîroc, he wanted to get nice, not drunk, just in case she showed up. Derek never drank but tonight his nerves were jangling. He didn't think she was going to show up. He never felt like this before.

His eye caught a flash of red and then he recognized her beautiful face. She had a natural beauty that needed no makeup. She was wearing a stunning red dress with red stilettos. She caught his eye but waited for him to approach. He glided over.

Derek said, "Hey, beautiful. It's good to see you."

Monique replied, "Hey. It's good to see you as well."

"I really didn't know if you were going to show up."

"How long were you going to wait?" Monique asked.

He shrugged. "If you weren't here at 7:31 I was out."

They smiled at each other.

Then Monique said, "I thought about waiting outside until I saw you leave. Then I was going to pop up. Like, where you going?"

Derek laughed. "Oh, so you do have a sense of humor. You seemed so serious when I met you. I like."

She smiled. "Yeah, intelligent, beautiful, and funny. Just some of my attributes."

"And humble too," he replied. They both laughed. Derek put his hand on her waist and they headed towards their table.

Derek added, "Hopefully you're hungry too because the food here is great."

Monique said, "Momma is always hungry. I worked today and I didn't have time for lunch."

"Sounds right. You had to get ready for me."

She tossed her head. "Something like that. This hair takes forever."

Appreciatively, Derek looked her up and down, "It looks great."

The waitress hovered over their table. "Good evening. May I start you with something to drink?"

Derek said, "Would you allow me to order for us. This is my spot so I can match everything up for a perfect meal."

Monique eyed him with a smile. "Taking control. Okay." She had never let a man order for her before but his confidence made her curious. What he described made her mouth water.

"We'll take a bottle of Rose Champagne," said Derek. For appetizers we'll take vegetable dumplings and crispy tuna sashimi roll edamame. For dinner we will have soy ginger glazed salmon with udon noodles and spinach. Also we'll have the roasted Thai Buddha chicken."

The waitress asked, "Any sides?"

Derek said, "Yes, we will have the Asian green stir fry. Thank you."

The waitress replied, "Very good. Everything blends well. I'll be right back with your bottle of Champagne." As she left, she winked at Monique. Monique smiled back. Derek was feeling right.

Monique said, "You did good because I don't eat beef or pork."

"Momma is healthy too."

They laughed.

Derek added, "I won't say I don't eat pork but if I'm at a barbecue, I'm eating me some ribs. As for beef I will have a steak once and awhile. I try and eat healthy myself."

Monique eyed him critically. "You look healthy."

Derek asked, "So how long you been working for the MTA?"

"Almost ten years," she answered. "It's a cool job with a pension."

He replied, "I ain't mad at you. It seems cool, but I wouldn't want to be stuck in that box all day. How's that?"

Shrugging, she answered, "I don't like it but you get used to it."

"Any kids?"

Monique laughed. "The interview has officially started. I have a daughter. Malaysia. She's seven. What about you?"

"Two boys and a girl. Derek, Michael, and Catherine."

Monique said, "Nice. That sounds like a lot. I have a hard time with just my daughter. That's why I work midday. Lucky for me my mother helps me. I couldn't do it without her."

"I have my grandmother to help me. I definitely couldn't do it without her. She is a better parent than me. She is a saint."

Monique patted his arm. "Don't say that. As long as you are doing the best you can. I think kids see that. They're very smart."

Derek shook his head. "I come from such a fucked-up childhood it's intimidating being a father. I don't want to be like my parents . . . or should I say parent."

She gazed at him. "I'm assuming your father wasn't around. So if that's the case you are already a better parent because you are there for your kids. That says a lot about you."

Derek said, "I guess."

Monique leaned forward. "There's no guide to parenting. I just took out the bad stuff from my parents, kept the good stuff, and added my own stuff."

Nodding approvingly, Derek said, "So what happened to your baby daddy?"

"Serving a life sentence in federal prison."

"Damn. For what? Gotta be murder."

Lightly but with an underlying sadness, she answered, "For murder and drug trafficking."

Derek asked his name, although he already knew it. You make the Hood news for a life sentence.

"Mohammad Asan. You heard of him?"

He nodded. "A street legend. He was from Brooklyn, right?" Derek had known him vaguely. He had still been small time when Larry was running the streets, about eleven years ago. Derek chose his people wisely just because of what happened to him. Smart guys always learn from other street dude's mistakes.

The waitress brought over the appetizers. At Monique's suggestion they talked about more positive things. Derek learned that her favorite color was red and her favorite rapper was 50 Cent. They shared a favorite TV show in *Martin*. That she loved the Knicks. And her inspiration was Malcolm X.

Derek found it so easy to tell her about himself. He had never felt this way before. He liked Grand Puba but he thought Jay Z was the best. His favorite color was green. The inspiration in his life was his grandmother and kids.

As they ate, Derek said, "I really like you and I hope we can keep in touch."

Monique gave him a glowing look. "I guess since you don't have a phone, I'll give you my number." As they chuckled, she asked, "Why don't you have a phone?"

Derek shrugged as he lied glibly. "No one pays attention to each other anymore. It's just rude. So I'd rather not participate in society's new trend."

Monique, "Okay. You know, I don't even know your last name?"

Derek said shortly, "Mason."

"What do you do for a living, Mr. Mason?"

More lies. "I buy homes and then sell them for profit. Not exciting but it pays the bills."

The waitress brought over the main course.

"Anytime you're the boss it's a good thing," Monique said. "I wish I could do that and spend more time with my daughter."

Derek winked at her. "Maybe we can be partners."

She smiled. They finished dinner and Derek gave her a ride home. Derek usually didn't talk much to anybody. Shawn knew him best and that's who he talked to the most but even that was limited. So this was new. He found it easy to talk to Monique, and he liked it. Most females questioned him to see what they could get out of him. Not Monique. He drove slowly because he was enjoying her presence, and he could tell the feeling was mutual. As he pulled up in front of her place, he hugged her and asked if she wanted him to walk her upstairs. She told him no. They agreed to see each other again soon.

#

Raekwon was a free man. He spent a week in jail for a suspended license then he hit the streets running. All he wanted to do was see Jocelyn. She couldn't wait to see him as well. She picked him up from Queens central booking. She was a little late because she didn't know what to wear. She settled on a black skirt, black shirt, and black stilettos. When she finally pulled up, his eyes went wide. He'd only seen her in jeans and Jordan's. She got out of the car and they kissed. The other newly released inmates gazed at them with envy.

Jocelyn asked, "Are you okay?"

Raekwon reassured her, "I'm fine. Easy time."

"There is no such thing," she insisted. "Anything can happen at any time. I'm just glad you're all right."

Raekwon said, "Being in the Syndicate means a lot in there. I had no problems."

"With a war going on," Jocelyn admitted, "I was worried. Because what happens in the street carries over to the jail."

Raekwon replied, "True. I was fine. I appreciate your concern."

They were at an intersection. She glanced over at him. "You hungry or do you want to go home?"

Raekwon leaned back and stared at her up and down appreciatively. "Let's get some food to go because I can't control myself seeing you in that skirt."

Jocelyn said with smile, "Take-out it is."

Chapter 41

BLOOD HOUND

Trevor needed a win. With Cecil in his Suburban driving through the Latin Cartel territory were his own people, Mark and Tiny. They were hunting like blood hounds. They circled the block a few times without seeing any of the Cartel until they saw four young Spanish dudes drinking beer, talking loud, and listening to music. They would be Plan B.

But those same Spanish dudes had watched them circle the block a few times. They knew about the war so they were on alert. Small-time hustlers, they were in the game. While the Suburban had crossed a street out of view, they had loaded up their weapons and were waiting for something to happen. They placed them in the wheel barrel of the car.

Cecil told Mark to pull over. "We were going to hit the boys on the corner."

Mark said, "Are they part of the Latin Cartel?"

Cecil said, "At this point it doesn't matter. Tiny, you get out here and walk up the block. Stay out of sight and if anybody runs shoot 'em. We'll meet you around the corner. Cut through the middle of the block."

Tiny nodded and got out of the truck. Cecil sat in the back on the driver's side.

Mark asked, "You ready?"

"Remember, don't speed off," said Cecil. "Drive smooth."

"Game time," said Mark. But when they turned the corner, their prey started shooting. Mark slammed his foot on the accelerator and sped away, with Cecil getting off a few rounds, hitting two people. One dead, one wounded. The coward out of the crew that ran was met by Tiny. All five-foot-five of him. Tiny shot him right in the chest twice. Tiny tucked the gun in his waist and started to run. He followed Cecil's directions and cut through the block and was blocked by a fence. He scrambled over it and dropped, and then felt the gun slip down his pants. He grabbed at it and heard the bang as he felt a searing pain in his thigh. He made it to the truck but he was bleeding bad.

Tiny groaned, "I'm hit."

Cecil looked down at bloody leg. "I got you. We're taking you to the Hood doctor. Just hold tight. Mark, now you can speed."

Cecil was pissed at Mark but now wasn't the time to address it. Cecil was most upset about not knowing how many he'd hit of the corner boys and how bad he'd got them.

In front of the Hood doctor's office, Cecil sent the text and they were soon met by the big white guy. Mark wasn't allowed in. The big guy searched both of them and then the Russian lady appeared.

"It'll be ten thousand to see the doctor."

Tiny, groaning and in pain, winced at the amount of money, but Cecil peeled the bills off from his roll and handed it over. He was paying for his freedom because if Tiny went to the hospital and the detectives questioned him, he might talk. So ten grand was worth it. They were told they had to wait, the doctor was seeing another patient.

Cecil shouted, "More serious than this?"

The Russian lady didn't bat an eye. "The same. Sit."

When the patient came out of the doctor's office, they recognized one of the Spanish dudes from the corner. He was in bad shape, helped by one of his boys. It took a second but the corner dudes recognized them too. They watched one another warily but no one did anything. They were all just trying to save their homies.

Cecil helped Tiny into the next room, and the doctor was at his desk drinking whiskey. He smiled at them. "The streets were busy tonight. You will be easier than my last patient."

The doctor cut his pant leg off and then he went to work. Cecil left in haste as Tiny passed out. The doctor took his clamps and felt around for the bullet in Tiny's thigh. He found it and pulled it out. The pain woke Tiny up, and he screamed in agony. The doctor then sewed him up and cleaned the wound. He shot him up with morphine and gave him some oxycodone for later. Tiny was semi-conscious but he knew he was going to live. Cecil was called into the office to get him.

Mark drove them to one of Cecil's people and dropped off Tiny so the police couldn't get to him. Then they went to see Trevor, who was staying at the Hilton in Brooklyn under his real name. They went straight up to his room. He had two guys outside of the room and men across the hall.

Without asking about Tiny, Trevor said, "What do you have for me?"

Cecil answered confidently, "We killed one and wounded another."

"They were Latin Cartel?"

Cecil said, "Yes. I recognized them."

Mark shifted uneasily, but all he wanted was to get paid.

"Good," said Trevor. "I want these motherfuckers to know we aint't no pussies. They can't fuck with the Brooklyn Bullies. We need to hit them again. Maybe take out a lieutenant."

Cecil had a bad feeling about this. "Most of them are in hiding," he said. "I think we should hire some outside professional help."

Trevor snorted, "Let some of these young boys prove themselves."

Cecil knew there was no arguing with the boss. "Okay. I'm on it," he replied.

#

Shawn's love for his family couldn't surpass crew love. He would never leave the game, so Carla had to leave him. Carla decided not to pack but to go right over to her mother's house and pick up her son and go. She didn't want to have any type of physical altercation with Shawn. She was going to leave like Kim did and then call him. She would always let Shawn see his son, as long as there was no drama. She just wanted to separate herself and their kid for a while to let him know how serious she was.

She stepped outside and saw his truck. Slowly, feeling nervous, she approached. Carla said warily, "This is a pleasant surprise."

"Just wanted to take my lady out," Shawn said casually. "Little man with your mother?"

Carla nodded. "Where are we going?" Shawn said, "There was a new restaurant in Harlem I heard about so I wanted to take you there. Like a soul Thai fusion. I just heard it's off the chain."

Carla said, "That sounds crazy. I guess I'll hold my thoughts on that and give it a shot."

Shawn turned up the music which meant he didn't want to talk. That got her upset and sent her thoughts back to leaving him. When they pulled up to an Ethiopian restaurant on 125 Street and Malcolm X Boulevard and parked, Carla started a slow burn. They both got out and he started walking fast. She trailed him a little bit and was about to walk away when he turned to her.

"I forgot where the restaurant was exactly. I should have written it down."

Carla snarled, "Ya think."

Shawn sighed. "I wish we could just eat at your restaurant every day. You're the best cook I know—don't tell my mother I said that, I would deny it!"

Carla said, "We can't do that because you got your head up Derek's ass. You could just give me the money but you act like I'm a gold digger and it's a scam."

Shawn stared at her, "Damn. You fucking up the mood."

Carla rolled her eyes. "The mood. You got a lot to learn."

Shawn pointed at the brownstone on the corner. "What would you say if I said we should open up a restaurant here?"

She looked around. "In Harlem?"

"Right here. Right here in this brownstone."

Carla started to tremble. "Don't play with me."

Shawn said, "The realtor gave me the keys. Let's take a look and see how you like it."

Speechless, Carla followed him up the steps. He opened the door and let her enter first. "Take your time and walk around."

"It's beautiful," Carla breathed. "It still has the original wood and stained glass windows." As she walked around, she visualized the kitchen on the second floor and the seating on the first. She knew where she'd put the bathrooms. She took a look at the backyard. It had a brand new deck. She loved it.

Shawn said, "I think we should live on the third floor."

Carla heard him but it took a second to process. "You would move out of Queens?"

Shawn said, "I would think about it."

Carla shook her head. "Never thought I hear you say that. How much do they want for this place? It has to be two million. You gotta let me help you negotiate."

Shawn said, "It's already done." He handed her the keys.

She cried and hugged him tight. "I love you. Thank you so much."

"I love you too."

Carla said, "This is for our family. This is fantastic. We are going to have to do major renovations and hire a staff. This is crazy. I need a drink."

Shawn went over to the refrigerator and took out a bottle of Champagne and two chilled glasses. Carla almost fainted. "You thought of everything."

Shawn said, "This was what I do." As they laughed he poured them each a glass. They toasted.

Carla said, "Here is to our family's future. I look forward to spending the rest of my life with you. We legal!"

They kissed.

#

The countdown had begun. Alison unpacked her clothes and took inventory. Maybe she had packed too much. Would she need a dress to go out in? It might be misunderstood if she brought leisure clothes. A decision had to made in the next ten minutes. Her ride was going to be there in ten minutes. She didn't want to be late for her first day with the agency. Leisure clothes out. If need be she would buy them. Two business suits, three sweat suits, shorts, socks, and underwear. She was nervous but ready. She repacked and went downstairs to wait for her pick-up. She didn't know what to expect. No one had told her anything, which she suspected was mind games. She had some egg whites, yogurt, and a glass of cold water. She didn't want to eat too much because they might work her out hard as soon as she arrived. The little bit of confidence she had was that Rob had chosen her. He was an excellent cop to her so he knew excellence. She had also made it through an interview with the Chief so two people approved of her. She sat on her couch and meditated. At 10 AM sharp came a knock on the door. It was time.

Special Agent Duncan asked, "Ma'am, is Ms. Hale home?"

Alison answered, "Yes. That is me sir."

After inspecting her driver's license, Special Agent Duncan said, "I will be escorting you this morning to your destination."

Alison grabbed her luggage and locked up the house. She went out to the black Suburban and got in on the passenger side. They were off.

She found it strange they ended up in her old precinct. Maybe this was a test. Would they take her to the block where she had the gun arrest? The mind games had begun. They pulled up to a project building and Special Agent Duncan got out. He returned with Malik. Malik got in on the rear driver's side.

Malik said, "Good morning. Malik Sanders."

Alison said, "Good morning. My name is Alison Hale."

They shook hands. It was a quiet seven-hour ride to Williamsburg, Virginia.

Malik thought about having to say good-bye to his mother. He packed heavy. He had his dancing shoes and a few outfits to party. Play hard, party hard. He concentrated on his cardio right after he spoke with Rob. He felt if he was in great physical condition it would help all other aspects of his training. This world was new to him. So he was ready. Plus, the Chief had interviewed him and he was impressed. So he had the blessings of Rob and the Chief. Let the chips fall where they may. Rob had arranged for him to be sworn in as a NYPD officer two days ago, and Rob and the Chief had showed up. It was official. He was a part of the solution now.

Alison was wondering about what kind of training it would be. Would the CIA give her some training or would she get the full training? After all, she was NYPD. She had watched a lot of CIA movies leading up to this to help her.

Sitting in the Suburban were two people who were going to be trained together and possibly work together. This ride was part of their bonding. This was executed by the Chief. He had come to accept and understand Rob's vision. The seeds were planted for life after the Unit. Choir girls and boys. Innocence and Integrity.

#

Mike and Dwayne did most of the money pickups for the Syndicate. They had formed a friendship and they were running the streets together. It was all good information for the Unit. Dwayne took pictures of the money when he could. He mentally documented all of the Syndicate's locations, which he would later put in a report at the Bat Cave. He fit in well. When Mike gave him a gun to carry, Dwayne sent the serial numbers to Stella. Dwayne played his role well because he knew he had the training and understanding of his powers. So he just acted like a drug dealer. He was working with the Syndicate and would kill for them. Self-defense as would be written in the police report. Dwayne had more than enough to start a case on the Syndicate. Nothing to connect Raekwon, Shawn, or Derek. Just that there was a drug business in existence. His role was paying off for the Unit.

Stella kept an eye on him and he knew that. He felt confident about his well-being.

#

Counter-intelligence is definitely not a science. Alex and Rob were sitting in front of an apartment building because Stella have given them information that the contract killers were there. She also got from wiretaps that there was a hit put out on them. When something goes wrong with witnesses or money sometimes the killers were killed. No evidence, no arrest. So for the third night in a row they sat and waited. They watched, recorded, and ate fast food. The worst part for Rob was not the boredom of waiting but the annoyance of Alex. He talked too much, he smelled, and he was almost always drunk. Alex was ecstatic to be working with Rob. Dat all.

At last, a car pulled up and two male Hispanics got out, dressed in all black. Long trench coats to cover their automatic weapons. Game time. Alex and Rob got out and followed. They both had their Glock 19s, police issue, and MP5s with silencers, CIA issue. Their bulletproof vests were visible. Entered the building soon after their prey, Alex and Rob saw the elevator stop on four. They rode up. They could hear the commotion as soon as they get off the elevator.

They listened for a few seconds and then Alex kicked the door in. Rob killed one and wounded the other, using the MP5 with the silencer. The contractors shouted, "Don't shoot!" with their hands in the air. They had no weapons. Scared out of their minds, they thought the police had just saved them. Two white guys killed the Hispanic guys. Who else would they be? In the Dominican Republic police corruption was rampant so if they were dirty no surprises there.

Alex picked up the weapons while Rob covered him. Then Alex grabbed the wounded man and dragged him over to the window. He opened the window.

Alex said, "Listen, you piece of shit, tell me who you work for or I'll throw you out of this window!"

Renaldo spat, "*Andate a la cresta*."

Alex shouted, "Fuck me? No, fuck you!" He shoved Renaldo halfway out of the window. "Tell me who's paying you!"

Renaldo yelled, "*Te vere en el infierno!*"

Alex threw him out of the window. This was to scare the other two. It worked. He handcuffed them and then went through their personal belongings. He knew their identifications were fake. He also knew they were from the Dominican Republic. Alex picked Hector to question first because he was visibly nervous. Alex directed him to sit in a chair. He did without hesitation.

Alex commanded, "Do you speak English?"

Hector cried, "*Si*. I mean yes. Just talk slow, please."

Alex mocked him. "Just talk slow. Okay. Did you shoot up the store on Linden Boulevard?"

Hector pleaded, "It was just business, my *amigo*."

Alex shouted, "Two young girls getting shot isn't business. That's murder. Are you with the Latin Cartel?"

Hector answered, "We work for whoever pays our price."

Alex leaned in. "Who paid you?"

"His name was Manuel. We don't usually meet the person—it's just a money transfer."

Alex grabbed his hair and yanked his head back. "Except you made numerous calls to this number from the lobby phone. Who were you calling?"

Hector cried, "Takeout food. I was ordering food."

Alex sighed. "We were doing so well." He pistol whipped Hector and asked the question again.

Hector groaned, "Manuel. I was calling Manuel."

Alex asked, "Did you meet anyone else while you've been here. Don't lie to me." He lifted his gun and Hector pleased, "Please no. Only him."

Alex and Rob had brought pictures of the Latin Cartel. Alex showed Hector a picture of Sosa, and all other lieutenants. Then he showed him a picture of Louie.

Hector said, "Yes, that is Manuel. That's him."

Alex asked, "Manuel from the Latin Cartel?"

"I don't know about that. Like I said, we had very little contact."

Alex asked, "What did you do with the weapons you used for the shooting?"

"Manuel took care of all of that."

Alex pushed his gun against Hector's chin. "What about the car? Did he pay you yet?"

Hector wept but answered. "No. We'll get paid when we go back to Dominican Republic. He wires it to us."

Rob nodded at Alex. They had all they needed. It was time to get rid of these pieces of shit that killed two innocent young girls. There were probably numerous bodies they were responsible for. They would blame this and the deaths of the girls on Louie and the Latin Cartel. They argued over how to do it. They both agreed shooting them was too nice. Rob won the argument. They handcuffed both of them and got the car keys from the dead guy. They put them in the back seat of the dead guy's car and Alex drove off in it. Rob followed. They drove to Staten Island. They went to the old sanitation dump. Fresh Kills. It was just a huge lot now. Soon to be a mall.

Rob got out and opened the back door to the other car. With a hammer he broke both their elbows. They screamed in pain. Then Alex and Rob both pulled them out of the car and then placed them in the front of the car. Rob walked back to his car and popped the trunk. He took out three pieces of Semtex and C-4. He placed one each in the laps of Hector and Ramon. Both had the exact same timer on it. He then placed the same explosive in the back seat of the car with a little longer time. Hector and Ramon both knew what was about to happen but they couldn't move their hands because their elbows were broken—all tactics Rob learned at the Farm. Rob lit all three and walked away. Alex stayed a little closer because he enjoyed the screams from the car and he wanted to see the explosion. In sixty seconds the bodies exploded then after thirty more seconds the car exploded. There were no more screams. There was no turning back now—Rob was a killer. This felt good to him. No arrest, no trial, no acquittal, no bullshit. A confession and then justice.

#

Derek knew the Latin Cartel was going to win the war with ease. Which was great because Louie was a competent businessman and Derek looked forward to working with him. Trevor would have been a disaster. He decided to reach out to his new partner. Louie, who shared his low estimation of Trevor, agreed to meet. They did it like gentlemen. Just the two of them at a bar on Parsons Boulevard. They sat in the back booth and talked.

Derek asked, "*Sauvé*, how were you? It's been a minute."

Louie said, "Yes it has. I'm trying not to get killed out here. This whole thing ain't good for business."

Derek said, "Unless you win!"

They both laughed. The waitress took their orders. Two Bacardi lemons and Coke. Derek said, "My treat. I know you're not making any money."

Louie answered, "Tell me about it. Terrible."

They both laughed.

Derek began. "Listen, the Italians were out of commission for the foreseeable future. So we lost our connect there. I have a new connect from Columbia and I would share him with you for a surcharge."

Louie said, "Just like the Italians. The connect is power."

"Exactly," Derek replied. "But I'm not going to do you like the Italians. With me it would just a ten-thousand-dollar markup on each key. What do you think?"

Louie said, "That sounds fair. Can I meet the connect to make sure everything was cool?"

"You know the rules. No!"

Louie said with a shrug, "You were being so generous I had to try."

Derek said, "We will figure out delivery schedules and more when you are back on your feet. Hopefully that will be soon."

Louie agreed. "I hope so. We were taking a killing. Speaking of which, you must be doing great with all the clientele coming your way?"

Derek shrugged. "I'm not complaining. Even though I wouldn't wish war on anyone."

Louie said, "Me either. Still not worse than stickup kids."

"I totally agree."

They both laughed. The waitress brought over their drinks and some nuts and potatoes chips to eat. They talked NY Knicks. The Knicks cross all religions, ethnic groups, and wealth.

#

Nigel's tier had all new correction officers after the incident, but he didn't feel safe. He knew from the Hood news that Trevor was almost done and he was reading the newspaper in his cell when a C.O. entered. He looked at the C.O. warily. It was after hours so it was unusual.

The C.O. said, "You are an important man. I'm your new guardian angel."

Nigel looked at the huge Spanish C.O. with suspicion. None of the other C.O.s had ever said anything like that. They never said anything they would have to testify for in the future.

The C.O. continued, "Gang Intelligence got word that there was a hit out on you. So I'm going to show you some photos and let me know if any of them are a threat. I'll take care of them on the low."

Still suspicious, Nigel said, "Okay."

The C.O. showed him a series of photos. Nigel didn't see anybody that was a threat but he did point out his two new bodyguards to let the C.O. know they were all right. He didn't want them harmed.

C.O. said, "Okay. I'm going to move you to a more secure location so turn around so I can cuff you. Then I will walk you over. It's night so nobody would see you."

"Cool," Nigel said, and turned around to be cuffed. He felt the C.O. wrap his arms around his neck but there was nothing Nigel could do. The C.O broke his neck while he choked him out. He then hung Nigel in his cell like he committed suicide. He took Nigel's shirt off and made a noose which made it look like Nigel did this to himself. The C.O. then calmly called over his radio for assistance.

#

Derek just happened to be in the area with flowers, candy, a gift card to Chipotle, and a box set of *Martin*. He glided down the steps while Monique was hard at work, arguing with a homeless man about getting on the train for free. As soon as she saw Derek she buzzed the man through. Once through he said, "Fuck you, bitch." But she didn't care. She was ecstatic to see Derek.

Derek said, "Sorry to interrupt you. It looked like you were about to whip his ass."

Monique sighed. "He is a regular. Sometimes you have to tell them no. It wastes time."

Derek shook his head. "I couldn't do it. I would just let them all in."

Monique replied, "Word would get out and they would be lined up every day at your booth. You have to hold your ground, especially as a woman. Welcome to my world."

"I like your world," said Derek. "Listen, you were on my mind so I brought you a few things."

She opened the token booth's door so he could hand her the bag. She had a great big smile on her face. "What did I do to deserve this?"

Derek said, "I had a great time the other night so I just wanted to do this. Anyway I will see you on Saturday for dinner. Restaurant to be determined."

Monique said, "Okay, Mr. Mason. I will see you then. Thanks again. I really appreciate it."

Derek said only, "Be safe."

#

Rob and Stella had a meeting with Captain Gallagher at the Bat Cave. Rob had called this meeting. Rob got there a little early to brief Stella on what they were handing Gallagher. Detective Stella told him about planting a story with her contacts in the media that the Brooklyn Bullies had done the killing and the bombing. The Latin Cartel ordered the hit and then didn't want to pay the contract killers so they killed them as well. These Drug Cartels were terrorizing this city and they had to be stopped. They should be treated like enemy combatants. Good work," he said as the captain entered.

Rob swung around and said, "Good morning, Captain. I have a big development for you in the death of the two young ladies. It was gang related as well."

Captain Gallagher smiled grimly. "Great news."

Rob went on. "Sosa Colon from the Latin Cartel was responsible for hiring two contract killers from the Dominican Republic. We have wire taps and physical surveillance to substantiate everything."

Captain Gallagher asked, "When are we arresting him?"

Rob replied, "We decided to give it to you. We have enough work with Dwayne working the Syndicate. We have to ensure his safety. This by itself needed a lot of manpower and attention. You can make the arrest and give the news right to the Mayor. It's a welcome to the unit as well."

"The city really needs this. Thank you for your hard work," said Gallagher.

Rob said only, "This was what we do."

Gallagher added, "We will make the arrest immediately so the Mayor can have his press conference—I mean, so we can get these killers off the street."

Stella said, "Word on the street is the Cartel put a hit out on the contract killers because of the young girls being killed. They wanted to get rid of all evidence that pointed to them. Even they know killing young girls is bad for business. So I'll keep you abreast of that situation as well."

Gallagher replied smugly, "Please do."

Rob said, "Here is the case file. Stella can walk you through it if you have any questions. Good hunting."

Gallagher looked down at the case file in his hands and then at Rob. "Probably sounds insincere but I apologize for the rough start."

Rob waved away the apology. "Don't worry about it. We're on the same team."

He watched Gallagher leave and sprang to work. He had to get Dwayne out now. What Rob and Alex were about to do could get Dwayne executed.

"Get an arrest team to take him down," he ordered.

#

As Mike and Dwayne drove to their first pickup they saw lights and sirens behind them.

Mike muttered, "I didn't do anything."

Dwayne frowned. "Yeah, there were no stop signs or lights on this road."

Mike pulled over. When he did three other police vehicles surrounded their SUV. He immediately thought it was Syndicate-related issues. He turned off the ignition and awaited his fate. He and Dwayne watched as masked gunmen exited their SUV and surrounded them. "This a hit?" Dwayne asked but Mike said nothing. They were told to exit the vehicle and lay on the ground. One walked over to Dwayne and stood over him. "Are you Dwayne Johnson?"

Dwayne said yes and the gunman said, "You are under arrest for identity theft, stolen property, and grand larceny. All felonies, sir."

"You're cops?" Mike asked. The masked officer searched Mike and then did a warrant check over the police radio. When it came back negative he was allowed to leave.

Cuffed in the back of the police car, he watched Mike drive away, knowing he would go straight to the club and tell Shawn. As the police car he was in pulled away from the scene, he relaxed in the seat. He didn't know why this was happened but he trusted Rob with his life so he knew it would be explained to him soon. As usual he was "Soul on Ice."

Chapter 42

WARRIOR

Fighting the Brooklyn Bullies was easy as predicted. So Louie was getting comfortable. He went back at the pool hall to pick up some money from the cash from the safe. He was meeting Sebastian Castro, the correction officer hired by the Cartel to kill Nigel to give him his ten thousand dollars for the hit.

Castro followed him into the back room to talk. Castro was very nervous, his legs shaking as they walked. He believed he was walking to his death. He was carrying his duty weapon, a Glock 19mm semi-auto pistol. Louie figured he was armed but he had no worries. Plus, Juan had his eyes on him and his hand on his gun.

Louie asked, "How are you, my friend? We need Warriors like you in the Cartel."

Castro said, "Listen, I did what you asked but that's it for me. I'm out. I want to keep my job."

"Relax," said Louie. "I have your money. No problem. Did something go wrong?"

Castro shook his head. "It's just too risky. If there is another suicide or murder on my watch they will investigate me."

Louie said, "You're right. We appreciate what you did. I just have to ask you a few questions. Who was protecting Nigel?"

Castro had found out who was protecting Nigel. The names meant nothing to him but he wrote them down for Louie. Tony Battle, Maurice Depes, and Ronnie Laurel. The names meant something to Louie. When he read them he knew they all worked for the Syndicate. So Derek had probably started this war for his own benefit. Fat Boy had told the truth: the shooting happened out of nowhere. It always had been about money.

Derek was making a power move. Louie had to decide what to do with this information. If it were true, then Derek was dead. But he needed the new connect. When the war was over they would need drugs. And a lot to catch up for lost money. They had been with the Italians for twenty years. They never needed to have a connect. Connects were difficult because the Cartels charged a lot if you were new and you had to have their money on time or you were dead. It was better to go through a middleman.

Castro interrupted his thoughts, "Can I get the fuck out of here. Please."

Louie nodded. "Take your money and go, *hermano*. If you ever need anything from us just give me a call."

Castro grabbed the money and he was gone. But Louie knew had control over Castro forever. He owned him. In the future if they needed him he would do whatever they asked. There was no statute of limitation on murder.

#

The weather was perfect. A cool 69 degrees with a light breeze as well. For Trevor, it was the perfect weather to smoke outside in his backyard. For city boys, his backyard was a city corner. Usually in front of a bodega so the beer didn't run out. Losing money, Trevor had decided to go back to selling weed again. He told himself that if he personally sold it, it would be easier to flush out the Cartel. Once out he could start killing them. He would make money and kill the enemy. A no-brainer. But the real reason was he was cheap and money hungry. He was told not to set up shop until after the war was over. Again he went against the street rules. So tonight he was on his most lucrative corner, Linden Boulevard and 136 Street.

He decided to put two guys out in the open to sell and he had three trigger men spread out in case there was trouble. He set up the stash and was talking to his guys because they were nervous. They all noticed a Dodge Charger circle the block twice. It had what appeared to be two Spanish dudes in it. The Cartel was out already. Cecil was there watching Trevor's back, locked and loaded. Trevor figured this was a good time to show his men he was in it with them. He asked Cecil for a gun and he was handed an old 38 revolver.

New York City blocks were long. The car couldn't sneak up on them. They saw it coming. Cecil knew it was wrong because he wasn't sure who was in the car. Once they have a shootout there would be no selling in the area for a while. This was the money corner. If they fucked this up, his pockets would really be hurting. The Charger made the right and was headed up the block. Trevor stepped in between two cars and waited, Cecil behind him. The other guns were further up the block. Trevor waited for the Charger to pass and then he fired three shots at the back window. He missed but the one of his soldiers hit the front passenger side.

They had just shot a cop. Captain Gallagher had put undercover narcotic officers around the Latin Cartel and Brooklyn Bully territories. The Charger was the bait. Anybody with a little streets smarts could have figured that out. Better yet, if he had spread some money around he could have had a source straight from the police department. Stupid and stingy.

In the Charger, Detective Jamie Toves got hit in the leg and stomach. Detective Jose Salas was driving. He put it over the radio and he sped off to Jamaica Hospital. "Central, we have an officer down at Linden and Jamaica. We are not waiting for transport; we are headed to Jamaica Hospital."

Central replied crisply, "10-4 Unit. Give us your route so we can block off streets."

There was another car from the same unit watching the movements on the corner after the Charger passed. The four Detectives in that car responded to the shots fired. This was personal. They came from the opposite direction. Two on foot and the other two in the car, Trevor and his crew never saw them coming. With an entire precinct responding to the area. Detective Brennan and Jacobs ran up on Delon, Jamero, and Lemar and emptied their magazines, thirty-four rounds split between the three. Detectives Sean and Solomon put on the lights and siren and drove up the block. Bingo. Two males started to run, which meant they were guilty.

Trevor and Cecil kept running up the block. Cecil cut through a yard, while Trevor was headed toward his car. He drank a lot of juices but he smoked weed every day. He was already out of breath. As he ran across the street, Detective Sean aimed the car right at him. Trevor went flying in the air and hit the ground was a thunderous force, knocked unconscious. Cecil was in the wind.

At Jamaica Hospital there were cops everywhere. Detective Toves had expired. The bullet had ruptured his femoral artery, and he had bled out before they reached the hospital. It would have been better to wait for the paramedics and just put pressure on the wound. Fatal mistake. The hospital was a zoo. Officers crying. Officers throwing stuff around. It was a long night. Word had spread that two perpetrators were dead, and one was in custody. One was outstanding.

His Unit went to Toves's house and brought his wife to the hospital. They were newlyweds. It was a pure tragedy. As soon as she arrived, the officers transferred their grief to support for the family. This was who police officers are. They ran towards the danger and most times they never had adequate time to grieve themselves. They never took off the Superman suit. This no dubitably led to domestic violence, drinking, and abusive power. Yes, slapping your wife, drinking and driving, and beating up prisoners was common. Violence begets violence. It was a vicious cycle. The pain and stress had to be released in some shape, form, or fashion.

#

Louie decided to kill Derek. He couldn't hire his usual Dominican killers. There was no time for that. He would have to use his guys. He gave it to Flaco. He was discreet but he told his gun guy he needed a clean weapon for a hit on a big boss. *Un mal jefe negro.* His gun guy was on Shawn's payroll. He called him immediately. Shawn knew right away the hit was for Derek. Derek wasn't upset; it was the right thing to do. Nigel being killed had revealed a lot. This was part of the game. He was exposed. This scenario had been factored in. If he caught Louie, he would have done the exact same thing. It was business. Derek wasn't even going to change his movements. The Hit was official and wouldn't be canceled even if Louie was killed. Derek put out a hit on Louie. Portia was on it. She worked fast. Shawn heard that with Trevor locked up, Louie he was back at the pool hall. Sosa was still in the shadows.

Louie was holding court in the backroom when he saw Portia on the camera. He sent a drink out to her and she declined. It intrigued him. He went out to meet her.

"You don't like apple martinis?"

Portia purred, "I like to see who is buying me a drink."

"Okay," said Louie. "Suavé. No problem. Can I buy you a drink?"

Portia nodded. "A Coconut Cîroc. Please."

Louie called the waitress over and ordered a bottle of Coconut Cîroc and two glasses.

Portia asked, "So why am I the lucky girl?"

Louie looked her up and down appreciatively. "You know you're gorgeous. This must happen all of the time."

Portia laughed. "You are too kind. Trust me, it doesn't."

They played a few games of pool together as they drank the Coconut Cîroc. And they ended up back at Portia's apartment, just like she planned it. She slipped him a Quaalude and Louie was tied up in less than thirty minutes. Awake, he couldn't move. But he felt good. The high was great. With Portia was standing there in her matching red panties and bra and those red stilettos, he thought he was in heaven. She used the feather to ask him questions.

Portia asked, "Do you own the pool hall?"

Louie was ready to impress her. He told her he owned the pool hall and he was the boss of the Latin Cartel.

Portia asked, "What is the Latin Cartel?"

"The biggest Cartel in New York City. Pronto." Louie told her they sold everything except for weed so if she needed anything he could get it for her. He told her he had a $100 bag of cocaine in his pants pocket. "If you want to party we can use it."

She already knew that because she had searched his clothes. "I'd rather just play with you. The alcohol is enough."

Louie panted, "I'm fine with whatever you want."

The fun took a turn when Portia asked about the location of the stash houses. The whole scene flashed in front of his eyes. A pretty girl walked into the poll hall and now I'm back at her place. We are at war. Big mistake. He knew in a situation like this he was dead but he had to fight. Louie said, "Listen I have a safe in the pool hall that has $250,000 in it. It's yours if you let me go."

Portia ignored him. "I want to know where the new stash houses are and what type of protection you have guarding it."

Louie pleased, "Why go through the trouble of stealing and then selling drugs when you can have straight cash?"

Portia demanded, "I want the address of the stash house and I want to know where Sosa is hiding." She took out her metal slapper and started to hit him across his face. The pain was instant. The drugs couldn't help him. Steel is steel.

Louie gave up the address of the stash house and a fake address for Sosa. Portia didn't care about what information he gave; he was a dead man. She set up the garbage bags beneath him. She took out a needle that had pure heroin in it. With it, she penetrated his vein in his right arm. It only took three minutes for the drugs to move through his system. His body went into violent convulsions. His mouth overflowed with vomit. He was dead in twelve long minutes. Sosa was now the leader of the Latin Cartel.

#

Alex and Rob thought they knew where to pick up Derek: at the strip club. But Derek was on his third date with Monique. This time it was lunch before she went to work. They went to Chipotle, her favorite, simple. As usual the conversation was great. For the first time he was thinking about settling down. Maybe he could bring her home to his grandma. He dropped her off at work and headed to his office. When he pulled up he was still daydreaming, so he didn't see the two white guys waiting for him. When he got out he saw them exit their vehicle. When they walked towards him he knew they were cops. And that they were there for him.

Alex said, "Mr. Mason you need to come with us."

Derek held up his hands. "Okay, gentlemen. No problem. Can I see some identification?"

Alex showed him his NYPD shield and I.D. card. Derek was confused as to why they didn't handcuff him. He thought it meant he wasn't under arrest. If all they had were questions, he had no answers—they could talk all night for all he cared. Alex opened the rear passenger for him and he got in. Rob drove them to a satellite office they had in Astoria, Queens. It was their official interrogation location, with all the tools they needed.

When they pulled up Derek was again confused. But he thought to himself that maybe they were part of a Federal Task Force. They all walked in and Alex told Derek to take a seat and asked for his identification.

Derek gave him his driver's license.

Alex eyed it. "Is this your current address?"

Derek said nothing.

In the interrogation room, Rob was setting up the chair and lights. He filled up three buckets of water and folded a white towel and placed that on the arm of the chair. Alex poured himself a drink. It was going to be a Johnny Walker Black night. Rob came out and escorted Derek into the room. He sat him in the chair and waited for Alex.

Rob said, "Listen, we just want to ask you a few questions. This could be done the easy way or the hard way."

Derek nodded his head but he wasn't going to talk no matter what. Fuck the police was the motto and there was nothing that could be done to change that. He wouldn't even give his name.

Alex entered the room hoping for the hard way to be applied. He stared at Derek for a moment. Could he be as cool as he was acting? They would all soon find out. Game time.

Rob started. "We know you are the leader of the Syndicate. Right?"

Derek stared at him.

Rob continued. "Don't waste your rebellion on stupid questions."

"Don't waste your time asking me stupid questions," Derek retorted.

Alex came up behind Rob. "Relax, big guy. You have no one here to put an act on for."

Derek said, "I'm not acting. You're NYPD. I don't respect beat cops, only the feds. They don't ask questions. They already have the answers."

Alex punched him in the face. Derek felt the pain spread across his cheekbone. He stared at Alex. Alex punched him again. Rob then tied down both his arms, leaving the right arm looser, his stronger one. Giving the impression that he could free himself. Giving him hope. Hope kills. Reality saves lives. The objective would be that he breaks his own arm trying to free himself.

Rob said, "Let's start over. You are going to answer our questions. So let's stop wasting time. You're the head of the Syndicate so we know you are smart. Do what's best for you because the rest of your team will roll on you. They always do."

Derek just stared straight ahead.

Pumped up, Alex got in his face. "We want confirmation on your status as the leader of the Syndicate and then we want you to name your lieutenants and connections. If you don't answer these questions I'm going to go to work on you. You have terrorized this city for years so we are going to treat you like a terrorist. You don't deserve the rights of a citizen."

Derek continued to stare straight ahead. Rob was impressed, but Alex was eager to get to work. The first phase of CIA torture was brutality. Alex put on his black gloves. Derek knew what that meant. Alex started low. He punched Derek in his ribs and stomach. Derek felt the pain but his mind went elsewhere like when his mother's boyfriends use to beat on him. It hurt but he was determined not to cry.

Rob advised, "This was fun for us so just say when. You were making this hard for no reason."

Alex said, "You killed two little girls, motherfucker. We are just getting started." Wanting to break his ribs so that he would have trouble breathing, Alex went to work. He cracked two ribs instantly. They were following the interrogation play book to the letter. The Chief would be proud. Next was waterboarding—a U.S. citizen getting waterboarded on U.S. soil.

Derek saw the set up with the buckets but he didn't know what waterboarding was—too much Sports Center and not enough CNN. He was about to find out all about it. Rod tied his feet to the chair legs. They both walked away for effect. A few minutes later Alex came back with a vengeance. He kicked the chair backwards. Derek fell back with a bang, and stared up at the ceiling.

Rob said, "One last chance, Derek?" When the man didn't answer, Rob put the towel over his face and Alex poured the water over it. Derek felt like he was drowning. He tried to get his arm loose but he couldn't. Rob and Alex did this for a while and then they took a break. They continued this for a few hours. Derek was in pain but he realized after a while that he wasn't going to die so he put his mind in that space again.

Rob advised, "We can do this all day. In the end you are going to talk and this could have all been avoided. You don't get cool points for this. It's actually stupid. You are a boss, so you know better."

Derek stared straight ahead. Alex put on his rubber gloves, his grounder. He then set up the car battery and cables. He put a sponge the tip of the cable so it would ground the currents. He tested it and the sparks were real. Derek saw this and knew right away he wanted no part of it. He tried to loosen his arm. He thought he could get his right arm out. He broke it. Rob saw this and figured that they had broken him.

Rob said, "You're ready to talk, aren't you?"

Derek still said nothing, but Alex was ready to motivate him. He touched Derek's chest with the cable. Derek's body shook with so much intensity it scared both Rob and Alex. Rob immediately turned down the voltage. He didn't want to kill him. He just wanted him to talk. It's not that he cared about him he was just focused on this night. He made the mistake before of only targeting the two people that killed his father. If he would have taken down the whole organization, he may have saved the two young girls' lives. This time he was going to do it right and take down the Syndicate completely. But Alex just wanted to hurt Derek and impress Rob. And if he died in the process, oh well.

Derek fell unconscious. Alex took a cigarette break.

#

The other interrogation was going smoothly. Trevor, handcuffed to a hospital bed, was in a talking mood. His excuse tonight was the police were angry, so he understood. An officer had been killed. Captain Gallagher was there at the hospital but Captain Breaks was in charge. It was his man who was killed in the line of duty.

Breaks asked, "Who was the mutt who got away?"

Trevor answered, "I didn't shoot that officer so I'll cooperate. What can you do for me?" Breaks shook his head. "There can be no deals. What's his name?"

"He's the boss. His name is Cecil Jerdon. I'll give you his address and cell phone number."

After he did, Breaks said, "Give me the names of the other knuckleheads."

Trevor again gave him everything he knew. He was looking to push the blame and get a deal. "I can give you numerous murders and other shit. Drug locations, whatever you need. Let's make a deal."

Breaks knew who he was dealing with. A coward. He started talking before the first question. So there was no need to make a deal. He would spill his guts because that was his character. Plus, you don't make deals when you have a dead officer. The fool had still had the 38 revolver on him when he was caught. Even Breaks knew after you shoot someone you're supposed to throw it away. ATF had done a Triple 9 computer check on the 38 Revolver and it had come back for two homicides.

Breaks interrupted Trevor's whining. "You've been busy with your gun."

Trevor blinked. "What?"

Breaks continued, "Your gun came back with two bodies on it. You're done. You're a cop killer and you have two more murder charges."

"That wasn't my gun," shouted Trevor. "It belongs to Cecil."

Breaks laughed. "It was in your possession, so it's yours. Bodies and all. Cause you know Cecil was going to say the gun belongs to you." He was done with this bozo. He would give the paperwork to Gallagher so he could give the mayor the good news.

#

Shawn was in charge while Derek was gone. It was written into their rules. Weiss had used all of his connections to try and find Derek in the system with no luck. Shawn had done the same with his street contacts. There was no word—not even a rumor. There was a video of two white police officers taken Derek into custody in front of the club, so Shawn decided Weiss would hold a news conference at his office and show the videotape to put pressure on the NYPD to confirm his arrest. Then Weiss could get to Derek and take on his case. Shanika would be only one at the news conference with Wiess. Weiss wanted her to cry to get some sympathy from the public.

Weiss introduced her as Derek's fiancée. Her tears were for real because she actually did care about Derek and she was genuinely worried. She had a bad feeling that he was hurt. Weiss invited all the major media outlets so they would all broadcast the videotape. They all showed up because everybody was curious as to what happened to Derek Mason.

Showing the videotape at the news conference, Weiss said, "We can clearly see the NYPD has taken Mr. Mason into custody. We just want to know that he is okay. As a citizen he is entitled to two phone calls and representation. I'm his lawyer and I want to see him and talk to him.

One reporter called out, "Did you contact the NYPD and ask them about the arrest?"

Weiss replied, "Yes, I went over to the 103rd Precinct and I was thrown out. Just for asking the whereabouts of a citizen who lives in the confines of that precinct and was arrested in the confines of that precinct."

The same reporter followed up. "Who did you speak to at the 103rd Precinct?"

Weiss said, "Captain Monahan, the Commanding Officer."

"What do you think happened to Mr. Mason? Could it have been federal agents?"

Weiss spread his hands. "No matter who arrested him, he would still have to be arraigned. We checked both the state and federal facilities. He is not in either."

Another reporter asked, "Is Derek Mason the leader of the Syndicate, the most notorious drug gang in the city?"

Weiss replied, "No. And keep in mind that this is about due process. Which every American citizen is entitled to."

Monique saw the news conference. She had been worried about Derek. For a man who didn't carry a cell phone he was a great communicator. Since she had met him they had spoken every day in some form or fashion. Not hearing from him for two days was unusual.

The mention of the Syndicate confused her. It and its vicious reputation could not be part of the man she knew. This all had to be a mistake. Derek would be able to sue and they could move out of NYC and get married—or something like that. She just wanted to see and talk to him.

Councilman Jackson had viewed the news conference with the rest of the City Council. They were all curious as to Derek Mason's whereabouts as well. The Republican side, which was all white, gave the NYPD and law enforcement community the benefit of the doubt. If he had been arrested, then he was guilty and he would eventually be found when the time was right. The Democrats, both white and black, wanted to know the circumstances of his arrest and his whereabouts. Councilman Jackson had called the Police Commissioner directly. He didn't have any time to waste on finding this young black man. The Police Commissioner had promised answers within the hour.

Detective Mullin had watched the news conference. He had been told to stay off the case, but he had a hunch. If he was right, then this could get a murderer off the streets of New York. Mullin called Assistant District Attorney Noble. Every good detective had a contact at the D.A.'s office and Mullin had a few. ADA Noble was his go-to for any major case. She was the best. The thing that separated her from the rest was that she didn't play politics. She wasn't trying to get promoted or impress her supervisors. She just wanted to prosecute bad people. He explained to ADA Noble the complex nature of the case. She understood. She was also familiar with Derek Mason. His victims and cohorts had all been in front of her. So if she had the opportunity to prosecute him she would, with optimal intensity.

Mullin said, "I was told to leave this case alone but I have some evidence I can't ignore. If I'm right, he is responsible for two murders."

Noble replied, "If you're right, we are going to arrest and prosecute the mutt."

All good ADA's have judges they can go to for subpoenas and warrants. She had a few. For this case she would go to her biggest fan, Judge Hachette. He was not a fan of her work but her ass. He wanted to fuck her and he had told her that on many occasions. Anything she brought in front of him would not be scrutinized. His only question when Mullin and she brought up the situation in his chambers was, "I hope this detective is not your boyfriend, because then I would have to deny your request."

She laughed off his comments and said, "We just need a subpoena for corroborative evidence he has just found. Which has established probable cause."

Judge Hachette said, "Done."

And they were off. They drove right over to the strip club, where Shawn and Shanika were. They called Weiss and sent him a picture of the subpoena. He told them it was legit and they had to cooperate. They believed it had to do with Derek being missing. So they were happy that the NYPD had started to investigate it. They gladly cooperated. Plus, no Syndicate business was done at the club so they weren't worried about that. They even offered coffee and water. Mullin got right to work on searching for his final piece of the puzzle.

Shawn asked, "Do you need me to show you how to operate the system?"

Mullin shook his head. "No. We got it. Thanks."

Mullin searched for the date of the carjacking. He couldn't wait to take the tapes back to the Technical Assistance Response Unit (T.A.R.U.). If he messed up, tampered with, or mistakenly destroyed the tape, the evidence wouldn't be admissible in court. No evidence, no case. He didn't care that this was a selfish move but this was his case and lead.

Sure enough, the tapes showed the Honda Accord with his two victims in them. At that moment in time they were two carjackers unaware of the identity of their prey. A few minutes later they were dead. Mullin had found what he was looking for. He took the tape and they were off. Noble, knowing the details of the case, understood what she saw. Mullin drove straight to Saint and Sinners on Roosevelt Avenue. He also took the liberty of ordering for Noble. "Two Steak pies, and two Guinness's."

He knew what she liked because they used to date. They were now both unhappily married. They messed around before and after they were married but had stopped. They were just friends now, with great respect each other's expertise. Mullin decided he had to tell his boss, which would put the burden on him to do something with this new evidence. Noble wanted to draw up the warrant and just arrest Derek Mason. She had no fear of anyone. Let the chips fall where they may. The problem was Mullin's fall could ruin his career and retirement. Reluctantly Noble agreed to do it his way. The objective was to get a drug dealer and murderer off the streets. Noble would notify her boss as well. This would be so the NYPD couldn't hide the facts. It would essentially put them on the clock.

The Chief had watched the news conference as well. He was very pleased about the footage. He knew that his men had taken the enemy combatant to their offsite for questioning. He could only imagine what the conversation was about and what they used to motivate him to talk. The combination of Alex and Rob was perfect. It was no act they were really good cop, bad cop. When this routine was done naturally it really worked. He hoped that maybe they had taped the session. If not, he would appreciate a verbal account. He knew Alex would inflict pain and Rob would ask the right questions. He knew they would get all of information they needed and then some for a successful arrest. He also knew if the public knew it would only be a matter of time before his bosses were asking questions about the program. But anything could be explained. Murder, rape, robbery, anything.

Chapter 43

WRONG PLACE

Shanika missed Derek and she was worried about him. But there was nothing she could do and that made her furious. As she was walking the strip club, looking for trouble, it walked in with a nice smile and killer body. Sofia. This bitch! She never saw it coming.

Shanika shouted, "Bitch you late!" and punched her in the face. Caught off guard, Sofia fell to the floor. Silence fell over the strip club as everyone stared.

Shanika glared at her. "You're getting too comfortable around here. We got rules and you better obey them."

Sofia slowly stood. And then rushed Shanika. She tackled Shanika and swept her off the floor. She beat Shanika's face with her fists. Rhonda and Mercedes jumped on Sofia, pulled her off Shanika, and began whipping her ass.

Sofia defended herself and then said, "Fuck this place." She stormed out. Shanika looked around at everyone staring at her. She felt embarrassed but she was still the boss. Sofia was gone!

#

Fat Boy hadn't heard from Louie in a few days. He was getting antsy, so he did what he does when he was nervous. He ate. He wanted his favorite, IHOP. He figured he would go to New Jersey to avoid any confrontations. The IHOP in Elizabeth, was a lot quieter than the city. He got his usual: three pancakes, two sausages, two strips of bacon, and ham. And the strawberry syrup. He drenched his pancakes in it. He took time to notice his pretty waitress. It helped that she was Latin. She was older than him but her body was amazing. He did the usual: he left his number and a hundred-dollar tip. Of course he complimented her every time she came to his table. Nothing more to do.

Fat Boy got a text from Madeline from IHOP while he was in House of Hoops shopping for new Jordans. He wanted another pair of the "Two's." He got her a pair as well, taking a guess at her size. He was back to pick up Madeline after her shift, after washing the truck and making a playlist to impress her. He was early so he parked around the corner until 9 PM exactly.

When Madeline walked out, the Range Rover impressed her. She had guessed from Fat Boy's look he'd have an old Tahoe. She would have been happy with that. But this shit was crazy. $100 tip! She got in and melted in the seat. He leaned over and gave her a hug.

For Fat Boy, the hug was a test. She passed. He had to make sure she wasn't going to act all high post and be like, "Don't touch me. I don't know you like that." He felt good about her. She was down to earth and real. He turned on the playlist at the first light. He was so confident he didn't ask if she wanted to go back to his place. He just drove there. When he pulled up, he got out and carried her bags inside. She followed with no hesitation.

As she looked around his place, Fat Boy said, "Here's a towel and washcloth if you want to shower."

Of course she wanted to shower. She smelt like food. But she went into the bathroom and checked the door for a working lock. It had one. She looked around for cameras and anything suspicious. She saw nothing. So she took off her clothes and showered.

Meanwhile, Fat Boy ordered some Chinese food. He was supposed to be laying low, which meant staying away from his own house. It was easy to break rules for pussy. Especially when Louie wasn't around.

He heard the water stop and then her voice, asking him for a shirt. He pulled out a T-shirt—a short one—from his clothes and passed it to her in the bathroom. The food arrived and he prepared their plates in the kitchen, where the smell of the food brought her. As soon as she kissed him, he knew he'd handled everything correctly. He kissed her back. They felt each other up. He led her to the couch. As they humped each other, he inserted his middle finger inside of her. She was wet. He sat back and put her on top of him. She straddled him. No condom. He was in. He wanted her to ride him because he didn't want to come quick. Not this first time. He would just sit back until she came. After that he went to work and nutted himself. They dozed off for a few minutes then washed up. He set out the food.

"Do you want to watch a movie?" he asked.

Madeline smiled and stretched lazily. "Okay."

He asked what she wanted to see. "El Cantante," she answered.

"Nice choice," Fat Boy said, nodding approvingly.

They ate and watched the movie. Perfect day for Fat Boy. Food, Jordans, and pussy. Not necessarily in that order.

#

The Commissioner found out quickly that the men in the video were his. He breathed a sigh of relief because it was believed they were part of a Federal task force, some type of special unit. This meant he could separate them from the department and blame the FBI, DEA, HSI, or ATF. Any agency would work. He just needed time to find out who was in charge of the particular task force. As for his two men themselves, Alex Dunne had a great arrest record and a few shootings. On paper he looked great. Off the record he was hated and the rumors said he had a drug problem. Robert Grey had an excellent arrest record. He was educated and good-looking, and his reputation was just as good. Nothing to worry about with him. Bonafide superstar. So if need be he could talk them up but blame their federal authority. Problem was the information for their current unit was classified and the boss was unwilling to cooperate. Frank Coppice, head of the NYPD Intelligence Department. Not a lot on him because he was an outsider. Only the commissioner had authority to look at it and release the information. Coppice was hired under another P.C. and probably made a deal with him to keep all information classified. So this was taking a little longer than usual. The commissioner sent out messages to the head of the NYC offices of FBI, HSI, DEA, and ATF. Until then he wouldn't be taken any phone calls.

Meanwhile, Councilman Jackson knew when he didn't get a call back quickly that the NYPD was a part of this new disaster. He made a few more calls but no one knew anything they could tell him. Of course the P.C. wasn't taking any calls due to a city emergency. So he had to ·sit and wait. What he could do was prepare a speech for his own news conference. He was going to be direct, self- righteous, and accusatory. His opening statement would be to let the city know he was ready to be the mayor this city needed. He had a sure thing with re-election to the city council. The pay and power were good but if he could be king!

#

Rob needed to check his phone but he had to make sure Alex didn't kill Derek while he was gone. So he made Alex step outside as well. Rob went to his car and checked his phone. Stella had called over twenty times. She texted 911. He called her back.

Stella picked up right away. "You guys all right?"

"Yes. What's so urgent?" "There was a videotape of Alex and you taking Mason away."

Rob paused and then said, "Okay?"

Stella continued, "So it's like the whole world is looking for him. They think the NYPD arrested him and threw him off the face of the earth. There was a news conference."

"Damn!"

"The Mayor and Police Commissioner called. I think if we just produce the body and show he is okay, the timeline can be adjusted and explained."

Rob thought a moment. "Let me call you back."

"Hurry up," Stella replied. "The city is looking for the three of you."

Rob said, "Thanks for the heads up."

He took the steps three at a time. He had to explain to Alex that this was over. After they had electrocuted Derek he still had not spoken. This was their first torture but even they knew this was not normal. Derek Mason was really tough. Not rap music tough, street tough. Maybe they would have better luck with another member of the Syndicate because this one wasn't talking.

Alex was still waiting outside the door. "Alex, we have to get him to a hospital."

"Why? What happened?"

Rob said, "They have videotape of us taking him from the club. The Mayor and P.C. are looking for us."

Alex shrugged. "We're covered because he's an enemy combatant. We should call the Chief and let him know what was going on."

But Rob knew it wouldn't be so simple. They had been using CIA directives on a U.S. citizen. The Mayor and the commissioner had said they would do whatever it took to protect New York City, which is why they had hired the Chief. The Chief had given the Unit CIA training and told them that they were authorized to use it on American soil. The problem was it hadn't been tested. There was no case law or examples to study or reference. The City Council had already questioned the Unit's authority once. It would all be under review soon.

Alex and Rob stood over Derek as he lay on the floor without moving. They needed to get him cleaned up before anyone from the public saw him.

Rob said, "If we take him to any hospital, it will be a nightmare. His face is all over the news—as ours is."

Alex shrugged. "So? We're the police and he resisted arrest. What we tell the public was what happened. I'm not worried. He's just another nigger to me and the world."

Rob said, "The problem is there was a video of us taking him away. There was no confrontation. It would be a hard sell."

Alex said, "Are you going to believe me or your lying eyes." Alex chuckled but Rob didn't laugh.

"I guess we have no choice," said Rob. "Let's at least try to clean him up before we leave."

Alex shook his head. "I don't do cleanup work." He walked out of the room.

Rob swore. He started to drag Derek towards the bathroom. He was in great shape but it was difficult to drag dead weight. Alex saw this and was amused.

"I know a place where we can take him," Alex suggested, "and the public will never see him."

Rob looked up. "Where?"

Alex said, "The Hood Doctor."

Rob stopped dragging Derek. "What the fuck are you talking about? The Hood Doctor?"

Alex told him about the doctor who had lost his license from selling drugs out of his clinic. How he still worked the Hood, charging perps.

"How do you know about this guy?" Rob asked.

"An informant," Alex had answered. He's also used the doctor a couple of times for some rich drug addicts. Alex knew the average price to see the doctor was ten thousand dollars.

Rob nodded. "If you think we can do this without being seen or caught I'm in."

Alex waved off his concerns. "Stop worrying about being caught. That's how you get caught."

Rob said, "Funny. How do we pay him?"

"I'll take care of that."

Rob said, "Let's do this."

They bundled Derek into the car.

"Do you have raid jackets in the trunk?" asked Alex. When Rob replied that he had full gear in the trunk, Alex said, shortly, "Good. We were going to need it."

At the Hood doctor's, Alex grabbed the raid gear out of the trunk and started putting it on.

Rob asked, "Should I do the same?"

Alex shook his head. "I just need you to stand in front of the door with the patient."

Alex made the call while Rob stood by the door with Derek draped in his arms. When the Russian lady and security opened the door for Rob, Alex rushed in. They believed the two white guys were cops so there was no resistance.

Once inside, Alex said, "Everybody keep your hands up. You." He pointed to the Russian lady. "Call the doctor out here."

She called to the doctor, asking him to open the door. The Hood doctor could see all of this on the camera. He opened the door, believing these were cops. They looked like cops. The Doctor recognized Alex as a face he knew. He thought his prior visit was probably part of his investigation.

"We have a sick friend that needs medical attention immediately. We can't pay you now but I promise that I will come back with your money soon."

The doctor winked at Alex. "I would rather do this as a favor to you and the department."

Alex smiled. Rob and security went out and carried Derek in.

The doctor placed Derek's right arm in a cast and did what he could for everything else. The ribs would just need time to heal. He cleaned up all of the blood. He gave them some pills for the severe pain. Alex took a few of them for himself. Rob thought that Derek looked presentable. Rob would just get him a change of clothes.

They thanked the doctor and left. As soon as they did, he pulled the tape from the security cameras and put it in his safe. It would be insurance.

Rob drove to Old Navy on Jamaica Avenue and got Derek some new clothes. He then drove to the 103rd precinct and booked Derek Mason for narcotics sales, disorderly conduct, and resisting arrest. The desk sergeant knew who was in front of him. He notified the commanding officer immediately. It didn't take long for the news media to arrive. The precinct had to set up police barricades out front to control the growing crowds. Weiss was on the way. Councilman Jackson was on the way. Gallagher was on the way.

#

The Chief knew only a Cuban cigar and dark rum would be appropriate for this occasion. He lit a Partagas Lusitania and sipped a glass of Angostura 1919. He didn't fear the NYPD or the New York City Council. The Mayor wanted him, and the former commissioner had signed off on the task force. His lawyer had prepared the contract. He was safe.

It took Weiss a few minutes to get to the precinct but he was allowed right in. Derek was drugged up but he could talk and write. His broken arm looked the least of his injuries. He was in a great deal of pain. Weiss demanded answers but police weren't giving any.

Derek told Weiss that he had been waterboarded and then electrocuted. Weiss was taken back. If he didn't know Derek and seen the injuries himself, he would not have believed his ears. Weiss took photos with his cell phone. He went outside and made a statement to the media.

"I'm glad that Derek Mason is alive but I'm very upset by his treatment by the NYPD. I was told by Mr. Mason that he was tortured by the two officers that arrested him. I'm asking the Mayor and Police Commissioner to take immediate control of this situation and ensure Mr. Mason's safety. That was all I have to say now. The more I say, the more his life will be in danger. I need to talk to government officials about this."

A reporter called out, "Can you give us more details about the torture he said he endured?"

Weiss shook his head. He needed to get back to his office and gather his thoughts for his next move and assemble his team.

Councilman Jackson arrived at the precinct but he was not allowed to see Derek Mason. He did talk to the C.O.

Monahan said, "Listen, these were not my guys so I can't tell you anything about the arrest or what happened before they entered my precinct. What I can tell you is that while he is here, I guarantee his safety."

Jackson said, "What did the officers say happened?"

C.O. Monahan said, "Under their union rules they don't have to speak to me for forty-eight hours. So I don't know what happened. We had EMTs look at Mason. He was okay. The officers were allowed to go home."

Jackson shook his head. "His lawyer said he was tortured. I have a feeling this is the beginning of a crazy situation." He looked for Weiss but he was drawn to the cameras. A speech in front of the precinct would be monumental—live in front of the world. CNN international. This could launch him into a viable candidate for mayor. He had his aide announce to the reporters that he would be making a statement. Blue suit, white shirt, light blue tie. Showtime.

Councilman Jackson said, "Good afternoon everyone. I'm here today as a proud New York City councilman, and even more proudly as a citizen of this great state and country. The reason for this greatness is we are all entitled to some inalienable rights. These rights cannot be repealed or restrained by any human or organization. This includes the mighty NYPD. It is the biggest police department in the world and one of the best but it still has to follow the NYS penal law and U.S. Constitution. It appears that the NYPD has tried to circumvent due process again. Mr. Mason's attorney has claimed that his client was tortured by the officers who arrested him. His injuries seem to support that. Also the officers did not need medical treatment at any time.

I don't want them to say later that Mr. Mason assaulted them. This only seems to happen to black men in this city. I don't need to go over all the names of the past victims of the NYPD. I have access to police data for all precincts. In this same precinct, the 103rd, there is a Ku Klux Klan chapter. They have a building on Guy R. Brewer Boulevard. They have not received any summons, not one, not even for double-parked cars. There was a report of child pornography and transport of illegal guns. But no arrest or even an investigation was because they had police officials and judges as members. The City Council passed this information on to the FBI and they decided to do nothing. But here we are again with another black man receiving the wrath of the NYPD. This was one city so there has to be one rule of law. So I'm asking the Mayor and Police Commissioner to ensure the safety of Mr. Mason, one of New York City's citizens. I'm not going to take any questions because I need to get in contact with the Mayor and the rest of the City Council immediately. Thank you everyone."

The Council walked off with his assistant running after him as reporters shouted questions. He was happy with his performance.

Monique saw the news conference. She believed now that Derek Mason was a drug lord. The NYPD was in the wrong but they wouldn't waste their time with a low-level target. Derek had to be a boss to garner so much attention from the NYPD, a private lawyer, and a councilman. She was still glad she met him. But she had been through this before, with her baby daddy locked up for life. But Derek was very different from her ex. Her ex was a killer and he had always in that mode. He talked violent, he practiced violence, and he fucked violent. Derek was different, more intelligent. He was no doubt violent but it seemed more like business for him. Her ex would kill anybody if he felt threatened or disrespected. He killed often and now he was behind bars for life. Still both of them were similar.

Shanika saw the news conference. She was happy Derek was alive. She felt hopeful for him because he didn't touch any of the work. He had separated himself years ago. He was an excellent businessman. The NYPD didn't have any evidence on him. He would be released and then sue them. She would see him and they would always be together. Even if Derek didn't know that.

Gallagher watched the news conference, knowing he had gold in his hands with Derek Mason's. He didn't believe that Mason was tortured. Shit like that just didn't happen in America nonetheless, New fucking York City. Old school beatings, maybe. But not torture. The lawyer and councilman were just rabble rousers. Police Officers were good people—not here to hurt anyone. Black-on-black crime was what they should be addressing. Gallagher was going to take the case file straight to the Police Commissioner. He wanted full credit for this. It could save the Police Commissioner's job and the image of the department. Once they announced Derek Mason as a murderer it wouldn't matter what happened. Alex and Rob would be heroes They would get commendations and shake hands with the mayor, live on T.V.

#

Back in his office, Weiss called in his partners to consult with him. They asked the question: Did he believe Derek Mason? He did. He had known Derek for over ten years and Derek had never lied to him about anything. Even in the underworld, your word mattered. Weiss made working in this world palatable to himself by comparing it to the most corrupt profession in the world, politics. He believed they were all felons. So he made his living in the hood with the Syndicate and other clients. But no matter what anybody thought about the underworld or specifically the Syndicate, all American citizens were innocent till proven guilty, all entitled to representation and due process.

So to his partners Weiss talked up Derek as if he were a real-life Robin Hood, and he defended him as such. The other partners knew the monetary value of the Syndicate to the firm. So they went along with what Weiss was saying. The first thing would be to get him released on bail because he wasn't safe in the system, whether he had been deliberately tortured or just beaten. So that was their immediate concern. The arraignment was in just a few hours.

Into the meeting walked Shawn with Shanika. They wanted answers. Weiss told them that they were trying to get Derek released on bail first. Shanika understood. She just wanted to talk to him and touch him. Shawn wanted to kill the motherfuckers who beat or tortured him. Of course Weiss told him that was not an option. Shanika and Shawn headed over to Queens Courthouse on Queens Boulevard, but Weiss had an important stop to make before he went to the courthouse. At Councilman's Jackson office, he described what Derek had told him— he had been water boarded and electrocuted. He described his injuries.

Councilman Jackson exploded. "This is unbelievable! We all need answers for this. Trust me when I tell you that you have the full support of the New York City Council behind you."

Weiss held back his grin of victory. "I appreciate that sir. Can you be at the arraignment this afternoon?"

Councilman Jackson said, "I didn't want to be a distraction but if you think it would help, I'm there."

They shook hands. Weiss's plan had worked. He wanted to put pressure on the Mayor and Police Commissioner for answers and wanted to leverage the violence used against his client for his freedom. And of course the Councilman wanted to attend the arraignment. Every major news organization would be there. It was primetime, which meant it was his time.

Chapter 44

GOD'S SON

The courthouse was a mad house. The court officers had to set up barricades to control the citizens and the media who pressed to enter the courthouse to witness the arraignment. Every civil rights leader in the city was there: Reverends Sharpton and Dougherty, and many others. The crowd was already in a frenzy. The reporters were just as bad. They all wanted to get the best picture and a chance at a question. So they needed to be in the very front for that.

Shanika and Shawn were already inside. Shawn had used one of his contacts to get in—a court officer from the neighborhood who helped him avoid the lines. They were sitting when Derek was brought in the court room with four other prisoners. Derek noticed them. Shanika saw that his arm was broken and that he looked as if he was in pain. Shawn saw a man who survived police brutality and racism—his boss. He knew they would get through this together.

Weiss walked into the courtroom with three other lawyers. He usually worked alone but today he needed a team to ensure Derek Mason got the representation he deserved. Weiss nodded at Derek. Derek winked back. Weiss saw Councilman Jackson and Councilman Andrew seated in the front row; they had entered through the employee entrance. ADA Lynch was prosecuting—a challenge, Weiss knew, as he had no police statements and, of course, the arresting officers were not represented. There was nothing in in the basic arrest paperwork about Mason's injuries. Weiss knew the most important person in the courtroom was Judge Laura Bailes. Considered liberal, she thought of herself as a commonsense-oriented person. Weiss felt good about the evidence he had against the police and the judge he was presenting it to.

Court officer said, "Order in the courtroom. All rise for the honorable Judge Bailes."

Judge Bailes said, "Please be seated."

The Court Officer proclaimed, "First case was Docket Number 73, New York State vs. Derek Mason."

ADA Lynch stood. "Your Honor, Mr. Mason has been charged with narcotics sales, disorderly conduct, and resisting arrest. He is the leader of a major drug cartel called the Syndicate. We ask for no bail."

Judge Bailes turned to Weiss. "Mr. Weiss?"

Weiss took a breath and began. "Your Honor, Mr. Mason is the alleged leader of a fictional drug cartel. Everything the state has is theory. They don't have one bit of evidence to offer the people. More importantly, we all know the attention this case has caused, as witnessed by the attendance in the courtroom and outside. But I would say the facts of the case are simple. The facts we have were my client's injuries. There was nothing in the paperwork given to us that would justify his injuries. No officers were hurt during his arrest. Yet he has a broken arm and several broken ribs."

ADA Lynch objected. "The officers involved are both highly decorated. Their word is trusted."

Judge Bailes said, "Sustained."

"Mr. Mason," Weiss continued, "is the only one who sustained injuries in the vicious attack. Also there is no proof of narcotics sale or his rank as the leader. At least not in the paperwork we received. Does the state have new evidence that we were unaware of, Your Honor?"

Judge Bailes looked at Lynch. "Anything new to offer the court?"

"No, Your Honor," Lynch said.

Weiss continued. "There was no causation here because there is no probable cause to arrest. This is police brutality and abusive power. The officers should be on trial, but they are not here to defend the attack or explain the arrest. So, Your Honor, we ask that Mr. Mason be released immediately without bail."

ADA Lynch shot up. "We object. We ask that he be remanded until trial."

Judge Bailes said, "Unless you have any more evidence, I can't under reasonable treatment and judgment hold Mr. Mason."

"Your Honor," said ADA Lynch, "is the court going to take the word of a drug dealer over two honest officers? This is outrageous!"

Judge Bailes said calmly, "We deal with the facts and evidence presented. You have no evidence and the officers are unavailable to appear. This was what the court was presented with today, Counsel."

ADA Lynch tried again. "The people of this state can't be punished because the officers belong to a union that grants them forty-eight hours before they have to make a statement. The people shouldn't have to be victims if this subject is let go to once again terrorize the streets of New York City."

Weiss strenuously objected to the language used. "He is definitely not a terrorist. The terrorists are the people who did this to him." Weiss pointed at Derek. The entire courtroom looked at the cast on his arm and the pain on his face.

ADA Lynch sat back down. "This is an insult to the people of this great state."

"The insult," Judge Bailes said, "is when trumped-up charges support a theory."

Nothing more was said from either side. The judge had decided. "The defendant will hand over his passport to the court and any major monetary accounts will be frozen. Mr. Mason is released on his recognizance. Next case."

Weiss couldn't have asked for a better result. Shanika and Shawn went over to Derek to walk him out of the courtroom with them. The councilmen beamed—they didn't support drug dealers or police brutality.

Shanika said, "They can't keep God's Son in a cage."

When Derek was released, Weiss, Shanika, and Shawn took him to a real doctor who confirmed that he had a broken right arm and two broken ribs. He was given medication and told to stay in bed. Shanika was in charge of keeping him in the house and she was eager to do so.

Shawn was running the business, and everything was going smoothly. But he was looking for a way out. If Derek lost the trial it would make it easier for him to do so. Carla's voice and the restaurant against the game. You can't win. Even you get killed or end up in prison. Unless you are Jay-Z.

Shanika was glad that Derek was alive. She thought that his injuries would give them more time together. She had dreams that this would make him cherish life more and propose to her. Wishful thinking but anything was possible.

Chapter 45

THE WAR REPORT

Too much time had passed. The mayor and police commissioner needed to make a statement. The mayor wanted to be defiant and stand behind what the two officers had done. The police commissioner wanted to blame it on the federal task force. Only one of them was running for re-election. It was time for the War Report.

The mayor said, "Good morning, everyone. I would like to address the events that have happened over the past few days. I made a pledge to the people of New York to keep them safe. After 9/11 we deliberately made a choice on how we patrolled and surveilled the city. We can't guarantee that we don't have another attack but we can do everything possible to stop one. This new process might not look pretty at times but you have to trust us. We have New Yorkers' safety as our main priority. For the process to work I gave the Police Commissioner unlimited power to protect the city, and the officers involved in the arrest the other day are an example of the new police tactics. Remember, terrorism us the use of violence and threats to intimidate citizens for any reason. This produces a state of fear and submission. This is a terrorist's method—and the terrorist can be a jihadist or a drug dealer. Drug dealers use violence to intimidate and control whole communities. These communities are always poor. So this is not about race because the people we are saving were mostly African American and Latino. So we make no apologies for anything that has been done because it was for all New Yorkers."

The police commissioner spoke up. "The department and the entire city stand behind the officers who arrested the most notorious drug dealer in this city. The facts of the case will bear this out, soon. Every time the Syndicate killed somebody, it was our fault, because we knew who they were and what they were doing. We had to stop them. How many more school kids must die before these animals are stopped?

Well, we stopped them. We should applaud the detectives. You don't need probable cause, Miranda warnings, or due process for an enemy combatant or terrorist. For now, we ask New Yorkers to trust us and let the process matriculate."

Councilman Jackson could have cheered. The leaders of the city had again called Derek Mason a terrorist and essentially proclaimed him guilty before he had a trial. He cleared his throat and began. "Derek Mason is a citizen of this city and deserves the presumption of innocence. He has been denied his due process. The evidence against him doesn't suggest that he is a drug kingpin. There is no evidence to support the NYPD's theory. There is no evidence at all—all we have is a severely injured young man. This was not the seventeenth-century nor is it a Star Chamber. We can't just say, 'Off with his head.' There is a process: probable cause, arraignment, grand jury, and a trial. You can't circumvent common law and fair treatment. This is oppression. This is abusive power. Anybody arrested, no matter the charges, deserve the basic human courtesy granted by our criminal justice system. It is built in—we don't have to do anything extra to receive or distribute it. I'm calling on the mayor as the leader of this city to apologize to Mr. Mason and all the citizens of this city for his accusatory language. The mayor should give Mr. Mason the same standard of innocence he gives the KKK chapter. For all of the citizens who are appalled by the NYPD and the mayor's behavior, we will be holding a Day of Outrage march this Friday. Please come out in peace and let the world know that New Yorkers won't stand for this abuse and corruption."

#

Derek was in extreme pain but he refused to take his medication. He didn't drink or use any drugs. Not even prescriptions. He didn't like being laid up basically under house arrest. Derek had needed some time alone to figure out his next move. So he was in his office in the basement while Shanika was watching T.V. on the couch. She had cooked but he wasn't hungry.

When she fell asleep watching Judge Judy, he decided to sneak out and visit Monique. She had been on his mind the whole time, even when he was being tortured. He showered and was out. He took an Uber X to her job in Far Rockaway. He knew her schedule. She was in shock when she saw him slowly walk down the steps. She broke all the MTA rules by running out of the token booth. She hugged him and started to cry.

"Why you crying?" he asked.

Monique answered, "I missed you. I was so worried about you."

Derek hugged her more tightly. "I'm here, baby. Relax."

Monique said, "Fuck you, Mr. Cool. This is me, I cry."

"I can't stay long but I just wanted you to know that you are on my mind because you are important to me."

Monique began uncontrollably and even Derek had to control his emotions.

Monique sobbed, "Fuck, I'm a mess."

Derek said, "It might be a while before I see you again. If a Mr. Weiss comes to see you, that's my lawyer. So you can trust him. I gotta get back. Be safe out here."

Monique said, "You better be safe. We just met. We have a lot of things to talk about and do together."

Derek said, "I got you babe."

#

Captain Gallagher waited for the optimal time and then headed over to the police commissioner's office. He had to wait forty-five minutes but he finally got in. He looked around at all of the pictures and certificates on the wall. He then took a seat on the couch. He was feeling confident.

The police commissioner said, "How can I help you, Gallagher?" "I have a case file on Mr. Mason for two murders." He put the case file on the commissioner's desk.

The commissioner stared at the file without touching it. "Don't bring no bullshit case in here that will put us in worse shape than we are in now."

Gallagher said, "Sir, this is for real. It has nothing to do with any drug business. Two idiots tried to carjack Mr. Mason and he killed them both. The investigation started over four weeks ago."

The got the commissioner's attention. "Who knew about this?" "Just the case detective," Gallagher replied.

"This was the best news I've heard in a while," the commissioner said. "Pick him up right away before he kills again. I'll let brief the mayor on this case. Keep me posted on the arrest. Don't discuss it with anyone."

Gallagher went right to see Detective Mullin and his bosses. He let them know that they could draw up an arrest warrant and get Derek Mason. Mullin and his bosses knew they were being used but there was no downside because the case was solid. Gallagher just wanted to be updated every step of the way.

Detective Mullin and Sargent Collens went to meet with ADA Noble and her bosses. Everybody wanted to take Derek Mason down. The best way to do that was to draw up the arrest warrant quickly so that nobody could change their minds. With Judge Hachette, the whole process took less than hour. They had what they needed to arrest Derek Mason.

ADA Noble at this point was more excited that Mullin. She thought Mr. Mason would fall through the cracks again, so to be a part of his arrest made her very happy. She would see Mr. Mason again on Monday morning!

Judge Hachette's secretary, Lola Presley, was from 40 Projects. She filed for overtime she never did every week. She made over $100,000 a year doing forty hours a week. So she could take a little touching and inappropriate jokes for that price. She heard their whole conversation about the arrest warrant and the subject. She knew Derek Mason. They grew up together. But her obligation was to Shawn. He paid her for information. She went to a pay phone outside and called him, telling him everything she heard. He promised her $10,000 by the end of the day.

Shawn called Derek and they met at Weiss's office. Weiss was blindsided but Derek wasn't; in his world things from the past come up when you least expect it. So he always expected surprises, and just dealt with them. Shawn did the same.

When Weiss found out there was no video of the shooting—just a timeline from the Strip Club to the traffic light—he began to feel better about the case. Except for Shanika. Derek trusted her, but Weiss didn't want to test that theory. To Derek and Shawn Weiss floated the idea of a self-defense plea because Shanika and Derek were the victims of an attempted carjacking. The tough part would be explaining their driving off and throwing away evidence. Weiss presented Derek with two options: fighting the fact there was no visual evidence, or pleading self-defense. Derek told him he was going to take some time and think about it.

Weiss insisted, "Derek, the one thing we don't have is time. They could arrest you when you leave this office. Let's talk about this now and figure out the best way to proceed."

Derek said, "I definitely understand what you're saying, but I need just a few hours to gather my thoughts. I'll give you a call later." He had just been tortured by two NYPD detectives. He didn't stand a chance. Derek knew he was going back to jail and he promised himself he never would.

Shawn knew that Derek had made up his mind but wanted to wait to tell everybody else. So they would just have to wait. It was Friday and Weiss figured they would arrest Derek Sunday night for a Monday news conference.

#

Fat Boy didn't know what was going to happen to the Latin Cartel without Louie running things. There was nobody who could replace him. He was tough and smart. Sosa had gotten word that Louie was dead. He also knew that Trevor was locked up. So Sosa had gone back to the pool hall to set up shop and decide what to do. He wanted to come out of hiding to show force. He was nervous so he surrounded himself with a lot of gunman. They were all eager to get back to work. Fat Boy wasn't so sure.

What he was sure about was his new girlfriend. Madeline and he had been seeing each other every day since they'd met. Today he was just stopping by for some takeout. She brought him his lunch. She got into the car and placed his food on the floor mat.

Fat Boy said, "Hey."

"Hey," Madeline said. "I missed you."

They kissed.

Fat Boy grinned. "I know."

They laughed and then she said, "Recline your seat back."

He knew what that meant. Blow job. Before his seat was all the way back she had unzipped his pants and pulled out his dick. She went to work. She sucked his dick with passion and skill. It didn't take him long for him to come. She cleaned him up with her tongue.

Fat Boy sighed, "Damn!"

Madeline smiled, "Pick me up at ten."

She jumped out of the car and went back to work. He drove around the corner and ate his pancakes, eggs, and bacon. He was in love. All along he should have been dating women his age or older. Maybe then he wouldn't have had all that drama. Madeline was cool and low key. She appreciated him and what he did for her. Most importantly, he trusted her.

#

Seventy-eight degrees and sunny: perfect weather for a Day of Outrage. A lot of people had showed up for the Saturday rally. Councilman Jackson was very happy with the turnout. The organizers estimated about 350,000 people, although the NYPD would report 100,000. There was a slew of speakers—a few actors, rappers, and singers—but Jackson was the headliner. The cause was just and the mood was positive. The people knew why they were there but still enjoyed the synergy of the each other. Councilman Jackson had a big announcement.

Council Jackson stared out over the crowd and began. "Thank you everyone for coming out today for this very important issue. Police brutality is very serious and the black community has been dealing with it since slavery. The NYPD and the black community have a very bad history. In 1966 we had the Wylie-Hoffert Murders. We had two white women killed. They framed a young black man for those murders. It led to Miranda warnings and a TV series, *Kojak*. That was 1966. In 2014 we had Eric Gardner. No more!"

The crowd went crazy.

Councilman Jackson waited until they had quieted. "We don't hate the police—or anybody. All we want is accountability. Accountability if one of them makes a mistake or commits a crime. That's all this is about. All the retraining, wasted money, and time can be replaced with equality."

The crowd went crazy again.

"On Monday morning," Jackson continued, "the City Council will hold hearing with the Police Commissioner and other city officials to answer questions about a secret police unit trained by the CIA and specifically the torture of Mr. Derek Mason. We will get the answers that the citizens of this city deserve. We will ask for federal oversight of the NYPD. Our permit ends at 6 PM, fifteen minutes from now. So I ask that you obey the police officers out here that are protecting us. Go in peace. Thank you for showing up."

The crowd clapped and cheered.

The police commissioner, the Chief, Captain Gallagher, and Rob were all ordered to appear in front of the city council at 10 AM. Monday morning. The Chief was the only one looking forward to appearing.

#

In Derek's business, he never wrote anything down because it would become evidence. Tonight he was writing.

He wrote out a statement saying he was the leader of the Syndicate drug gang. He took credit for the murders they committed under his watch. He did this so the families of the victims could get some closure. This was, in part, his closure as well. He wrote that his cause for sinning was his violent childhood. He grew up with one parent who was a drug addict. He had been physically abused until the age of twelve. He was not making excuses, just being truthful. He had had a hard life but he didn't blame it on the system. It's just what the streets created: The government gave black people drugs to sell and use. Then they turned around and made it a business filling up prisons.

At first he had thought he had been getting revenge for all that had been done to him but then he realized that he had become a version of the evil that his mother was and who she had dated. He was no Nino Brown and this wasn't New Jack City. This was real life and he was no rat. He was taking full responsibility for everything. But because of the life he created for himself he couldn't do a day in jail. When you enter that cell your life didn't flash before you. It's more like a slow nightmare. He never wanted to experience that again. He would never be caged again. America built him so they would have to take some ownership for him. Starvation, physical and mental abuse, poor education, government & police corruption, and racism. He was raised on the streets and in jail. This was the end product. But with all of that he never hurt anyone who wasn't a part of the game. He never went after babies and women. He obeyed the street code. He never tatted on friends or his enemies. If he had a problem, he settled it in the streets. No snitching. So he was proud of his life. He would go out in a blaze of glory on his feet. He was the leader of the biggest and baddest crew in New York. He would take that to his grave.

He listed his lieutenants as Sosa and Trevor. His last line was, "I'm guilty!" He signed below it.

He was leaving this letter of admission with Weiss and also instructions for his assets. He left Portia his hideaway condo in Baltimore. It was paid in full. He also left her his Range Rover parked in the Poconos and $500,000. He left full ownership of the strip club to Shanika. Plus, he gave her his house with a suggestion to sell it for cash. It was paid in full but he believed she should have a fresh start. He left two properties to Monique and $250,000. He was in love with her. He was also happy that he didn't have time to fuck it up—they were ending on good terms. She didn't have to date another drug dealer and he didn't have to mistreat another woman. He had never felt this for a woman before. It felt good. It was enough for him. He left the millions to his kids to spread out over twenty years. He left the connect to Raekwon and his blessing for him to take over. Raekwon would be happy with the number one spot and with Jocelyn, his future looked bright. For Shawn he left a second chance at a normal life—naming Sosa and Trevor as his underbosses.

Derek drove to Weiss's house and gave him the letter and instructions on the money and properties. He gave Weiss a suitcase with a million dollars in it for his work. Derek didn't say much. He was out. Weiss thought that if he ran he would be caught soon. Derek was smart but they eventually got Whitey Bulger so no one was safe. Weiss faxed over the confession to Councilman Jackson's office.

Derek was staying at the Sheraton on South Conduit Ave in Jamaica, Queens. This was to avoid his pending arrest. He was never going back to jail. He was not an animal. Jail made everyone an animal. He took a very long hot shower, about an hour. Dinner was jerk chicken and cabbage with Fiji water. He put on his favorite Nike black sweat suit and his ACG Nike boots. He then loaded up his two Smith and Wesson S&P 45-caliber handguns. Two magazines with ten rounds a piece. Between the police and hit men it was only a matter of time. He decided not to hide.

Derek had found out through a source that Shawn had brought a restaurant for Carla in Harlem. He was jealous and suspicious as to why Shawn didn't tell him. They had always told each other everything. It was their creed. No secrets meant nothing and nobody could come between them. He had driven up to Harlem to see for himself. When he pulled up Carla and Shawn were talking to the contractor out front. So it was true. Derek was very angry. Did Shawn lie about anything else.

Derek was in the middle of a war he didn't trust anyone. It took him a minute but he realized that Shawn did this for Godson and Carla. They were legit which meant and a way that Derek was too. He would live through them. Something good had come out of this chaos. His mood changed. He drove off in peace.

Raekwon was ready and built for war. He would knowingly stand and die with Derek without hesitation. That's all Derek needed to know. It would be a selfish move to have either of them die with him. Because this wasn't going to end until he was dead.

Derek had called some hired goons to meet him at the strip club. He arrived at 11:16 PM. He could feel the heat when he walked in. The Latin Cartel knew this was his spot so they had people watching. The goons were waiting inside. They didn't know the imminent evil threat that awaited them outside.

Derek says, "Listen I've known all of you a long time so I'm going to be straight with you. We are at war with the Latin Cartel so there's going to be some serious violence soon. If you're in I'm paying a G a day for your gun. If not I understand. Walk now.

There were ten guys there. Two walked.

Derek says, "Everybody holding?"

They shook their heads yes.

Derek says, "Cool. Brandon set them up at the front and back door. After that take Shanika home."

Brandon says, "On it. Are Shawn and Raekwon okay? I can get more guys."

Derek says, "There good. Thanks."

Derek went to tell Shanika she had to leave. It didn't go well.

Derek says, "I need you to go home. I have arranged for Brandon to take you home."

Shanika says, "What? nah I'm good!'

Derek says, "Listen this is real. I have beef with the Latin Cartel and they can strike at any minute. Let Brandon take you home and we'll figure out a system tomorrow."

Shanika says, "We got beef with the Latin Cartel. So tell where you want me?"

Derek says, "I love you for that Shanika, but this is real. Please leave. Let's talk about this in the morning."

Shanika did tell her girls to go home. Then she walked away to get her gun in the safe. At that point Derek noticed Robin standing by the bathroom. What made him standout was he wasn't paying attention to any of this. He was one of Derek's people but he was Spanish. Derek knew the look. It was happening now which is what he wanted.

He didn't want Shawn and Raekwon to die for this. This was his idea so it was his responsibility.

He always said he would never go back to prison. So dying so his family could live was easy for him. Shawn was right this King of New York shit was a bad idea. Shawn was legitimate so, so was Derek. He had no Plan B. Raekwon was going to be a good boss. He would take care of Jocelyn and the rest of the Syndicate well.

Robin had already made the phone call. The killers were on the way. Everybody would get what they wanted tonight. Everybody!

Derek checked both of his Smith and Wesson's. He was loaded and ready. He took his regular seat in the back where he could see everything and ordered a Hennessy and Coke. He didn't drink but tonight was a special occasion.

Robin acted as if he was taking the garbage out so he could open the back door. Derek didn't even try and stop him. The two knuckle heads at the door never had a chance. There was no knock just a straight barrage of bullets from two Tech Nines. One named He tor, the other named Willie! The sound was beautiful and Rhythmic. The two guys at the back were dead. Brandon had to forcibly carry Shanika into her office. He then barricaded the door with a desk.

Derek was still sitting at his table Ready to Die. The four at the front door didn't know what they had signed up for. It was complete silence now and it was deafening to them. They had guns but they wanted to run. Everyone knew what was on the other side of that door so they took cover.

Derek had a gun in one a drink in the other. The other gun was sitting on the table. He could hear Shanika yelling and screaming in the office. Trying to get out.

She bit Brandon on his finger down to the bone. Out of anger he punched her in the mouth. He broke her jaw and literally knocked her out. He was bleeding profusely. The second barrage hit the front door and killed one of the goons instantly. Only seven left. Six of them not build for this. Alex just started shooting at door. Wasting his bullets and letting the gunman know where he was. The professional just turned his Tech towards the muzzle flash and let loose. Two more goons down. Jason took his chances and ran out of the back door. Now the killers were just having fun. They waited till he crossed the street and thought he was safe. Chi Chi walked up on him and shot him in the head. He knew the girl walking towards him was wrong but it was too late. She took a picture of him and kept moving towards the alley. Covering the back door. Derek was in a strip club with three dudes he didn't really know. At least Brandon was with Shanika.

He knew him from the block. These were his people. There are not many who could stand up to this fire power. Only other professionals could really counter with a chance. Shawn and Raekwon were taught well Derek so they would have killed a few more but this was a no win situation. Steve got up and tried to open Shanika's office door.

Steve says, "Brandon it's Steve let me in!"

No reply. When Steve tried to pry the door open one shot by Brandon took him out. It was the right move because Brandon didn't know who was with Steve on the other side of that door. It was now

Three the Hard Way on the dance floor. Derek was ready the other two were shaking and crying. One of them, Mike called 911.

Mike says, "Hey there are shooters at the (Name of SC). Please come quickly."

He then texted his girl goodbye.

Mike yells, " I called the police there be here shortly. You better get the fuck out of here."

It was game time. The third barrage started and it was different. Louder and more rounds came in. It stopped and then three images ran in and took cover. Derek aimed and hit two with no problem. The third took out another goon. The numbers weren't on his side. He knew the end was near, so his thoughts went to his childhood and what got him here. His mother, Reagan? It really didn't matter because he had absolutely no control of his childhood! But he did have control of his ending. He felt some satisfaction in that. He had made lemonade. Black lemonade but still it had hydrated many people. From the Syndicate and beyond. He had even paid for a few houses for police officers off of the overtime they got investigating him. Shawn had made it out with his family. The Syndicate was now legit. It was in the restaurant business. Who would have thought it. Raekwon would run the streets now for as long as skills would allow. Hopefully Shanika would live. She deserved too! His kids would be better off without him because he would never shake his demons. His love for them was real and everlasting, but it was the lack of love for himself that had destroyed him. Some Spanish dude would probably be the one to pull the trigger but Derek had killed himself.

She was patient. She walked into the Strip Club as if someone was expecting her. She was beautiful with her long black hair in a ponytail. It draped perfectly against her black shirt. She wore all black. Black panties, bra, socks, pants, belt, and shirt. Soon Derek would be wearing the same color scheme. The weapon she carried was special. An automatic machine gun made specifically for spraying and killing. It shoot a hundreds rounds per minute. She was fully loaded with a thousand rounds. He was a good aim but it was no need to be.

Derek reloaded both pistols and took a deep breath. He wanted to die on his terms. On his feet! Fifty Cents Many Men was playing low. The jukebox was on automatic.

Song, "Many, many, many men wish death pon me."

Derek rose to his feet and started firing towards the front door. He was shooting with his right hand first. No time to reload so once that was empty he would toss it and keep firing. Right was empty. He tossed it. Shifted the other gun to his right hand and before he could pull the trigger he saw fire. He had time to see it was a machine gun and that it was a very pretty girl behind it. Then he saw blackness. There was no pain. The bullets penetrated through his body so fast his brain didn't have time to send a message of pain. He was gone!

She directed her attention towards the office. It was quiet but she knew someone was in there.

Brandon knew the sound of what he heard wasn't good. That was military firepower on the other side of that door. So he did his best and move to the corner of the room and took cover.

She swept her gun two times across the room. Brandon was dead before he could return fire. Shanika was laying on her stomach behind the desk. She could hear and she flashes of the bullets. With the pause she crawled over and got Brandon's gun and then then draped his body over hers. With the gun in her right hand between his legs pointed at the door. She laid there like she was dead. If she was going to die she would take someone with her. Another barrage of bullets came through. Brandon was dead but he got hit a couple more times. His flow of blood made it appear they were both dead. The door open and the first one through the door was Pacheco. He saw the sprawled bodies and blood and assumed they were both dead. The second through the door was Hector. He thought the same but shot at the bodies a few more times. He then signaled for her to walk in. She did to see her work. It was messy but she had did what she was paid to do. In record time. They had orders to track and kill Derek no matter how long it took. Collateral damage wasn't a consideration. Women and kids, everybody goes. It had only taken her three days. Juan and the Cartel will be impressed. She saw the eyes open and look at her. She thought it was sad that this person would have to feel more pain. She walked over to deliver the head shot. She saw the hand and gun but it was too late. Shanika let that clip empty. She hit her in the stomach four times, and hit Pacheco twice. Hector jumped out of the way. When the clip was empty he delivered the fetal headshot to Shanika. She saw it but didn't feel anything.

#

This wasn't supposed to be easy. The most power and secretive NYPD Units office was hidden so no one could find it in the department. Perpetrators had no chance. But when you have a drug addict posing as a Detective with a real drug addict girlfriend then anything is possible. He had broken the rules and let Lisa drop him office at the office. Around the corner of course. You can't be too careful. He was too high to drive. She was high also but could manage the steering wheel. Of course she watched to see where he went. She brought her dope from the Cartel and they had seen him waiting in the car a few times. So they checked them both out. They knew he was a cop. Know thy clientele. A rule in the drug dealing business. So to get the location out of her, it only took a hundred-dollars' worth of dope. Sold.

So under the dark blue sky professional hit men were going to takedown cops. Money makes anybody a target. There were six NYPD targets inside; Alison, Shelia, Lance Bonner, Joseph Rogers, Alex, and Rob. The instructions were to kill them all.

Alison was on the computer. Lance and Joseph were updating the board. Shelia, Alex, and Rob were in the conference room drinking Jack Daniels celebrating Derek's demise. News travels fast on the street. This was bad karma, celebrating death.

Shelia says, "That's a fucking lie. No way you went into a Crack House by yourself and fought off fives addicts and three killers. No ducking way. I didn't believe when my Sergeant told me about ten years ago and I don't believe it now."

Rob says, "The only difference is the person that was there is telling you!"

Shelia says, "Get the fuck out of here."

They all laugh. Alex got a text on his phone.

Alex says, "I'll be back in a few."

She wasn't supposed to drop by unannounced. At all for that matter. This could get Alex in big trouble. If the Chief found out he would get launched out of the Unit and be back on uniform within 24 hours. What the love of narcotics does to you. He was happy to see her. He planned to fuck her in the backseat of the car. Might as well enjoy the Jack Daniels the right way. As he walked towards the door he could see her. She was shaking like crazy. She looked like she needed a hit badly. He thought she was there to get money for a hit. He opened the door to kiss her and her eyes opened so wide it sacred him. The gun was at his temple before he could figure things out. She ran off. Alex put his hands up. He couldn't see them but there were four masked gunmen there. No peripheral just tunnel vision. It was cold steel. A gun. It made you follow instructions.

Alex says, "Take my money. It's in my left front pocket."

The masked gunmen smacked him in the back of his head with the gun. Alex was stunned. The gunmen searched him and took away his duty weapon.

Masked Gunmen#1 says, "Just let us in and everything will be okay. Don't do anything stupid. Nice an easy."

They started moving inside. There were cameras but nobody was watching them.

They entered the computer office first. Lance and Joseph turned around and saw a masked man with a gun to an Alex's head. Before they could react two masked gunmen that were hidden appeared and killed them with a short barrage of shots. They kept moving with Alex. They split up. Two and two.

Shelia and Rob heard the shots. Alex wasn't in the room so Rob knew this evil had to do with him. They both had their duty weapons out and they took cover behind a desk.

Alison was sitting on the toilet when she heard the first shots. There was no mistaken what it was. She had seen Alex walkout, but she didn't understand what was happening. She got up quickly and opened the bathroom stall door, she then edged herself feet to head wall to wall. Just as she got set the bathroom door opened. The masked gunmen ducked down and saw no feet so he kept moving to the next room. She took her gun out of the holster and tactically started moving.

Two gunmen entered Rob's office with Alexa's their cover. Shelia and Rob didn't have a clear shot.

Gunmen#1 says, "Throw down your weapons and we won't kill you."

Alex was shaking his head no. Rob knew what that meant. They were going to die regardless. Shelia looked at Rob. Rob knew Alex was probably correct but he wanted to try and save his life.

Rob says,"We are going to put down our weapons. Please don't shoot."

Shelia threw down her weapon then Rob. Gunmen#2 killed her with a headshot. Alex tried to grabbed the gun from gunmen#1. Rob went for his backup weapon.

Alison had hid under a desk and when the two gunmen passed her, she took them out quickly. Heads shots. Her first kill. She then started moving towards Rob's office because she heard the gunfire. She was moving with a purpose.

Rob took out one of the gunmen but he didn't have a clear shot because Alex was fighting with the gunmen. They were fighting for the gun. Rob ran over to help. The gunmen got his finger on the trigger and started firing. Alex tried to keep the weapon away from him. He was fighting for his life. He heard a grunt. He knew what it meant but he didn't look towards Rob. Alison entered the office and shot the gunmen in the head. They both ran over to Rob. He took two rounds to his chest. He was in bad shape. There was blood everywhere. Alison held him. Alex fell to the fetal, and began crying. He knew this was his fault. Alison called a 10-13 on her radio.

Rob says, "Tell my wife and kids I love them."

Alison shook her head yes. If she spoke she would cry.

Rob says, "Kid I choose you to be the future of this Unit for your Integrity and Pride. You're the Blue Angel that will watch over this city. You owe me nothing. But you do owe the city."

Alison was speechless. Rob's eyes were closed. She performed CPR. Backup was knocking at the front door.

Alison yelled, "Alex. Alex go open the fucking door."

Alex woke out of his stupor and opened the door. Cops and EMS rushed in. When they got to Rob he was gone. Now Alison was crying.

#

Alex was with Lisa at the dope house on Rockaway Boulevard with Lisa. He ordered two bags of the Darth Vader Heroin. The dealer looked at him and said, "You know you have to dilute this shit. Or else it'll kill you." Alex assured him he knew what he was doing. He took the two bags and went upstairs to enjoy it right away. He pulled out his needle and poured the whole bag in it. Lisa looked at him like he was crazy but she said nothing. She used a quarter of the bag. She shot up and her body went right into enjoyment. Alex shot up and his body went right into shock. He was dead within ten minutes.

#

With the possession of the confession from Derek Mason and Robert Grey's death, Council Jackson was in full control of his own destiny. He was running for Mayor. Even in his time of selfishness the councilman did something humane. After he found out that Alex overdosed, he put the full blame on Alex and his drug problem. He was a murderer who had tortured Derek Mason. On Monday morning he asked for a department funeral for Robert Grey and full benefits for his family. The rest of the Unit was free to continue their quest to clean up the city. The Council agreed.

Chapter 46

GOD LIVES THROUGH

Derek's funeral was a celebration for the hood and the last of the old hustlers. It was a different time. The game effected sports and music. All basketball players portrayed themselves after the wannabe tough rappers but the fake rappers got it from the real hustlers they knew or heard about. Except for Jay Z, DMX, and Fifty Cent! Everything else was either an exaggeration or lie. The limos rolled in. Derek's family was there: Grandma and the three kids. Shawn and Raekwon. Shawn reflected on their past and the come up. He was sad but he also knew all they had done and seen was never to be mentioned to anyone. Raekwon, angry, was dressed in black with a black 45 in his waistband. He wanted revenge. Jocelyn had to take the gun away from him. He was looking to use it on anyone at any moment. Shanika was okay until they took his casket out of the hearse. She fainted at the sight of it. Monique sat in the back. She couldn't stop crying. She only could think of what could have been and it made her sick because she thought they would have been in love for the rest of their lives. Carla was extremely happy and her Cartier shades hid that fact. She was glad Derek was gone because it freed her man. All she cared about was her family. She had a restaurant and a future with her family.

The reverend kept it short. He talked about Derek and his remaining kids. He said, "Derek was now free as a bird and he was flying towards heaven. Where he belonged."

#

The Mayor and Police Commissioner were seated in the front. They attended reluctantly. But they both refused to speak. Rob's wife didn't care about them. She was holding her two kids and crying uncontrollably. Rob's mother was draped over the coffin and crying. The Chief was there.

He sat in silence. Bowtie straight, shoes shined. Alison was there and she had cried her eyes dry. She watched the man that her saved her life die in front of her. He had put her in this unit and made her a Detective. She felt she owed him so much. There was a lot she didn't know about him and that was probably for the best. He told her debt was the citizens of New York City. She would take this seriously. Malik was by her side. He too didn't know the man well but felt he owed him so much. He was eager to start training. Council Jackson did speak. He spoke well of Rob and the police officers who protect the city. He was preparing his path to run for Mayor of this city in the next election. There were a lot of other Police Officials spoke as well. Robert Grey was beloved in the NYPD. The remaining members of the Unit were there dressed in their Class A uniforms. They were the Poll Bearers. Captain Gallagher presented Loren Grey with the American Flag. After the service was over she got in the awaiting SUV with Malik. They were on their way to the CIA FARM for training that Robert Grey had arranged for them.

#

Instructor Baron and Phillips were upset that Malik and Alison weren't theirs—they would go back to their agency when they graduated.

Baron asked, "Why wasn't Malik's last name listed?"

Phillips replied, "That's what the Chief wants."

"Say no more," said Baron. "Malik X it is."

"You give them the good news," said Phillips.

At a knock on the door, Phillips called out, "Come in."

Malik and Alison hustled in and stood at attention.

Baron said, "Relax. We just wanted to tell you that you made it extremely hard to choose between the two of you for class leader so we are going to make you both the class leaders. This is only the second time in our storied history. So it is a big deal."

Alison and Malik X said, "Thank you, sir."

Phillips went on. "Wear it proudly because you earned it. Congrats. Now get back to class."

Alison and Malik X both hustled out of the office.

Malik says, "I think I understand now. Rob created us because he knew his own fate. From his evil we are reborn. This training will give us new life so that we can clean up the city.

Alison says, "So from his ashes let's defeat evil."

It was time to begin…again.